LITTLE FALLS

LITTLE FALLS

A MYSTERY

Elizabeth Lewes

CROOKED
LANE

NEW YORK

Copyright © 2020 by Elizabeth Crouse

Published in the United States by Crooked Lane Books, an imprint of The Quick Brown Fox & Company LLC.

Crooked Lane Books and its logo are trademarks of The Quick Brown Fox & Company LLC.

Library of Congress Catalog-in-Publication data available upon request.

ISBN (hardcover): 978-1-64385-506-6
ISBN (ebook): 978-1-64385-507-3

Cover design by Nicole Lecht

Printed in the United States.

www.crookedlanebooks.com

Crooked Lane Books
34 West 27th St., 10th Floor
New York, NY 10001

First Edition: August 2020

10 9 8 7 6 5 4 3 2 1

For my daughters.

Sometimes in life you feel there is something you must do, and in which you must trust your own judgment and not that of any other person. Some call it conscience and some plain obstinacy.

—John Masterman

Survival...is an infinite capacity for suspicion.

—John le Carré,
Tinker, Tailor, Soldier, Spy

I remember fragments: the color of the desert burning, the smell of the blood drying in the sun, the sound of the glass shattering under fire. Never what happened after. Rarely what happened before.

But sometimes . . . sometimes, I remember everything. Time slows, crystallizes. I see everything, I smell everything, I hear everything. I *feel* everything.

Then something . . . snaps. Fragments.

It just happened. Here. In the barn. Flakes of snow are melting on my jacket; they're damp on my numb fingers. It happened when he looked up, when he turned toward me, when I saw her blood matted in his long hair, his hand on her face.

Then I fired.

This is what happened before.

1

Dust: long, fat streamers of it rose from the wheels of my truck as I drove up into the hills of Jeremy Leamon's ranch. It was dry that Friday, dry as early August in Okanogan County usually is, but Leamon's black steers were still bent low in the parched pastures, scrounging for tufts of yellow grass under the orange morning sun. The windows in the truck were down, and I was tapping my fingernails on the window frame, but not to the beat of the honky-tonk on the radio.

An outcrop shot up out of the pasture and became a ridge. I steered the truck around it, bounced over the stones that had crumbled off, and powered through a mess of tree roots and washouts that made the steering column jerk and the axles whine. Not long after the truck stopped bucking, an outbuilding peeked out of the stand of ponderosa pines that washed down the hillside. Its corrugated steel paneling and wooden barn door had seen better days. Hell, better decades. But the thick padlock on the door was shiny and new.

Suspicious? Yeah.

The country is not that peaceful, you know. Drugs—we got plenty. Prostitution, too. And guns. Jesus Christ, do we have guns. In the years I had been inspecting properties for the County Assessor's Office, I had seen more than my fair share out on the back roads, in the hidden valleys, and in forgotten forest clearings just like the one I found that day on the edge of Jeremy Leamon's property. That's why I carried my official ID in my pocket and my unofficial Glock in my right hand. Why I let the truck roll through the potholes until I turned a bend, then switched off the ignition and listened long and hard before I got out to take a look.

I remember that when my boots hit the ground, puffs of yellow dirt rose around my ankles, drifted on air heavy with the smell of sunburned pine needles: dry, hot, resinous. The smell of summer. The smell of fire.

I padded through the trees. A hundred yards in, I saw the back end of the building above me on the hill. I came up on the south side and approached the tree line, then doubled back to the north side. No sounds from the building, not even the whisper of a ventilation fan. So why lock it up, all the way out here in the hills?

My finger slipped closer to the Glock's trigger.

Slowly, cautiously, I approached the building. There was only the one door and no windows. No way to see what the padlock was protecting. But as I rounded a corner, a gust of wind blew through the trees, and a steel panel on the side of the building swayed with it. I held my breath, waited for some sound, some shout, from inside the building. When it didn't come, I caught the edge of the panel with the toe of my boot. It swung out easily, and daylight shot through holes where nails had once secured it to the building's wooden skeleton.

Inside was a stall for an animal, a horse maybe. Beyond it, open space, sunlight pouring through a hole in the roof onto messy stacks of last year's hay. The air glittered with dust and stank of decay, the funk of rot. But there was something else there too, something sweet and high and spoiled. And buzzing, buzzing that filled my ears, that vibrated my brain . . .

I ducked under the steel panel and clambered in, breathing shallowly. Holding my weapon at the ready, I rounded the corner of the stall, and then I saw him.

Hanging.

Hanging from a loop of braided wire stretched over a wooden beam. His fingers were at his neck, but not to scratch it or run over his scant, patchy beard. They were stuck. Stuck in the noose. Stuck when he'd clawed at it, tried to pry it away, tried to make room to breathe.

I'm sure he tried.

Because he hadn't jumped: there was no chair, no ladder. Nothing kicked away, nothing standing.

Nothing but the kid and the flies.

* * *

4

I don't remember much of what happened next, but I know I went back to the truck, and I must have made a call. Because I know I watched the helicopter erupt over the rock and sweep down the hillside and land in the track I had driven down. And I can still feel the dirt from the downwash blasting my face and the icy cold steel of the stairs when I pulled them out just after the bird settled on the ground. And I remember not understanding why everyone was acting so strange, why the doctor set down her things in slow motion, and the pilot just switched off the bird and strolled to the trees to light up a smoke and why both of them were so casual, like they were going to the park. But then I felt a hand on my shoulder, and I turned around. And everything snapped into focus.

Sergeant Darren Moses. My God, you should have seen him that day, in his mirrored sunglasses and chocolate-brown uniform, his black buzz cut and those high Indian cheekbones. He was always good looking—even when we were kids—but I guess I hadn't seen him for a while.

He asked me how I was, reached out and touched my shoulder again, looked concerned. I had on this green tank top, and the rough pads of his fingers were cool against my skin. He was standing close, almost intimately, his aftershave musky and faint. But I stood there and watched my reflection in his sunglasses and was an asshole.

"I'm glad to see the Sheriff's Office hasn't cleaned out the stables yet."

Darren laughed, smiled broadly, his teeth flashing white in the sun. "You know I'm the kind of shit that sticks to the floor."

He moved his hand away. My shoulder was suddenly cold.

I smiled, tried to laugh, then grabbed another bag instead.

Darren held out his hand to take it. "You don't have to haul our gear, Camille."

I shrugged. "May as well. I'm here."

"Really."

"It's not a big deal."

Darren's smile disappeared. "I'm sorry. I need you to stay here."

My fingers tightened on the handle of the black Sheriff's Office duffel. "What are you talking about?"

"I can't let you into the crime scene."

I shook my head. "I've already seen it. My fibers or whatever you're worried about are already in there."

"It's procedure," Darren said, his shoulders lifting slightly. "No exceptions, not even for old friends."

"That doesn't make any sense."

"And you've had a shock. Listen—Lucky's on his way up here. He took a truck so he could stop and talk to Leamon. He can take you back into town, and I'll drive your truck down after we're done."

I frowned. "What? *No.*"

"Camille. If you're right and he's . . ."

"Hey, Moses!" someone shouted.

I spun toward the building and saw a second officer standing by the peeled-back panel of corrugated steel: Deputy Jesus Moreno. His voice tight and flat and deathly calm, he said: "You need to see this."

Darren took the duffle from my hand and jogged over to the building. I followed. I'm not good at following orders. Never have been.

Inside the building, the two men stood side by side, their chins lifted, their eyes fixed on the corpse. Moreno was frowning, his arms crossed over his chest. He looked like a man at a museum: interested, but removed, distant. Darren looked like a man taking it personally. His jaw was clenched, his neck rigid, his thumb twitching on the safety catch of his holster.

In the corner, the medical examiner—a small woman with graying curls—busily set out her equipment on a bale of hay she'd draped with a white sheet. When she turned, she was zipping a white jumpsuit closed over a blue buttondown shirt.

"It's just decomposition, gentlemen," the examiner said. "Part of the natural process."

"How long would you say?" Darren asked, still studying the corpse.

"Three or four days," I said without thinking.

Darren shot me a look and started to say something, probably to tell me I was violating his procedure, to threaten me with arrest if I didn't get out of his crime scene. But the examiner was faster.

"Yes." She adjusted her glasses, squinted at the body, then said slowly, like she was really thinking about it: "It's been hot—hot enough for that much bloating—and the maggots are pretty far along. So, yes, that's a fair assessment."

Darren glanced from me to the examiner and back again, then opened his mouth.

6

"Aren't you going to introduce me, Sergeant?" the examiner said.

For a moment, Darren was caught between irritation and manners. He was staring at me like I had strung up the kid myself, his eyes dark and intense, a vein in his neck jumping. The examiner was staring at *him* like he was a naughty schoolboy.

"Doctor Marguerite Fleischman, Camille Waresch," Darren said. "Camille found the body this morning, Doc. She works for the County Assessor's Office."

"And?" the doctor said, looking over her wire rims at Darren.

"And she's leaving," he said, taking a step forward, one hand reaching toward my arm.

The examiner raised her hand to him. "Not until she answers my questions," she said, then turned to me. "How is it you know the body's been there for three or four days?"

I shrugged. "Just a guess."

"Camille was a medic, Doc," Darren said through gritted teeth. "She was in Iraq."

I clenched my jaw, looked away. "And Afghanistan."

"I see."

Doctor Fleischman pulled on a pair of latex gloves, snapping them against her wrists. Then she squatted and rifled through one of her bags. When she stood, she was holding a notebook and pen out to me.

"My recorder is broken. You remember how to take notes?"

* * *

We had been at it for a couple of hours when a truck pulled up outside. The engine died and one door, then another, slammed. I stood up quickly and backed toward the wall, skittish, my eyes on the big door by the road.

"I'm telling you," a male voice said outside, his voice escalating from exasperation to anger. "That ain't my building. I don't know what your problem is, but it ain't mine."

Leamon, Jeremy Leamon. My dad had known him. I had knocked on his front door and chatted with him about the weather that morning when I arrived at the property for the inspection.

"All right," another man said in this sort of soothing, persuasive voice, the kind of voice you want in commercials for condoms or caramels. Lucky

Phillips, it had to be. He was Darren's partner back then. And he was an outsider, one of the few people who'd moved *into* the Okanogan instead of out.

"I believe you, Jeremy," Lucky said. "But you know I'm a curious kind of guy—I just want to see if any of these keys work."

"It ain't mine," Leamon growled, but there was panic in his voice.

Someone thumped the door and fiddled with the padlock, its steel loop rattling against the cleats on the door. The door jerked open, sliding to the side on the top rail. Lucky stepped into the doorway, all tall and broad in his brown uniform and flaming orange hair. And beside him, his arm clamped in one of Lucky's big hands, was Jeremy Leamon, a man with too much denim wrinkled around his body and a halo of gray stubble on top of his head.

"What's that then, Jeremy?" Lucky asked, still cool, still smooth.

Leamon ducked out of Lucky's grip, his gnarled, liver-spotted hands clenched in enormous fists. But Lucky was younger and faster. He stepped forward, taking the older man's arm and spinning him, forcing him to look into the building, to look *at* the body still hanging from the beam, still crawling with flies, dripping slowly onto the packed earth floor.

Leamon staggered back. "What *is* that?"

"What do you mean?" Lucky said in mock surprise. "You aren't going to introduce us to your new neighbor?"

"Neighbor?" Leamon's face went white as butcher paper, his knees wavered and shook. He shoved Lucky to one side and, bent double, ran outside, his hand clamped to his mouth as he began to retch.

*   *   *

Later, much later, I could still smell the decay, hear the smack of flies against the inside of the plastic body bag after Moreno finally cut the kid down and zipped him up. I was fine when they loaded him into the helicopter, fine when Darren asked me how I was for the second time that day. He said he knew I'd seen things before, but did I want someone to drive me to my place? I shook my head again, told him no. Then he climbed into the helicopter and I stowed the stairs, and I *was* fine until the bird disappeared over the rock, until even the sound of its rotors faded away, and I was alone again, alone in the narrow track, dust clinging to my jeans and caked in my hair.

That's when the shaking started.

I fell to my knees and tried to not let it happen, but sometimes it just does. Sometimes the movie inside my head just won't stop, and I see the sniper bullet blow off half that staff sergeant's skull, see that corporal go limp on the table in the field hospital when everything went wrong, see that lieutenant's eyes gazing blindly into the deep, blue desert sky while his blood sank into the sand. And then the mortar rounds, the streaks of fire in the night sky, the staccato burst of AK-47s in the bone-dry morning, the sudden sick rocking of an IED going off under the tires of the forward Humvee.

After some time—God knows how long—I stood up and half-stumbled, half-ran to my truck and threw myself into the cab, then tore down the mountain faster than I should have. The assessment didn't matter; the rocks slamming against the chassis didn't matter; the cattle scattering wildly at the reckless rumble of the truck didn't matter. The only thing that mattered was getting out.

I still don't know how I got back that day. I just remember looking out the window of my one-bedroom apartment, my hair wet, my skin raw from the shower, watching people drive into the gravel lot below, go into the mart—*my mart*; felt strange to remember that, to remember that my father had bought it for me when I came home from the desert for the last time, that it was supposed to be my unwanted salvation—then leave again, a half rack of beer or a gallon of milk in hand. Across the street, my neighbor's trees, their leaves still green, waved in the heat rising off the pavement of the two-lane road that went through my two-street town. Behind them, behind the trees, the hill rose yellow and pale, dried-out green, the dirt streaked with orange. Like it was rusting.

Numb. I was numb. That's how it is at first. First bomb. First kill. You're scared out of your mind, scared straight. Get shit done, accomplish the mission. And then—it gets quiet. You're out, you're back at base. You're safe. And then numb. It's like floating, and nothing can touch you, nothing can make you feel. You're floating through the day, through the tour, through life. Then someone shoots down your balloon and it's all pain.

Most days, I miss the desert. But what I really miss is that numb.

*   *   *

As the shadows were lengthening, a key turned in the front door.

I was sitting at the scuffed kitchen table, staring at the property report for Jeremy Leamon's ranch in the black binder I'd had with me on-site that morning. My hair was dry and sticking to the sweat on my neck, so it must have been awhile since I had gotten back. I leapt to my feet—bare feet—grabbed the Glock, cocked it, and held it down, but ready, my index finger hovering next to the trigger. God, I must have looked insane when the door opened and my teenage daughter walked in.

"Uh, hi," Sophie said and dropped her backpack on the floor.

"Hi," I said without breathing.

"What's with you?"

Sophie sauntered into the kitchen. Hastily, I slid the Glock under the county map draped over the table.

"Nothing."

Across the narrow room, Sophie raised her eyebrows. I looked away, my jaw clenched. *Be calm. Be normal.*

"How was work?" I said, trying and failing.

"Okay."

Sophie opened the fridge, rummaged, smacked things around until she found the last can of soda.

"Crystal was okay?"

"Yeah, Crystal was okay." Sophie stood up, closed the fridge, and popped open her drink.

"Roseann dropped you off?"

She paused.

"I asked if Roseann dropped you off."

"No," she snapped, her back still toward me.

I ground my teeth.

"She had to go to Coulee City for something," Sophie said before I could open my mouth. "She said she wouldn't be back until late."

"Why didn't you call me?"

"I got home." Sophie hesitated, her back stiffened. "I mean, I got back okay, didn't I?"

And that was it, really. Home. Her home was my home: the white farmhouse I had grown up in, the same place she had grown up after I left her to join the Army and then after I came back, when it was too much for me to take care of myself and take care of her too. And it had stayed that way, me in the apartment over the mart, her and my father in the old farm-house thirty miles away. Until he died that May. After that, home was . . . well, not my apartment.

"Who brought you?" I asked as evenly as I could. "Who brought you back?"

"A friend."

Sophie turned quickly and stalked past me until, like a toy tied to her with string, I sprang up and reached out to grab her. But then she stopped and the string broke. My hand snapped back.

"Who?" I insisted, my voice cracking with the strain of holding back the fury, the anxiety and fear.

"Just a friend."

"A name. *Give me a name.*"

Sophie glared at me, then bent to pick up her backpack. I rushed forward and put myself in her path. Her brown eyes—flecked with gold like mine—flashed dangerously, just like her father's had when he'd been pushed too far. Just like mine must have too.

"Jason," Sophie said through clenched teeth. "Jason Sprague."

I stared her down. "Never heard of him."

"You wouldn't have," she sneered. But then she dropped her eyes, dropped her head, and a lock of dark hair fell over her forehead.

"Granddad thought he was okay."

She said it so quietly, almost reverently, her eyes so downcast that her long lashes fanned over her cheeks. Even I felt tears welling. But my father thought everyone was okay; he was everyone's hero. And here's the thing, here's what I had learned about being a mother during those few months that Sophie and I had been the only ones left: your kid is the predator and you are the prey. They smell blood. They smell fear. And then—just then—Sophie was playing with her food.

"Fine," I said, biting off the word. "I'll meet him next time."

I let her push past me. She slammed the bedroom door behind her; I stomped to the kitchen, poured a glass of water, and took it to the table.

Hours later, I was still there, trying to write my report about Leamon's ranch on my laptop when Sophie burst out of the bedroom. Her eyes were wild, and her long black hair flew behind her as she darted to the front door.

11

"Where are you going?" I demanded, rising from the table.

Sophie was pulling on her shoes, didn't even glance up when she said, "To Tracy's."

"Why?"

"I just am," she said dismissively, snarling in that way that burned through all my nerves.

"No."

Pulling the laces tight, her face away from me, she muttered, *"Fuck you."*

In the blink of an eye, I was standing over her, the muscles in my arms screaming against the force it took to hold back my fists. *"Stop."*

Her head jerked up: trails of tears streaked down her face, smeared mascara haloed her eyes. "What the hell is wrong with you?" she shouted.

The heat of her anguish drove me back to the kitchen counter. Fury I could deal with, but anything else, anything *more* . . . My chest tightened, my vision narrowed, darkened. Pinholed. I closed my eyes, shook my head, pushed down all the thoughts, the impulses, and the screams. And when I opened my eyes, there was just Sophie. On the ground. Crying and tying her shoes like a child. *My child.* I dropped to my knees.

"What's going on, Sophie?" I said quietly, tentatively. "Why are you— why do you need to go to Tracy's right now? It's late."

"Because," she wailed, then breathed deeply, the air shuddering in her chest. "Because Patrick is dead."

I shook my head. "Patrick?"

"Yeah, Patrick."

"Okay." I nodded. "Who is Patrick?"

"A friend," Sophie said impatiently. She scrambled to her feet, grabbed her bag.

"A friend."

Sophie wove to push past me; I wove too, pushing back.

"Like Jason?" I said too sharply.

Sophie's eyes flashed through her tears. "No. He's my—he's just a really good friend. From school."

"From school," I repeated, trying to keep myself in check.

Sophie rolled her eyes. "I mean, he just graduated in May."

What?

"Patrick?" I whispered, looking past Sophie, looking over her shoulder into the distance where I could still see a male, his bloated body black and purple with pooled blood, patches of peach fuzz on his face, hanging at the end of a length of braided wire.

"Yeah, Patrick!" Sophie hitched up her backpack. Fresh tears were puddling in her eyes, her shoulders were tense. "He hasn't been around for a couple of weeks and now—" Her shoulders rose, her voice shuddered. "And now someone found him up in the hills and he's . . . he's *dead*."

My heartbeat quickened. "What do you mean in the hills? Where?"

"I don't know! Why would I know? Tracy just called me, okay?"

But I couldn't believe the kid that morning had been Sophie's friend, that the casualty was that close. I couldn't believe the medical examiner would have released an identification that early, that she could even know yet who the dead boy was. And why would some kid—why would Sophie's friend—know about it anyway?

Then everything sort of slowed down, came into focus: the tears on Sophie's cheeks crept down to her jaw, the smell of her shampoo—green apple—filled my nostrils; the dim light from the lamp by the sofa was suddenly blinding.

"Who found him?" I asked, my voice sounding tinny and distant in my ears.

"I don't know!" Sophie was shrieking now, her voice echoing in my brain, overloading every circuit. "How would I know?"

"How old was he?" I said urgently. "How old was Patrick?"

"It doesn't matter; he's dead!" She tore my fingers from her arms, even though I didn't remember—don't remember—grabbing her.

"*Tell me.*"

"Nineteen, okay?" Released, Sophie lunged for the door. "He just turned nineteen!"

Nineteen.

I had written nineteen on Doctor Fleischman's yellow notepad that morning.

"Victim is a Caucasian male, approximately nineteen to twenty-two years of age," she had said from her perch on the ladder. "Death likely caused by asphyxiation, *likely* involuntary hanging, but"—she had leaned closer, peering through a magnifying glass at the discolored skin on the

13

kid's chest—"what appear to be electrical burns were inflicted to the torso prior to death. Two, maybe three days prior."

She had pulled back then and shifted her attention downward. "Other indications of torture include nails missing from digits two through four of the right hand, pre-mortem bruising and lacerations on the left side of the face, including the eye . . ."

Downstairs, the heavy steel door slammed.

*　*　*

I waited for Sophie to come back, waited while I was stretched out, rigid, on the couch, with my jeans on and my boots lined up on the floor by my feet. All the lights in the apartment were off, so I studied the ridges and valleys on the ceiling by the yellow light of the sodium streetlamp.

Around two, I heard footsteps on the gravel in the parking lot, and then the door downstairs opened. She crept up quietly; I smiled because it sounded like she'd even taken off her shoes. When her key turned in the lock of the apartment door, I threw my arm over my eyes and pretended to sleep.

Later, I crept to her door and opened it silently. Inside, the bedroom that had always been bare when it was mine was now anything but. Clothes were scattered everywhere, books were stacked in uneven piles. Sophie's pink backpack had been slung onto the chipped wooden desk. In the middle of it all was the girly white bed my parents had bought her for Christmas one year when I couldn't—or wouldn't—come home. She lay on the covers, curled in the fetal position, her hair tied up in a messy bun, her hands balled up under her chin.

I walked into the room, fighting the urge to pick up the mess, and watched her in the light that seeped through the thin, frilly white curtains that had once hung at the window of the bedroom we had both spent our childhoods in. At just barely fifteen, she still looked like the child I had watched growing up during visits two or three times a week for years. Her cheeks were thinning but were still rounded; the skin on her arms peeking out from under her T-shirt was still silky and down covered. Regret surged through my body as though it were a physical force—a shock wave. I closed my eyes to keep it in.

When I opened them again, the first thing I saw were the freckles sprinkled over her nose and cheeks. She looked like her Colville father, like

Oren, with her dark hair and pale brown skin and almond eyes. Only her freckles were me.

Her phone, clutched in her hand, buzzed. She stirred but didn't wake. I glanced at the screen, then did a double take. The phone background was of her and a boy. He was a little older than her, but sort of wholesome looking—if you looked past their glassy eyes and flyaway hair and flushed cheeks. I thought I recognized the boy, imagined there was some resemblance there to the kid who had been hanging in Jeremy Leamon's barn. But then the screen went dark, and I glanced back at my daughter, her rounded cheeks not so childlike, her arms more sinew than down. And I looked past the freckles and saw a lot more of me.

2

I didn't sleep that night. Every time I tried, *there was heat and sand and sweat dripping in my eyes. Then a fist pounding hollowly on a door and the crack of wood breaking against the butt of an M16 and air brushing past my face, air thick with decay and cool as a tomb.*

I woke, shaking. Again and again, I woke.

3

Numbness fades into fear. Paranoia. *Obsession.*

My brain went on repeat. During the day, the same questions—*Why him? Why me? Why Sophie? Who did this?*—and the same guesses, played over and over. No answers. No resolution. At night, the dream—the heat, the pounding, the stench—dozens of times, *hundreds* of times, cycling through until I threw myself off the sofa, pulling at my hair, choking on the scream in my throat.

Just before five AM on Sunday, I pulled on my running shoes and flew downstairs, then across the gravel and into the road. When I reached the bottom of the hill, I was sprinting, tearing across Jim Horn's field, the dew on the browned grass splashing onto my calves, turning the dirt to mud. While the stars winked out, while the sky colored crimson, then orange, then peach, I ran circuits around the lake until I couldn't breathe, until my throat burned. Even then, every detail still rang inside my head: every note I took, every one of Doc Fleischman's gory revelations, every tear streaming down Sophie's cheeks. So I kept running until I couldn't think.

Back at the apartment, my thighs dull and heavy, my skin still steaming from the shower, I sat down to write my report on Leamon's property, but the first paragraph was nonsense, the second unfinished. My attention kept straying to the county map, the one with Jeremy Leamon's property. The one without a barn, without any outbuildings at all. Not that that was surprising. "No permit, no problem," right? But there was something different about this, something I couldn't let go. Something about the kid, about the barn. And something about Jeremy Leamon and why his reaction didn't fit.

"Neighbor?" he'd said. Like he knew better. Like he knew more.

Snap. The lead in my pencil broke, splintered where I was driving it into the surface of the table. I had to get this shit out of my head, had to push the blood and the terror and the dreams back into the dark corners. To do that, I needed answers. I needed the kid to be put to rest. I called the Sheriff's Office, but no one answered Darren's extension. I called his cell and got no joy there either. Not like I expected him to tell me anything, even though we'd known each other since we were five. He was a professional; that much he'd made plain at the barn. So instead of trying again, I grabbed my keys.

When I arrived at the county building just before noon, the parking lot was empty, the guard station deserted, the hallways silent. The only sound was my boots padding across the carpet, then tapping on the concrete stairs, and then on the concrete floors, until I arrived at a heavy gray door in the furthest corner of the basement. After unlocking it, I walked past the old wooden desk and the coffee cup that was always half empty, and into the rows of cabinets stacked up high.

I pulled the map of Jeremy Leamon's place and spread it out on the long table in the corner where snowmelt trickles in through a crack in the foundation every spring. There was the track I had driven down two days before. It started at the county road, then wound up and hugged the property line until it circled back around to where it began. Must have been a logging road once upon a time. But there weren't any buildings alongside it, and the file didn't include any permits for one. So I pulled the map for the neighbor's place, lined it up alongside. And there it was, on the edge of the property, uphill from a little house and the head of a long drive going down to the county road that went past my front door: the barn where the kid had been strung up to die.

When I left the building, the late afternoon sun stung my eyes so badly, tears seeped from the corners. Wiping them away, I got in my truck and drove north up the highway. It was thirty minutes from Okanogan to my mart, but only another ten minutes from there to Leamon's neighbor's place. I'd go up the gravel drive and flash my county ID if I had to in order to trek up that hill and get to that barn. I'd do it because I needed to, because I had this visceral need to know how Patrick had gotten there. But by the time I arrived, the sun was sliding behind the mountains, and the trees were reaching over the gravel drive with long, dark fingers. Wind swept through the window of my truck and froze the sweat on my face.

I shivered.

I rolled up the window and stared out the windshield, watched the leaves dance in the breeze, listened to it whistle and hum through the cracks in the body of my beat-up truck. I was being stupid. I was being paranoid. I was making things up. There was nothing up there. Nothing wrong. *I* was wrong.

I threw the truck into gear and drove away.

4

The flies. My God, the flies.

It was dark, so dark in the passageway that the door at the end was just a darker blot in the gloom. But beyond it—so loud we could have found the door just by listening—buzzing, humming. Thousands of pairs of wings roaring, drowned out only by the pounding of a private's M16 against the old, dry wood of the door.

Then, crack.

The wood splintered. The private's foot thundered against the door and it swung open, and that smell poured out, high and thick and sweet. We filed in: one soldier from the left, two from the right, then me. All of us with rifles at the ready, pointing into the dark corners, looking for a skull to smash in.

"Jesus," one of them said.

The second didn't get anything out, just dropped his rifle onto the packed earth floor, doubled over, and puked.

Me, I stood there, staring. Staring at him hanging from a heavy metal hook screwed into the ceiling: bloated, blackened, unrecognizable. His chest bare, his feet bare, the strings of his Army-issue pants loose around his ankles. I stared at him hanging in the beam of the third soldier's headlamp, the soldier who stood there, transfixed, horrified, drinking it in for long, still moments before looking away. Before plunging the kid into darkness again.

5

I returned to the county building just after seven on Monday morning. Inside the County Assessor's Office—third floor, last door on the left— the cheap metal receptionist's desk had that waiting look of a place unused, and the frosted glass panel in the door to my boss's office was still dark.

On the other side of the room, I unlocked another door and slipped into my cubicle. *All clear, thank God.* I plugged in my laptop, then set up the file transfer when it had booted up.

"I'll be damned. If it ain't the Ghost of Christmas Past."

I clenched my jaw. Gene. He loomed at my elbow, one arthritic hand on the outer wall of my cube, the other clutching his beloved NRA coffee mug. A vicious smile spread across his thin red lips, splayed by an underbite as bad as a chihuahua's.

"Does that make you Scrooge?" I asked levelly.

I watched him slurp his coffee. "What brings Your Holiness in today?" he said. The boss liked me. I knew it and Gene knew it. And this was his way of trying to punish me for it.

I stared at him blankly for a long moment, then turned back to my computer screen.

"What the hell is wrong with you, Waresch?" he snarled, the chihuahua gone rabid. "A man says good morning, and you—"

"You didn't say good morning."

Gene sputtered. "I'm the senior man in this office. I expect you to—"

"I'm filing a report."

Dramatically, I clicked "Submit," shut down the laptop, and slid it into my backpack. That's the best thing about being a property tax inspector; aside from filing reports, there's no need to be in the office.

21

"See? All done. Parcel 15981-2851: you can check it yourself."

I stood up and Gene immediately stood up taller. We shared a moment of furious silence; then I slung my backpack over my shoulder and brushed past him.

Before I got through the door, Gene said, "Parcel 15981 . . . 2851?"

I paused, my fingers gripping the doorframe like it was a live thing, a sudden surge of anger whipping my spine straight.

"Ain't that out there where they found that kid?" Gene asked.

I turned back, ready to lie, ready to argue, ready to tell him to mind his own damn business, and—and nothing. I saw the gray stubble coating his sagging jaw and the spot of food—egg, maybe—crusted on his short-sleeved shirt. His coffee cup was chipped and stained, and his hand quivered just a little, like he wasn't quite strong enough to hold it anymore. And I remembered that his wife had died a year or two before, and he was on his own now: like me, but not like me.

"Beale," Gene said softly. "His name was Beale. Local kid. Hurt pretty bad, I heard."

My fingers tightened on the doorframe and I leaned into it; pressed my palm against the wood, dug my fingernails into the white paint, willed away the horror show in my head before it started again. But, no. That smell, that rotting *stench*, and the flies and the bloating and the muddy purple skin peeling—no. *No.*

Gene sniffed.

I said, "I gotta go."

Downstairs, I darted past the security desk, pounded out the doors, and stood at the top of the stairs, sucking down the cold morning air. A woman in a fringed shirt and feathered hair glanced at me sideways and hurried past. I smiled tightly and grabbed the railing, walking down slowly, steadily, then scrambled back up when a group of kids poured around the corner. A tide of little brown and blond and red heads swirled across the sidewalk in front of me. I wondered how old they were. *Eight? No. Six?* The same age Sophie was when I came back from Iraq for the last time. The age she'd been when I had barely recognized her at my mother's funeral.

As quickly as they had appeared, the children passed, following their teenaged chaperones down the sidewalk and into the old county courthouse.

More slowly this time, I walked down to the sidewalk. It was shady in front of the building, but when I crossed the street, the sun was so fierce it burned through my hair. I hurried past the wide windows of the drugstore and on to the place on the next corner, the Do-Re-Mi Café, its windows lined with red vinyl booths and tables shingled with plates of pancakes and eggs and bacon.

Inside was Lucky Phillips, rising from a booth in the back corner, and Darren Moses, still seated, drinking coffee from a mug the same shade of brown as his uniform. The bells were still crashing against the glass door when I slid into the seat Lucky had left behind.

"Moses," I hissed.

"Camille." Darren smiled thinly and pushed his half-finished plate toward me. "You want some hash browns?"

"Why haven't you called me back?"

He shrugged. "I don't have anything official. I can't tell you anything."

"At least tell me what you got out of Jer—"

Darren, reaching for his wallet, glared at me.

"At least tell me what you got out of the property owner," I said.

"Sorry."

"Oh, come on. Did you get him to say it was his or not?"

"He says it isn't."

"What about the hay?"

Darren glared at me again, so I whispered instead: "The padlock?"

Darren dropped a twenty on the table and put the salt shaker on it. "He admitted those are his, but he says the building belongs to the neighbor."

I nodded. "It does."

"You been doing my job?" he asked, gazing out across the restaurant, his eyes sliding over the people hunched over scrambled eggs and coffee, out to the far wall, where an old, grease-slicked poster of Mount Rainier hung in a blue frame.

"I've been doing *my* job," I shot back. "Reviewing the records. Research. You should try it sometime."

Darren cracked a smile. "I will." He yawned, then swallowed the last of his coffee. "Lucky's going over there to ask, anyway."

"What about the kid?" I asked, knowing I shouldn't have.

He shook his head. "Sorry."

"At least tell me his name."

Darren's eyes were cold as he put his wallet back in his pocket.

"Everyone already knows, Darren."

He stood up, settled his belt on his hips, and glanced out across the restaurant again. "Come on. I'll walk you to your truck."

Fine. Maybe he'd talk away from other people. Maybe he'd tell me the kid wasn't my daughter's friend after all, that before the rot and the insects set in, he hadn't been the stoned boy in the photo on her phone. But when we got outside and I started for the truck, he didn't tell me anything at all, just offered me a piece of gum.

I looked at him and said, "No, thanks."

Darren pointed to a brown truck with a faded county seal on the door. "That yours?"

"No, it's the green one on the next block."

He nodded, kept walking with long, loose strides.

"Look," I said after we stepped off the sidewalk at the corner, "all I want to know is whether you've identified the kid."

"The doc got some good fingerprints," he said, his voice low, even though the street was deserted and all the buildings were closed tight to hold in the AC.

"And?"

"And what?"

"Do you have a name?"

Darren stepped between two cars and crossed the street diagonally. I followed, hurrying to keep up with his long stride.

"I can't tell you that," he said.

I stopped in the middle of the pavement, my keys gripped tightly in my right hand. "Then why does Sophie know?"

Darren stepped onto the sidewalk, then turned toward me. "Your daughter?" He was curious, but not surprised.

"She knew him. They were dating," I said, without knowing the truth.

"No way. He was too old for her."

"Nineteen?"

"Yeah." Darren frowned. "What name did she give you?"

"Patrick." Then I added the name Gene had mentioned, again without knowing the truth: "Patrick Beale."

"Did you know him?"

"No." I paused. Then, not sure if I was right or just crazy, I said, "But he—the kid at Leamon's place—he looked familiar. I mean, sort of. Maybe I met him, saw him with Sophie. Or maybe he came into the mart."

Darren folded his arms across his chest, leaned back on his heels. "Recently?"

"Maybe."

"You got a camera at your mart?"

"Yeah."

He nodded once. "His folks have a place a few miles from you."

I shook my head, but then I remembered seeing them, their faces pale and worn, in front of the little white church down the street from my mart the day before. "Ed and Christine? He was Ed and Christine Beale's son?"

Darren just kept walking.

"You gotta get a better rig," he said when he saw my truck. Then he went around to the passenger side.

I followed him, stared him down. "You're not going with me."

Darren wrapped one hand around the door handle, placed the other on the side panel. "Yeah, I am."

"What are you gonna do if I say no? Impound my truck for asking inconvenient questions?"

"Just open the door, Camille."

But like I said, I'm not good at taking orders. I went to the driver's door and unlocked it, slid onto the torn vinyl seat, then turned the key in the ignition. Darren, his brow creased over his mirrored shades, his mouth set in a thin line, knocked on the window, hard. I put on my sunglasses, leaned over, and stared him down again. Then I let him in.

When he'd closed the door, I cranked the wheel hard to the left, pulling out into the street while he was buckling up.

"So, where we headed, Sergeant?"

Darren pointed straight ahead. "North."

We drove through town—what there is of it, anyway—crossed the river, then got on the highway and accelerated. I asked questions, but he stonewalled me just like when we were kids, just like when I went for the bad boy instead of him in high school. I guess it's a sort of patience. Or cussedness. Probably both.

I shut my mouth, but over the steady whir of the tires, my mind wandered to all the dark places. Until—

"Pull over!"

I slammed on the brakes and swerved to the side, one wheel going off the side of the pavement and into the dirt, throwing up a cloud of dust. A red and black Chevy Suburban swept past, the driver leaning on the horn and a passenger gesturing out the window. In the seat next to me, Darren had a death grip on the door.

"What the hell?" I shouted.

"You missed the turn," he said, sounding more calm than he looked.

"You couldn't just tell me that?"

"I did. Twice, Camille."

"Oh." I swallowed, stared at my hands on the steering wheel. They were still shaking. "I, uh . . . I was thinking about something."

From the corner of my eye, I saw him staring, wondering about things I didn't want to tell him. Didn't want to tell *anyone*.

Instead, I nodded, flexed my fingers, and glanced at the rearview. Empty highway and brown grass ran to the hills. "Where was the turn?"

"About a half mile back."

I made a wide U-turn and veered onto the county road Darren pointed out. After a few minutes, we passed a long, narrow track that went off into the fields and then plunged into a gulch.

I glanced at him. "You took a risk highjacking my truck back there."

"Oh?"

"Yeah. I could take you down one of these roads, and no one would ever see you again."

He smirked. "I don't know. I can think of worse things than going down one of these roads with you."

I pushed down on the accelerator and powered the truck around an uphill curve. Out of the corner of my eye, I watched him—a married man—smiling to himself.

"You sure?" I kept my eyes on the road, watching a blue car approach at reckless speed. I guess I was feeling existential that day. Finding a dead body can do that to you. "I mean, I could have killed that kid. It's a good way to get away with murder, you know, calling in the body."

Idly, unconcerned, he said, "Did you kill him?"

I rolled my eyes. "No. I'm just saying."

"We've known each other a long time, Camille." He paused, smiled slyly. "Besides, at least twenty people saw you leave the Do-Re-Mi with me. That's enough to start an investigation."

"Yeah, and how's this investigation going, Sarge?" I jutted my chin at the road. "You got any leads?"

But Darren was good at silence.

A few minutes later, we passed the sign for "Little Falls, Population 72." A moment after that, Darren told me to pull into the lot of my mart. Out front, Rhonda Faye, the woman who ran the place for me, had set out baskets of her mother's vegetables in the shade of the awning. Another woman hustled out of the mart to a dented cream sedan idling by the gas pump, a kid wailing in the back seat.

I parked the truck in the shade in the back lot, jumped out, and slammed my door. Darren closed his. I started toward the door to my apartment.

"Where you going?" Darren said, still standing by the truck.

"My place." When he looked surprised, I added, "Don't you want to see the property records? My research?"

He shrugged. "Not really."

"What'd you come out here for then?"

"The video, Camille." I must have seemed confused because he added, "The security video from the mart. You said the kid may have come in."

I smiled. "So it was Patrick. You admit it."

Darren turned away, walked around the side of the building. I followed, but he went through the open doors of the mart before I could catch up. Inside, Rhonda Faye was behind the register, watching a telenovela, her way of learning Spanish so she could work the harvest in her fiancé's orchards that fall. She smiled at me, then raised her eyebrows high when she saw Darren's uniform. He stopped and held out his hand to her.

"Don't worry about him," I said to Rhonda while I unlocked the office door. "We're just assisting in his inquiries."

"You must be Rhonda," Darren said in a voice that was all honey, no sting.

From inside the office, I heard Rhonda get to her feet and reply abruptly, then the creak of the stool when she sat down again. He kept her talking for a minute or two about what usually happened at the mart while I was away, even got her to laugh a couple of times. Then he was standing behind me, the office door closed, only the high notes of Spanish melodrama audible from the mart.

I had the system up on the computer and clicked the "Play" button. "I've got fourteen days of footage."

The security recording played back on fast-forward, the digital black-and-white picture showing everything happening at lightning speed: Rhonda opening on Friday morning. Rhonda setting up outside. The first few customers darting in and out, cups of coffee and Rhonda's cinnamon rolls in their hands. Cars filling up their tanks in seconds, then speeding back out into the street. Rhonda rearranging the displays, her arms moving like a snake's tongue, flicking up and down and around. Me taking over at five, then closing at seven thirty. Everything was dark for long, steady moments, until the sun broke through the windows again, and there I was, breathing hard, walking past the door after my run. A little while later, me opening the front doors on Saturday and the slow, steady trickle of people who come through at the weekend went on for mere moments before I swept up and locked the door and then night fell, and the place was silent, dark, all day Sunday. And then, on Monday—

Darren leaned closer to the computer. "Wait, play that again. At normal speed."

I clicked on an earlier point in the timeline and then hit "Play."

On the screen, a small pickup parked in front of the open doors, and a kid with tufts of shaggy hair poking out from under a ball cap slid out the driver-side door. He walked in with the sort of narrow-hipped swagger you'd expect from the star player on a high school baseball team. Maybe he had been. Inside the mart, he nodded toward the counter, and I saw Rhonda, fiddling with a display, nod back and say something. There was no sound with the video, but I imagined what she'd said, probably something about how the cinnamon rolls were already gone and she had another pot of coffee brewing.

The kid wandered out of the image but returned a few seconds later with a bottle of soda and a packet of jerky. Rhonda walked around the counter and rang up his purchase. While she was counting his change, he turned and looked up at the camera for a long moment, his face tilted up

28

so I could see his chin and his mouth, his eyebrows knitted up like he was wondering if the camera was real. His hand, strong and long-fingered, was resting on the counter, but then he reached up to scratch his neck, to scratch the skin under his patchy stubble . . .

My spine turned to ice.

"That's him," I whispered.

I glanced at Darren: his jaw was clenched, and he was squinting at the screen—not at the kid, but at his truck. I handed him a piece of paper and a pen, and he scribbled down the license plate number. On the computer screen, I watched Patrick Beale turn back to Rhonda, flash her a smile, then take his change, go out to the truck, and drive away.

Darren picked up the phone on my desk and called in the plate, then held his hand over the receiver while he waited for the registered owner's name.

"Can you make me a copy?" he said quietly.

I nodded. "Yeah, I'll email the files to you."

"No," he said quickly. "On a drive. A USB or a disc or something."

By the time I found a USB, he was off the phone and pacing the office, his dark eyes stormy.

"Can you get all the footage on that?" he asked.

"What, all fourteen days?"

"Yeah."

"Probably."

"Great," he said, then slipped out the door.

His frown shifted to a smile for Rhonda Faye. He questioned her carefully, opaquely, about customers in the mart, while I transferred the files. But Rhonda's no idiot, and neither am I.

Later, as I drove Darren back to town, he got a call. The truck didn't belong to the kid or his parents. I asked him if it belonged to the people who owned the property next to Jeremy Leamon's, and how Lucky's talk with them had gone. He stonewalled me for twenty miles before finally giving me a name: CLA. The truck belonged to some company out of Delaware, a company called CLA LLC.

I must have said something like, "So what? The kid had a job."

His jaw rigid, Darren shook his head.

* * *

Okanogan County isn't big enough for a real morgue. It isn't even big enough for a real coroner, only the visiting kind who are called out when needed. You just have to hope they're nearby when you do. Doctor Marguerite Fleischman was one of those, an itinerant doctor who brought her tools to a vacant hospital suite near you.

The hospital in Omak—largest town in the county by far—was a slick, white, sprawling place built with federal funds and Colville casino dollars. I parked in the first spot I saw and practically ran to the building, suddenly afraid she'd been called out on another job. I was half-right and, thank God, only half-paranoid.

"Doctor Fleischman!" I shouted from across the parking lot.

"Ms. Waresch," she said, shielding her eyes from the midday sun. "You almost missed me."

"I'm glad I didn't."

She smiled. "Thanks again for your help the other day. It made the whole thing go much quicker."

I nodded. "Sure. Is it done? The autopsy, I mean."

"Just submitted my report. I'm heading out. There was a combine accident out on the Palouse. I have to be in Ritzville by five."

"What happens if you're late?"

She shrugged, smiled again. "He'll get up and walk away."

I laughed but stopped when she started for her car again. "Doctor Fleischman?"

She was a small woman, but I had to hustle to catch up with her. When I did, she said, "You know, I'm going to look you up the next time I'm here. I bet you've got some good stories from the field."

"Yeah, sure. But—"

"The stuff that you all were trying out there six, eight years ago is just now starting to trickle into the journals. Did you know that? Ridiculous that it's taken so long."

"Yeah."

"I just read about this material that expands in a wound to staunch it *from the inside*. Did you ever see that stuff?"

"Sure. But Doctor Fleischman," I said loudly when she darted between a couple of cars.

She didn't even turn her head, just said, "Yeah?"

"What about Patrick Beale?" I asked. "What did you find?"

She stopped, glanced around the parking lot, waited for me to catch up, then took off again, more slowly this time.

"You know what we saw at the barn." She pushed a strand of hair off her forehead, turned her head, looked around the lot again. She was worried, but about what? "It was worse, much worse."

She shuddered. I stopped in my tracks, my memory flashing like a television set: scrambled pixels, then for a moment, a millisecond, clear.

"Electrocution to the genitals and rectum," I said automatically, the words appearing in my mind without introduction, without context, as though they were on a teleprompter. "Cigarette burns on the inner thigh."

Doctor Fleischman stopped suddenly and turned, her eyes darting over my face, boring into mine. I looked away.

"I've seen it before," I said, uncertain whether I ever had or whether my imagination was running wild. I stared past her, out over the cars to the weedy empty lot beside the hospital. "I've seen it before," I said to myself, not sure if I believed it. I squeezed my eyes shut, willing the black and white lines in my head to settle into a picture again. When I opened them, the doctor was squinting at me in a clinical way.

I brushed past her, pointed to a car at the end of the row. "Is that yours? The gray one?" She didn't answer, but I went to it anyway. A moment later, she was at my side again.

"Where?" she demanded. "Where have you seen it?"

"Out there. In the field."

Again, I looked away, out past the dirty apartment building at the end of the lot, past its scrubby yard behind a weathered chain link fence, to the desert and the ghosts in my head. Unless—

"Ms. Waresch? Camille?"

The doctor's hand was on my arm, her brow creased.

"What else?" I said slowly. "What else was there?"

The doctor's mouth twisted. "His jeans."

"His jeans?"

"They were filthy: dirt, urine, feces."

"He was wearing them when he was tortured." Then, realization dawning, I said, "That was part of the torture."

The doctor nodded. "And soot. All along the hem of his jeans and smeared on the knees."

"A fire?"

"Yeah. One he tried to fight," she said. "There was fire retardant on his hands."

I frowned. Then the doctor dropped her bombshell.

"And chemicals. There were chemicals caked in the fibers."

"From a fire extinguisher?"

The doctor shook her head, her graying curls bouncing. "No. Ephedrine. Toluene. Ammonia. All the major ingredients for—"

"Meth," we said at the same time.

The doctor's eyes pinned me. "You know."

I shrugged.

"But you suspected." Doctor Fleischman sighed. "I probably should have too. But I haven't seen much lately. Ten years ago, yes—a couple cases every month. But none in the last year."

"What about the torture?" I said. "Have you seen that before? With meth involved, I mean."

She shook her head, but she wasn't looking at me. She was staring hard off into the distance, her brow furrowed, one hand on the trunk of her beat-up sedan, the other clutching her keys so tightly she might have cut herself.

* * *

It was nearly three o'clock by the time I stopped the truck at the foot of the gravel drive of the property on the back side of Jeremy Leamon's. I half-expected to see Lucky Phillips's patrol car come rolling down the hill or hear him shouting, threatening to arrest me for trespassing. Because that's what I was doing. I had the map of the property in my big black binder and I had my county ID, but I still had no official reason to be there. Not if they called my boss. It was a strange feeling, going somewhere I wasn't supposed to be. It had felt like that when I first started working for the Assessor's Office, but it went away after a while; after all, I had the county behind me. But when I went up that gravel drive, I wouldn't anymore.

I drummed my fingers on the steering wheel. How much was this worth to me? How badly did I want to know who killed Patrick Beale? Or, the real question: How badly did I want to put all the nightmares back into their box and shove them to the back of my mind? Pretty fucking badly.

I gunned the engine.

A little way up, the rutted gravel drive forked, but that was on the county map: take the right or the left and you'd end up in the same place. The top of the circle, the easternmost part, was about halfway up the property—the rest of it was just topographic lines, first wide, then narrower and narrower the closer they got to Jeremy Leamon's land.

I went left.

Ten minutes later, I killed the engine at the top of the circle and slid out of the truck onto the gravel. It was quiet up there, peaceful, the wind whispering through the trees. I leaned down, took the Glock out of its lockbox, checked that the topo map was still in my pocket. Then I took off on foot.

A little way off the drive, the trees opened to a sort of meadow, a field of long, dry grass glowing in the sun, rippling between two stands of pines like a river of gold. I slid on my sunglasses and skirted the trees: there had to be a path up to that barn somewhere near the road. Thirty yards along, I found what I would have found faster if I had just stayed in the truck. A narrow track curved up from the main drive and kept going straight into the grass until it stopped abruptly at a circle of scorched earth, forty, maybe fifty feet across.

At the center, a clutch of pipes were melted, twisted like demonic fingers. The blackened timber sagging around them shimmered in the sun. And the grass at the fringe of the circle was singed, none of it yet regrown. It was a fresh burn, so new I could almost feel the heat on my face.

Outside the circle, the plastic wrapper from a bottle of brake fluid—curled and charred, but still readable—had been blown into the brush. And a little farther along, there was a narrow paper receipt, curled up on itself. It was just like the receipts the register at the mart spat out. Blue-black ink, rough paper, no date, a few numbers: 1.19, 1.29, 5.99, plus tax. Just enough for two sodas and a pack of cigarettes. Two people, maybe three. And not long ago either: the receipt was barely dirty, definitely hadn't been through a rain.

I turned back. On the property record, there was a house. Small. Built in the fifties. Flammable. But a house fire this far from town would have taken out the entire hillside, maybe more. This was neat. Tidy. Controlled.

This was someone who knew what they were doing. Someone who knew to dig a firebreak, to bring fire extinguishers and a buddy to help him keep it under control. A buddy. A kid, maybe. A kid like Patrick Beale.

I never found a path to that barn from the burn site. But after some trial and error, I found a dilapidated horse fence and followed it up the hill. I went over my tracks from the Friday before, those that hadn't been obliterated in the downwash from the helicopter. I even found the last bits of Jeremy Leamon's lunch dried on a tree trunk at the edge of the clearing. But there weren't any other tracks: not in the meadow, not in the trees, not on the dirt road. It was like Patrick Beale had been spirited into that barn and hung by a vengeful ghost.

* * *

Sophie came in late again that night.

She volunteered nothing about where she'd been, or why she smelled like vodka and gasoline, or who was driving the car that rumbled away just before I heard her boots hit the stairs. But I knew enough.

Still, I stayed in my seat at the table, mute, fists clenched on my thighs, nails biting into my palms. Words of rage and frustration and fear screamed through my mind, held back only by my grinding teeth. I had no protocol for this. I had no training.

So I did nothing.

I didn't look up when she slammed the door, or when she stumbled past to the bathroom, or when I heard the vomit crash against the porcelain bowl.

Instead, I kept my eyes on the reports spread in front of me: county tax records listing three used trucks, a forklift, and a brown helicopter, a Sikorsky S-76. It was everything that CLA LLC owned, including the black Dodge truck that Patrick Beale had driven the morning of the fourth day, the truck he had parked below the window I was sitting beside.

6

The rotors roared; the wind tore at my uniform, tore at my hair. In the cockpit, the doc shouted into the radio, "No, we don't need an OR—this one's cold."

I huddled in the corner, my eyes fixed on the cloudless sky. It was watery blue, that pale, pale blue you get on the hottest days in the desert.

"You all right?" the medic, a new guy, shouted from the seat next to me. I nodded a little, smiled a little, but I couldn't look at him.

"This the guy?" the medic shouted.

The mountains leapt over the window frame when the pilot banked to the right, then fell away again when he straightened out the bird.

"Hey! Is this the guy?" the medic shouted again. His hand pushed against my shoulder, his head lurching into my line of sight. His eyes were black beneath the visor of his flight helmet, his chin bulged around the strap.

"What?" I said.

"Is this the guy you went out to retrieve?"

I nodded and hair flew into my eyes.

The medic pulled the mic closer to his mouth. "Yes, sir. She says it's Beale, sir."

No, I tried to say. I tried to shake my head, but it was stuck, locked, uncontrollable in the depths of the dream. The other medic was staring at the floor of the helicopter, and then the bird lurched, dropped, and he swore and grabbed the handrail. Something in the bag shifted and hit my foot, and I recoiled, kicked it away. A fly crawled out, crawled onto the outside of the bag. It rubbed its front legs together—quick, quick, slow, quick, quick, slow— before taking flight.

7

When I walked out of the bathroom Tuesday morning, Sophie was standing in the kitchen in pink underwear and a ratty yellow T-shirt. I stood in the threshold, my hair dripping onto my shirt, my fingers on the switch for the bathroom fan, and watched her pour a cup of coffee, take a sip of it black. She made a face, clutched her stomach. I smiled a little when she tilted the cup up for another mouthful, then shook my head when she rushed to the sink.

I turned off the fan and walked over to the counter that separated the kitchen from the living room.

"Sophie."

Still leaning over the sink, her hair tangled at the base of her neck, she said, "Yeah."

"From here on out, you're to—"

When her head snapped toward me, I stopped, reassessed.

"Please call me," I said hesitantly, then got my nerve back. "Call me if you're going to be back later than eight."

She didn't say anything, just slumped over the sink again, the thin fabric of her T-shirt tented between her shoulder blades.

Do you hear me?

She spat into the sink, then turned back to the coffee. "Yeah."

My fingernails dug into the particle board under the countertop. It was time I put on the brakes, or she never would.

"And if you're going to be drinking," I began. Her back stiffened. "If you're going to be drinking, you aren't getting your learner's permit. Or your license."

Sophie pulled her shoulders back and held her head high and rigid, then turned to the sink and poured out the coffee in a long black stream.

She placed the cup delicately on the counter, and then turned and glared at me with a hatred, a viciousness, I hadn't seen for years, hadn't seen in anyone's eyes except her father's. I shrank back, even as my hands coiled into fists and acid seared my throat. Sophie walked away.

After pulling on my boots, I snatched my keys from the counter and almost ran down the stairs, then slammed the door of the truck shut behind me.

She was just a kid. A teenager with a filthy temper and a mouth to match. A punk. Not a threat. Someone to instruct, to command, to rein in. Just like a soldier. Easy. So, why was my adrenaline racing? What was that sharp terror I had felt upstairs? Why did I flee? She was just a kid. *My* kid. My responsibility.

I texted my neighbor, Roseann, made sure she was coming to pick up Sophie, to take her to work down at Crystal's in Chelan. She was a couple of minutes away, no big deal. My temperature cooled, and the sweat on my hands dried while I waited.

Roseann's green hatchback pulled into the spot on the side of the building. Thirty seconds later, the door at the bottom of the stairs burst open and Sophie bolted out, a blur of blue jeans and orange tank top and flying black hair. Just a kid. She climbed into the hatchback and the car backed up, then turned onto the side street. A moment later, I glimpsed it on the other side of the store, accelerating toward the highway and the morning sun hanging in the sky.

The breath I had been holding leaked out of my lungs.

Just a kid. My kid. And her father's.

Sitting in the sun, I shivered, then grit my teeth and cracked my back. *Not going there.*

I flipped open my phone and called a friend at the State—Harry German, a buddy I knew only on the other end of the line, a guy with the answers when all my county resources had dried up. He promised to do some digging—confidentially—on the company that owned the truck Patrick Beale was driving before he was killed, and then he asked if I was okay.

"Yeah," I said, but he knew I was lying. You get a feeling for it out there in the field, out in the dust and the sand. Harry had been there too. That's why he broke the rules for me sometimes when I really needed it. Because we both knew.

"What's going on, Waresch?" he said gruffly.

"Nothing." But I could hear him waiting, so I told him something. It was mostly the truth anyway. "Sophie."

"Yeah," he drawled. "That was always gonna be rough, but I been telling you that for years."

"I don't know how you do it, man."

Harry laughed loudly, a great barking belly laugh that always made me smile. He had five kids, all of them doing well, staying out of trouble. Unless *he* was lying.

"Well, it helps to start 'em young. Even when you're deployed, Camille. You gotta come home and get back into it as quickly as you can."

"Yeah, I know. I screwed up. Shoulda had her with me a long time ago."

"What did she do?"

"I don't know, but she's been drinking. Came home puking last night."

Harry whistled long and low. "Didn't she just turn fifteen?"

"Yeah."

"What'd you do?"

"I talked to her this morning."

"Did you lay down the law?"

"No. She already hates me; that would just make it worse."

"She ain't your friend, Waresch," Harry growled. "She's your kid. You gotta get that straight."

"Yeah. I know."

"So you gotta do something."

"Like what?" I snapped. "Wash her mouth out with soap? Chain her up like a dog?"

Harry sighed. "Structure, soldier. Kids need structure. Just like you and me."

He was right. That had been the hardest part of coming home from the Army: no cage to climb up. No cage to throw myself against. I got past it eventually, built the right walls inside my head. But building one for my kid . . . I didn't even have a hammer.

"Think about it," Harry said.

"Yeah." I shook my head. "Just, uh . . . just call me when you find something, yeah?"

Afterward, I turned the key in the ignition and drove the truck out of the lot, the tires crunching the gravel and spitting it out, pinging on the wheel wells. Then, on a whim, I yanked the wheel to the right and pulled into the lot at the front of the mart.

On the walkway in front, Rhonda was pouring a bucket of fat, stubby cucumbers into an ice-filled metal tub. I said good morning and walked straight through to the office. A minute later, Rhonda was placing a cup of coffee and a cheese Danish beside the keyboard.

"So," she said, instead of hello. "What's with the cop yesterday?"

"Oh, you know."

"He thinks we got something to do with that kid's murder?"

"Yeah." I clicked through the files on the desktop until I got to the security footage. "He thinks we kidnapped him and fed him pastries until he hemorrhaged."

Rhonda didn't laugh. "What'd he want with the camera?"

As far as I was concerned, there wasn't anything to tell, but Rhonda was like a pit bull: once she got something in her jaw, she wouldn't let go.

"I told him—" I began, and then thought better of it. "I told him I heard the dead guy everyone's talking about might have been a local kid, and I told him he could check the footage if he wanted. Maybe he could establish the last time anyone saw him."

"You didn't look at much of it yesterday."

"Yeah, well . . . I had things to do, so I just made him a copy. Alright with you?"

I looked away from the computer screen, craned my neck to look up at Rhonda. She towered over me even when I was standing. Sitting down and looking up, I could barely see past the mountain of her boobs stuffed inside a frilly red shirt.

"I'll tell you the last time I saw him." Rhonda crossed her arms under her breasts. "It was a little over a week ago. Week and a half, maybe."

Surprised, I turned back to the computer and opened the file.

"You won't see it on there," Rhonda said.

I clicked on the playback bar to where I figured ten days ago began. "Why not?"

"Because it wasn't here," she said, snot dripping from her voice.

I pushed the chair back and crossed my arms too. "Oh yeah?"

Rhonda dropped her arms. "It was in Oroville. At a diner."

"Did you tell Darren that?"

"No." She paused, sneered a little. "He didn't ask."

"Yeah. That's awesome, Rhonda."

"I'm telling *you*."

I shook my head and turned back to the desk, rummaged in the drawers for another USB drive.

"He was with some other guy," Rhonda said. "Someone I didn't recognize. Tall, tattoos everywhere."

"What else did you notice?"

"Long hair, dark. Really tan—or maybe he was Latino. Older than the kid. Twenty-five, twenty-six. Something like that."

At the back of a drawer, I found another drive. It was caked with dust, but the light at the end glowed when I plugged it in. I dragged the files into the window and waited while the light flickered on and off, green then dark, until all the video had been saved.

"You going to eat that?" Rhonda said, pointing at the Danish. "It's a good batch."

"Yeah." But I didn't touch the pastry.

Rhonda sighed. "Hey, I gotta leave a little early today. Have to go try on my wedding dress."

"Yeah, okay. When?"

"Four thirty."

"Okay, I'll be here."

Rhonda swept out, then back again, leaning on the doorjamb. "You're coming to the wedding."

"Uh, yeah," I said, but I was watching the video, not paying attention to her.

"I'll pick up something nice for you to wear, put it on Tim's account. You can pay him back later."

"Yeah." My eyes flicked over the screen, following the black-and-white people and the black-and-white vehicles racing through fourteen days. "Sure."

*   *   *

Later, I packed a box of Danishes. Then I got in the truck. At the edge of the parking lot, I turned left toward the hills, drove for a couple of miles before turning left again, and then again a few miles after that. As I came out of a long bend that wound down the side of a hill, I put on the brakes and turned into the driveway of Ed and Christine Beale's place.

Ed was in the yard; I could just see his blue coveralls bent over the engine of an old truck. He looked up when I turned into the drive, put his tools down when I slammed the door, and wiped the grease off his long fingers on a red rag streaked with black before he took the pastry box from me. But he didn't look me in the eye, not once.

"I was sorry to hear about your boy," I said softly.

Ed was still. I followed his gaze out to the field where his stock was grazing. Brown cattle, steers, their necks bent low, their tails flicking lazily.

"It isn't right," I said, "what they did to him."

Ed laughed. "Yeah?" he mumbled.

Surprised, I glanced at him out of the corner of my eye. Not that I hadn't seen someone grieve like that before. Not that I hadn't seen it a hundred times, just clothed in Army green, not blue coveralls.

So I waited, stood there like a statue and waited for him to say what he needed to say.

"He was a good kid," Ed said suddenly.

I nodded but kept my mouth shut.

Still gazing out at his fields, Ed said, "You know he played baseball all four years of high school? He was gonna play in college too."

"College?"

"Yeah. He was gonna go to Western. Coach was scouting him."

"But he didn't go."

Ed sighed. "Naw. Last winter, he comes and says to me, 'Dad, I'm through. I played enough ball.' And I said, 'Okay, son. You gotta do what you think is right.'"

"That why he stuck around here?"

Ed nodded.

"Did he stay here at the house?"

Ed slowly shook his head, the afternoon sun catching in his graying blond hair, shaggy and curling at the ears like he'd waited too long between cuts. Like his son's hair.

"No," he finally said. "I told him, 'If you ain't going to college, go get a job, put food in your mouth.'"

"Did he? Get a job, I mean."

"Yeah."

"A good one?"

"He was makin' money. Got himself an apartment down in Omak. Got himself a truck."

Not his truck, I thought.

Ed shook his head again, slapped the grease rag against his thigh. "It's too bad it wasn't working out."

I narrowed my eyes. "How's that?"

"Don't know. But he'd been talking about leaving, maybe going down to Texas. Houston, maybe."

Texas? Texas was big time for narcotics. Didn't take a genius to figure that out.

"Was he going to work for the same people?" I said.

"No." Ed clenched his jaw. "He said he wanted a fresh start. Something new."

"Don't we all," I said under my breath.

Angry, his brow compressed into ragged valleys, Ed said, "No. No, we don't all want that. Me and Christine like it just fine here. And I told him that, told him there was no point leaving the Okanogan. I told him there's no better place."

Ed squeezed his eyes shut, then raised his arms and pressed his hands hard into his eyes. His shoulders heaved and I reached out to the one nearest me. But he reacted like my hand was a high-voltage line: dropped his arms just as quickly as he'd brought them up and rounded on me, his black eyes fierce and sparking in his deeply tanned face.

"I should have told him to go," Ed shouted, his voice soaked with rage and grief. "I should have put him on the road myself."

"You don't know that would have helped anything. You can't know that."

"They wouldn't have found him hanging in that barn!" Spittle flecked Ed's stubble. "I know that!"

I locked my hands on his shoulders, held him at arm's length. "You don't know that."

But Ed was bigger and stronger than me; he broke free. "Goddamnit, Camille. I do. I *do* know it. And I'll take it to my grave."

For a moment I watched him, the hair on the side of his head splayed up violently in the high wind that came off the mountain, the collar of his coveralls flattened against his neck, the pain in his eyes. It was the kind of pain that makes you crazy. The kind of pain no one should feel and no one else should see.

Embarrassed, I looked away to his golden field, to the narrow valley and the red hills and the blistering blue sky.

"Do you know who he was working for?" I asked quietly. Out of the corner of my eye I saw Ed shrug. "Do you know who did that to your boy?"

But Ed just shook his head, shut his eyes. When he opened them, they were flat and black and depthless, like a mountain lake on a still day. He shook his head again, then picked up the box of Rhonda's Danishes and mumbled thanks. He turned and walked through the open garage door, disappearing into the house. He wasn't coming back. Not that day. Not ever.

So I got in the truck and reversed out of the drive. The last thing I saw before I headed back the way I came was Christine Beale peering out the window, a frilly white curtain framing her slack, puffy face.

* * *

There aren't many places in the Okanogan where you could store a helicopter—just a few small airfields—and it didn't take much to learn most of them didn't have any helicopters or a place to keep one. But over near Chelan, there's this airstrip with a cluster of private hangars off to one side. Every now and then, a tall, wide door will slide open, and a shiny four-seater will roll out of the air-conditioned gloom on skinny wheels and toothpick legs. It wobbles down the apron and then around the corner to the runway and speeds off, lifting up toward the end of the asphalt, its wings buoyed up by the dry winds that sweep down through the valley. When I was a kid, my dad would take me down there to watch them. He'd tell me about how they went up and came down again, why they stayed up there, and how sometimes, they didn't. He said they were like big, brittle birds, their bones too fragile to survive during the storms we get sometimes.

I thought about that a lot out in the desert, in Iraq. I spent a lot of time flying there, on helicopters mostly, going out to the field with one of the docs, a gurney, and a mobile medical kit. We'd sit around with the pilot in a shack out at the airfield watching satellite TV, waiting on an old plastic couch for the next call to come in. When it did, we'd throw on our gear and sprint out onto a dusty tarmac that shimmered in the heat, leaving the fat civilian guy, who always scoped my boobs, alone in the shed with the telenovelas and black-and-white Westerns and cartoons. I'd hang on for dear life when the bird lifted off, then tilted forward and soared out over the sand. And I'd pray to whatever was listening that I'd live to see my baby girl one more time. I'd pray that the bird's brittle bones wouldn't break.

In Chelan, in August of that year when everything started to go to shit, my truck rolled to a stop in front of the office at the airstrip. A golden dog sprawled on a patch of grass, its tongue lolling, dripping slobber on its paws and into its shiny metal dish. It smiled at me like I was a long-lost friend. Behind it, the office was gray and long and low—government issue, just like the shed back in Iraq. Inside, the air conditioning was cranked up so high you'd think you were in Baghdad. Squatting in the middle of the room was a cracked brown Naugahyde sofa, a layer of dust on the arm glowing white in a shaft of sunlight shining through a high window, CNN scrolling soundlessly on the TV in front of it.

"Just be a minute," a man shouted, his voice muffled. A moment later, a toilet flushed, a sink ran, and then a guy in an orange polo two sizes too small for his gut walked out from the back room, still wiping his hands on his jeans.

"How you doing?" He extended his hand. Instead of taking it, I flashed my clipboard.

"Camille Waresch. I'm from the county." I didn't bother to tell him *which* county. Chelan was outside my jurisdiction, and I wasn't exactly there on official business even if it had been. I was skating, lying, whatever you want to call it. In any case, betting he wouldn't look too closely at the paperwork.

His watery blue eyes walked down the front of my body and back up again. Then he took the clipboard. *Damn.*

"County assessor," he muttered and looked up, confused.

I smiled. "Property tax inspector."

His face hardened, his eyes narrowed.

I jerked my thumb over my shoulder. "Just need to take a look at a one of the hangars."

Then he smiled, his eyeteeth creasing his bottom lip. "You got a warrant?"

"Don't need one," I said, then took the clipboard from his hand. A wet thumbprint stained the page of the assessment order I'd drafted that morning. "I'm not law enforcement."

"Look, lady. You want into a hangar, you got to show me something more official than that."

"Like my boobs?"

That caught him off guard.

"I need to take a look at the odometer on an aircraft," I said before he got any ideas. "It's standard procedure; I'm not going to take anything."

He squinted at me so hard I could see the wheels turning in his head. Then he jerked his head toward the window that looked out on the airstrip. "Ain't you supposed to drive a county vehicle?"

"It's in the shop."

He jabbed a fat finger at my clipboard. "And if I called that number, someone'd tell me this is all legit?"

I held the clipboard out to him, the heel of my hand over the Okanogan County seal, and bluffed. "Go ahead." I was confident no one would answer the phone anyway.

He looked down at the clipboard like it was covered in shit. Then he looked at me like I was too. But he turned around and lumbered to the back room. A moment later, I heard squeaky metal hinges opening and he shouted, "Which hangar?"

"The one that has a brown Sikorsky."

I slipped my sunglasses on when I followed him outside and kept my distance down the gravel path to the seventh hangar. At the far end of the airstrip, a woman with a long gray ponytail under a John Deere green ball cap rode away from us on a mower, skirting the tarmac. When I turned back, the guy from the office was walking into the hangar, leaving the door open for me.

Inside, the Sikorsky S-76 perched like a bird of prey. It was mud-brown and glossy, its rotor drooping like wings at rest, its pointed nose like a raptor's beak, its belly just large enough to swallow a gurney, a pilot, and a couple of medics. It was just like I had pictured it, just like the photos I had seen online of rescue copters and medivac birds. Just like the birds I had ridden in Iraq.

The guy in orange was leaning against the wall, his hands tucked up into his armpits.

I nodded at the helicopter. "You ever been up in one of these?"

"Nope."

"Me neither," I lied. "They scare the piss out of me."

He laughed. I guess the tension was running higher than I thought.

I put my hand on the side of the passenger compartment, trailed it along as I walked around the airframe, peeking into the windows, the gritty dust and slick paint sliding beneath my fingertips.

"Like flying grenades, my dad used to say. He was in 'Nam, so I guess he knew."

"Yeah?" the guy said. "My old man went, too."

"He ever talk about it?" I tilted my head back to get a better look at the blades, four of them cocked at right angles from the rotor.

"Naw. He don't talk much anyway."

"My dad didn't talk about it either."

"He still around?"

I clenched my jaw, closed my eyes, just glad the idiot couldn't see me on the pilot's side of the bird. "No," I said as lightly as I could. "He passed earlier this year."

"Sorry to hear that."

I tried the pilot's door. *Damnit.* Locked.

"You got the keys for this thing?" I asked.

"Nope."

I leaned against the window, my hands framing my eyes against the glare of the fluorescents.

"This aircraft's got a lot of miles on it," I said, my voice extra loud in the echoing hangar. "I mean, for its age."

Through the windows of the passenger compartment, I saw the guy shrug his shoulders. "It goes out every few weeks."

"Taking tourists out over the lake or something?" I said absently and made a show of writing down what I could see of the odometer reading.

"No idea. I see a guy come and pick it up in the afternoon."

"Does it come right back?"

"I guess. I'm never here for the return."

"You work days?"

"Yeah."

"Who's the lucky bastard who gets the night shift?" I said, then laughed.

"Nobody." The guy glanced at his watch, a chunky black digital model. "There's no one here after five."

* * *

After the airfield, the day was mostly a lost cause. After hitting one property down south, I drifted back to Chelan when I got hungry. A BLT and an iced tea later, I lingered in the booth in the back corner of Dee Dee's, ignoring the dirty looks from my waitress and staring at the cursor blinking on the blank first line of my blank assessment report.

"Hey!" someone said. I didn't look up: the restaurant was busy and there was no reason why any of the sticky, sunburned tourists would "hey" me on their way back to the lake or out to the mountains.

"Hey, how's it going?" the same voice said, louder this time. Then he slid into the plastic booth opposite me. Lyle.

I forced a smile. "Hey."

"What are you doing down here, Sis?"

I hated it when he called me that, mostly because I wasn't—I'm not—his sister, not even his sister-in-law, technically. As far as Lyle is concerned, I'd long considered myself a victim of circumstance. I stared back in silence. He laughed in that high-pitched "ha-ha-ha" of the perpetually stoned.

Lyle swiped a wilted French fry from my plate. "On the beat?"

"Something like that," I said and closed my laptop. The USB stick in the drive flashed green.

"Yeah, I just, uh . . ." Lyle smiled a little smile that was sweet by design. "I just wanted to say hey. I haven't seen you for a while. Since the funeral, I mean."

To which he hadn't been invited. But I didn't want to be mean, so I didn't say that. Instead, I nodded and managed a disinterested "How have you been?"

Lyle's usual monologue began, the same one I'd heard at least a couple of times a year in every one of the five or six years since he'd gotten out of juvie. The theme was always different, but the message was always the same: *I know the last thing didn't work out, but now I'm doing this other thing that's really awesome, Sis, and you gotta check it out, I mean it's freaking amazing. And, you know, we're taking investments!* And that's where I'd frown and pull the laptop closer, and he'd say, *"I mean, not just yet, you know, we're working on a business plan, but a month, two months tops, and we're totally in the game and we're gonna make bank."* And that's when I'd smile and nod and say good luck and back away and try not to notice the hopeful, hangdog look he always gave me. Because that just ruined me, that look that said, *"Nothing's gone right yet, but I'm still tryin'. My big brother may have abandoned me, my mom may have driven off a cliff, but I'm still tryin'."* That look just ruined me. And he knew it.

But this time—miraculously—this time was different. This time, he was halfway through the usual story when I looked out the window and across the street and saw Sophie ducking out of Crystal's schmaltzy little tourist shop. Sophie with her cell phone at her ear and on her face the intense, lip-biting look of someone who's talking to someone she's really into, someone she'd really like to screw. Just the look I wanted to see on my fifteen-year-old's face.

Lyle twisted around, his grimy-nailed hand spread on the gold-flecked Formica.

"What are you looking at?" he said, still all excited. Then he added under his breath, "Oh shit."

"What?" I snapped, glaring at him like he was fresh meat.

He turned back toward me, his icy-blue eyes wide. "I am the worst uncle *ever*."

"That's news?" I said it without thinking, then immediately regretted it.

No use kicking the underdog, I thought. It was something my father had said about a lot of people, not just Lyle. But even though Dad knew Lyle, even though—hell, maybe *because*—he knew where he came from, *what* he came from . . . Let's just say that Dad was a helluva lot nicer to him than I was. And much as I hated the circumstances, he was the only other family Sophie had left.

"Yeah," Lyle said, drawing the word out to at least five syllables. "I totally forgot her birthday. I mean, I haven't hung out with her for a few weeks. Been busy with the new bizness. *Shee-it*, I even forgot to call her. It was last week, right?"

"Two weeks ago. Two *Wednesdays* ago."

Lyle's eyes darted back and forth, to me, to the window, to the grease-coated photo of Lake Chelan on the opposite wall. Then he slammed his hand on the table.

"I know! I got it!" Lyle shouted. Everyone on our side of the restaurant stopped and stared, including my snarly waitress. "I'll come by tonight." He pointed one long, bony finger at me. "I got the perfect thing for Soph."

I didn't have time to stop him, to persuade him to forget it. He slid out of the booth faster than he'd arrived and darted out the door, the smell of unwashed clothes and stale pot trailing behind him. I watched him walk out of sight, then looked for Sophie again. But she was long gone.

*   *   *

Rhonda took off at four thirty; I was there behind the counter for the afternoon rush. Five customers picking up beer for the evening and another two filling up their tanks. Soon, I was up one hundred and thirty-nine and change, plus a little completely bullshit gossip about the dead kid.

Around six thirty, I started sweeping up, pushing the wide, frayed broom across the worn wooden floor, down one aisle, around the corner, and down the next. As I worked my way around the room, a sedan pulled up in front of the mart. The engine shut off and a kid too small and mousy to be driving his mother's old Ford stepped out and strolled to the open door. I had seen him just that morning, driving with the windows down and the breeze from the road still ruffling his hair as he slowed to turn into the driveway of Ed and Christine Beale's place just after I pulled out. I had waved and he had waved back.

That evening, he walked into the mart quietly, respectfully. He even said, "Good evening, ma'am," before going to the cooler and pulling out a glass bottle of Mexican Coke. I watched him out of the corner of my eye, not quite sure there was a family resemblance. But he had his dad's hair, minus the gray, and his mother's thin face, and the same squared-off shoulders—even if they were a lot sharper—as his older brother.

"I'll be right there," I said, then turned down the last aisle, shuffling the push broom in front of me.

"That's alright," the kid said quietly. He set the soda on the counter and waited, his face toward the wall and his back to me. His spine was rigid, his shoulder blades sharp and bony beneath his red T-shirt.

I finished up, then leaned the broom against the wall beside the office door.

"It's, uh, it's Mrs. Scott, isn't it?" he said when I got to the register.

My eyes shot up, angry, startled. I had never been—*would never be*—Mrs. Scott.

"*No,*" I growled.

The boy stepped backward, raised his hands. "You're, um . . . you're Sophie's mom, right?"

Oh. *Sophie* Scott. I didn't have any reason to think of her that way. To me, she was just Sophie, my girl Sophie. And since my parents had custody, because the state had made them her guardians . . . Until that May, until my father died . . . God, it had been years—*years*—since I'd even thought of her last name. Scott. Like her father, Oren Scott. Like her uncle, Lyle Scott. But sure as hell *not* like me.

"Ma'am?" the boy said, his eyes round as a deer in my headlights. "Ma'am, are you alright?"

I shook my head, scraped my fingers along my scalp. "Yeah, I'm Sophie's mom."

"Sorry." The boy's face flushed pink, his mouth opening and closing soundlessly.

"No, *I'm* sorry." I held out my hand. "You can call me Camille."

He shook my hand, his fingers long and strong, his grip good, better than I'd expect from a kid as wiry as he looked.

"Whatcha got there, then?" I said and nodded to the soda bottle in his hand.

"Just a . . . just a Coke." He put it on the counter, then stepped back again.

I nodded and rang up the sale.

"Is she around?" he said, his voice small, nervous. "Sophie, I mean."

I reached under the counter for the bottle opener and slid it across to him, dodging his question. "You're Ed and Christine's boy. The younger one."

The kid glanced out the door to his mother's Ford. Then he nodded. "I'm Todd."

"I was sorry to hear about your brother."

He swallowed, his Adam's apple bobbing in his skinny neck. He nodded.

"Were you close?" I said without thinking, then regretted it. "I mean—"

But the kid just shrugged and kept staring out the window.

"You go to school with Sophie?" I tried.

"Yeah." He nodded, then turned toward me again. "I mean, yes. When we start back in a couple of weeks."

"Do you have any classes together?"

"I'll be a junior." When I stared at him, clueless, he smirked and said, "I tutored her in Spanish last year."

I swallowed, fought the blood staining my cheeks in embarrassment. I knew she had just finished her freshman year but had no idea she took Spanish. Not that I would ever admit that.

"Sophie was Patrick's friend too, right?" I asked.

The kid nodded again, looked away, but I saw the shadow cross his face. *Interesting.*

"I never met him," I said, hoping Todd would fill the silence by filling in the gaps.

He frowned. "Really?" His disbelief was angry, scornful. "They were, I mean they used to—"

"What?" I said, more intensely than I should have. When the kid backed away, I felt myself leaning forward, my shoulders tightening, my fingers spread on the counter, ready to pounce. Quickly, I pulled back, shoved my hands in my pockets, smoothed the edges off my face.

"Sorry." I tried to laugh. "It's been a long day. What were you saying?"

He swallowed hard, watched me warily. "They were dating. Or they used to, anyway."

"When was that?"

"I don't want to get Sophie into trouble."

"She's not in trouble," I said too quickly. "I'm just curious when it was, that's all. Was it before he got that job?"

Todd Beale shook his head but then turned the shake into a nod. He had dark blond hair that flopped a little when he did. It needed to be cut, but not as badly as his brother's had needed it. Or his dad's. In a flash, I wondered if anyone would ever think something like that about me and Sophie. How similar we are, I mean. But, no. No, they wouldn't.

"Yes, ma'am," Todd said, his voice certain and a little—yes, a little angry. Righteous anger? His parents weren't quite Bible-thumpers, but not far off. Or was he jealous that his brother had a girlfriend and he didn't? "They were dating before that. It was February when they got together, and he moved out in April."

"Were they still dating then?"

Todd nodded. Something more passed across his face, something dark.

"Was it a *good* job?" I asked as though I was just curious. "Did he like the people he was working for?"

"Yeah. He hung out with them a lot. I heard him say they had good parties."

"You ever go to one?"

Todd shook his head, his eyes unreadable.

"Not your crowd?"

"No, ma'am."

"He ever introduce you to anyone he worked with?"

Todd shook his head again. "I saw him driving through a couple of times. Him and another guy. They gave him a nice truck to drive, a Dodge."

A Dodge truck. A Dodge truck like the black Dodge on the fourth day of the footage from the mart's camera.

I smiled tightly. "He ever let you take it out for a spin?"

Todd shrugged. "No. I guess it was just for work."

"Nice truck for farm work."

"He wasn't working on a farm."

"Around here? What else is there to do?"

"He said it was supply chain management, distribution, something like that."

"Distribution," I said carefully. "What, like the guy who delivers the beer?"

"I guess."

"And the other guy did runs with him?"

"Yeah."

"Do you know him? I mean the guy he worked with."

"No," Todd said. "He had long hair. Patrick was saving up to get a tattoo like his."

"Yeah?" I said. "What of?"

"A snake, I think." The kid grimaced. "He said the guy had a snake tattooed on his neck."

All the scenes in the barn flashed across my mind's eye: walking in on the kid hanging from the wire noose, the helicopter landing in a cloud of dust, Darren and Moreno staring, Jeremy Leamon's face going from pissed off to shocked, to sick. And then the field examination with Doctor Fleischman, painstakingly taking notes of everything she said, every detail she noted. She hadn't said anything about a tattoo. Patrick Beale hadn't even had enough time for that.

Across the counter, the kid reached into his pocket, pulled out a brown wallet, said, "What do I owe you?"

I looked up, startled. *Todd, not Patrick. Todd, whole. And alive.*

"I heard he had a nice place down in Omak," I said, to keep him talking. "Did you ever visit?"

"No, ma'am," Todd said firmly, but there was that shadow again. *He's lying.*

"Really? I thought you were close."

The kid's jaw flexed. "Yeah."

"Your parents go down to visit?"

"No." At least *that* appeared to be the truth.

"But he was still dating Sophie when he moved out."

I turned my head toward the window, watched a spit of dust rise behind a passing truck and blow away. The shadow across Todd's face appeared again, and this time it didn't lift.

Todd dropped the cash on the counter, thrust his hand in his pocket, and pulled out the keys to the old Ford sedan. He grabbed the neck of the bottle of soda and turned and walked toward the door, his heels pounding into the old board floors with every step.

*   *   *

An hour later, I was locking the doors when a dirt bike pulled into the lot, the noise bouncing between the few buildings in town and shooting out across the fields beyond. In the orange light I saw the rider dismount by the gas pump. I opened my mouth to tell him the pumps were off, but then he took off his helmet.

"Hey, Sis!" Lyle said, pushing shaggy, sweat-soaked hair back from his forehead. "Is Sophie around?"

"Yeah. But, listen—"

"*Sophie!*" Lyle shouted, his hands cupped around his mouth. "*Soph!* Where you at?"

In the still air, I heard Sophie's heels hit the floor upstairs. "Lyle?" she said out the window in her best, girliest voice.

"I got a present for you!" he shouted, then loped around the corner.

I sent the deadbolt home on the mart's front door and hurried after him. When I got to the back lot, beside the big metal feed tub full of leggy basil that had gone to seed, Sophie was tearing cheap wrapping paper off a shapeless mass while Lyle, a sloppy grin on his unshaven face and an empty green backpack held limply in his hand, watched. The wrapping paper drifted to the gravel, and Sophie jumped into Lyle's arms, a stuffed animal bouncing off the back of his head.

"I love it!" she squealed, stepping back and holding the bear up. It was nothing special, really: a brown teddy bear with shiny plastic eyes and a bushy tail. But it wore camo gear and chunky black boots and an M16 strapped across its chest. If *I* had given it to her, she would have called me a fascist, but from Lyle, it was an adorable toy from her favorite—her only—uncle.

I stood a few feet away, my hands in my pockets, watching them chatter, Lyle showing her how to put the gun in Teddy's paws. He laughed when she pretended to shoot up the side of the mart, then laughed harder, his faded T-shirt rising and falling over his knobbly rib cage, when she pretended to let off a few rounds into his chest. Where he'd gotten the bear at such short notice—*why* he'd gotten it—I had no idea, but Lyle had always been strangely resourceful, even when he was just a little kid tagging around after me and Oren back in the day.

Then Sophie hugged the bear to her chest and said earnestly, "You ready to go?"

"Yeah," Lyle said. "Let's do it!"

"Where are you going?" I asked from the sidelines.

Sophie rolled her eyes, but Lyle turned, buoyant as ever, grinning widely. "Ice cream! You wanna go, Sis?"

"You know, that sounds good. I'll drive."

I don't know how Sophie managed to toss her head and stomp off in a way that screamed so much annoyance and anger and impatience, but she did it then, like she had so many times in the four months since we'd been thrown together again.

"Awesome!" Lyle exclaimed. "I'll just bring the bike around back. You don't mind if I put my stuff in your place while we're gone, do you?"

I was still staring at Sophie, still fighting to keep the rage bottled up. "What?" I said, refocusing on him.

"My stuff? Is it okay if I put it in your place while we're gone?"

"No. Put the bike in the truck. You can go home from the ice cream place."

* * *

Summer in Chelan can be a little crazy. The tourists come out from the cities with their motor boats and their beer kegs and their money. They buzz around the lake on water skis and have house parties and puke in the brown grass around their rentals. I'm not saying it turns into Vegas or something. I just hear from the boys in the Sheriff's Office that the city people can run a little amok.

But there are others—the young and the sober, I guess—who are good for business. They buy the trinkets in shops like Crystal's and rent canoes and take their kids out for sundaes at the only good ice cream place in town. And just about the time the little ones are packed off to bed, the teenagers descend, keeping stools inside and out, and even the concrete curb, occupied until the owner, a sinewy guy from Idaho called Hank, kicks them all out.

By the time we got there that night, the crowd was a seething mass of sugar and hormones. Sophie and Lyle, who had been chattering about nothing I could follow the entire way there, fell silent, their heads turning as the truck drifted past the big neon ice cream cone that clung to the side of the A-frame building.

"Omigod," Sophie said suddenly.

"What?" I asked, still looking for a parking place.

"Nothing."

I glanced at her sitting next to me, her skinny butt wedged in the middle of the bench seat. She looked at her uncle, who raised his eyebrows at her like he didn't know what she meant, but before I looked away, I swear I saw him wink.

After standing in the twenty-person-deep line to order, then escaping from the deafening din and sickly sweet air inside the place, Lyle and I waited for a table and our ice cream outside while Sophie flitted from table to table. I didn't know any of the dozen different kids she hugged quickly, urgently, or the second dozen she engaged in furious, enthusiastic conversation. Her face lit up with every loud giggle, every time a kid leaned in with some new story. Who was this girl?

Finally, a couple vacated half a table, and Lyle and I swooped in. A few minutes later, our number was scratchily called over the loudspeaker. Lyle went to pick up the ice cream and Sophie. She ate hers—bananas Foster with a mountain of whipped cream—while perched on Lyle's knee, then got up and said she was going to the bathroom.

The bathroom at Hank's place is on the outside wall, a steel door to a tiny unisex stall, so there's always a line. And near it, just before you step past the big plate-glass windows into semi-darkness, is the last table, the last set of orange metal stools. That night, a group of older kids sat on those stools and on each other, the rest slouching around the edges. The guys looked like they thought they were tough—tougher than bananas Foster, anyway—and the girls had long hair and piercings and dull, flat eyes. I wondered what they were doing there, right up until I saw Sophie bend down and say something to one of them, a kid—no, a *man*—with tattoos up and down his ropy brown arms and long black hair that didn't quite hide the ink on his neck. I wondered right up until I saw him grab her ass.

"—then we'll *sell* the extra stuff next summer," Lyle was saying. "I figure we'll have like a seven, eight hundred percent profit—Hey, what's up?"

I was crouching, one foot on the metal stool, my fingers splayed on the metal mesh table top, ready to vault over it. Lyle sat opposite, looking up at me, his brow creased, his eyes curious. Then he twisted around until he saw what I saw: Sophie bending over, talking to the man who had just grabbed her ass, her dark hair hanging in a curtain, hiding her face from me.

"Hey, who's that?" Lyle asked over his shoulder. He turned back to me. "Do you know him?"

"No," I said through clenched teeth. I glanced at Lyle. "Do you?"

Lyle glanced again and shook his head. I stood up, determined to deal with this, whatever this was.

"Hey, Sis." Lyle said it so quietly I barely heard him over the noise. He put his hand on my wrist; he was gentle, his fingers barely brushing my skin, but it felt like a thousand volts. "Sit down."

I glanced at him. He looked serious and—somehow—wise. For the first time I wondered if this loser, this complete failure, knew more about raising my kid than I did. I glanced back at Sophie, her thin wrist in the black-haired man's paw. Slowly, my eyes still on her, I sat down.

"Look, Camille," Lyle said. He shrugged. "Sophie's at a weird age, right? And everything that happened this year just makes it . . . *weirder.*"

"So?"

"So . . . cut her some slack, alright? She's got shit to deal with."

"Uh-huh."

"Yeah, like that guy, okay?"

Lyle jerked his thumb over his shoulder, to where Sophie was now standing in line for the bathroom, that man beside her, his arm curled down and around her back, his hand cupping her hip, murmuring into her ear.

"She didn't go over there right away. I mean, he's probably just someone she met at the shop or something like that. You know, one of these people from Seattle who come out for the weekend or something."

"It's Tuesday."

"You know what I mean."

Yeah, I did know what he meant and it made some sense, even though Lyle had been the one to say it. And, more than that, I knew what I would have done—how much *worse* I would have done—if my mother had dared to confront me about a situation like that. So I bit my tongue when she finally came back to the table, held it all the way back to the apartment. Instead, I drove, listening to the hum of the tires on the highway and gnashing my teeth while she sprawled in the passenger seat, her face glowing in the light of her phone.

Eventually, I pulled the truck into the dark lot behind the mart. The few streets in town were empty, the trailers and houses dark. Without a word, Sophie slid out of the passenger seat, then darted to our door, unlocked it, and went upstairs. I stayed in the truck, my hands still on the wheel, listening to the steady plink, plink, plink of the engine cooling. Time passed, I don't know how long, but the light in the bedroom upstairs stayed on. Then the engine was still, quiet.

I opened the door and stepped out of the truck. The gravel crunched under my feet as I walked around the building, to the front. Inside the mart, the red pinprick on the security camera shone near the ceiling by the coolers, the sallow light from the streetlamp casting deep shadows behind the shelves. I locked the glass doors behind me and made my way to the office. Something had been preying on my mind all day: that helicopter owned by CLA LLC.

Half an hour later, I knew which types of commercially available helos had a range to get me from Chelan over the rough, deserted back country of the county to the first major highway in the United States, or over the Canadian border and back again. I knew exactly how much weight each of those could carry. And I knew that the model in the hangar in Chelan was one of the best for the job: fast and so common it was easy to hide in plain sight or on a dirt track in a back field next to a disused barn. Perfect for moving as much meth as Patrick and his fellow felons could produce.

I plugged in the USB and opened the video feed from the mart's camera, then pressed "Fast-forward." I sat motionless, my eyes wide and unblinking, while the first few days played, until the footage I had seen the day before with Darren flew past. Then I slowed it down, watched the time pass. I hit "Stop." I hit "Reverse." At 5:57 PM on the seventh day, a Thursday, a familiar truck, a black Dodge, parked in front of the mart.

Patrick, wearing a baseball cap again, came through the doors, then walked out of the picture right away. The next person through the doors moved more slowly, swaggered. He stopped in the middle of the floor, coolly looked around, said something, then strode to the counter.

I paused the video and enlarged it, squinting at the screen until I was sure the tattoo on his neck was the same one I had seen from thirty feet away at the ice cream place in Chelan that night. Then I saw the tats on his arm, the dark lines blurry on the video, and I remembered what Rhonda had told me, and I wondered. Why had she told me she'd seen Patrick with some Latino guy in Oroville? Here he was, in the mart, in front of the counter she lived at for ten hours a day, five days a week. Here they both were on what could have been the last day Patrick was alive.

But after the swaggering Latino guy arrived at the counter, after Patrick joined him there, two bottles of soda in his hands, I knew why.

It was *me* behind the counter. Me, on a Thursday evening after Rhonda had gone home. Me, who handed Patrick's buddy a pack of cigarettes and took his money and put it in the till and smiled at Patrick when he probably cracked some stupid joke. Me. It had been the day after Sophie's disastrous fifteenth birthday, when I'd stayed home and made her favorite cake and gotten her everything I could think of that I thought she'd love. When I tried to be the mother I thought she wanted. Because it had been the first birthday we were together. Just us. Alone.

But she hadn't come home after work, and she hadn't answered her phone. I'd tried to give her space, tried not to worry, tried not to fly into a rage when she came home insanely late, clearly drunk, clearly unconcerned. But I still hadn't let go. She had gotten up the next morning, Thursday, grumpy and angry. I'd thought she was just hungover, but then she'd screamed at me about forgetting her birthday, about forgetting *her*. I stood there, in the kitchen, stunned. Her cake was in the trash where I had thrown it in a blind fury the night before. Her presents were in the office downstairs, still wrapped, where I had thrown them. And she *dared*—

She dared to be angry with me.

Even as I watched the video, I did not remember Patrick Beale or his friend, that tattooed jackass who knew my daughter, probably better than I'd ever want to know. It was like the rest of that Thursday had never happened. In my memory, there is only Sophie that morning, her face convulsed, her skin pale, her fists clenched tightly, running out the door.

* * *

I watched the rest of the video that night, watched it carefully, but Patrick didn't appear again. Around midnight, I called Darren's office, left him a voicemail about the sodas and the cigarettes and said I had something for him. I didn't say I had the receipt that had blown into the bushes on the property next to Jeremy Leamon's. I didn't tell him I now knew when the little house that had been there burned. I didn't tell him I thought I knew the last day that Patrick Beale had been unscathed, the last day he was just some stupid, foolish kid.

I shut down the computer and locked the steel office door, then the glass doors to the lot behind me. The day's heat radiated off the gravel. A few crickets played, and I tilted my head up to the night sky: black velvet, pockmarked with stars.

When I walked into the apartment a couple of minutes later, light leaked from under Sophie's bedroom door. I knocked quietly, then went in when she didn't answer. She was asleep, sprawled on the bed, her phone clutched in her hand and earbuds in her ears. I leaned down and brushed her hair from her face, then gently pried the phone from her hand.

Suddenly, she was awake. She pushed herself up on one elbow, her eyes wide and darting.

"What are you doing?" she demanded.

"You were asleep."

"That's mine. Give me my phone."

Instinctively, I looked down at the phone, still held loosely in my hand. Sophie pushed herself into a sitting position and held out her hand, her fingers splayed, her palm flat and hard. The phone buzzed and a text message from someone called Nick appeared on the screen.

Hey, baby, it read. *Where u at?*

"Who was that at Hank's tonight?" I asked without looking up from her phone.

"What?" Sophie said, convincingly confused.

"That guy, by the bathroom. With the tattoos."

"Who?" she said, less convincingly. "I don't know what you're talking about. Give me my phone."

I'm not proud of what happened next.

I gave her the phone.

I straightened up and tried to make light of it, tried to convince myself that nothing was wrong, that I was just being overly protective, irrational. Sophie snatched the phone from my hand and turned away from me. She clicked it on and began to type a reply. Her hair fell over her face as her skinny little fingers flashed over the screen. She hit "Send."

That's when I leaned down and snatched it back.

I didn't listen to her howls or her threats or the abuse she hurled at me as I walked out of the bedroom. I didn't listen to the pleading either, the wails that began when she realized I wasn't going to cave to her anger. I didn't listen to the whining or the sobs. I just put the phone in the back pocket of my jeans and laid out on the couch, stared unblinkingly at the uneven surface of the ceiling, and waited.

I didn't know what else to do.

8

There's a hill at the end of my run, on the way back to the mart. It starts slow and steady up the path from the lake, then it flattens out on the road. Every morning, I pound through a quarter of a mile of it fast, as fast as I can after however many laps. Then the hill climbs and I churn up it, sometimes running no faster than I'd walk. Every morning, my breath rips through my lungs until I reach the crest and see the mart off to my right, past the Mulvaneys' blue trailer and the little white house that's been empty and falling apart as long as I can remember. On the best mornings, the sun is just coming up, and the light is so golden and soft, even Little Falls looks good.

That Wednesday, the gold had already gone.

At the top of the hill, I stopped and panted, my fists on my shaking thighs. When I looked up, the sun was burning up the horizon. Unsteadily, I took off again, my heavy footsteps kicking up the dirt on the side of the road.

Twenty yards closer to the mart, a truck came from behind and sped past me, twangy country-pop blaring out of its open windows, a massive gust of wind trailing it, drying the sweat on my skin and pulling the doors of the mart open.

Open?

My quads screamed as I closed the distance at a sprint.

Hands cupped over my eyes, I peered through the window by the counter: unlit aisles; till drawer empty and open as usual; office door and cigarette case locked up tight. Probably Rhonda had just arrived early, but when I jogged around the corner, the only vehicle in the lot was my truck.

Only Rhonda and I had keys. So who was in there?

I unlocked the truck and retrieved my Glock from its lockbox under the driver's seat. Chamber loaded, sun at my back, I crept around to the front and pushed the door open.

"Hello?" I called.

Inside, the floorboards creaked under my running shoes, and water rushed down the pipes from the shower upstairs. At least Sophie was up. I prowled the aisles: chips and popcorn, candy bars, and canned goods on the shelves, beer and soda in the humming coolers. Nothing missing, nothing out of place. Just the doors, unlocked.

Then I looked up: the pinprick light on the security camera was out.

My eyes shot to the office door, but it was closed tight. Had I come in during the middle of something?

Slowly, I leaned over the counter, Glock first. Nothing, just bare floorboards and the old shotgun Rhonda kept under the counter. I padded around the ice cream cooler, closed my fingers around the handle of the office door, and gently turned it. Unlocked.

I took a deep breath and flung the door open.

Just a room with an ugly green carpet and boxes of beer and cigarettes stacked up in the shadows along the wall. And a desk. With nothing on it.

Shit.

* * *

I was still on the phone with the insurance company up in the apartment when Darren showed up. I heard the car on the gravel, heard him get out and walk over to talk to Rhonda at the table she'd set up in the shade. She had gotten there a couple of minutes after I had, walked into the mart all casual, saying "good morning" in that gossipy way she gets when she's got something good to tell. I almost shot her, but she didn't take offense. Instead, she gently took the Glock from my hand, told me to go call someone, and locked up. Then she found a table somewhere and started hawking coffee and pastries to the folks who'd stopped by, wondering what was going on. It was just like her to make lemonade out of my lemons.

A few minutes later, the bell rang.

"Good morning," Darren said after I opened the door to the lot downstairs.

"Hi," I said, standing there like an idiot and staring at him in that brown uniform.

He smiled a little. "You said you had a break-in."

"Yeah, in the mart."

"So aren't you going to let me in?"

I stared at him a moment longer: his sunglasses were resting on his chest, his black hair was slick and wet.

I blinked, shook my head, then pushed past him. "Don't you want to see the crime scene?"

"I'd like a cup of coffee more. I already tried Rhonda, but she said it's brewing upstairs."

"Crime scene first, then we'll talk about coffee."

He trailed me around to the front, then grinned when I asked him if he was going to dust for prints. "You're joking. Half the county's fingerprints are on that door handle."

"Uh, no. The doors stay open this time of year. No one except me and Rhonda touch them."

Darren sighed, pulled his phone out, but then thought better of it. "Fine. Let's see the inside, and then I might call Moreno and have him come up here with his gear."

I crossed my arms, frowned. "Wow. You are a model law enforcement officer."

Darren just laughed. "You gonna show me this crime scene, or what?"

I ground my teeth and glared at him.

"C'mon, Camille. I'm really looking forward to that coffee."

My stomach boiled, my fist curled, my arm tensed with the punch I couldn't throw.

I forced my fingers open, then put the key in the lock and used it to lever the door open without touching the handle. Darren grinned, then edged in through the door and held it open for me with his foot. While I fought down the bubbling rage, he walked the perimeter of the store just like I had, frowned at the racks of bottles and cans in the cooler just like I had.

"Didn't even touch the beer, huh?"

"No."

"That rules out a few folks."

After frowning up at the security camera for a few seconds, he turned back toward me. "You going to do your key trick on the office door too?"

I clenched my jaw and got the office open.

"What was on the desk?" Darren asked.

"Other than the laptop, you mean?" I said, my voice like battery acid.

He just looked at me, his face impassive. "You doing okay? You're a little . . . *angry* today."

"Yeah, Darren," I said. "Yeah, I'm good. I mean, my place was robbed while I was asleep upstairs, while *my kid* was asleep upstairs. But you know, I'm fine."

He nodded. "Okay, I get it."

I wanted to tear into him, wanted to scream at him that he was supposed to fix it, that it was his goddamned *job* to fix it. But then he cocked his head to one side and smiled softly, and I noticed that he hadn't shaved, noticed that he looked exhausted, that there was still a pillow crease on his cheek.

I closed my eyes, breathed levelly, and turned to the desk. I opened my eyes.

"The receiver for the camera." I pointed. "The cord is there, on the wall. That's why the camera isn't on. No power supply without the receiver."

Darren squatted, inspected the desk top. "No dust."

"I like it clean."

"That's too bad," he muttered. "Dirtiness can be a virtue."

In spite of myself, I laughed. "I'll keep that in mind."

He stood up and fingered the cord hanging limply against the wall. "And the camera doesn't record at the unit? Only at the laptop?"

I nodded.

Darren glanced around the room, saw my cache of extra beer and cigarettes. "None of your stock is missing from in here either?"

I shook my head.

"Great." Darren rubbed his palms together, cracked his knuckles. "So, how about that coffee?"

Upstairs, Darren called Moreno on my landline. Pulled him out of bed, by the sound of it. I pretended not to listen, but later I wondered why Darren had told him to keep it quiet.

"You hungry?" I asked when he had hung up the phone, not knowing why I asked, even as I did. I'm not exactly the domestic type.

"No. Go ahead though."

I leaned back against the counter and crossed my arms. "No, let's just get this over with."

"Why don't we sit at the table?" He jerked his head toward it. "More comfortable."

I hurriedly stacked the papers on the table and put the pile on the counter. Darren didn't ask about the property records or the county map spread in front of him. He didn't even ask about my list of last known sightings of Patrick Beale. He waited for me to sit down, then moved a chair closer to me and opened his laptop.

"Where's Sophie?" he asked idly while the laptop booted up.

"At work. Roseann picked her up a couple of minutes after I called you."

"Would she have gone down to the mart last night?"

"Maybe, but she doesn't have keys."

"Could she have taken yours?"

"No, I had them in my pocket all night."

"And while you were running?"

"They were in my hand."

Darren nodded and opened a new file, then typed in my name and the mart's address. He turned toward me. "So. When did you last see the missing items?"

"Two, two thirty."

Darren's eyebrows jumped. "PM?"

I glared at him coldly. "AM."

He shrugged. "Did you lock the doors?"

I nodded.

"And the laptop and the receiver were definitely there when you left?"

"Yeah. I went into the office to take care of something and they were definitely there."

"Did you hear anything during the night?"

"Nothing. And I had the windows open."

"Who do you think took your stuff?"

I shrugged. "No idea."

"It couldn't have been some kids who knew the laptop was there?"

"If it was just some kids, they would have broken the glass, taken the beer, something like that. They wouldn't have picked the locks. They wouldn't have bothered to go into the office."

"Who knew the laptop was in there?"

"You, me, Rhonda. That's probably it. Not that it would be hard to figure out. Lots of people have a computer."

"And there's no safe?"

I narrowed my eyes. "No."

"Even if there was," he said, then turned back to his keyboard, "nothing was taken from it, right?"

I glared at the side of his head while he typed. When he was done, he sat back, threw his arm over the back of the chair, turned toward me.

"So, what's your theory?" he asked.

I wasn't sure yet, wasn't sure if it was my gut talking or the paranoia making me see things that weren't really there. But if I was right, if it was real, only one thing made sense.

"I think it's about the video. About Patrick Beale on that video."

Darren cocked his head. "Why?"

"Did you watch all of it?" I asked.

He just stared at me, his eyes, his entire face, blank.

"Did you see him come in again? On Thursday afternoon?"

Nothing.

"That guy he was with, the one with the tat on his neck? I saw him last night."

"Where?" Darren asked.

"At Hank's, down in Chelan. You know, that ice cream place."

"What were you doing there?"

I told him how Lyle had come by with a gift for Sophie and how he'd wanted to take her out afterward for her birthday. I told Darren what he already knew, that I didn't trust Lyle. Not only because he was Oren's brother—and a complete fuck-up—but because there was just something wrong with Lyle, something I couldn't explain. And I told him how I intervened, how I took them both down there in the truck, and how Sophie had known half the kids in the place, but there was this one kid—this one *man*—she seemed to know well. Too well. I told Darren how Lyle convinced me to back off, to let her deal with her shit on her own. And I told him how I did because I thought maybe, for once in his life, Lyle was right, and like so many other times when it came to Sophie, I was wrong.

"Did Lyle know the guy?" Darren asked when I had stopped babbling.

I looked down at the table and saw that my fingernails were white, I was clenching my hands so tightly. "He said he didn't."

"Did Sophie tell you the guy's name?"

I grimaced but didn't look up. "Well, no, but—"

"What?"

"I think his name is Nick."

"Why?"

I looked out the window. It wasn't quite eight thirty, but the heat was already shimmering on the tarmac outside. I stood up and went to the window, leaned my back against the frame.

"After we got back," I said quietly, "Sophie came up here and I went downstairs. I was . . . I don't know—pissed off, worried. Furious, really. And I wanted to watch the rest of the security video. That's what I had been planning to do before Lyle showed up."

"Why did you want to watch the rest of the video?"

Astonished, I looked up. "Because I found him. *I* found Patrick in that barn. I want to know why."

Darren swallowed, then nodded.

"I wanted to see if maybe Patrick came in here again," I said. "If he did, then maybe we could get better information about when he disappeared or something." I shook my head, and a lock of hair tumbled into my eyes. I brushed it away.

"And he did," Darren said. "On Thursday night."

"Yeah."

I went back to the table and pulled my chair away from Darren, then turned it around and sat down. He still had his arm flung over the back of his chair, but now he shifted, faced me head on.

"On Thursday," I said. "I saw that truck first—the one registered to that LLC—and then him and then that guy from Hank's."

"And you're sure it's the same person?"

"Yeah." I nodded. "It's him."

"How'd you get his name?"

I leaned back in my chair and looked at the ceiling. "When I came upstairs, the light in the bedroom was still on. I went in to say goodnight, but Sophie was already asleep. So I went over to her bed to turn off the light. She was still holding her phone, so I took it to put it on her night-stand. She woke up and yelled at me. Then someone called Nick texted her while the phone was in my hand. He said something like 'Where you at, baby?' And . . . I don't know. I got this feeling. So, I asked who the guy in Chelan was, but she just grabbed the phone and started texting."

"Did she tell you Nick was the guy in Chelan?"

"No, it's—" I tilted the chair back, then let it drop to the floor with a thud. "It's just a feeling."

"Did you see his last name? His phone number?"

I shook my head, but he knew I was holding back. He was right, but I wasn't ready to confess to him that later that night, after she'd stopped howling and before I'd gone to sleep, I'd rifled through Sophie's phone, looked through her entire contact list, her Facebook feed, and everything else that would open without a password. And then I'd sifted through her photos, the boring ones of sunsets and random junk, the innocuous ones of her and various girlfriends, and the ones I knew I'd find in there some-where, the photos of her and older kids, their eyes always glazed over, their faces always a little slack; and in the background, always a plastic cup or a bottle of booze. I found the photo of her and Patrick Beale, the one on the background of her phone. And then I found another of them with a third man, the one from Hank's. He was shirtless, his arm around Sophie, his hair barely hiding the snake tattooed on his neck.

"Camille?"

I glanced at Darren, then told him to wait. A moment later, I was downstairs, my key turning in the door to the mart, not worrying about the fingerprints this time. In the office, I moved the carpet and the sheet of plywood beneath it and opened the safe. Inside was the cash I had put in there just before Lyle showed up the night before. And beside it was Sophie's phone, exactly where I had put it at two thirty that morning, just after I had confirmed my fears.

* * *

That afternoon I just drove: north over the hills to the Canadian border, down through the valley on the highway before turning east, then south toward the Colville Reservation. I told myself I'd go out, do a couple of inspections, then come back to meet the insurance agent later. But really, I just drove.

I had this itch, this feeling about Patrick Beale. About Nick, whoever he was. Darren had taken the phone number and the name and said thank you very much, leaving me with as little information as I had had when he walked in that morning. Moreno showed up not long afterward. He smiled and shrugged when I asked him how the investigation was going, whether they had any suspects. Then he was silent as he carefully dusted for prints and pressed film into the debris.

The office had been wiped. There were no fibers anywhere. Not even a partial print showed up on the door handle, the desk, the cable that was supposed to be plugged into the receiver. Still, he smiled when he left, said they'd let me know if there was anything else there.

But I didn't need Moreno to tell me; I already knew there was something else there. Something more than just some kids making a little meth. Something big enough to need a helicopter, that made it worthwhile to break into my place, to try to make me, a bystander, afraid.

But I know fear.

Fear comes after. It's after the rip of the adrenaline, the numbness of the shock. That's when fear settles in, deep and strong. Tidal.

I had felt it already. It fueled my growing obsession with this kid who had stood arm in arm, locked at the hip, with my daughter. Who had been dragging her into the maw of that man with the tattoos. I felt it when I realized that the kid had been put down like a dog.

But fear blooms. Into paranoia. Pain. Then—if you're lucky—anger. Anger that rages like a forest fire.

I had to accelerate the process.

So I drove.

I drove until I hit the national forest and passed into the trees. Then I pulled over and shut off the engine. While the hawks screamed in the updraft, I paced the white line on the side of the road, turning the options over in my mind and rejecting them all. Then I turned the truck around and faced my fear.

*   *   *

69

On the way out, there had been a truck pulled over on the side of the road. Maybe it sounds strange that I remembered it, but out in the county, you might drive ten miles without seeing anyone. So, yeah, I recognized it when I saw it again, coming from the other direction; I recognized its dirty cream paint job and faded wood panels and orange rust streaking around the wheel wells. I slowed down, idled in the middle of the road, because that's what you do when you see someone who might be in trouble.

"Hey," I shouted. "You need some help?"

"Yeah," the driver said from behind a set of enormous binoculars. "You can get the hell out of my line of sight."

I looked right, but there wasn't much: just grass and rocks marching up the hillside to a blue doublewide, then on to a smattering of raggedy trees on the ridge of the valley wall. I turned back. The driver balanced the binos on the window frame, his gnarled knuckles clenched around them, and glared at me from under a roughed-up Stetson. That's when I saw the rifle in the cab with him, its barrel pointing skyward. I glanced back to the trailer, saw a woman come out from around the corner with a laundry basket in her arms. *Shit.*

"What are you looking for?" I said, my voice friendly and upbeat while reaching down, grabbing the binoculars I always had in the door pocket, and taking the opportunity to also slide the Glock out from under the seat and into my lap. "Maybe I can help."

He grunted, then pointed to a spot behind me. "See that truck up there?"

I turned around in my seat, followed his arm to the ridge, and sure enough, there was a white pickup sitting there. Looking through the binoculars, I saw lumber piled up in the bed and coils of wire sitting on top.

"See that wire?" he drawled. "See those boys up there, having a smoke?"

"Yeah."

"They're putting in a nice new fence," he said, then added with a Nashville twang, "Electri*fied.*"

Oh. *That* kind of crazy.

"How long they been at it?" I asked carefully.

"'Bout a week. I put it out that I'd be out of town today, that's why they're doing this part now."

I swept the binos across the ridge line. A cluster of rough, stringy men stood in the shade under a couple of trees, smoking. To the east, a line of posts a half-mile long leaned drunkenly, waiting to be secured before electric wire could be strung between them.

"You been watching them for a week?"

"Since last Friday. I been out here in the truck, livin' on crackers and coffee, pissin' in the grass. Didn't even stop on Sunday."

"Dedicated," I muttered. I put the binos down and rested my arm on the window frame. "So," I said slowly, "what's it to you anyway?"

"What's it to me?" he roared. "That's my land! Those bastards are *fifty feet* into my land."

I whistled.

"And you know why?" he said, pointing his crooked finger at me like it was a gun. "Because there's water on my property, and there ain't none on theirs."

I nodded appreciatively. "You talked to the county?"

"Yeah, a lot of good it did me too. I been callin' and callin' and nothin'. *Nothin'*. The damn county won't even send anyone out to look at the place. They just tell me the documents say this, the documents say that. I don't care what the damn documents say! That's my land. It's been my land since I bought it forty years ago, and it'll be my land until the day the deed falls out of my cold, dead hand."

"Yeah?" I tapped my fingers against the side of the truck door, looked over my shoulder at the hillside, the tiny humans working at the top. "What's the best road to get up there?"

"County road, about five, six miles down that way." He jerked his head in the direction I was going. "You go up a couple of miles and it swings around."

"What's the address?"

He shrugged, bony shoulders rising under a T-shirt with a collar so worn it was shredded. "No idea. It's Randy Johnson's old place. Little brown house by the road."

I nodded, put the truck in gear.

"Hey!" he said, suddenly indignant, like I'd stolen his favorite toy. "What the hell are you gonna do?"

"You wanted the county," I said, shifted my foot from the brake to the gas, then shouted out the window as I drove away, "You got the county now."

Up in the hills, the road narrowed to one lane, then degraded into a packed gravel track. The wind sweeping across from the Palouse stripped all the moisture out of the air blowing in through my windows, but I was sweating so much my sunglasses were slipping down my nose. Eventually, I saw the house, only the third one in three miles. It squatted by the road like a rotting animal, chunks of brown paint missing and bald, weather-stained wood lurking beneath. Crouched in front, faded pink flowers dropped from a bush studded with parched leaves. I passed the house slowly, watching for movement around the place, but it looked like it had been abandoned since long before Randy Johnson—whoever *he* was—had sold it.

I steered the truck onto the packed dirt drive and took it as far back into the property as it went and then kept on going, following the tracks that a truck a lot bigger than mine had made. Rocks ricocheted in my wheel wells; the chassis creaked and whined over the ruts; dust rose and flew away in the steady wind.

I heard the drill first, the engine roaring, the bit clattering with every stone it hit. Then I saw the workers, six of them and a foreman, all of them with skin nut-brown from the sun, their clothes yellow with dirt.

I let the truck roll to a stop and made a show of getting out slowly, my big steel document case with the county seal on it in my hand. Some of the workers stopped and stared, but only until the foreman shouted at them to keep at it, that they had a deadline to meet. Then he walked toward me.

"Can I help you?" he shouted from twenty feet away.

"Maybe," I said. "I'm just curious what you boys are doing out here."

The foreman reached up, swept a faded red ball cap off his head, wiped his brow with the thick blond hair on his forearm, then put the cap back. "How's that any of your business?"

"I'm from the county." I shifted the document case so the gold seal flashed in the sun. "Routine inspection."

"Yeah?" The foreman cracked his knuckles, shifted his weight. Behind him, the team with the drill shifted to the next marker, a wooden stake with neon green tape that waved like a flag in the updraft from the valley. Two more men took their place, one with a bag of gravel, the other with a bucket of wet concrete. Even as they worked, they were watching. Waiting. Hungry.

The foreman looked over his shoulder, then turned back and, his eyes on me, spat a long stream of tobacco juice into the dirt. "What you inspecting, hon?"

"Your manners, apparently."

A couple of the guys on the crew sniggered, but they all traded knowing looks. Then one holding a couple of metal posts—a tall kid, scrappy, with thick shoulders under his stained white T-shirt—dropped one and shifted his grip on the second, held it like he was on deck and ready to swing.

Awesome. A cowboy.

The foreman took a couple steps toward me, grinned, then shifted the chew in his lip and spat again. "Well, my manners don't need any inspecting 'cause I'm a perfect gentleman."

"Of course you are. But I've got to inspect the property all the same." I opened the cover of my document case, unclipped the pen. "You got your permits handy?"

"Well, no I don't, darlin'. See, I don't own this place, just puttin' the fence in like I been paid to do."

"That's kind of strange, isn't it?" I said and cocked my head. "Most contractors get their own permits. At least, the good ones do."

His face colored, but that grin had been stuck on with super glue.

"Naw, the owner handled it. Happens all the time."

I made a quick notation on my pad, let him watch my pen flash over the page, then looked up. The crew mixing concrete had put down their tools, and those with the drill had left it silent, still on the ground. The kid with the fence post was slapping it softly in the palm of his hand. The wind gusted, tore a few strands of my hair loose.

"What's this owner going to do with this land, then?" I said. "Doesn't look like it's fit for much of anything."

"Can't see that's any of the government's business."

"Oh, it is. Impacts the value of the land for taxes." I jutted my chin toward the line of posts sticking out of the dirt. "Just like this fence you boys are putting in. Say, why are you using all that wire mesh? Expensive stuff, especially if you're going to electrify it anyway."

The foreman shrugged. "Electricity goes down out here, it stays down. Gotta protect the crop even when that happens."

Pen poised over my notepad, I asked, "What kind of crop?"

For a moment, he was flustered, but that wide grin was back right away. "No idea, hon. I got no idea what they're doin' up here."

"Who does?"

He shook his head. "Sorry."

"Who do you talk to, then? Who's your contact?"

The foreman touched the bill of his cap with one finger, then turned, his arm raised, and shouted at the crew.

"Get going, boys. We got work to do."

* * *

As soon as I had cell reception again, I called the surveyor's office, but a woman with a hornet up her ass told me to go to hell, more or less. Gene wasn't much more help, but at least he told me who owned the parcel where the fence was going in. It was another LLC—Gorgon Four this time—with a Mr. Jack C. Wyatt listed as point of contact. I asked Gene to look up the contact person for the parcel where Jeremy Leamon had his ranch.

"It's Leamon's land," Gene said irritably. "All you gotta do is call him."

"Could you just look, please? I don't have a connection where I'm at."

He grumbled but a minute later announced in a viciously self-satisfied voice that he had been right. It was Leamon's property, and he was the only person on the deed.

"Can you check the next parcel over?" I said. "The one to the west." The one with the barn where I had found Patrick Beale's body.

"Ohhh-kay."

I heard Gene's arthritic fingers tapping on the keyboard, heard the twangy, fuzzy strains of Merle Haggard playing from his old cassette player in the background.

"Parcel 16001-3829," he said at last. "Owner of record: Gorgon Six LLC. Point of contact, Mr. Jack C. Wyatt."

I mumbled my thanks, put off his questions, and hung up abruptly when he started to nag me about my manner, my professional courtesy, and half a dozen other things permanently stuck in his craw.

When I got to Chelan, I turned off the main drag and parked the truck on a side street where I could sit in the shade and watch the door of Wyatt & Johnson, Attorneys at Law. For two hours, I sat there in the truck with the windows open, trying to catch a breath of breeze, trying to figure out why I was even there. In all that time, one man entered the brick building on the corner with the big plate-glass window. He looked young, but not much younger than me, with buzz-cut blond hair, square shoulders, and a loping, relaxed kind of walk that didn't quite hide the handgun in the holster beneath his shirt. When he left, he glanced around, took his time to put on a pair of sunglasses—just enough time to take in every car and truck in sight. Then he walked around the corner and climbed into the back seat of an old black sedan gone yellow with dust. I stayed still, slumped down in my seat with a map open on the steering wheel, like I had been for the half hour since he'd gone in. The sedan pulled away from the curb and lumbered down the street and out of sight.

*　*　*

I got to Crystal's just before closing time. Her shop was the kind of place that has strings of glass beads and bells that crash against the door when you open it. It's the kind of place where you expect a wrinkly white woman in a worn sweatshirt to emerge from racks of touristy schlock and giant half geodes with action figures glued to them. You'd expect her to assault you with sweetness and maybe even a sucker for the kiddies, but you wouldn't be shocked when you glimpsed the knife edge hiding underneath all that sugar. And that's what you get. Crystal doesn't like to disappoint.

"Oh, it's *you*," she said, her bright smile fading like the Cheshire cat's.

I continued idly picking through a bin of polished rocks. The sign on the front proclaimed, "Genuine local garnets!" Never mind there weren't any garnets west of the Palouse. Never mind they looked like lava rock someone had dunked in a bucket of polyurethane.

"Sophie here?" I asked without looking up.

"She's in the back." The stink of stale cigarettes wafted off Crystal when she went past me to flip the sign on the door to "Closed."

I straightened up, slid my hands into the pockets of my jeans. "She doing all right? Doing what you need her to do?"

"That why you're here? Checking up on her?"

"I was in town," I said, rolling my shoulders back. "Thought I'd save Roseann the trip."

"Your daddy—may he rest in peace—did just fine with that girl, you know." She turned her head away and muttered, "Better than that woman did with you, anyway."

"What was that?"

"Oh, nothing."

Crystal smiled. She was local, had gone to school with my father and a few other people still kicking around the Okanogan. None of them were quite like her, though.

"It's just too bad you gotta work all the time," she said and sighed. "It's so hard on Sophie; she needs someone to take care of her."

I crossed my arms. "Uh-huh."

"But you're just like your momma, aren't you?" Crystal smiled again, her face creased like a dried-up apple. "Of course, she had your daddy to support her. We were all *so* disappointed when Sophie's daddy ran off. Now, if *I* were your momma—"

I rolled my eyes. "Everyone knows you had a hard-on for my dad."

Crystal's eyebrows shot up. "If *I* were your mother, that boy would have married you. Set you right."

Every muscle in my body tightened. Decades-old wounds throbbed. She was too close. I fell back; Crystal advanced.

"Your poor daddy," she breathed, her head shaking like a cobra's. "All he wanted was a good wife, a good little girl. But you and your momma . . ."

"He *loved* my mother."

But Crystal was an unstoppable force. "Best thing that ever happened to him was that woman gettin' herself killed."

Without thinking, I raised my fist, pulled it back—

"Crystal?"

From where I was standing, Sophie's voice was faint, like she was speaking from the bottom of a hole. But then the floorboards creaked, and in the corner, behind the register, the purple bead curtain parted, and Sophie appeared, smiling.

"I'll see you tomorrow—" Sophie said, then stopped, beads falling around her dark hair, one hand on the strap of her backpack, the other holding back the curtain. The smile drained from her face. "Oh. You."

"I—"

"Your momma's gonna take you home," Crystal said, turning on the syrup. She fussed over my daughter, who smiled and hugged her with the warmth and affection I'd never gotten from her. Never given either, I suppose.

Outside, Sophie slung her backpack over one shoulder, tossed her hair, and walked off.

"Hey," I called out. "The truck's around the corner."

Without turning around, without even looking over her shoulder, she said, "I'm not going back with you."

"You are."

"I'm going out tonight anyway."

"You are *not*."

Sophie whipped around, her hair flying. "I *am*. You can't stop me."

"We are going home. *Now*."

"I'm not going anywhere with you. No fucking way."

It was one of those moments that I will remember forever: Sophie, only Sophie, on the dingy sidewalk in shorts and ripped stockings, scuffed boots, and long wisps of her father's razor blade–straight hair, dark against a tight red shirt. Sophie, glaring at me with so much independence and rebellion and—yeah—hatred that the air between us crackled. I mean, it damn near burst into flame.

"Fine," I said, my jaw so tight it might have been nailed shut. I caught a glance of Crystal spying through the glass door, frigid disapproval on her face. I turned. And then I walked away.

"Hey!" Sophie yelled. "Hey!"

I kept walking, my legs rigid, my veins jumping.

"Hey!"

Then she was coming after me, the heels of her boots slamming into the sidewalk, the bangles on her wrists jangling.

"You can't just leave me."

But I could. I had. And I would again.

I kept on, went around the corner and squinted into the evening sun. Someone threw a cigarette butt from the window of a passing car, showering the street with a brief explosion of sparks. I stepped onto the tarmac, crossed diagonally, crushed the rolling cigarette butt under my heel as I went.

"Camille!" Like a toddler, Sophie stomped her foot. *"Mom!"*

That stopped me.

I waited with my back to her, and started walking again when she caught up. She accused me of abandoning her, threatened to call CPS. I listened for a while—grateful that at least she was talking to me—but it wasn't long before the only sound in the truck was the steady roar of the radials on the highway.

* * *

I'd like to say it ended that night, that there was a Brady Bunch moment, a saccharine resolution—cue the theme music—and now we're the best of friends. But it didn't and there wasn't. Nothing ended there.

* * *

I don't know why Sophie expected that after a show like that, after a screaming match on the sidewalk, I would be so stupid as to believe her when she said she was going to Tracy's, that they were going to watch a couple of movies, have some popcorn. I hope she didn't think I was so stupid I would just believe her when she said she'd be back before midnight and that I shouldn't wait up.

I watched from the window with the lights out, low profile like I learned when I deployed, my binoculars trained on her as she walked down the street and slipped into the yard of Tracy's parents' place. But the front porch light didn't go on, and a few minutes later a low-slung car turned the corner, its headlights spraying the cracked pavement with yellow light. It drove the two short blocks that measure the width of my town, then paused and idled just long enough for the doors to briefly open and slam shut.

After I grabbed my keys, I flipped the lights on in the apartment and ran down to the truck. I followed carefully, at a discreet distance, grateful these roads were quiet, but not entirely empty, after dark. After a while, I figured we were headed toward Chelan, maybe back to Hank's, but then the car blew past town and turned onto a long road that led into one of the fancy developments near the lake. I drove past the street where the car turned, then flipped off my lights and, in the darkness, turned around and followed the red brake lights. When the low rider slowed at the end of the road, I watched four, maybe five kids pile out of it.

Light from the house at the end of the cul-de-sac spilled out of two-story windows onto strings of cars parked haphazardly in a manicured yard. Kids in short shorts and T-shirts or no shirts glowed in the light. Loud music and shouting drifted to where I sat a hundred feet away, tapping my fingers on the steering wheel.

I had no idea what to do. Barge in and drag her out? Slink back home and pace the floor? I was damned either way. So I did the only thing that made sense: I watched. For two hours I watched, from the truck at first, then later from across the road, my knees in the dry dirt, my shoulder pressed against a tree, sweat rolling down my back inside a fleece jacket, the darkest thing I had in the truck.

It looked like a normal teenage party: cheap beer and vomiting in the bushes, crappy music and posturing, just at a nicer place than I'd ever been invited. The longer I watched, the more familiar it felt, the more I felt myself being drawn in. I half-expected Oren, my ex, my daughter's deadbeat dad, to walk around a corner, plastic cup in one hand, blunt in the other. He was tall and rangy, like the guy from the ice cream place. But the Oren I remembered was younger, cruder, volatility always flashing in his eyes. And after Oren there would be Billy Boykin, his buddy, his shadow. Billy who was two years younger than Oren, the same age as me, and complicit in everything—*everything*—Oren was up to. Billy, the black-haired Irish kid from town who hung out with Oren, the bastard, whose Colville daddy had abandoned the family years before, whose white momma was a bigger basket case than just about anyone else I knew, whose little brother Lyle was safe at home, tucked up in bed, too young for even Oren to corrupt. At least, that's what I thought then.

But it wasn't Oren or Billy who followed Sophie out the massive front door of the house by the lake. It was a different boy—a man—who appeared in the doorway after she'd plowed through it, a couple of girls in her wake, and stalked down the road. The man had hair cut like a soldier, his arms crossed over his bare, muscular chest, a pair of jeans hanging loosely from his narrow hips.

He called after Sophie, told her to come back. When at first she didn't return, his tone changed from smirking to commanding, and I saw her pause, saw her hesitate on the pavement. She turned, and for a moment, I thought she was cowed. But her friend opened the car door, and in the light of the cab I saw my daughter lift her chin and lift her hand to flip off the guy standing in the door. And I saw the anger flash across his face, saw him drop his arms and start down the stairs, saw the porch light glow on the muscles rippling across his back. Saw the narrow-eyed watchfulness I had seen before, outside Jack Wyatt's.

I darted through the trees, bent far over, branches tearing at my hair, until I reached my truck. By then the low-slung car had roared past, swaying on its crapped-out springs as a kid too drunk to drive drove anyway. I flung myself into the cab, but before I could tear after that car and force it to the side of the road and pull my daughter out of it if I had to, I saw soldier boy yelling and three—no, four—flunkies pouring out of the house. One of them was the guy from the ice cream shop, the guy from Sophie's photos. Nick or not-Nick, his long black hair stringy on his inked shoulders and a shotgun in his hand. All of them in pursuit of *my daughter*.

New threat. New plan.

I slid out of the truck and slipped to the rear, balanced my Glock on the tailgate, and squeezed the trigger until the safety popped.

Everyone except Nick was climbing into vehicles; he was shouting something I couldn't hear over the music and the roar of the partiers. But it made soldier boy stop even as the headlights of the forward vehicle— another dark-colored sedan—penetrated the darkness. I took aim, his head tiny and fragile, like a ripe grape, in my sights.

They exchanged a few words and the black-haired guy shouldered his weapon and turned back to the house. Soldier boy slammed the door of the sedan and followed, his flunkies slowly trailing him.

I released the trigger and breathed again.

It was only when I pulled out of the ditch several long minutes later that I noticed the dark-colored truck parked across the road. I lifted my foot from the gas, flipped on the headlights, and read the license plate as I rolled past.

I knew that truck.

And so had Patrick Beale.

*   *   *

That night, I watched the video again, upstairs, with the USB drive plugged into my work computer. It's not like I was going to sleep. And anyway, I hadn't watched it—*really* watched it, not just played "Where's Patrick Beale?"—all the way through, beginning to end. That's why I hadn't seen the light-colored truck with a guy with a blond buzz cut at the wheel. It was the guy from Jack Wyatt's office, whose shirt still didn't conceal his weapon. Soldier boy from the party. On the video, he got out and filled the tank at the pump in front of the mart. In the passenger seat was Nick, the sunglasses on his face looking like shit had been smeared over his eyes, picking his teeth with his fingernail. And in the back seat, there was a girl. She was looking away, her long, dark hair turned toward the camera.

I slowed down the video and watched soldier boy go into the mart and pay Rhonda. I watched him walk back out into the glare of the sun, two sodas in one hand and a lump like a pack of cigarettes in his pocket. Then he climbed into the truck. My face inches from the screen, I watched while he pulled away from the gas pump, clearing the view to the back seat of the club cab. As the truck rolled out of the frame, the girl turned her head. And I saw my daughter's eyes look back at me.

9

Sand blasted my face, skidded across my visor.

Heat shimmered off the tarmac, distorted the limbs of the orderlies jogging toward the helicopter slowly, so slowly, like insects in amber.

Sunlight danced on the table between them, flashed and played as its wheels bounced over ridges, dove into cracks from the munitions craters sunk into the airfield. Dazzled until the body bag was dragged onto the table and swallowed the light.

Then.

A tall corporal leaning against the hospital intake desk. His badge was Mortuary Affairs, but his smile blinded, his black skin gleamed. Too pretty to be an undertaker.

I said, "I'll help."

He frowned. I insisted. He scrutinized, then sympathized. He empathized. He mourned for me, for the loss of someone I loved.

"He was my soldier," I barked. "My soldier."

The undertaker's thick eyebrows rose.

"My *responsibility*."

Then.

The concrete block MACP. The mortuary. The morgue.

The pretty undertaker pushed the table in; I followed.

The pretty undertaker said no, tried to order me—a sergeant—out; I scrubbed down anyway. The same soap we used at the hospital—chemical bubblegum scented—stinging every one of the million cracks in my skin.

The pretty undertaker dialed a number on the phone; I suited up, marched through the big, black door.

Inside, the body bag was small under the day-bright fluorescents. It was a dark spot, like a bruise in the row of steel tables and drains and scalpels and . . .

I cringed when a white-suited private unzipped the bag.

Gagged when the smell, the high sweet stench of rot, poured out.

Winced when a fly's wings glinted in the yellow light.

Then.

"Waresch. Sergeant Waresch!"

A male in the gap between the big black doors, his cover still on, the sunlight at his back.

"Waresch; to me."

Then.

At attention, my thumbs pressed hard into the seams of my pants, my fists so tight my fingernails cut into my palms.

In front of me, behind the desk, the first sergeant. Graying hair. Deep lines etched into his dark face.

"Sit down, Waresch." But my knees were locked. "Take a seat, Sergeant."

I buckled.

"This isn't your fault, Waresch."

"I denied his request," I said. "I confined him to base."

"You were right," the first sergeant said. "He was too green. No business in the field." He passed his hand over the stubble cut high and tight on his head. "Probably what got him killed," he muttered.

A shiver went up my spine. "I failed, First Sergeant. I didn't do enough."

"He was AWOL, Sergeant."

"I didn't report him."

"For what?"

I kept my mouth shut. No use slandering the dead.

The first sergeant sighed, wiped his face with the palm of his hand. "This isn't your fault."

"But I—"

"He was your soldier." The first sergeant leaned forward onto the desk, the shadow of his shoulders falling over his hands. "But he screwed up. Not your responsibility. Not your fault."

I ground my teeth.

* * *

My eyes flew open. Grit crunched between my teeth. My face burned like it had been baking in the sun for years. Blood boiled through my veins, pounded in my temples. But yellow light snaked across the floor and died under the kitchen table. Cool, clean air caressed my sweating face. Fibers scratched my cheek, my neck where they touched cheap brown carpet. I was on the floor in my apartment. In Little Falls. In the Okanogan. *Not* in Iraq.

Slowly, I pushed myself to my feet, rubbed my shoulder. On the sofa, my pillow was undisturbed. But halfway across the room, my sheet was twisted and balled up, a white blotch on the carpet.

Every dream gave me more pieces. But the images that were so vivid in the dead of night were lost during the day. I had filled pages of a notebook with everything I remembered from Iraq, from Afghanistan, from every place I had been with a helicopter and an M16. But there was nothing there. Nothing that dragged up the memories that haunted me in the dark.

I sunk onto the sofa and leaned forward on my knees, stared at the brown carpet between my bare feet. A mud-brick room and a hanging body. A helicopter and a morgue and my first sergeant. That's all I had. It felt so clear, so real. But without a name, without an identification, my memories were just nightmares. I had to know what was real. I had to know who he was. I had to know the name of the soldier who'd died like Patrick Beale.

10

How, exactly, do you talk to a teenager about—I don't know—about things like *this*? In the military, it would have been simple. *Soldier, you are wrong. Soldier, you will report for disciplinary action. Soldier, you will report to the stockade.*

But a teenager is a wilder breed. Unpredictable. Unforgiving. Unreasonable. In the end, the only option I thought of was the worst possible option. Not that I knew it at the time, but I should have guessed.

I left a photo on the table that Thursday morning, a printout from the video I had watched the night before. Soldier boy—the man I had begun thinking of as the lieutenant—was pumping gas, the guy called Nick just visible in the front of the truck, the pump blocking the view of most of the back seat. The time stamp was in the corner.

I watched Sophie come out of the bedroom in the morning, waited for her to get her cereal and sit down at the table. I sorted through files on my computer and, from the corner of my eye, watched her a while longer, waiting for a reaction, to see if she would recognize the two men and admit it.

"Where did you get this?" she asked, her spoon halfway from bowl to mouth.

I didn't look up from my laptop. "What?"

"This photo."

She waved it in front of me; I took it from her hand.

"The video feed," I said.

"What video?"

"In the mart. There's a camera," I said, then corrected myself. "There *was* a camera, anyway. The new setup hasn't arrived yet."

Sophie seemed shocked, but I don't know how she could have failed to see it in all the years she had been coming to the mart. "You have a video camera down there?"

"I did. The receiver was stolen the other night with the laptop."

Sophie had gone pale. "Wha—What are you doing with this?" she stammered. "What are you doing with this shot?"

"That?" I said, as though it was nothing. "Rhonda's convinced one of them took something when she wasn't looking. She wants me to get Darren Moses to ID them."

"Did you?" Sophie stood up so violently her chair fell over behind her. "Did you give it to him?"

"Why? Do you know them?"

"N-no!"

She wrung her hands, pushed them through her hair. Then she ducked and picked up the chair. When she stood, her face was smooth, calm, but her eyes were still wild, panicked.

"You sure?" I said carefully, trying to look how I imagined a concerned parent might.

"Yeah."

I nodded, turned back to my work. "Anyway, he has the video."

Sophie pounded back to the bedroom, and the door slammed shut behind her. I waited until Roseann picked her up and then waited some more. But when I searched the bedroom, I didn't find anything that pointed toward those men or what she'd been doing with them out past town. I didn't find any clothes that smelled like wood smoke or brake fluid, nothing dyed red from phosphorous or blood, nothing that reeked of ammonia, and nothing—not even the bottom of her shoes—with any obvious chemical residue. I did find shirts reeking of marijuana and cigarette smoke, a handful of condoms, and a bottle of cheap booze. And I was glad that was all I found.

* * *

The building Patrick had lived in was on the fringe of Omak, just off the highway on a street right before the foothills broke off at a golden-brown cliff. Long gray streaks stained the yellow-brick building; the pavement in the parking lot was so cracked that my truck swayed like it was traveling over a dirt road.

I had gotten the address from Sophie's phone. It was buried in a long string of text messages and photos of things I would have given a lot to unsee. Kids I recognized as Sophie's friends smoking bongs or throwing flaming fireworks up in the air, the orange afterglow arcing through the night sky. Kids I didn't know, shit-faced and glassy-eyed, their shiny faces pressed too close to the camera. Sophie, nearly naked in her bedroom at my father's house. And a boy—Patrick—shirtless, his worn jeans hanging below his boxer shorts, standing in front of a mirror in a dingy, yellow-tiled bathroom. That was April. And then the texts dwindled, ran out. Nothing for a month. And then on July 7: *Where you at? Somebody wants to meet you.*

Somebody.

I could guess who.

Cars sped by on the street, but no one was around at the apartments. I parked the truck in the shade, then pushed my sunglasses up and went to the stairs: they were concrete, worn black nonskid strips peeled off in patches. On the second story, I hung a left and kept going until Christine Beale stopped me on the threshold of apartment 2D.

"Camille?" she said. "What are you doing here?"

I had no explanation, no story, no believable response. Nothing beyond the fact that I couldn't let go of her son's murder, that it haunted me. That his death was opening so many doors in my head, was pulling so many blood-soaked memories out of my brain that I was this close, this close to—

I shivered.

And then I lied. Badly.

"Sophie told me to pick her up here."

Christine shook her head. "Sophie?"

"Yeah, she said she would be here with a friend." I fumbled my phone, stooped, picked it up. I turned it on, made a show of looking. "It was, uh, the address was—"

"This is Patrick's apartment," Christine said, her voice hoarse. I glanced up and she shook her head, raised her fingertips to her forehead, smiled sadly before correcting herself. "This was—" she said, but then her voice caught in her throat. "God. This was—" She pressed her hand against her mouth.

"Oh," I said, faking the shock, but not the confusion. "I, uh—I guess Sophie gave me the wrong address."

We stared at each other then. Me, paralyzed, my brain spinning for the right thing to say. Christine, her watery brown eyes red-rimmed, her pale face puffy, her blonde hair slack. And behind her, open boxes, tidy stacks of clothes. A small stereo. A backpack on the ground, a couple of notebooks spilling out.

Christine sniffed, wiped her eyes, then her nose with a tissue that was already crumpled and damp.

"Can I help?" I said. "I could . . . I could keep you company."

Christine sobbed, closed her eyes, then opened them again. She smiled a little. "What about Sophie?"

"Sophie?"

"You were gonna pick her up?" Christine prompted.

"Right," I said quickly, remembering my lie. "Sophie. I'll just—I'll just call her."

So I went to the railing and pretended to call, said loud enough for Christine to hear, "Can your friend take you home? I'll be there a little later." Then I waited a moment to make it seem real, said something like, "Just helping a friend," even though that sounded even less believable than the truth.

When I stepped through the doorway, Christine was stacking kitchen things on the narrow stove. Two plates, three bowls. A handful of forks and spoons. Four glasses. While I watched, she wrapped them carefully in newspaper, nestled them in a box like so many tiny babies. She cried freely but quietly, her tears staining the newsprint as she dropped them one by one into the box.

"He was a good kid," she said, more to herself than to me. "My Patrick. My son."

I nodded. My throat was closed, my voice trapped.

"I found his things, you know," she whispered. Then she cleared her throat and, her voice suddenly firm, suddenly parental, said, "They was right there in the closet. Right there for me to see."

I glanced toward the back of the apartment, past the unmade queen-size bed to the cracked mirror on the closet door.

"It's a good thing it was me." Christine scrubbed her tears off her face, the heel of her hand leaving a trail of mascara. "If his father—if Ed had found 'em, he would have killed—"

Christine was quiet then, her mouth working over the words repeatedly, silently. *Killed him.* He would have killed him.

"But he didn't," I said, too loudly.

Christine's head snapped toward me. She looked at me like she had never seen me before, like I was an intruder. I guess—no, I know: I was.

"What didn't he find, Christine?" I said gently. "What was in the closet?"

"Magazines," she said hoarsely. "With girls in 'em."

My heart sank. *Porn? That's all?*

"And booze," she said. "I can't think where he got it. He's only nineteen. I mean—"

Was. He *was* only nineteen. No one needed to say it. It just hung there in the air.

Christine's head dropped, then she sank into a cheap, metal-framed chair and gazed down at the peeling yellow linoleum, her face in her hands.

"Was there anything else?" I said.

Christine shrugged, shook her head. "The police—the sheriff—they took some stuff. There's a list. They wrote it all down."

I glanced around the apartment, searched for something official looking. But there was nothing. Just debris.

"It's in my bag," Christine volunteered.

I didn't dare ask to see it, but she reached over and dragged a turquoise leather purse toward her across the table. Then she pulled out a piece of paper that had been opened and folded so many times it was ready to tear. She let it fall open on the table and read it silently, her lips forming the syllables. I read over her shoulder. An ounce of marijuana had been confiscated, a few prescription uppers he had no prescription for. An unlicensed .45. And a laptop. That was all. A short inventory for a short life.

"Christine," I said quietly.

But she just stared at the sheriff's list of her son's possessions, gently caressing the edge of the paper like it was her boy's cheek.

"He was a good boy," she whispered, though her words were against all the evidence.

"Christine," I said more loudly. I rested my hand on her shoulder, but she didn't budge.

I took up the newspaper and wrapped up the rest of the kitchen things. When she still hadn't moved, I put the clothes—neatly folded, the way a mother would—into the boxes that stood open on the floor. When I was done, Christine looked up at me, at the apartment, with flat, dry eyes. Eyes that had cried out all their tears.

She mumbled, "Thank you," but didn't stand until I held my hand out and helped her up. Then she took the box from the stove and walked out the door. I followed her down the stairs once, twice, five times, until the only things left were the dingy furniture and the stained mattress that came with the place.

We stood together in the doorway. I scanned the place to make sure we had everything. Christine bent down to pick up her turquoise purse. Then—

"No!" Christine said suddenly, her voice filled with panic.

I spun toward her: was this the break? Was cleaning out her son's place the thing that pushed her over the edge? Her knees smacked into the concrete floor under the thin carpet when she dove for the bed, her fingers tearing at a scrap of blue and white fabric poking out from under the bare box spring. When she craned her head over her shoulder, her eyes were wild and red, her face contorted with anxiety, with grief.

"Help me!"

I ran to her and heaved the mattress and box spring up off the floor. Christine fell back, pulling out the fabric. It was nothing special, just a man's buttondown that had seen better days. Old cotton. Pearly snaps. But Christine hugged it to her chest fiercely. And then she sobbed into it, her shoulders heaving with every breath.

I wrapped my arms around her then, held her as tightly as I could and waited for the shudders to stop. When they did, I got up and picked up her purse, walked with her to the threshold and stood by while she closed the door.

"Do you want me to take you home?" I said quietly.

Looking down, her fingers still on the doorknob, Christine shook her head. Slowly, she lifted her chin and set her jaw, then turned and walked unsteadily to the stairs.

I followed her to her car; told her to call me if she needed anything. Then, hands in my pockets, I watched her drive away.

Back in my truck, I sat and picked the tape off the flash drive I'd pulled from the wooden frame of the old box spring in Patrick Beale's apartment.

It had been right there under the bed. Right there for me to find. Why the sheriffs hadn't, I couldn't guess. But when I lifted the bed for Christine, my fingers closed over it, and as Christine began to sob, I ripped the drive off and put the bed down, pushing the evidence into the pocket of my jeans as I stood.

Right there in the parking lot, I opened my laptop beside me on the bench seat, slotted the drive into the USB port, and waited for the files to load. There were only a handful on the drive, but fewer that mattered. Photos mostly: a meth lab set up in a small kitchen with sunshine-orange countertops, the backside of a truck with a light-haired man leaning out the window, the inside of an aircraft—a Sikorsky helicopter; I would have bet my life on it. And an audio recording.

The sound was distorted, scratchy. It began with a roar like a toilet flushing, then a clatter. A toilet seat closing? Breathing. Not heavy, but near. And quiet, like someone was trying to keep it quiet. Then scraping, plastic against something hard. Someone standing on a toilet? Finally— faintly, like it was coming from the bottom of a well—a man's voice.

"Tuesday."

A moment of silence.

"Yes, sir," then a few seconds later, "Yes, sir," again.

A semi's horn blared, swept by in a wave of sound. And when it had passed: "Drop point is forty-nine point—"

In the background, water rushed loudly enough to drown out the rest of the coordinates. And in the foreground, quiet and desperate: "Fuck."

The water stopped. Air swept across the mic. Then a long, faint squeal, like a hinge that needed to be oiled, followed by the thud of wood slapping against wood.

"I don't have it yet," the voice at the bottom of the well said.

Then: "I said I would get it." He was impatient. Irritable. "*Sir.*" Insubordinate.

"Yeah," he said more meekly. "Tomorrow."

That creak again. Plastic under strain. That scraping sound, plastic against something hard. A grunt from nearby. Skin slapping against something flat: concrete?

Then the distant man said: "What about the support personnel?"
Breathing, heavily. Right by the mic.

"Fine," said in a voice that made it sound like it wasn't. "Yes, sir."

Boots, shifting, scraping on a hard surface. Boots walking away.

Rubber soles slapped against concrete. Plastic clattered.

Then loud, so loud over the speakers I had turned up to maximum volume: a whisper, the sound of lips moving quickly against the microphone: "That was Nick. I told you about him. He's workin' with someone else. I don't know who. It's a California number, eight six eight seven nine—"

A thud like a heavy ring slamming into wood, that squealing sound again.

"Beale!" barked the same voice that had been faint a few moments before. "The fuck are you doin' in there?"

And that voice, that young, near voice, saying loudly over the rustle of fabric, "Jesus. Can't a guy take a shit?"

Then nothing. That was the end of the track. Two minutes and three seconds.

I didn't have to wonder what Christine Beale would give to hear those two minutes and three seconds. To hear her boy's voice one more time, to be proven right, that her son *was* a good kid. I knew that's what she would want. I knew that was the right thing to do—in the universal sense, the *human* sense. I knew it when I listened to it the third time and the fifth. When I dropped the drive into an evidence envelope while I stood in front of the desk at the Sheriff's Office. While I wrote out a note explaining how I had come by the drive, where I had found it and when. When I handed the envelope over to the deputy behind the desk and gave him an order: "Give this to Sergeant Moses. Darren. Darren Moses."

And I knew then I'd hate myself for doing the right thing. Right is a relative term.

*   *   *

By the time I got to Jeremy Leamon's place, the fields behind his drab gray house were already shrouded by the long shadows of the mountains. The house was small and square, the windows framed by narrow white shutters that needed paint. In front, the grass under the tires of Leamon's truck was brown and stubbly, like his cattle had gnawed it down to the ground. Barren flower beds lined the foundation.

When I knocked on the front door, there was no answer, so I turned the handle quietly and called his name from the crack.

"Mr. Leamon? You in there?" I said in my county voice. "May I come in?"

A weary voice said from somewhere deep in the house, "Who is it? What d'ya want?"

I opened the door a fraction wider. "It's Camille Waresch from the County. I was out here last—" I faltered, remembering Leamon's reaction when Lucky made him face Patrick's corpse. "I was here last week."

"You're Lee Waresch's girl, ain't you?" the same voice said, but with a softer tone; less wary, but just as tired.

I said I was, and he said what a good man my father was, how sorry he was to hear he'd died. He'd said the same thing when I'd introduced myself the Friday before.

Inside, the curtains—dingy and yellow with ruffled edges—were drawn over all the windows. Plastic slip-clothed furniture in the sitting room and a dusty dining table lurked in the dim light that made it through.

My Glock was in the truck; my fingers twitched in its absence. I stopped, forced myself to breathe, to stop peering suspiciously into every corner, stop skirting the walls, watching the doorways.

"Your dad was a good man," Leamon said again, so close this time I nearly jumped out of my skin. Then I saw him through the next doorway, a week of grizzled stubble on his cheeks sitting at the kitchen table in a flannel shirt rolled up to the elbows, stray pieces of hay stuck to it.

"Thanks, that means a lot," I lied.

But Leamon wasn't listening—that was clear. A coffee cup sat in front of him on the table, but the stale air reeked of cheap whiskey. Every muscle in his body was still, rigid, waiting for something. Even when I pulled out the chair in front of him and sat down, his detached gaze never wavered from his cup.

"Can I talk to you, Mr. Leamon?" I said quietly. When he didn't answer, I repeated myself, louder. When he still didn't answer, I just asked the question.

"Whose barn is it, Mr. Leamon?"

He smiled, but faintly, a ghostly smile. "Used to be Don McEnroe's."

"But it isn't his anymore, is it?"

"Naw, Don sold up a few years ago."

"Whose is it now?"

Leamon shrugged, his shoulders moving jerkily under his shirt.

"Have you ever met the new owner?" I said.

He just smiled.

"When did you start using it?" I asked.

"Five years ago? Six?" He took up the coffee cup, his hand shaking slightly, and drank deeply from it.

"And the owner, they never said anything? Did they use it too?"

He shrugged. "Maybe."

Maybe like he didn't know, or maybe like he didn't *want* to know?

"What did you see?" I said.

He glanced up and away so swiftly it might not have happened at all. "Nothing."

But that was too easy an answer. "Did they keep something there? Fertilizer? Medicines?" I pressed. "Anything?"

But Leamon wasn't biting. He began to hum, trying to drown me out.

"Did they have a helicopter?" I said, then, when his humming faltered, "Did you see it?"

"Patrick was a nice kid, wasn't he?" Leamon said it as though it was the most natural thing to say in the world. "I guess he got caught up in the wrong crowd."

"You know who killed him," I said and immediately regretted it.

Leamon's lips thinned and his hand darted under the table. I pushed my chair away from the table and leapt to the door. His hand back on its surface, Leamon laughed, a sort of thick, phlegmy chortle, like tar bubbling out of his throat. I was furious, but I swallowed it, dragged the chair farther from the table, and took a seat.

"Had you seen Patrick before?" I asked. "At the barn, or maybe next door?"

Leamon, still laughing, didn't answer.

I tried again. "There was a house next door, wasn't there? Did you see him there?"

"You mean Don McEnroe's place?" Leamon said, still smiling. "I haven't been to Don's place for years."

I watched his face. He was still smiling, but smiling like he'd just laid down an ace.

"But someone else has," I said.

A shadow passed over Leamon's face.

"What were they doing there?" I said. "What were they using Don's house for?"

Leamon shrugged, looked away.

"What did you see?" I probed. "Deliveries? Someone keeping odd hours? Were there any strange smells? Chemicals, maybe?"

Instead of answering, Leamon just picked up the coffee cup and drank from it, drank deeply and didn't even wince. I tried a different tack.

"When did it burn, Mr. Leamon?" I said. "When did Don's place burn down?"

At first I thought it had worked, when Leamon looked back at me with a little smile. But then he said, "It didn't burn. He sold up. I told you."

"It burned. I've seen it."

"Naw," he said, waving his hand at me. "It never."

"Fine. What's going on over there, then?"

Leamon stuck out his lower lip, rolled it back and forth between his fingers, but didn't say anything.

"Did they pay you?" I said. "Was it Nick? What did he pay you?"

Leamon's eyes narrowed. "My father didn't like your dad, you know. Said he was a bad influence."

I shook my head, confused. What the hell did my father have to do with anything?

"And I listened. I listened to everything my father told me back then. Listened to what he told me to do, who he told me to see. But he was a difficult man to please."

I tried to steer Leamon back. "What about Don? Did your father like Don McEnroe?"

"How could he? He was already dead when Don bought that place."

"I'm sorry," I said, chastened.

Leamon laughed, though it sounded more like a bark. "He deserved what he got."

"What did he get?" I said tentatively.

"Same as that kid." Leamon nodded to himself, his gaze far off, his mouth set in a vicious, self-satisfied smile. "Got hisself killed."

What?

My eyes narrowed, my hands closed into fists on my thighs. "Did Patrick deserve what he got?"

Leamon nodded again, absently, like he was remembering something that happened a long, long time before.

I leaned on the table, my fingers spread, my arms tensed to fight. "I said, did Patrick deserve what *he* got?"

Leamon's eyes shifted toward me; then he grunted, looked away again. "The hell should I know?" He ground his teeth and his eyes grew wider. He said more quietly, "It weren't my fault, anyway."

"Whose fault was it?"

"Hisself."

I sat back, studied him. His jaw worked like he was chewing on his thoughts, then his eyes widened, narrowed, and widened again. His shoulders shrunk in on themselves, and he clutched the coffee cup closer to his chest.

"You're afraid," I said bluntly.

Leamon didn't respond, but his eyes darted to me and away again.

"Ain't got nothing to be afraid of," he said.

"What do you know? What do you know that they don't *want* you to know?"

His eyes grew harder, darker. His mouth opened slightly, and I thought he might talk, but then he shut it again.

"They been out to see you again?" I said. "Since Patrick, I mean?"

Leamon remained silent.

"Did they threaten to do the same thing to you? String you up in the barn?"

But Leamon set his jaw, clenched his teeth, and stared past me out the kitchen window.

"Did you see them cooking?" I said. "Did you see them burn the McEnroe place? Did you see them with Patrick?"

But he wouldn't look at me. He was staring hard over my shoulder, hard enough to punch a hole in the wall.

I slammed my hands, open-palmed, on the table, leaned forward so far I could have spit in his eye. "Did you see them torture him? Did you see them electrocute that kid?"

His eyes, black and thick, focused on me hard. But there wasn't nearly as much anger there as terror. He hadn't known. He hadn't stayed in the barn long enough that day to see exactly what they had done to Patrick Beale.

"Who was it?" I shouted. *"Who?"*

Leamon looked away, lifted the mug to his lips, drained it, then let it drop onto the table, where it tottered and settled, the handle pointing at his chest. When he stood up, he was fast, purposeful, lithe. When I stood up, startled, the chair behind me crashed to the floor.

Leamon laughed, the same barking laugh as before, but harsher, like the whiskey had torn his throat.

"You need to be more careful, Miss Waresch."

My cheeks burned hot; I reached for the weapon I didn't have.

He looked out past the dingy net curtains in the window, out to the fields and the deserted blacktop. He watched, seemingly waiting for someone. And then he said quietly, "You go digging too deep and they'll kill you too."

11

A beige door, thick hollow metal and wire mesh in the glass.

   Knock. Knock. Knock.

A male voice, harassed, from inside the room. "Enter."

The door swung open. The male—crackling blue eyes, a fuzz of black hair, desert tan—looked up from a laptop that was open on a scratched steel desk.

My voice, distantly: "Major Brittan."

The man behind the desk leaned back, picked up a pen. "Sergeant Waresch."

"Sir. Is there any news, sir?"

He smiled crookedly, clicked the pen. "There's always news."

"About my soldier, sir. You wanted to think about the evidence I gave you on Tuesday."

"Oh." He frowned, and his eyes faded to gray. "That."

"Do you agree with my assessment, sir? The inventory records clearly indicate he was stealing from the medications locker. Narcotics, sir. And you have my account of him removing items from the hospital."

"Sit down, Sergeant." The major clicked his pen twice, then a third time.
"Sir?"

He pointed to the green steel chair opposite him. "Take a seat."

I nodded, sat down.

"The command is grateful—I'm grateful—that you feel such a sense of . . . loyalty to the Army and to the soldiers under your command."

"They're my responsibility, sir."

"Let me finish, Sergeant." The sleeves of the major's uniform strained against his biceps when he leaned on the desk. "The command is grateful. But your duty is to continue the mission."

"I am, sir. I just got back from a retrieval."

"Yes. Another well-executed task, I understand."

"Thank you, sir."

"You have a good record, Sergeant. Exemplary even. It would be a shame to muddle it now."

"Sir?"

The major gathered his brow, dropped his chin. "You need an opportunity to refocus, reorient yourself."

I shook my head. "I don't understand."

"I'm sending you out to the field, Sergeant." The pen clicked again: once, twice, three times. "Tomorrow. Pack your ruck, Sergeant. You'll muster at zero four thirty."

"What about—?"

"You're dismissed, Sergeant."

Click.

A gray door, heavy steel, just a dark blotch on a concrete-block building in the dead of night. No window.

The tumblers scraped in the lock. A breath of stale, chemical-laden air—bubblegum and formaldehyde—escaped as I slipped inside.

By the pinpoint light of a tiny flashlight, I darted through the big, black doors edged with rubber like on a meat locker, across the concrete floor, and past the stainless steel tables and the deep porcelain sinks. Through another door—hollow steel and a window embedded with metal mesh—left ajar. Inside: a desk, a telephone, a computer, filing cabinets.

Autopsy files, drawers full of them, with no logical order—all the names, all the words in dream script: disordered, distorted. Then one word of many: "torture." More: advanced state of decay. Electrical burns, cigarette burns, premortem blunt force trauma. Asphyxiation. But where's the name?

I need a name.

I pawed through the file, flipped through it a hundred times, over and over again, my fingers flying, my eyes scanning every page.

Until.

There was one page in my hands, one page scrawled with unreadable script. But at the top there was a name, the name that had to be there, the name that had been swimming in the darkest corners of my mind since I heard the first fly buzzing around Patrick Beale:

Pvt. Havers, Paul Kerry
Male; Caucasian
MOS: 68W, Health Care Specialist
Date of birth: April 29, 1986
Date of entry: September 11, 2004
Date of death: August 13, 2005

Then, like a movie on fast-forward:

Havers, the newest member of our squad, reporting for deployment the morning we flew to Iraq. He was tall and thin, his cheeks baby smooth, his smile too knowing.

Havers, his face grim and set, running past me to the OR after a call for all hands over the loud speaker. And later that week, Havers, his spine straight, his eyes unflinching and hopeful, asking to be sent out with a convoy. Me, denying the request, telling him, "You aren't ready. Maybe next month."

Havers, at attention, his eyes steady and wide and far too innocent when I ordered him to account for items missing from the stockroom. Havers, claiming that everything had been there when he did inventory the day before. Me, giving him the benefit of the doubt.

And the next month, Havers flashing a too-confident smile, carrying a box of supplies out the side door of the hospital. "Taking them to the quartermaster, Sergeant," he'd said. "They're surplus."

Early in the morning a week, maybe two, after that, Havers carrying a box of exam gloves out to the back of the hospital during the crack between the night shift and the day. "Garbage," Havers had said and smiled that same smile. "Sat in the heat too long. One of the docs said they were useless." I didn't stop him, didn't check to see what was actually in the box. Didn't exercise my right—my duty*—to make sure my soldier was doing the right thing.*

The following month, Havers again requesting permission to go on convoy. Me, denying him again, watching his lips compress, his jaw clench, his cheeks flush, his eyes darken. Havers requesting instead to take a few days R&R back home. Me, denying that request too. Me, knowing my choices were right.

Then a month later, Havers failing to sound off during morning roll call. Havers, conspicuously absent. A few minutes later at the barracks, his bunk neatly made, his gear neatly stowed, and that familiar feeling of absence, of loss heavy and near. Later that morning, after I'd combed the dining hall, the barracks, the movie theater, the hospital, and everywhere else on base I could think to look for my dirt-bag kid soldier . . . that's when I went to see Major Brittan behind his desk at the hospital the first time, the major who liked me and my exemplary record. The major with his lips thin, his fingers angrily punching in the number of the base commander's office, his voice tense and low when he told the commander about a soldier who'd gone missing, who was absent without leave.

A few days after that, Havers, in the cool, stale air of an abandoned, half-blown Iraqi residence.

Havers, hanging in the beam of a soldier's flashlight. Hanging at the end of a length of polypropylene rope, his chest bare, his feet bare, only the pants of his uniform slung over his narrow hips, the strings meant to secure them at his bony ankles dangling limp instead.

*   *   *

And then I woke.

My shirt was drenched with sweat, my jeans plastered to my thighs. Blood pounded in my ears like surf breaking on the shore.

I threw my legs over the side of the sofa, forced myself to breathe slowly, calmly. Listened to the night outside; listened to the insects hum and the wind sigh; and, far away, a coyote howl. Eventually, the tide ebbed.

Havers. Private Havers.

He died like Patrick Beale. He *lived* like Patrick Beale: arrogant, greedy, and criminal.

But was he real?

As Friday dawned, I found what I needed to prove that my dreams were memories, not just nightmares: a black and white and red web page, crude. It screamed for justice for Private Paul Havers, for a soldier whose death the Army had tried to cover up, tried to pawn off as enemy action. Its manifesto dripped with venom, the words mostly crazed, but some of them . . . some of them were so rational, so *clear*, they might have been the truth. So plausible that I nodded as I read them, heard myself saying, yes, he couldn't have died by enemy action, not in the friendly town in which his body was found. Yes, the Army's failure to return his personal effects, the contents of his footlocker and ruck, couldn't have been an accident—maybe they *had* been purposefully destroyed. Yes, taking four months to release his remains was suspicious, and God knew what they had done with them in the meantime. And were they even his? They were just ashes, after all.

The page appeared to be dormant, no recent posts, just the same rabid words screamed into the void of the internet for years. The Facebook page it linked to was similarly quiet, the most recent post a three-year-old, misspelled note from a random veterans group that sounded like it identified more with Hitler than Uncle Sam. At the top of the page was a banner with "Justice for Pvt. Paul Havers" printed across a photo of a wiry white kid, his eyes laughing at the boot camp photographer, his green dress uniform pristine, the flag hanging limply behind him like the ruffles on a girl's skirt. It stopped me cold. He seemed familiar, but in a far-off way. Like I'd seen him somewhere before, but not in my dreams. He was different in my dreams. But nothing in a dream is real, not *really* real, like you could put your finger on it.

Below the veterans group post, the comments were like acid, cutting and ignorant. "You're a fucking traitor. US Army is USA!" "Some towel head shot your brother." "You should have been in the sandbox too." The words of people who had never been. No wonder the page had gone so quiet.

I tried to message the organizer, but hit a login window. I opened an account under an old email address and reached out to a guy by the name of Mike Havers, whose profile picture showed a young man with a shaved head and a grin behind a pair of sunglasses.

I have information. Are you Havers's brother?

I glanced at the clock in the corner of the screen. 4:53 AM. It was a long shot, but I waited anyway. After a few minutes, I got up and made a pot of coffee. When I sat down again, I was surprised to find a response in the chat window.

What do you know?

But I wasn't ready to spill my guts yet, especially before I knew whether I would get anything for doing it. So I responded in kind: *Are you Pvt. Havers's brother?*

I sipped coffee, growing more anxious, more doubtful as each minute slipped by. Twelve minutes after I sent my message, Mike Havers was back.

Why do you want to know?

Why *did* I want to know? Why did it matter, if he had the information I needed?

I want to know I'm talking to someone who cares, I typed. It sounded fake, even to me, but it was the closest thing to the truth I had to offer.

And, anyway, that wasn't *really* what Mike Havers wanted to know. He wanted to know why I was contacting him, to know I wasn't just some random person on the internet, another crazy who was going to make fun of him, tell him he should be dead too.

My cursor flicked on and off in the chat line. My palms began to sweat, my fingers poised over the keyboard.

Finally: *Are you a journalist?*

Relieved, I dashed off an answer. *No. I was stationed with him. I knew him.* I hit "Send" before I could stop myself.

Oh. Then: *Yeah. I'm his brother. Mike.* And on a new line of dialogue: *When did you know him?*

I needed his trust. But I also needed him to be hungry. I couldn't give him too much too soon.

In the Army.

When?

His reply had been immediate. I had his attention and I had to keep it. The question was, how much to tell him? The simple truth: 2005? Or the provocative truth: when he died? In the end, I went with simple.

2005. You all are from Arizona, right? Do you still live there?

Yeah. Were you with him in Iraq?

I stalled, tried to pull him out a little more. *He always said he didn't mind the heat.*

No. He went out in the desert a lot when we were kids.

Interesting. Private Havers had been rebellious before the Army. Or maybe just stupid. Only one way to find out.

What was he doing? I typed.

Don't know.

He ever take you with him?

No.

Did he have friends he went out there with?

Don't know. Maybe.

Do you know where he was going?

No answer. Seconds dragged into minutes, dragged into a quarter of an hour. He could have been driving. He could have been at work. Or I could have pushed too much.

A breeze swept down from the mountain and through the window. I shivered and shifted my chair into the sunlight stretching across the room. When I pulled the laptop toward me, Mike Havers had reappeared.

Who are you?

It was a good question. I chose a cop-out. *Just a friend. I want to see justice, just like you.*

OK. Then, a few seconds later, *What do you know?*

I know who killed your brother. I typed it and for ten minutes, stared at the letters on the screen. Did I? I thought I did. But I couldn't prove it. Yet. I deleted the message and logged off. Better to leave him hungry.

12

Later that Friday morning, I was on the road, way out in the county, following up on what Harry German had given me. It was gold, he'd said on the phone that morning, gold he had dug out of the state records: every property owned by any company that looked a little fishy and every property that had Jack Wyatt's name associated with it.

"If there's anything there," he'd said, "you'll find it at one of these places."

He'd listed them out, address by address, on the phone, well aware that giving me state records was against the rules, smart enough to not put anything in an email or to send it through a fax machine. The list began with Gorgon Four's future pot farm up in the hills and finished with Gorgon Six's barn, where Patrick Beale had hung, rotting, for days. And in the middle? I was making my way through the middle.

I'd left the mart just after the sun rose, driven past the town sign and on past the lake, shining like a mirror in the rising heat. I'd been heading out for an inspection when Harry called, but after we hung up, I swung the truck around and went the other way. By ten o'clock, I had already seen two places: one empty and forgotten, farmland untouched for so long that trees sprouted in the furrows like ghosts rising from a burial ground, and the other a respectable place with a tidy little house and a tidy little garden and a couple of kids out doing chores. I skipped the next few, turned north, then headed east down a narrow road just north of the Colville Reservation.

I was coming around a curve, the sun in my face, when a black truck came screaming down the hill so fast, so recklessly, I thought its brakes were out. I swerved off the road, my tires skittering wildly on the edge of a fifty-foot drop. I wrestled the wheel, fought for purchase on the dry dirt that spilled over into nothing. Two wheels, then three, and finally four stabilized, spun on solid ground. I slammed on the brakes and the truck lurched, stilled except for the engine idling. I jerked my head over my shoulder to get the license plate number, but the truck was long gone. The tarmac of his lane was completely clean; thick black streaks of rubber snaked wildly in mine.

"Mother fuck," I said and folded over the steering wheel. When I stopped hyperventilating, I gave the engine a little gas and gritted my teeth as the tires slid in the dirt before catching, and the truck finally lumbered back onto the pavement.

Past the crest of the hill, stands of trees swept down toward the road, and the scent of musty pine needles drifted through the open windows. A couple of miles further, the trees opened, and dried grass rippled in a broad clearing bordered by a long gravel track. Beside the track was a battered mailbox, its old plastic numbers peeling off but clear enough to match to the address on my list.

I drove down the gravel slowly, the dust barely rising from the truck's rear tires. The trees closed in again, and the hill tapered down. Just after I crossed over a trickling stream boxed up into a culvert, I saw the trailer. It was a double-wide, cream-colored and mushroom-like in a small clearing off to the side. A car, broken up for parts, lurked under a tree. Spots of oil speckled the dust in the drive.

I did a three-point turn and parked the truck with its nose pointing toward the road. The clearing was quiet, calm; just the wind rifling through the trees until, far away, a hawk screamed. On the metal-mesh doorstep of the trailer, there was a bottle of bleach—a big one—and a box of rags like you'd get at an auto shop, a narrow receipt peeking out from under one corner.

I rapped on the hollow metal door, but the only response I got was the faint twang of country pop on a cheap stereo somewhere inside. I tried again, but no one stirred. Around back, the music was louder, drifting out an open window. But there was no response when I knocked on the back door or when I shouted, "Hello!" So, I circled the trailer, glancing casually into every window, all of them wide open, every room empty, until I reached the last one.

Inside was a bedroom, big and open, with seafoam-green walls, tatty yellow linoleum, and a gold-flecked bathroom through a partly open door. But there was no bed, no nightstand, no clothes hanging in the open closet. Instead, there was a plastic tarp decorated with dried blood and a wooden chair with rubber straps hanging from the arms. In front of the chair, where a seated person's feet would rest, a truck battery with clawed metal leads and a pair of pliers rested in a disposable aluminum pan, a pool of blood in one corner.

I backed away from the window, stumbled over my own feet, and landed on my ass. My heart pounded in my chest, the sound of it echoing in my ears. I sprang to a crouch, scanned the clearing like it was a war zone. No camera. No watchers. No weapons. I spun in a tight circle, my fingertips in the dirt, my thighs tight and strong, ready to charge. I scanned the trees, but there was nothing. I was alone.

At the nearest tree, I slid down the trunk and closed my eyes, pressing my hands into my face. Battery. Pliers. Blood. That tarp. They'd tortured him. That's what the doc said. That's what I had known, even when I didn't know what I knew. They beat him. They burned him. They ripped out his fingernails at the root. Here. In the cream-colored trailer. On the sunshine-yellow linoleum. And then they washed their hands in that golden sink, and they took him out and strung him up to die alone, in the shadows, in the dark. They'd made him *bloated, blackened, unrecognizable. His chest bare, his feet bare . . .*

Jesus Christ, *make it stop.*

My eyes flew open. The trees were still. The grass in the clearing was still. But the radio played on. Who'd left the music on? *The truck.* That truck tearing down the mountain like the driver had forgotten something important. *How long ago was that? How long a drive to the nearest store? How long until the devil returned?*

On the radio, a commercial ended, and a steel guitar beat out a frantic tune. I tore my phone from my pocket and went back to the window, photographed everything I saw from every angle I could capture. And then I fled like a rabbit, ran to the truck like I had a battery of rifles on my tail, throwing it into gear and barreling up the dirt track and out onto the county road, my eyes shifting frantically between what was in front of me and what was behind.

There was no cell signal, so I called Darren on my county sat phone, told him to get the hell out there, that the trailer was everything he needed to nail Patrick Beale's killer. By the time I saw the sheriff's cruisers flash past the gas station where I had pulled over, there was more adrenaline than blood flowing through my veins. I sat in the truck, both of my county phones on the bench seat beside me, waiting for Darren to call me back, to tell me that they'd gotten the evidence and grabbed the guy who put it there, the guy responsible for spraying Patrick Beale's blood all over the floor.

But the call didn't come. Instead, he pulled up alongside me where I was parked in a sliver of shade. Then he got out of his cruiser, opened the door of my truck, and climbed into the passenger seat.

"What the hell are you doing?" I said. "Your boys went by here ten minutes ago."

"Nice to see you too," he said and tossed a piece of gum into his mouth. He took off his sunglasses and wiped the lenses on the fabric stretched tight over his leg.

"What about the evidence? What about the photos I texted to you?" I said, my voice rising. *What about the asshole who did this?*"

"Lucky's got it under control." His gum popped between his teeth.

"What the fuck, Darren? Lucky isn't enough." I fumbled with the keys, slotted them into the ignition, and turned. I shouted over the roar of the engine, "That guy will be back soon, I swear it. The radio, the bleach! He's going to fucking clean the place, Darren. It's all going to be gone!"

"Camille." Darren's voice was soft, but the hand he curled over mine on the truck's gear shaft was firm, unyielding. Gently, he moved my hand to my thigh, then reached over, turned the key, killed the engine. "Relax. It's under control. Let me do my job."

I clenched my jaw, closed my eyes, but that only made the images play more vividly against the black backdrop of my lids. Blood and flies and stained denim. Bloated flesh. And the smell. The smell I couldn't get out of my nostrils, out of my mind.

I opened my eyes, watched the heat rising off the blacktop and studied the scrubby hills, golden in the sunlight, off to the west. They were pure, clean. They were here, now. I breathed—in, out, in, out—and felt the pressure in my veins drop. Then I leaned across the cab, opened the glove box, and handed him a plastic bag.

"What's this?" he said, turning it over in his hands.

"A receipt," I muttered. "It was there today, under the bottle of bleach. There's a label in there too, for brake fluid. That's from the place behind Jeremy Leamon's."

Darren's eyes were black, inscrutable. "How did you find out about that?"

I shrugged. "Why does it matter?"

"Tell me."

I narrowed my eyes. His face cleared, the naked intensity from only a moment before disappearing behind his usual cloak.

"County records," I said, curiosity overcoming my fear, my urge to flee. "It's what I do, Darren."

"When did you go there?"

"Monday."

"What did you see?"

"You mean other than the big fucking burn pit?"

Darren nodded. He didn't seem surprised.

"Just that label," I lied and pointed at the plastic bag. There was no reason for him to know about the receipt I had found out there also, the one from my mart. No reason at all.

"Did anyone see you?"

"No," I said quickly.

"Did anyone see you today?"

I pursed my lips, gritted my teeth. Had anyone? Could I be sure there hadn't been anyone in the trailer or the trees? Could I be sure no one had stayed behind?

I shook my head minutely.

"You're sure?" Darren said urgently.

"No."

Darren turned his head, looked out the windshield to the golden hills. His jaw was clean-shaven, his collar pressed, but his eyes were bloodshot, ringed with dark circles.

Softly, he said, "Please stop."

"What?"

"This." He pointed to the plastic bag. "This . . . *investigating*."

I cracked my jaw, turned away.

"Don't get me wrong, Camille. I appreciate the tip today. It looks promising. But you've gotta let me do my job. And you—you've got to live your life."

"This *is* my life."

"No, it isn't. You've got your job. You've got the mart. You've got Sophie."

"Goddamnit," I snapped. "That's what this is about, Darren. It's about—"

A voice crackled over the radio pinned to Darren's shoulder. He turned the volume up, listened to the message. Even with the static, I recognized Lucky's voice. Even with the static, I knew it wasn't good news.

"Shouldn't you be going?" I said, my throat tight.

"Yeah. Are you—?"

"I'm fine," I said tersely. "I'm *fine*."

That's when he slid his hand over mine, still on my thigh. His skin was dry and cool. Mine was hot, my veins pulsing with fevered blood. I froze.

"You did the right thing," Darren said, like that was supposed to be comforting.

But my jaw was locked, so tight I couldn't say any of the vicious things going through my mind or scream away the terror or tell him to never move his hand.

I shook him off and saw the hurt flicker across Darren's face before the shield came down again. He opened the door and stepped out onto the pavement, but he turned back before closing it.

"Call me," he said. "We should . . ."

He paused then, long enough for me to realize that I was waiting for his next words, that I needed them in a primal way. But all he said was "We should talk."

13

That night, the boys, Patrick, Havers . . .

They spoke to me.

They spoke to me where they hung. They raised their heads and stared at me, their eyes swollen with gas, crusted with flies, weeping syrupy fluid.

They said the same thing over and over again.

I was alone in the darkness, but each time I turned away from them, something pushed me back.

Each time, they said: You know. You know.

And each time, I screamed at them: I don't! I can't.

And I didn't. I didn't know. And I couldn't help them.

But I couldn't stop. Wouldn't stop.

No.

The boys just stared.

I woke in a pool of sweat.

14

Before that Saturday, I had been to only two funerals.

The first, my mother's, was surreal. I was twenty hours off two straight days of flights from Baghdad. I still had Iraqi dust under my fingernails, could still smell the spicy sweat, the cordite, the dog piss. But the wool fabric of my dress uniform scratched against clean skin, skin scrubbed so hard in the shower at my parents' place that it was raw.

I remember standing at the edge of everything, standing right up next to a tree in the cemetery out on the bluff above Okanogan. And I remember the looks that people gave me: awe turned to curiosity, turned to cautious fascination when I wouldn't budge from the tree, when I couldn't stop scanning the crowd. Turned to fear when I acknowledged them with a pointed glance at their hands, their pockets, their faces. When I barely said a word.

And I remember watching a little girl in a white dress reach up and put a lily as big as her head on the coffin. Briefly, I wondered whose kid she was. Then she reached up and took my dad's hand, and I realized she was mine, that she was Sophie. I hadn't been home for over a year, had requested that my deployment be extended, had made the case over and over again that I was indispensable to the command, to the mission. And the commander had believed me, taken me at my word. Despite what Major Brittan told him. Despite my first sergeant's growing wariness. The commander had been more sympathetic. My phone calls to my folks, to Sophie, grew shorter and less frequent. Because the desert was home. Home was where the rockets flew and the blood ran and my best friend was my M16. Where I had a purpose. A mission.

But mostly, I remember standing in the cemetery and fearing the silence.

Dad's funeral was different. It had been just that May. Sophie was there, but not there for me. I had moved into Dad's house after his heart attack the week before. I wasn't much of a mother then—hell, I never have been—but I knew enough that a fourteen-year-old girl had no business being in a house by herself. I hadn't told her yet that we were both going to live above the mart, that, yes, I was going to rip her out of the bedroom that had always been hers, that had once been mine. I couldn't admit to her that nothing in that house was right anymore, that, for me, too many ghosts walked the halls, too many of them crouched beside my bed and gnashed their teeth at night. But the funeral was nice.

Patrick Beale's funeral was another thing altogether.

It was on the football field of the high school down in Omak, the aluminum stands ablaze in the morning sun, friends and family and hangers-on perched up there in their Sunday best and sunglasses that reflected the dark casket overflowing with flowers. The preacher from the faded church in Little Falls gave the eulogy, his voice creaky on the loudspeaker, the crowd wincing every time the microphone screamed when his hearing aid got too close.

After the service, after the sighing and the crying and the kind words about a life lived too quickly, the mourners and the merely curious trickled off the stands like sweat, pooling onto the field below. To one side were the church people and their profane neighbors, all of them slowly pressing forward to shake Ed's hand, to hold Christine while she cried. And to the other side were the kids, Sophie and her friend Tracy and a lot of others I didn't know, ebbing and flowing, hugging each other and parting, their hands held loosely together until their bodies were too far away to maintain the bond.

But still sitting on the stands was Todd Beale, alone, his dust-colored head resolutely facing his brother, facing the box. Or maybe the other side.

"You going to say hello?" someone said, his breath hot on my ear.

I turned fast, swinging, and Darren caught my elbow.

"Hey," he said before letting go. He settled back in the row behind me, the last in the bleachers.

I turned back to the field, my face burning. "Didn't know you'd started a conversation."

"Thought I'd let you ruminate." He stood up, stepped down to my row, and sat beside me, much closer than the woman who had vacated the seat at the end of the service.

"Big word."

I was sorry the moment I said it, but Darren just laughed. And when he did, he leaned forward, his elbows on his knees, his thigh so close I could feel the heat of him through the thin fabric of the only dress I owned, the one I'd worn to my father's funeral.

"Well?" Darren said and turned his head toward me. He was wearing his uniform and the same aviator sunglasses he'd had on when he stepped out of the county's helicopter the week before. My tongue traced the edge of my lips.

"Well, what?"

"You got it figured out?"

"Thought you didn't want me investigating."

Darren's smile didn't break. I looked away.

"Maybe," I said.

"Did the bastard show his face here?"

I shrugged.

He nodded and looked out at the field. Then he touched my leg, one fingertip quickly brushing against my bare skin. He pointed his chin out at the parking lot. I pressed my knees together.

"You seen that truck before?" Darren asked.

I scanned the mostly empty parking lot. "Which one?" I said, then took a guess. "That brown Chevy?"

"No. In the far corner, under the trees. The Suburban. Black with red stripes."

I scanned again and saw what he meant, crouched in the shade beneath a giant cedar, its windows tinted and windshield pointed away from the field. I had seen it that day, and I had seen it before too. Out of the corner of my eye, I saw Darren watching me, and I knew he knew I had. But did he recognize the long black sedan next to it? The one with its windows rolled down and its side panels dull with dust; the one with no one in it. I did. He didn't.

He put his hands on his knees and sat up straight. His shoulder brushed against mine, strands of my blond hair snagging on his brown uniform when I turned my head to look at him.

"What do you think of the brother?" I said suddenly, instinct, or maybe obsession, moving faster than my brain. I had nothing on the kid, just a feeling. A weird feeling.

Darren frowned and glanced at the field. "Todd?"

I followed his gaze and saw what he saw, a teenager standing near his parents, hugging a woman with curly hair the color of yellowed teeth. Just a normal teenager, his hair burnished in the sun, his face drawn and pale, the edge of the collar of his pressed blue shirt dark with sweat. A slight girl in a little black dress and church-mouse brown hair stood at his elbow. She took his hand in her thin fingers when he let the old woman's shoulders go.

I nodded.

"Nice kid," Darren said.

"Yeah?"

"You don't think so?"

"Doesn't seem to like his brother much."

Darren shrugged. "Boys will be boys."

I nodded again and doubted myself.

"You want to grab some lunch?" Darren said. "I know a place. It's good and it's close. Sophie can come too, if she wants."

"She's going to lunch with some friends."

Darren stood and held out his hand for me, but I ignored it and started down the stairs.

He had his cruiser, so I followed him out past Okanogan, then down a road to the other side of the river, until he pulled into the driveway of a little brown house shaded by the wide branches of an oak tree. His house. The engine still running, I leaned out the window of my truck.

"What's this? Making a house call?" I said, playing dumb.

He slammed the door of the car and started walking. "The line's shorter here."

He unlocked the door and disappeared inside, the screen door slamming behind him, the front door wide open.

Tapping my fingers on the steering wheel, I glanced back at the road in my rearview, at the road in front of me, and then at the house. Sighing, I threw the truck into first gear, rolled it into the drive, and parked.

Inside, the house was dark, the front hall lit only by the afternoon sun sneaking in through the cracks of the curtains in the living room.

"How's your wife?" I asked.

Somewhere beyond the living room, a refrigerator door opened. Glass jars clinked and something slapped onto a counter. As my pupils dilated, I took inventory. In front of me, the living room was all but bare: I could see the arm of a leather couch—a light-colored T-shirt thrown over it—a squat coffee table in front of it, and a TV balanced on a cardboard box directly opposite. Doors to the right, closed. And on the wall at my elbow, a shoe stand—unoccupied—and above it, hanging askew, a kitschy wooden sign that read "Welcome to the Moses home."

"You mean Meredith?" Darren said eventually.

"Yeah." In the hallway, I stepped back, frowned, tilted the welcome sign to the right.

"She's gone."

"Out doing a trial?" I tilted the sign a little to the left.

"No. Gone. Moved to Oklahoma a year ago."

I stopped, my fingers still touching the not-quite-perfect sign. No wonder it was crooked.

"You want a beer?" he said when I got to the kitchen, then handed me an open bottle before I could say no. I set it on the counter and stepped away.

"Divorce was final in December," he said while slicing a tomato. He looked up and flashed me a wide smile. "She took a job with one of the tribes down there. It was good for her."

"What about you?" I asked warily.

He shrugged. "It's good for me too."

There was nothing more to say, so I offered to spread the mayo while he washed the lettuce. A few minutes later, we were sitting on the steps of his back porch, balancing our plates on our knees and listening to the water slowly glug through what was left of the creek.

After a while, I asked him again about the day before. About the trailer.

After another while he told me: "Nothing. There was nothing."

"What do you mean, *nothing*?"

"We were just too late. The place had been sprayed down by the time we got there. The bleach was so strong, we had to air it out before anyone could even go in."

"But what about the chair, the—the leads, the battery? What about the bloody pliers, the bloody *tarp*?"

He was looking out across the yard to the stream, frowning, his fingers restless, peeling the label off his beer bottle. He shook his head. "They weren't there."

"But you *saw* the photos I took," I said, setting my plate aside, getting up to retrieve my phone from the house. "You *saw* them, didn't you?"

"Yeah." Darren nodded, his head bobbing like it was no big deal. "Yeah, I saw them."

"Well, they didn't just disappear. It was thirty minutes—no more than thirty minutes—before your boys drove by."

Darren frowned briefly, doubtfully, then nodded.

"I thought Lucky was going to handle it," I pressed, staring down at him. "When did he get there, Darren? Who was first on the scene?"

He didn't respond.

"Fine." I crossed my arms. "There must have been tracks. You got a tire imprint, or something."

"Sure, Moreno took some."

"So you can find him that way."

He snorted and looked up at me with a disgusted, or maybe just exhausted, smirk. "What do you think we are—*CSI*? *NYPD Blue*?"

My anxiety and my heart rate were rising at a furious pace. The truck. I hadn't told Darren about the truck the day before. How could I have forgotten? What *else* had I forgotten? I sank to my knees.

"Did it match Patrick's truck? There was someone in it yesterday. He forced me off the road."

Darren shifted, his brow creased.

"There was a truck, a black one, just like Patrick was driving in that video. It forced me off the road yesterday while I was driving out to that address." I pressed the palm of my hand against my forehead. "He was totally out of control, driving like a demon."

"There was no truck."

My head snapped up. "*I saw it!* He almost killed me!"

"Camille," Darren's voice was soft, calm. Patronizing. "*The tracks.* The tracks didn't match Patrick's truck."

"It was black, like the one Patrick drove."

Darren shook his head.

"But—" I hesitated, scraped my fingernails through my hair, over my scalp. "What about the other one? The one that blond guy was driving in the video. Or that Suburban."

Again, Darren shook his head. "The tracks were from a standard American-made sedan, Ford or Chevy or something. Something easy to hide around here."

"Like the car next to the Suburban?" I snarled.

The creases on Darren's forehead deepened. "When?"

"At the funeral."

"Tell me."

"Standard American-made sedan, Ford or Chevy or something," I said mockingly.

Darren's face hardened. The wall that had been eroding sprang up between us again.

I sat down, breathed. Lowered my voice. "It was black." I turned toward Darren. "It was beside the Suburban. And I've seen it before."

"Where?"

"It doesn't matter," I said, anticipating the hell he'd give me for lurking outside that lawyer's office. So when Darren opened his mouth, I added quickly, "But I saw one of the guys from the mart's video get into it. When I saw it before, I mean."

"Which one?"

"That blond one. Tall, buzz cut, sort of lanky. Former Army, I'd guess."

"He wasn't with Patrick in the video," Darren said bluntly. "Where did you—"

"No," I said sharply, not wanting to go there, not wanting to get into how—let alone how *much*—I knew about the lieutenant. "It was later. Day four of the feed. And you're right. He wasn't with Patrick. But he was with the guy who was. The one with the tats. They're both involved. Somehow."

Darren nodded, took a long pull from his bottle of beer, and stared out at the yard, his eyes hiding whatever he was thinking through.

"Did you hear me?" I said, my voice rising.

Darren glanced at me, his entire face blank, impassive. My pulse quickened: I was right.

"What's his name?" I barked. "Who is he?"

Darren drained his beer and set the bottle on the wooden porch, green paint peeling from the weathered boards.

"Was it him on the recording?"

The skin of Darren's forehead creased. "What recording?"

"Patrick's recording."

The frown on Darren's face deepened. "You have a recording my victim made?" He cracked his jaw. "And you didn't give it to me?"

"I left it for you," I said, my anger, my exasperation, matching his. "At your office. I told the guy at the desk to give it to you."

"*When?*"

"Yesterday afternoon. I told him to give it to you. I said your name. I wrote it down."

His eyes narrowed. He shook his head.

"Who else would have taken it?" I said. "Moreno?"

"No," Darren said quietly.

"Lucky?"

Darren glanced away, ground his teeth. He didn't know. He didn't *know*, but he suspected. Like I suspected. Lucky at the barn. Lucky at the trailer. Lucky at the Sheriff's Office. Lucky everywhere.

His eyes on me again, Darren asked, "Where did you get it?"

"Patrick's apartment. I was . . ." But I didn't want to tell him why I went there in the first place. "I was helping Christine pack up his things. It was just there, a thumb drive taped to the bottom of his bed frame."

"What was on the recording?"

"A phone conversation. Patrick was hiding somewhere—a bathroom, I think. He recorded a conversation someone was having on the phone, someone giving coordinates and asking for instructions."

"Did you keep a copy?"

"No. I gave it to you. I did the right thing."

Darren turned away from me then, so I couldn't see what he was thinking. But I saw it anyway, the muscles of his jaw tightening as he ground his teeth, the blood pounding through the artery in his neck, saw him finger the safety strap of his service weapon as he adjusted his utility belt.

"Tell me his name, Darren!" I shouted. "For Christ's sake, I can help. I *am* helping!"

"*No*," Darren said, his voice low, forbidding, his face still turned away from me.

But I would not let it stop there; it *couldn't* stop there. "Fine," I said quietly, trying to hold back the rage. "What about the receipt? You've got him on the receipt, right? You can tie him to my photos, at least."

Darren shook his head. "It's not enough."

"What do you mean?" I snapped. "It's all there: the bleach, the rags. Time of day. Everything. It's everything you need."

He shook his head again. "Paid in cash, no video, and the clerk can't describe who bought the stuff."

My pulse spiked, pounded in my neck. Suddenly, I was standing over him, every muscle in my body tensed. "What about the landowner?" I shouted. "You got my message last night, didn't you? Didn't you find anything?"

"Nothing." Slowly, he stood up. "It's just a company. It was formed to buy the property about six months ago and hasn't done anything since."

A gust of wind swept through the yard. It might have come from the top of Mount Rainier, it chilled my skin that much. Or maybe—

"What if he saw me?" I whispered.

I backed away, glancing around the yard, the stairs, the porch—looking for safety, for a safe position out of the open, somewhere with something solid at my back. Darren squared off, his eyes dark, his brow creased. And I saw him do it: I saw his hand stray to where his gun rested on his hip.

"I'm not crazy!" I shouted. "Jesus Christ, this was supposed to be over. That was supposed to be everything you needed. That was supposed to end it."

"Hey," he said softly, trying what was probably meant to be a warm smile. "Camille. We'll get them. You'll be fine."

"No, I won't. They broke into my store. They stole the fucking evidence, the fucking evidence that *I* found. And they—they sprayed that place down. They bleached it, erased it. They *erased* Patrick's blood and shit and, and . . . and . . ."

Darren stepped forward, but I went rigid, my muscles coiled to fight. He stopped, held a hand out, appeasing.

"It's okay. They're not going to get away with it. They're not going to do anything to you."

"Do you know what they did to *him*?" I said, fighting myself, fighting the urge to scream. "Can you even imagine?"

He nodded. "Yeah," he said quietly. "I saw the doc's report."

"Then you know what they would do to me. You know what they'll do if they saw me, if they know who I am and what *I* saw."

Then, suddenly, a new panic shot through my veins like ice water and pulled me through to the other side, the side where I had lived for years in the desert. The side where everything is black and white and afterward . . . Afterward, everything is fragments.

"Oh my God," I breathed. "Sophie."

*   *   *

That afternoon was blurred fields and hills receding in my rearview as I sped to the next place I thought I might find her, damning her for not answering her phone the first time I called, then the fifth and the fifteenth. I went to all the places to eat in Omak, in Okanogan, all the way down to Chelan. I went to Crystal's shop and Hank's, the ice cream place where she'd flirted with that tattooed motherfucker. And then I went to the first place I should have gone.

It was one of those perfect days at Lake Chelan: dry and sunny and hot, the sound of motor boats and distant, distorted music ricocheting in the hills. I turned onto the street where I had followed Sophie the Wednesday before. During the day, it was quiet, the street deep in the shade of ponderosa pines, the yards perfectly sculpted around the huge houses set back from the road. But there was the driveway where the black Dodge truck had been parked, and there were the shrubs that had picked my fleece jacket apart, and there was the house my daughter had stormed out of late that night, the night when she'd had a shotgun at her back.

I stopped the truck on the street, and for a long time I watched and waited. The entire street seemed deserted, but no house more so than the one where the party had been. All the blinds were drawn, the driveway empty, the yard pristine. Eventually, I tucked the Glock in my hand, held it rigidly at my side, and walked slowly to the front door, the nerves in my body so tight, a feather would have made them snap.

I knocked on the door with my left hand, my right forefinger hovering over the trigger. Out on the water, someone whooped and a speedboat engine roared with all its cylinders, but the house remained silent. I knocked again. Nothing. So I walked the perimeter, keeping my head low and my guard up while trying to be as inconspicuous as a woman in a little black dress in the middle of the day can be. Finally, I found a window where the blinds weren't completely shut, but there was nothing to see: no plastic cups, no overflowing ashtrays, no empty beer cans, not even furniture. Nothing to indicate that anyone had ever been there.

I circled back around to the front, wondering if it was the wrong house, if I had driven down the wrong road, if I had dreamed the whole thing. There are times when I can't trust my memory, can't trust my mind. But then I saw it: a cigarette butt tossed aside and missed under a shrub beside the front walk. And I remembered when, at the party, the blond lieutenant was angry, how he shouted at my daughter and threw aside a cigarette hard and fast, orange sparks exploding on the pavement in the dark. And I remembered watching the glowing butt roll off the pathway and wink out.

Faintly, I heard my county phone ring, and my heart almost exploded as I sprinted back to the truck. When I picked it up, the caller ID was for the mart, and I guessed it was only Rhonda Faye, irritated that I'd destroyed her entire Saturday.

I answered, apologies at the ready, and—"Camille?" Sophie's always irritated voice said. "Camille? Are you there?"

I'd like to say I read her the riot act. I'd like to say I raced home and at least hugged her or told her I loved her. But I didn't. I couldn't.

On the phone, I told her to stay put, to stay at the apartment, that I'd be home soon. Then I tore up the highway, my heart bursting with fear and relief and joy that she was okay, that they hadn't gotten to her, that she hadn't been punished for my sins again.

But when I opened the door, the apartment was silent, the air suffocating and stale. Only a wisp of her shampoo—green apple—lingered.

"Sophie?"

The bathroom door was open, the one to her bedroom closed. Padding across the floor, Glock in hand, I approached the far end of the apartment at a wide angle. Reflected in the bathroom mirror were the plain white wall and the rose-colored toilet. Half a step further and I saw the shower curtain hanging limply, gathered at one end of the tub.

"Clear," I breathed.

I advanced to the bedroom. Shoulder blade against the doorframe, I reached around the corner and turned the knob of the bedroom door slowly before flinging it open. Silence. Blood pounding in my temples, I pivoted into the opening, pointing the gun into every corner of the room. Sheet twisted at the foot of her empty bed, laundry piled on the floor, pink backpack slouched beside the white desk. Disarray. Normal disarray.

She was gone.

I flipped open my county phone, the one she had called an hour and a half before, and dialed her number. It went straight to voicemail. Pacing hard, the heels of my pretty black pumps ripping into the carpet, I tried again and again. Where the hell had she gone?

That's when I saw the note.

It was on the counter, on top of the day's mail. In Sophie's loopy scrawl, it read: *I need a new phone.* And there, beneath it, was the phone I had been calling all afternoon and again only minutes before. It was broken, mangled, crushed under the tires of a car. Or a truck. Or a Chevy Suburban.

She was with them, those assholes in the black and red Suburban. The note didn't say it, and she hadn't said it on the phone, but I knew it was true. Willingly? Maybe, but that wasn't any better.

On the table, the screen of my work laptop reflected the last burning rays of the sunset. I snatched my phone off the counter and sat down, booted up the computer, and opened the files I had taken from Sophie's phone after confiscating it earlier that week. Then I dialed.

He answered after three rings, fumbling, scratching like he had his hand over the receiver. And in the background, there was thumping bass almost drowned out by a roaring fan.

"Yeah," he drawled, distracted.

My free hand tightly fisted on the table, I demanded, "Where is she?"

"What?"

"Where is my daughter?"

"Who is this?"

There it was, a slight accent, like a slant in his voice. It was him, the black-haired, tattooed Latino from Hank's and the mart video and Oroville. I had been right: this was Nick.

I stood up, grabbed my keys, prepared to run wherever, to do anything for her, for my girl. "Where is my daughter?"

"The fuck are you talking about?"

"If you touch her, if you . . . I swear to God, I will rip your throat out with my teeth."

He laughed, giggled like a little boy tormenting a fly.

"You some crazy bitch," he said and sighed. Then, his voice hardened, sharpened. "But you got no idea who you messin' with."

The line went dead.

*　*　*

Sophie came home later. I wanted to rage, wanted to scream. Instead, I cried. Ran to her.

She pushed me away.

15

Just after the boom, after the orange flash and the heat on my face, the screams piercing my ears. Just after the horror, I was on the floor, my rifle in my hands, locked and loaded. The corner: it was the most secure point. I low-crawled, my weapon in front of me, then crouched against the wall, high enough to see out the window, low enough to not get shot. The long steel barrel of my rifle balanced on the ledge.

Outside: an inferno.

A rocket. It must have been a rocket.

But I hadn't heard the whine of its entry, hadn't heard the alarm. A moment later, that didn't matter because below me, outside, someone was running toward the flames, running with something in his hands, another bomb, another incendiary. Something. And when I saw, I screamed in Arabic: *Get away! I will shoot!* But before I could aim, before I could trap the asshole in my sights, the screaming was closer, louder, the crying panicked, shrill.

I pivoted on my knee, aimed my weapon at the immediate threat: a little brown girl, her huge eyes wide with terror, rags hanging off her too thin shoulders, hands held high, begging. *Ya Allah.*

Outside, another blast. More shouts, running. Then the roar of a fire extinguisher briefly eclipsed the crackle of burning oil.

Inside, the freckles on the girl's face danced in the light of the flames. And I remembered that I have freckles, that my daughter, my baby, has freckles too.

I looked down at my rifle, but it wasn't my M16. I looked at my hands and saw the fine wrinkles. Looked at my legs and saw bare skin.

I looked up at the girl, cowering, quivering.
And then I saw.
My daughter.
Myself.
The rifle fell from my hands.

16

That night was terrible: the fire and explosions and filthy black smoke rising from my bombed-out truck quickly faded under the onslaught of a circle of neighbors with fire extinguishers. Then the sirens and wild red lights when the sheriff's boys finally arrived, the whole population of Little Falls standing huddled in their pajamas, drinking beer because there was no point in letting a spectacle go to waste. But I couldn't watch.

Instead, I threw Sophie's clothes into a duffel bag while she sat, shaking and white-faced, her eyes wider than wide, on the edge of her bed. Then I picked up the phone. Booked her a flight to Detroit in the afternoon. Called my aunt, Martha, who I hadn't talked to since calling to say Dad had died. Before I could ask, she said she would be at the airport to collect Sophie. Before I could explain, before I could say anything, she said she would do anything. Because blood is thicker than anything else. Just like it had always been between me and her.

Then I called Lyle to take Sophie to the plane in Seattle. I didn't want him involved, didn't want to explain, didn't want to trust him. But he was the only person I could think of at two o'clock in the morning who I thought loved Sophie as much as I did. And I had to get her out of there, had to get her out of danger, away from *me*.

When Lyle arrived an hour later, when he pulled into the front lot in the crappy old car he was driving back then, I hustled Sophie down the stairs, threw her duffel into the back seat, pushed my cell phone into her hand, and slammed the door. She looked like a refugee. Staring, but not seeing, her knees drawn up against her chest, the seat belt cutting into her neck. She looked like a little child.

I stood there in the raging darkness long enough to see Lyle fire the engine, but then I turned away. I didn't watch her leave.

It was the first time she'd ever obeyed me.

The next morning, long after my truck had stopped smoking, long after it had been towed away to the Sheriff's Office in Okanogan and everyone had gone home, I went downstairs and sat down on a milk crate at the edge of the parking lot. My head was pounding, fogged. All I wanted was sleep, but sleep would bring dreams—of the explosion the night before and other explosions from nights and days long before.

I couldn't handle any more dreams.

"You sure you don't want me to make some coffee?"

I shook my head.

"A couple of eggs? Toast?"

I leaned farther forward, cracked my spine.

"Bowl of cereal?"

I yawned, hid it badly. Then I looked over my shoulder at Darren, sitting beside me on another milk crate.

"You saying you're hungry?" I said.

"Yeah, actually."

The skin under Darren's eyes was puffy and dark, and his jaw was peppered with stubble.

Slowly, I sat up, cracked my neck. "I didn't ask you to stay."

"What are friends for?"

I arched my back, reached behind me, and tightened my ponytail. Out of the corner of my eye, I saw Darren watching me.

"You don't have to stay." I leaned forward again, forearms on thighs.

He pursed his lips, slapped his hands on his knees, and for a second I thought he would just leave. Panic, burning like battery acid, rose in my chest. Instead, he reached back, pulled his phone off his belt, and started typing. I balled up my fists, breathed deeply, forced myself to stare at the singed branches on my neighbor's tree.

"Don't look so relieved," Darren muttered.

Startled, I jerked my head around. "The hell I do."

He grinned, kept typing.

"So, what now?" I said after a while.

"You call your insurance company, I guess." He lifted his hip, tucked the phone back into its holster. "I wonder how much they're gonna raise your rates now. I mean, if they don't just drop you. You make two claims in one week and I'd drop your ass."

"Thanks," I snarled. "You're *such* a good friend."

I heard a vehicle pull too quickly into the lot out front, gravel grinding under the tires, popping and bouncing in the wheel wells. I rocketed to my feet, ready to run. There was a blast of classic rock when the door opened, the engine left running. Then boots grinding the gravel, then knocking on the glass doors. "Rhonda?" the guy yelled when he realized the doors were still locked. A few moments later, the truck's door slamming shut, and its engine revving, then its thick, throaty roar, like a big man gargling whiskey, when it shot out onto the road.

Wearily, I sat down, said, "We're closed."

I pulled up my knees, put my head down, but the explosion was still there on the inside of my eyelids. When I opened them again, Darren was standing, looking down at me, his eyes worried, thoughtful.

"Moreno should have something for us today," he said quietly, then sat down again. "About the explosion, I mean. It won't be complete, but he should have a good idea of what set it off."

I nodded.

"We'll have to get the feds involved."

"Good." I nodded again. "When do you want me to talk to them?"

"They'll only talk to me. They just review the evidence."

"That's it?"

"Yeah," he said, like it was obvious. "Standard operating procedure."

"Jesus," I muttered.

"What?"

"Oh, come on," I started, then thought better of it. Instead, I leaned down and pried a piece of gravel out of the dirt, dug it into the skin of my finger and thumb.

"Tell me," he said.

I swallowed hard. He had looked at me the day before like I was nuts. Had gone to draw his gun because he thought I was cracking up. And maybe I was. *Fuck.* Maybe I was just jumping to conclusions, letting the paranoia surge. I mean, engines burn sometimes, don't they? Spark plug goes and *poof*. Up in smoke. But in the middle of the night? I ground my teeth, tried to sift through the thoughts swirling in my mind, to spot the ones that were crazy, so I wouldn't say them out loud.

Finally, I said, "They're connected. The laptop and the truck."

Darren frowned, then stooped to pick up his own piece of gravel. He tossed it at one of the potholes in the lot, and it smacked into another loose piece; both shot off like BBs.

"I know they're connected, Darren."

"What's your theory?"

"This is about fear. They're trying to scare me."

"You said yesterday they were going to kill you."

"They must think I don't know enough to kill."

"Who's 'they'?"

Nick. But I didn't want to explain, didn't want to admit to Darren what I had done.

"Whoever killed Patrick Beale," I said instead, which I thought was the truth anyway.

He tossed another piece of gravel, then another and another. The silent treatment.

"Darren."

"Yeah?"

"This is about Patrick Beale."

"He blew up your truck?"

"Ha," I said. Neither of us laughed.

Darren threw another rock out into the lot.

"It's about the video. And . . ." I paused, then plunged on. "And that trailer: the bleach and the . . . the *equipment*. I was right. And they want me to back off."

"You don't know that."

"They know who I am, Darren," I snapped. "You know it and I know it."

"You said no one saw you," Darren said quietly.

"What?"

"At the trailer." He jutted his chin toward the trailer across the road—a dead ringer for the one I had found in the trees two days before. "You said no one saw you at the trailer. That there was no one there."

"No, but I . . ."

I couldn't tell him that I'd brought this down on myself, on my daughter. That I had called Nick, threatened him. Or that I wasn't sure anymore, not sure about what I had seen or *not* seen. That if I hadn't remembered about the truck that had almost run me off a cliff, then maybe I was forgetting other things, more important things. Of course, it didn't help that I had so little information to start with—

"Camille?"

"I don't know what they"—I threw my arm wide—"whoever *they* fucking are—know. I don't know what anyone knows because no one will tell me a goddamn thing."

Darren grabbed my hand, ducked down, hissed at me to keep my voice down.

"It's just meth, Darren," I said, ignoring him, snatching my hand back. "It's been here forever. Why string up a kid over it?"

"Just let—" Darren grabbed my wrist again. "Just let Moreno figure it out before you jump to any conclusions."

"Yeah?" I yanked my hand back. "And when he says my truck was bombed by some crazy-ass Mexican, what are you going to do then?"

Darren's eyes narrowed. "Who?"

Shit.

"What else?" I said quickly, frantically redirecting. "What else could this be?"

"It could be anything, Camille." But his eyes were still narrowed, his brow still creased. "*Anything.* It could have been a kid you wouldn't sell beer to."

I shook my head, rolled my eyes. "Yeah, right."

"It could have been an electrical problem."

I clenched my teeth.

"Or maybe you pissed off someone else, someone completely unrelated to this investigation." Darren ran his hand through his short black hair. "I mean, Christ, you've got a talent for it."

"What does *that* mean?"

"I *mean* you need to stop asking questions, stop going where you shouldn't. I told you—" he said angrily, then relaxed his jaw. "I *asked* you to stop."

I stiffened, said too loudly, "Have you been following me?"

Darren snorted. "You think I've got those kinds of resources?"

"No, I guess not. Look," I said. "*I found his body.* He showed up on *my* videotape. I found that trailer and that . . . *stuff.* I feel responsible, like I've got to do something about it. And I can't let some motherfucking pyromaniac stop me."

"Innocent bystander," Darren said calmly, but he was watching me, waiting for yesterday's panic and fury to reappear. "That's all you are."

"No," I said savagely. *"No."*

A spark of frustration flashed across Darren's eyes. "It's not like you killed him."

Surprised, offended at his dismissal, I spat out, "Neither did you."

But the look on his face, the stony, grim determination there, made me pause. It made me wonder if this was how all cops worked a case, even the grisly ones, even the ones that involved a tortured nineteen-year-old kid. It made me wonder what else was going on in the background, what was going through his head. But then, faster than it appeared, the look was gone.

Darren sighed. "So, why aren't you just an innocent bystander?" he asked, calmer, but the edge was still there.

"I've been doing some research."

Darren breathed out, his face tense again. I steeled myself for a fight, for the fight that would start when he told me again to stop investigating. But all he said was "Research."

"Yeah. That barn where I found Patrick isn't on Leamon's land. It's across the property line. It's on the land where that house was burned down."

"So Leamon was trespassing."

I shook my head impatiently. "That doesn't matter. The land is owned by this company, Gorgon Six LLC. It doesn't own any other properties in the state, but I found some other companies that I think are related."

"Gorgon Six?"

"Yeah," I said. "And there are others."

"Okay. What do they have to do with the kid?"

"There might be a marijuana grow at one—"

"Where?" Darren said, suddenly all business.

"Place just north of the Res, out east. But there's nothing there yet. Probably won't ever be now."

Darren frowned.

"There was a crew up there. They were building a fence. One of them said there was a crop that had to be behind an electric fence."

"How do you know it has anything to do with Beale?"

"I looked up the property; it's owned by another company, Gorgon Four. And the same lawyer is connected to that place and the one where Patrick was found. Jack C. Wyatt."

Darren's lip curled. "He was Meredith's lawyer in the divorce."

"What? But he's a . . . I don't know *what* he is, but he's not a divorce lawyer."

His lip still curled, Darren nodded. "Yeah, he is. A real prick too, but my guy rolled over him. That's why I got the house."

"But he's involved. His name is all over the documents."

Darren shook his head. "No, he's small time. Maybe he filed some stuff, but that's it."

I clenched my jaw, ground my teeth. "You think the meth is small time too?"

Darren's face instantly went blank. "We still talking about Wyatt?"

I said, "Maybe," but that didn't interest him. "Patrick Beale, anyway."

Darren picked another piece of gravel out of the dirt, flicked his wrist, skipped the gravel shallowly like a flat rock across the surface of a pond.

"Patrick *was* into it, Darren," I said in a low voice. "I'm not making this up. He had cash. And he had plans to leave."

"Everybody's gotta have a dream."

I shook my head. "No one knows where he got the money, who he was working for, what he was doing. Not his parents, not his brother. No one."

Darren shrugged.

"His dad, Darren," I said, even quieter. "Ed Beale's blaming himself. He thinks he made the kid stay. He thinks he got his son killed because he made him stay in the Okanogan."

"Survivor's guilt."

"Survivor's guilt?" I snapped.

Darren's jaw tightened.

"Fuck you," I said with a sneer, and he finally turned his head, finally looked at me. "Fuck you," I said again, too loudly. And then I stood up too quickly, and all the blood in my body rushed to my head.

"You don't have the right to say that. You don't have *the right* to just throw that away," I shouted, and then a black halo clouded my vision, obliterated the blue sky and the fried trees and the gravel, everything except Darren's face, hard and dry and fierce.

And then the halo closed and I stumbled forward. Darren caught my wrist with one hand and the other wrapped around my waist, holding me up.

"Hey," he said quietly. "Hey, you okay?"

"There's something big here . . ." The halo was fading, but stars were still bursting. "Something huge."

"You're tired, Camille. You've had a shock." Darren's left hand was warm and wide on the small of my back, his right hand strong and gentle on my arm. His lips were dry, cracked, just inches from mine . . .

"Just trust me," he said. "Let me do my job."

I closed my eyes, shook my head to clear it. "I'm fine." I opened my eyes, pushed him away. "I'm fine," I said again, but I swayed like grass in a gale.

Darren put one arm around me, and then both his arms were around me and I leaned into him, pressed my cheek against the rough cloth of his uniform, my forehead into the soft skin of his neck.

At that moment, I wanted to tell him about the night before, about the explosion, about how I was back *there*, back in Iraq, with the noise and the fire and the black, acrid smoke. I wanted to tell him about how I took up my weapon and almost fired. Wanted to tell him about Sophie, how I'd aimed my rifle at her, how I didn't see her—didn't really *see* her—until it was almost too late. But I knew how that would turn out. So I told him what happened after.

"I sent her away, Darren."

"Who?"

"Sophie," I whispered.

"Where is she?"

"Michigan, with my aunt, Mom's sister. Lyle took her. He's taking her to Seattle, to the airport."

Darren held me more tightly then, pressed his cheek against my head and waited for me to breathe again. "She'll be fine," he said. "It's better this way. We'll figure it out and then she'll come home."

I looked up, looked him in the eye. And for a moment . . . for a moment, there was something there, something for me. But all I could think of was what I had done.

*   *   *

Rhonda's fiancé loaned me a truck, an ancient Bronco he could spare from the orchards for a couple of weeks. Its springs creaked and its old four-cylinder whined the second the speedometer hit forty miles an hour, but it was transportation.

Darren had told me to stay home, to keep my head down and let him do his job. Instead, I took the Bronco back into the hills, through the orchards that climbed their flanks, all the way to an unnamed back road, and then onto a pressed gravel driveway. At the end, I parked it behind an old shed with peeling yellow paint, and sat there until the cloud of road dust had blown away. I sat a while longer and stared up at a house with white siding and dust-streaked windows and a porch that sagged a little on the north side. In the yard behind it, the silver leaves of aspens fluttered like ghosts.

I slammed the truck door behind me, padded across the dirt drive, and walked up the creaking front steps. Like I'd done a million times before, I slotted my key into the lock, then pushed open the door. In the front hall, the air was hot and dry and smelled of old clothes and old food and fresh paint, just like it always had. And when I pushed the door shut behind me, the glass rattled in a way that was so familiar my blood ran cold.

Home.

My parents' home, and then my father's home and Sophie's home, and then no one's home. But if I listened carefully, if I closed my eyes, I could still feel them all like there was only a moment, only a shred of space and time, between us. If I only listened hard enough, I'd hear my mother's fingers tapping on the keyboard of her computer in the back room, where it was so cold in the winter that she wore fingerless gloves while she typed her manifestos. I'd hear the tractor's engine rumbling outside, and then the sudden silence when it shut off. I'd hear my father's footsteps on the back porch, the thwack of the old wooden screen door slapping shut behind him, his footsteps on the hall floor, and his voice humming something soft and country. I'd smell the dirt and the fertilizer and that fleeting scent of green leaves and ripe apples as he walked past me into the kitchen. And if I waited just a moment longer, I'd hear little footsteps above me, then running down the stairs, pounding with joy and excitement. My heart would quicken and I'd smile, grin with joy, and Sophie would dart down the hall, and there'd be a little squeal of delight and a whiff of the Johnson & Johnson's that my little girl always smelled like back then, back before everything broke.

But everything did.

And in the space of a moment, I wasn't there anymore: I was standing in an old house that smelled like time.

I sucked up the snot streaming down my nose and wiped away the tears. Then I turned into the kitchen, went to the door by the old electric stove, and opened it, then pulled the chain on the bare lightbulb screwed into the wall. But the electricity had been switched off since May, since Dad's funeral, so I climbed down the stairs in the half-light that seeped in through the narrow window above the washer and dryer.

By the light of my cell phone, I wove my way through the racks of stuff in the basement. My mother's books, her articles and research, copies of all the crap she wrote for all the campaigns she waged: farmer's rights, worker's rights, clean water rights. Everything. And I kept going, past the racks full of Dad's fishing gear and our old tent and the tidy row of sleeping bags. It got darker the farther in I went, but I knew exactly where I was going. I knew exactly which box of supplies I needed from the shelves lining the north wall. Which weapons I needed from the heavy gun safe to replace the Glock that had gone up with my truck. How the smooth wooden stock of the shotgun Dad had used in the orchards felt under my fingers; how the butt of the Beretta M9 I'd bought at a pawn shop when I was fresh from the field settled comfortingly into the palm of my hand.

When I had packed it all into my old duffel, when I had raided the ammunition that Dad wouldn't need for hunting season that year, wouldn't need ever again, I pulled the last box, a small one, off the top shelf. Inside, my medals rested on black velvet: red, white, blue. Yellow. Purple. I pushed them aside, pulled out my dog tags. At first, the chain was cold on my neck, but moments later the metal was warm, warm as blood.

* * *

Sophie called me from the airport in Seattle. Flight announcements and chatter buzzed in the background, but her voice was loud and clear and fearless. Icy, angry, accusatory. Hours later, she had gone far enough to hate me again.

I understood.

* * *

Late that night, I sat in the kitchen with a glass of ice water, my work laptop open on the table, flipping through the photos I had downloaded from Sophie's phone the week before and the ones I had paid some shady friend of Lyle's two hundred bucks to pull off the wreckage that afternoon. Most were the same, but in the thirty-six hours after I'd given the phone back and before it was crushed, she had taken several more: a melancholy shot of Patrick Beale's coffin on the fifty-yard line, the midmorning sun harsh and glaring on the white lilies piled on top; candid glimpses of teenagers embracing on the field, their clothes pressed, their hair glossy, their eyes puffy and red. Then silly shots of girls in black, sitting at a diner, pulling ridiculous faces, boys in blue buttondowns drinking milkshakes.

And the last two. First, through a dusty plate-glass window, a window in the same diner maybe, a black Suburban with a red stripe through its belly and a dark-haired man with a tattoo on his neck in the driver's seat. Nick. And the last shot from inside the Suburban, the photo that turned the blood in my veins into rivers of ice: Nick behind the wheel, his brown skin dark against upholstery that was red like dried blood. He was facing the camera, his eyes hidden behind sunglasses, his hand reaching out toward the phone. And through his fingers, glimpsed through a sliver of air, another man in the back seat, blond stubble and shiny skin stretched tight over his tanned skull. The lieutenant.

But who *was* he?

He had been at the party, at that lawyer's office, in the video. But he wasn't eating ice cream at Hank's the week before. And here he was again, in a position of power—chauffeured by Nick. And my daughter. *My daughter.* Suspicious enough to take photos. Worthless enough to let go after flipping off the lieutenant at the party. Threat enough to crush her phone. And daring enough to get into the Suburban. *My* daughter.

On another screen, I checked the arrival time of her flight. There was another forty minutes before she would text me to say she had arrived, that my aunt had met her at the airport in Detroit. That she was safe. From them. From me. From herself.

I closed the window. I closed the files from her phone. I closed my notes and my maps and my video feed. Then I logged into Facebook.

Mike Havers hadn't sent any more messages. Then again, I hadn't responded to his.

It made sense for him to ignore me. I was just somebody on the internet, picking at his old wounds. He had asked if I was a journalist. Maybe he thought I was going to do some exposé that made his brother look stupid or wrong or guilty. Maybe he'd been burned that way before. I didn't know. But I had this suspicion that Mike Havers knew something that would help me. So I bluffed.

On the screen of my laptop, in the Facebook messenger conversation I had started days before, I typed, *I have more information.*

But Mike Havers wasn't stirring.

So, I waited. For the next breath of breeze to filter in through the window and dry the sweat on my neck. For Mike Havers to come online, to tell me I was right, to validate my dreams and my suspicions about his brother and Patrick Beale, about how similarly, how uniquely, they had both died. For Sophie to tell me she was okay, that despite everything I had done and left undone, she still loved me. But there was nothing, not even a whisper.

Until.

Around 11 PM, I woke, startled, lifted my head up from the table where it had rested for too long. My left arm was numb, my neck was stiff and screaming, but on the screen of my laptop was the message I had been waiting for: *This had better be good.*

With my right hand, I dashed off a response. *Someone blew up my truck last night.*

Breathlessly, I watched the message window, hopeful that Mike Havers was still online. He was. *That sucks.*

Then, a few moments later. *What does that have to do with my brother?*
It means I'm getting closer.

To what? Then, the little prick added, *You're wasting my time.*

I started to respond angrily, then stopped myself. I had to give him something to get something.

Someone else was killed just like your brother.

Mike's response was immediate. *Who?*

A kid. About his age.

Where? Iraq?

No. Washington. Out in the hills.

So what?

It was the same. Look, I know, okay? I typed that fast, then hesitated. The images of Paul Havers and Patrick Beale rotting at the end of the rope surged in my head. The putrid smell swept into my nostrils. The buzzing of the flies . . .

"No," I said aloud. "No," I said again as I stood quickly, my left arm still stinging while the blood surged and the nerve endings reconnected.

Mike's response appeared. *I don't think you know shit.*

"Oh yeah?" I shouted to my silent apartment, then bent forward and pounded out a response.

I know how your brother died. I found his body.

I hit "Enter" before I could second-guess myself.

Outside, a coyote howled. On the screen, my cursor blinked lazily.

You're lying.

I wasn't lying, but I might have been manufacturing the story. I screwed my eyes shut, pressed my fingers into the ridge of my brow. Stars burst behind my eyelids. I opened them, squinted, groping for the memories I needed to get what I wanted from Mike Havers. There was nothing there except my dreams. Everything else was a blank slate. But I had to start somewhere. Had to get him comfortable enough to tell me what I needed to know.

I did recoveries, I typed on the screen.

Recoveries of what?

Bodies, I typed, then added, *Soldiers.*

Bits and pieces, I didn't say. Torn limbs and bloody stumps and holes blown clean through their chests. But sometimes . . . sometimes there would be a guy slumped over against a building or in a Humvee, a soldier who looked perfect, his helmet on, his hands ready on his weapon. Like he was asleep. Until you pulled him away and saw the blood that trickled from his nose, his eyes that stared at nothing.

But you never knew what you'd find when you got the call. Then and now, that sound is still in my head. Imprinted on my brain. The phone at the hospital with its persistent beeping, electronic and brash, and the red light flashing on the black handrest on the white Formica counter that was permanently stained by the orange dirt that traveled everywhere in Iraq. If I closed my eyes, if I hunted in the deepest reaches of my mind, the memory would unfurl like a bloody flag.

Yes.

There was that stale medical smell, that chemical bubblegum tang of soap blooming in my nose. The red light flashing as my hand reached out to pick up the handset. I answered with name and rank. A male voice was at the other end of the line.

In Little Falls, on that hot, dry night, I typed, my fingers dragging across the keyboard like I was asleep. I typed what I heard the man's voice say in my memory: *We got a tip. A soldier in a village.*

"Go now," the voice on the phone ordered.

So I sprinted through the white-and-green halls at the hospital, through the door to the airfield, and hit a wall of heat that made my eyes water. Sprinted across the tarmac . . . and then . . .

I was in a helicopter touching down at the edge of a stubbled field, the remains of a harvest brittle and crumbling into the parched earth. The bird rocked and settled. One, two, three soldiers in tan desert gear rolled out, their M16s at the ready, black barrels swallowing the morning sunlight. I was last out of the helicopter and last into the bombed-out remains of the whitewashed building a hundred feet away. Methodically, we swept through room after room, each of them littered with the shredded remains of domestic life, the air growing cooler and more stale as we reached spaces that looked like everyone had just gone out for a walk: small carpets rolled up and nestled against the wall, cushions piled in the corner, toys scattered on the floor, a calendar four months old curling on the wall. And then, at the end of a hallway, that heavy wooden door. That stench that seeped from the crack at the bottom. That buzzing . . .

My eyes flew open.

The last message from Mike Havers was impatient, disbelieving. *Paulie died in combat.*

I found him in a village. I responded. *In a bombed-out building.*

No.

It was in the morning. I typed as the memory faded, as its edges blurred. *It was August.*

August 13, 2005, Mike typed. *In a skirmish. He was shot.*

I shook my head. *He suffocated. He was hanged.*

They tried to save him at the field hospital where he worked, he responded.

There was nothing we could do. He had been dead for days, I countered.

Mike's next message appeared immediately, urgently. *You're full of shit!* Then: *You don't know anything! My brother died in combat.*

Is that what they told you? I shot back. *You were right, you know. On that website. You said they weren't telling you everything.*

He was in combat.

No.

He wasn't supposed to be. But he was. He was a hero. Someone told me. The Army just won't admit it.

I snorted. This man didn't want the truth. He wanted a fantasy, a golden dream about a golden brother who never existed. But I had only the truth.

He was tortured, I typed. *He was murdered.*

There was something about those words. *Tortured. Murdered.* Something plain and chilling and stark. That's why I had typed them. That's why Mike Havers paused.

By the ragheads? he said after a while.

I cringed at the term—stupid and racist and above all, *wrong*—then corrected him.

No. By an American.

141

17

Jack Wyatt.

The firm name—"Wyatt & Johnson"—was printed in black and gold letters on the glass set in the door. Wyatt's name was below. Johnson's had been filed off. Beyond the glass, a woman with light brown hair shot through with gray was filing. She looked up when I opened the door.

"Good morning," she said in a voice that made it sound like it wasn't.

I nodded. "Is Mr. Wyatt in?"

She closed the filing cabinet and sat behind a cheap wooden desk, pulling an appointment book toward her. "You don't have an appointment."

"Is he in?"

"I'm sorry, dear," she said, poisoned honey dripping from her voice. My spine went stiff. "Mr. Wyatt keeps a very tight schedule."

"Alright." I breathed out, gritted my teeth. "When is his next available appointment?"

She picked up a pencil and drew it down the list, then without looking up, "He has a few minutes at ten thirty."

"Great. I'll wait."

And I did, for two hours, watching Wyatt's secretary on the phone, filing, typing up documents. She barely glanced at me the entire time, didn't offer me water or coffee, despite the pot off-gassing in the corner.

Finally, at ten thirty, she ducked into his office. There was murmuring and then she emerged.

"Ms. Waresch," she said drily, then sat down.

I walked into the inner room, a place that looked like I'd always imagined a lawyer's office would. It was dark and stuffy, lined with leather and dark wood and old books that looked like they hadn't been moved in fifty years. Window dressing; a set for a play, and here was the leading man.

Wyatt unfolded from his chair. He was long and wiry, his face lined and suntanned, his white hair a little wild. When he smiled, his teeth were tobacco-stained; his eyes flat, calculating.

He sat down, shifted his worn leather chair closer to the desk, creased his brow. "What can I do for you, Ms. Waresch?"

What exactly did I expect from this man? I had no more idea of *that* than I did of how I would get it or where he was in the chain of command. Was *he* the one in charge? Was he calling the shots? Maybe. Probably not. All I knew was that he was connected—maybe even the connector—and I hoped he had answers.

I tried the subtle approach. "I'm thinking about buying some property. A friend suggested I speak to you."

He leaned back, smiled his thin smile again. "Alright. Where's the property?"

"Here. In the county."

"And what will you do with it?"

This was the question I had wrestled with since I had decided to seek this man out. How much to tell? How much to bluff?

"I've got some business interests in mind."

"Agriculture?" He smiled in a way that should have looked benign, like an old man making a harmless little joke, but it wasn't. Not by a long shot. "That seems to be the thing to do around here."

"You could say that."

"Wheat? I hear the market is coming back."

"A specialty crop."

The lawyer folded his hands on his chest, nodded slightly. "That can be complicated."

I inclined my head. "I understand you're experienced with complicated things."

Wyatt's eyes were still flat, but I could see the wheels moving in the shadows behind them. "Who did you say your friend is?"

"Let me put it this way." I smiled and smoothed the air between us with the palm of my hand. "My friend said you set up a company for him. It's called CLA LLC."

Wyatt frowned, his untamed eyebrows knotting as he studied me. "CLA?"

"Yeah," I said. Then—compulsively—corrected myself. "Yes, sir."

He smoothed his mustache with gnarled fingers, shook his head. "I'm sorry. I don't know that name."

I was prepared for that, had prepared my bluff that far. "Your name is on the records online, on the state website."

It wasn't, but it was in the documents Harry had gotten for me. Wyatt didn't need to know the difference. But he was no idiot; I should have figured that out by then.

He smiled faintly. "Is that so?"

I watched him expectantly, as though I demanded a response there and then. He picked up a letter opener shaped like a golden snake, ran his finger down the edge and back again, still smiling that faint smile.

"Will you do it or not?" I said impatiently. "I don't have much time."

He made a show of looking at his calendar, drawing his middle finger like a claw across the tiny, cramped handwriting scrawled over the week ahead. And then he shook his head sadly, almost sorrowfully.

"I'm afraid not, dear." He looked up, his eyes full of fake concern. "But perhaps I can refer you to another practitioner in the area?"

He knew it and I knew it: I had overplayed my hand.

* * *

The glass in Jack Wyatt's office door shuddered when it slammed behind me. I marched down the street, took a left and then a right at the end of that block, then climbed into my borrowed Bronco. Inside, I gripped the steering wheel so tightly it should have broken in two. I was a fool. Screaming, I slammed my fist into the ceiling of the truck once, then again and again.

This was part of it, the rage. Part of my trauma, my "condition." It wasn't just anger. Anger I had wanted, craved for days. *Anger* banished fear, made it go and hide in a dark corner where it could be forgotten. Anger fueled. But rage . . . rage destroyed. Rage was—*is*—it's like staring into the sun, standing so close my skin smokes, my eyes melt. It's like a geyser in my chest, the pressure building and building until it's all let loose through my fists.

When my vision cleared, I was panting, hunched over the steering column, knuckles scraped raw.

Fool.

They wanted me to fear them. They wanted me to back off. So why not kill me? Why not just hang me up in a barn like Patrick Beale? Because they didn't think I was close enough yet to go to the trouble. And now? Had I said anything to that lawyer to make them think differently? Or was I still just flailing around, blind and deaf in a locked room?

I sucked the blood from my knuckles, scanned the busy streets and the quiet buildings of summertime Chelan. The phone rang.

Darren.

Sergeant Moses.

He never called me. So, why? Sophie was safe in Michigan—she had texted me when she landed the night before. Looking into the truck would take days, and it's not like he'd report to me about any other evidence. Had Wyatt called me in? Had he reported me for harassment, intimidation? Yeah, because that was exactly what he would think of me after my half-assed impression of a drug dealer. What then? Darren calling to tell me to lay off the investigation, probably. Maybe someone had seen me at the lawyer's office, or maybe the lawyer had a contact at the Sheriff's Office.

The ringing stopped.

I slid the key into the ignition and held it there, the wounds on my fingers starting to sting and throb. At the end of the street, a family turned the corner, walked lazily toward me. Mom with light hair, dad with dark, two kids in shorts and shirts faded by the sun, sprinting ahead, then skipping back, their small voices piping. I reached over and rolled down the window, hung on to every word, every shout, and the thick coconut scent of sunscreen that lingered long after they'd passed. Family. It sounded so right, smelled so right, so sticky and sweet and reckless. But that was the closest I was ever going to get. An observer. A voyeur.

My gaze fell. Blood seeped from the scrapes on my knuckles, dripped onto the smooth gray plastic of the steering wheel, and ran.

Focus.

I fired the engine and while it coughed, I glanced over at my phone again, lying on the seat beside me. It was ringing, the sound drowned out, but unavoidable. Darren's number on the screen again.

"Where are you?" Darren's voice was harsh, clipped; his sheriff voice. *Shit.*

"What?" I said and revved the engine. "Can't hear you."

"Where are you?"

He was checking on me, checking that I wasn't interfering. That lawyer *had* called me in. I guess that gave me some kind of answer about his involvement, his reach: he was letting the sheriff do his work for him. Why waste his own guys when the sheriff would do it for free? Or did he have the entire office on the payroll?

"Camille?" Darren said, his voice rising.

The street was empty, but I was exposed. I threw the truck into reverse.

Faintly, barely audible over the whine of the gears, another voice on the other end of the line said, "Where d'you want the tape, Sergeant?"

Something scraped against the mouthpiece of Darren's phone, his hand maybe, because then, his voice muffled, so faint I almost didn't hear him, he said, "There."

I pressed hard on the phone's volume button, cranking it up as far as it would go.

"Sure you don't want it on the gate?" the other man said.

"Yeah. Use the stakes," Darren said, then so loud it hurt my ear, "Camille?"

"What?"

"Where *are* you?" He said it like I was a suspect.

"Why?"

"Just tell me."

"In town." Slowly, I pulled into the street, my foot perched over the gas pedal, ready to slam it to the floor.

"Omak?"

"No."

"Okanogan? Are you at the building? Good. Stay there—stay in your office. I'm gonna send someone over."

"No."

"No?"

"I'm not at the office."

"Goddamnit, Camille," he said, but his voice was strained, eroded somehow. Frustrated. "Don't fuck with me right now. Just . . . just tell me you're safe."

Safe?

My heartbeat quickened. I glanced in the rearview, the side mirrors; quickly scanned the street and the sidewalks.

"What do you mean? What's going on?"

At low speed, I rolled past Hank's, the ice cream place where I had been with Sophie and Lyle a few days before. I didn't recognize any faces.

"Hold on," Darren said.

Again, there were other voices on his end of the line, muffled by the palm of his hand. I rolled up the window, but all I heard was something about a shotgun and a rag. And then, out of the static, a name: Leamon.

"Leamon?" I said, then shouted Darren's name.

When he finally brought the phone to his lips, all he said was, "I gotta go."

"What happened to Jeremy Leamon?" I said. But he didn't hear me; the line was dead.

From Chelan, it's an hour and a half to Jeremy Leamon's front door, depending on how many big rigs you get stuck behind. I made it in an hour and ten.

At the foot of the drive, a little way back from the big wooden gate, a deputy stood in front of a line of police tape, sweat streaking down his face. He was crimson under his wide-brimmed hat. Beyond him, a quarter mile across a stubbled field, sat the house I had walked into uninvited just four days before. And parked in front of it were a couple of sheriff's cruisers and an ambulance, its rear doors open, its lights off.

"How you doin', ma'am?" the deputy on the drive said, hunching over a little to look in the window of the Bronco.

I pointed up at the house. "What's going on here?"

"Nothing to worry about, ma'am." He tilted his hat forward, wiped the back of his neck, then winked at me. "Just a little po-lice matter, ma'am."

So that's how it's going to be.

"Huh." I rolled my shoulders back, tried to smile. "What kind of matter is that?"

He grinned broadly, his teeth stained and ragged. "Nothing to worry about."

You said.

"Well," I said, trying to simper, "I got something for Mr. Leamon. I'll be real quick. You won't even know I was here."

"Sorry, darlin'. Can't let you through." He extended his hand, pointed with a finger too stubby for his height. "See that tape? That's po-lice tape. No entry, not even for pretty gals like you."

We'll see about that.

"You think he might come down the road to get it?" I pressed.

The deputy—"Walker," his badge said, "F. Walker"—slid his pink tongue over his lower lip.

I'll remember that, Walker.

He hooked his thumbs in his belt, rocked back on his heels, and looked back at the house. Everyone else was inside or out back or someplace other than around the vehicles. I had switched off the truck and the engine was cooling, its steady plinking the only sound except the scrape of the deputy's boots when he took a step closer to the Bronco.

"I reckon I could take it to him."

I blinked, long and slow, but before my little smile cracked, the front door of the house opened. A black-shirted male backed out, then descended the stairs, carrying one end of a stretcher, a black bag on top of it, swollen, zippered shut. I didn't know it, but I felt it. A shotgun and a rag and Jeremy Leamon. *Murdered.*

"I mean," the deputy stammered, "I could take it up to the house. If you want to leave it."

I swiveled back to Walker, clocked his discomfort, his realization that I knew his game.

My little smile was gone, my shoulders were steeled, my voice was all business. "Sergeant Moses here?"

Walker shook his head. "No, ma'am. He was, but he left."

A new knot formed in my stomach.

I turned the key in the ignition and when the engine roared to life, I threw the truck into reverse. When I looked up, the EMTs were nowhere to be seen, but a moment later, a brown-uniformed man walked out from behind the house, his stride long and loose, his hands cupped around his mouth as he lit a cigarette, his hair blazing red in the sun.

Lucky Phillips. *Why are you always there, Lucky Phillips?*

He slid something into his pocket, and pulled out his phone, dialed quickly, spoke briefly, and put it away. Then he turned and shaded his eyes, squinted . . . and saw me. The phone reappeared in his hand—

"Ma'am?" Deputy Walker had remembered his job, was pulling out his notepad. "Ma'am. I'm going to have to get your name."

"Not today, Deputy." I put my foot on the gas and reversed, the Bronco bucking in the potholes, spewing a thin cloud of dust into Walker's mouth as he ran after me.

*   *   *

Lyle.

By the twenty-sixth of August, I had already seen him more in a month than I had all year. He had always been on the edge of my life, first with Oren, later with Sophie. I'd ignored him mostly, swatted at him like a fly, shunned him like a leper. But he just kept coming at me, kept showing up. Unstoppable. Unbeatable.

That day, he came over to my table in the old casino, wearing sunglasses and a battered, long-sleeved T-shirt, even though he was inside, even though it was the dead of August.

"Hey, Sis. What are you doing here?" he said, his jeans whispering as he slid across the red Naugahyde of my booth like a mouse sneaking into an occupied room.

Startled, I looked up from my laptop. My nerves were shot, my paranoia acute. I'd been holding my breath, intent on the dots and lines splayed across the map on my screen, desperate to quiet the anxious thoughts bouncing through my head like Ping-Pong balls. I gulped in stale air, tried to answer. Failed.

He swiped one cold French fry and then another, dangling them in the puddle of ketchup on my abandoned plate before stuffing them into his mouth. But he winced when he opened his jaw, winced again when he began to chew.

"You okay?" Lyle asked.

"Yeah," I said, fascinated, repulsed, watching him shovel more of my leftovers into his mouth, like he always did. He was like a vulture, always waiting for carrion. But he didn't eat like one, didn't have the sort of slow, relaxed cadence of a bird that knew its dinner wasn't going anywhere. No, Lyle always ate like it was a desperate act, like he had to get it all in his stomach before the plate was taken away. It was like watching a refugee with an MRE.

"What are you doing here?" he mumbled, his mouth half full, his eyes still fixed on the plate.

"Eating lunch."

"You ever even been in here before?"

I hadn't, but it was the only place I could think of where no one would look for me, not even Darren Moses. For the hundredth time since I had arrived, I scanned the room, touched the butt of the M9 in the holster under my jacket. It felt good to have it back, reassuring.

"Why?" I said, snot dripping from my voice, then turned back to the screen. "Am I on your turf?"

Lyle laughed at that, but thinly.

"What's with the sunglasses?" I said.

Lyle laughed again, unconvincingly. "Nothing."

"Yeah, 'cause it's real sunny in here."

"It's a new style." He looked up; his eyebrow bobbed like he was winking behind the dark lenses.

"Yeah, like *Miami Vice*," I said. "Okanogan Vice."

For a moment, Lyle smiled blindingly, his strangely white teeth shining, and I knew that behind the glasses, his blue eyes sparkled. This was "The Smile," the one he trotted out when you'd been a good little boy or girl. It was a gift to you, from him.

But then he reached for the bottle of ketchup, and I saw the wince that crinkled the skin around his eyes. And I saw what he wanted me to see when the cuff of his shirt rode up. I seized his wrist and held on when the tendons beneath my fingers tightened, strained to break free. But he stopped, yelped, when I pressed too near the cigarette burns, black and crispy, ringed with tender skin that was too pink. In the tussle, his sunglasses slid down, and the bruises, fresh and dark and ringing his eyes, showed.

"Nothing," I sneered.

I loosened my grip; he snatched his hand back. "It was just a little disagreement," he muttered, pushing the sunglasses back over his eyes.

I closed my laptop, put it to one side, and waited: he'd talk if I gave him enough empty air. He always did.

"With one of my business partners," he said.

With spectacularly bad timing, the waitress arrived. Lyle started to sidle out of the booth, but I put my foot up to block him, ordered him a Coke, and glared at the waitress until she took the hint.

"Who?" I said when she'd left.

Lyle, doing the little boy act, collapsing in on himself: "No one you know."

"*Who?*"

"Look, I'm fine."

And maybe he was. It wasn't the first time he'd been knocked around, and it wouldn't be the last. He liked the pain, I think, liked playing the underdog. It was a sort of justification.

"Was it that guy at Hank's," I said carefully, "the one with the tats?"

"Nick?" he said, conveniently forgetting—or maybe not forgetting at all—that neither of us was supposed to know the dark-haired man's name. "No, it wasn't him." The tip of Lyle's tongue appeared at the corner of his mouth, traced a crusty split in his lip.

"What about the other one?" I said quietly, uncertain how far I could take my suspicions about Lyle's involvement in the underbelly of Okanogan County, uncertain how much he remembered about that night at Hank's, who was there and who wasn't. Lyle had always acted stupid—the harmless loser, the victim—but even back then, I had never really bought the act. "What about the blond one?"

His eyebrows darted above the rim of his sunglasses. "Who, Jimmy?"

"Yeah," I said, like it was the most obvious thing in the world.

He shook his head, took another French fry, skipped the ketchup. "Naw, it wasn't King."

Jimmy King. Yeah, that fit the cocky blond lieutenant, pumping gas on the video, and the ripped, shirtless bully who flicked a lit cigarette into the bushes rather than go after my daughter with a shotgun.

I watched Lyle finish the food on my plate. His golden-brown fingers were rough and dry, the nails peeled down to nothing, just like when he was the little blond ten-year-old I'd known way back when. When he tagged around after his big brother Oren, already out of high school and living in the trailer out on the corner of the Res, living the high life with his buddies.

Because Oren had been like their dad, big and tall and broad shouldered, a "model" Indian straight out of some crass Western movie. And he was absent, distant—like their dad. He was always telling Lyle to stay out of it, to go home, to go keep their mom—already teetering on the edge—company at the apartment on the fringe of Omak. And at the time . . . at the time, I guess I thought Oren was being mean. So I was nice to little kid Lyle who took after their slight, weak, blonde mother. I bought him chocolate milk when Oren wasn't looking and gave him a ride home when he still managed somehow to show up just in time for Billy Boykin, Oren's right hand, to smack him upside the head or stick out a foot to trip him. Even though everyone would laugh, even Lyle. Everyone except me.

And then . . . I don't know why I said it. I don't know why I say *anything* sometimes. The pathways in my brain, the neurons or whatever, they go to a lot of strange places since the war.

"Was it Billy?" I said quietly, my eyes narrowed.

Lyle looked up, the skin between his eyebrows bunching. *"Who?"*

I studied his face, watching for a lie. Then said, just as quietly, "Billy Boykin."

Lyle snorted, shook his shaggy head. "Billy *Boykin*?" Then he laughed, shook his head again. "No, Sis. He's down in Seattle. In the pen."

"Prison?" I said, surprised, but not surprised. "What for?"

But Lyle wasn't telling any more. He shrugged and flashed that perfect smile again. And there was that tickle again, way back in the corner of my brain.

"Who's this business partner?" I asked eventually.

In a neat flyby, the waitress set a tall glass of Coke on the table. Lyle unwrapped the straw instead of answering me, then sucked the glass dry, hunting down the last dregs of soda from the joints between the ice cubes.

"Lyle." I snapped my fingers in front of his face. "The business partner. Who is it?"

"How's Sophie?" He was bent over the table, the straw almost brushing the five o'clock shadow on his chin. But behind the sunglasses, his eyes darted around the room.

"She's fine," I said, even though I didn't know if it was the truth. The truth was I hadn't spoken to her, had just received a short text saying she was in Michigan, and then another a couple hours later saying she had gotten to my aunt Martha's place safely. And that was enough for me. The truth was that I had no idea how she was, not that she would have told me if I'd asked.

He nodded his head like he was bouncing to a beat. "That's good. That's real good."

"Yeah." I leaned forward. "What are they into, Lyle?"

He shrugged, the bones of his skinny shoulders lifting the thin fabric of his shirt.

"I know they're into something. Nick and King and . . . and Patrick Beale."

Lyle raised his eyebrows and looked squarely at me. "The dead kid?"

"He was working for them, wasn't he?"

But Lyle just shrugged, looked away again.

"Is it meth?" I said quietly, maybe too quietly to be heard over the tinkling and beeping of the slot machines on the other side of the bar.

He turned toward me again; I could feel the crystal-blue stare coming through his dark lenses, even if I couldn't see it. Then he leaned back, laid one arm on the back of the booth, and slid, putting one foot up on the seat and scrunching up in the corner.

"Well?" I said.

He looked over his shoulder, and then he said so quietly I almost didn't hear it, "You didn't hear it from me."

"And Sophie?" My jaw was tense; hell, every muscle in my body was tense. "Is she involved?"

"She's a good kid, Sis."

I snorted. "So was I."

I sat back in the booth, tried to see what he was seeing out among the sullen lights of the casino. But there were only machines and a few old women with flowers on their tatty sweatshirts and the ghosts of curlers in their hair. Hardly anything worth whispering over.

"How is she anyway?" Lyle asked. When I jumped, he added, "Sophie."

"You already asked."

"Oh." He sucked a thin layer of Coke-tinted water out of the glass and kept sucking, the harsh, manic burble shredding my last nerve.

"Where did you send her again?" he asked, his lips still around the straw.

"To my aunt. In Michigan."

"I didn't know we had family in Michigan."

"*We* don't."

His shoulders fell, caved. For a second, he was that little boy again, shaking the ice in his glass like it was a beggar's cup. And for a second, I felt like an ass.

"Look," I said, trying to make up for it, but not really. "Whatever you're into, you can tell me about it. Maybe I can help."

He winced when he looked up, then slowly took off the sunglasses and used a dirty napkin to wipe a fresh tear of blood away from a gash in his cheek, a gash like a ring might make upon impact with human skin.

"Jesus, Lyle. Whatever it is, it isn't worth it."

When he looked up at me, his face had that sad look, the one he trotted out every other time I saw him. But above his lips pursed in pain, inside the squinting rims of his eyes, his pupils were hard blue icebergs caught in a lacy web of broken capillaries. They were their mother's eyes: hard, calculating, greedy—even at the end.

Then—something snapped in my head, and I wasn't at the casino anymore. I was in my apartment, and it was the other night, the Saturday before, when the truck blew and I got my rifle, and there was so much fire, so much smoke, so much noise, and I called Lyle and told him to come now, come for Sophie—

Sophie. She ran to him when he got there that night. He came up the stairs and pounded on the door, and I shot up like a rocket from the couch where I had been sitting with my head between my hands, trying to hold everything in. When I opened the door, he was upset, he was excited, he was— And then the door of Sophie's room flew open, crashed against the wall, and she ran, sprinted past me, crashed into him, sobbing. He'd held her like a child, smoothed her hair, whispered in her ear. And when he looked up at me, all I saw were those eyes, those hard blue icebergs: triumphant. Like he had won, and the prize was—

Jackpot.

The siren on a slot machine wailed, plastic chips crashed into a plastic basin. A woman squealed.

I blinked and there was Lyle in the casino, Lyle staring at me with those eyes, Lyle clutching the bloody napkin. But then he tossed it away and put on his sunglasses without wincing at all.

"Thanks for the fries," he said, sliding out of the booth. "And the Coke."

Then he swaggered off past the bar and disappeared into the thicket of machines.

After a while, the waitress came back and cleared the table.

Little boy Lyle. Playing the innocent, pretending to be the fool. The one everyone took advantage of. The one it was easy to pity. But he was also the one who knew everyone and everything useful in the Okanogan. At least, useful for certain things. Was he right about Jimmy King? Was *I*?

I opened my laptop and connected to the internet.

It's easy to find a dead soldier. Obituaries litter the internet. Just search for "U.S. Army", and you'll find hundreds. It's a lot harder to find a survivor. There are some news stories that name names. Mostly, the articles date back to when the war was hot, when the public was still horrified by the blood and the body count. Before they became numb to the photos of sand and rockets, grungy soldiers and tattered civilians. Before the atrocities of war became boring. That's when I was there. In the early days. But you won't find my name in any news story. I'm just another anonymous soldier who went and fought and was sent home alive. Sometimes the obits seem like they were written for the lucky ones. But Jimmy King was not one of the lucky ones.

I searched for what felt like hours, in and out of every corner of the Web, using every name I could think of that was similar to Jimmy King. Department of Defense sites. News sites. Archives for every local newspaper I could find. Archives for the whole internet. Then, finally, an obit. Not for him, but for his brother. Lee Kingman had stayed home when President Bush, the second one, had stumbled over 9/11, even after he called for Saddam Hussein's head. Lee, the brother, had stayed at his job in retail, fighting the good fight in Thanksgiving Day sales for minimum wage in Oklahoma. And when he died, on July 19, 2005—the obit didn't say how— he left a grieving mother, a girlfriend, and a brother—James Kingman, Captain, U.S. Army, stationed in Iraq with the infantry.

2005.

The last year I was there. The last year Private Havers was alive, stationed at a forward medical facility with me and the infantry, out there in the sandbox, keeping as many as we could alive. How ironic that Kingman's brother gave me what I wanted. Maybe another brother would too.

I opened Facebook and messaged Mike Havers, not expecting anything after the bombshell I had dropped, but hoping that he had thought about it. That he had realized that what he thought he knew didn't stack up. That his brother hadn't been killed in combat, that there wouldn't have been any reason for the Army to hide that. Location, time . . . yeah, maybe they'd hide that. But not the raw fact of combat. Maybe Mike Havers had realized my truth was the truth, and now he would remember something important. Maybe the name—Kingman or Jimmy—would jog his memory of something his brother had mentioned. Something that would tie Jimmy King to Private Havers, that would make him the link between Havers and Patrick Beale.

I sat in that booth for a while longer, hunched over the laptop, waiting for a response, flipping between Facebook and a search for federal prisons. By the time I found the number I needed, Havers still hadn't responded. So I shut down the computer and headed for the doors, waiting for a human being to pick up at the federal detention center in Seattle as I wound through the flashing lights and electronic blare of the machines. Outside, I squinted in the glare of the late afternoon sun, my cell phone pressed against my ear as I struggled to hear the prison guard on the other end of the line. Visiting hours were Tuesday afternoon and, no, I wasn't too late to sign up.

As I tore up the highway, the stench of manure and the funk of fertilizer flying out the windows of my borrowed Bronco, I crossed my fingers and hoped my luck would hold.

* * *

I spent that evening driving all over the county, my mind spinning as fast as the wheels on the Bronco. Havers smuggling supplies—narcotics, other precursors of synthetic drugs—from the hospital. Patrick, meth precursors caked into his jeans. Both of them cocky and sure—too sure—that they were above the rules. Both of them trying to get away from the humdrum, from the middle-American numbing boredom. Running to something new and exciting and different. Running into the jaws of a monster, then trying to retreat when they realized that what they knew, what they had done would be their undoing. But both of them were tethered like sacrificial lambs by the people who held them back—Havers by me, Patrick by his father. And both of them were tortured and strung up to die.

Before, they were just two sad stories. But now I had Jimmy King. Jimmy in Iraq and Jimmy in the Okanogan. Jimmy on the video tape with my daughter and that punk, Nick. But could I prove he knew Havers? Was he really the link?

I pulled over for the tenth time that evening and checked Facebook on my phone. When the message icon appeared on the refreshed screen, I killed the engine and waited breathlessly for Mike Havers's response to load.

Fuck.

Mike didn't remember his brother mentioning any Jimmy or James or King or Kingman. Not any captains; not any officers at all. He had sent me a message about that in the late afternoon. Then—maybe he had kept thinking, or maybe he had remembered more—an hour later, he had sent another message that scrolled down the screen, a hundred times longer than anything he had ever sent before. It was like a fire hydrant had broken, and all the frustration and anger and suspicion were gushing out of him. It was like I was his therapist instead of some random chick on the internet destroying his dreams about his not-so-heroic brother.

He knew some guys in the infantry, but I don't got names. He said once that they took him off base to shoot up shit in the desert. He told me I had to keep quiet about it because his sergeant was a real bitch.

He told me this one time that he was going out to some village to pick something up. I asked him what he was gonna pick up, and he got all defensive, said I didn't hear him right. That I was making shit up. Then he hung up on me.

You asked about him going out to the desert at home. He beat me up bad when I told Mom about it, so I wasn't going to say anything about him doing it in the Army. I was just a kid when he went in.

The soldiers came to the house a couple weeks later and said he was dead. I was at school. Mom told me after that he got shot. She said they told her he would be home soon. But it was weeks before they sent him. And then there was no body. That was serious for Mom. She don't want the ashes they gave her, said to the guy who brought them to the house, how am I going to visit my son? You burned him up! How do I even know this is him???

It was real tough on her. So I called them in Arlington and asked why they didn't send Paulie's body. But no one would give it to me straight. Just kept passing me from person to person who said they didn't know. But that's all bullshit. They're supposed to send the body with a flag. We all seen it on the news. You ask me, the US Army didn't want us lookin' at the body. They didn't want no one to know how my brother died.

We had the funeral anyway. I got a flag and we put it on a stand with a wreath at the church. There were lots of people.

A couple months later, Paulie's stuff came in the mail. Mom couldn't look at it. Just cried. So I opened it. It was just this little cardboard box with a uniform and his dog tags and a Bible. My brother never read the Bible in his life. Growing up, Mom tried to make him. Took him to church same as me. But he wouldn't read it. No way. I don't think it was his stuff. I mean, where was his wallet? Where was the watch my uncle gave him when he graduated from high school?

We got this letter once too. It was from a bank in Panama. Said there was a lot of money and Paulie needed to get it out because they had had it too long. When I told them he was dead, they wouldn't talk to me without a lawyer. But you need money for a lawyer. We don't have money.

Anyway. You find anything else? Mom's been sick. I want to tell her some good news.

I started to type a reply, but it was all wrong. Angry and frustrated and suspicious. Just like him. And just like his message, it wasn't going to get me anything I wanted. Instead, I watched the cursor blink until the screen on my phone went black.

I didn't *feel* anything. Not like Mike Havers. Not like his mom. I was just angry that he wasn't giving me what I wanted, that he wasn't fitting together the pieces of my puzzle. And that's no feeling to have about a dead kid. Or his brother.

My fingertips were white, I was gripping the phone so fiercely. Slowly, I put it down on the seat and curled my hand around the steering wheel again.

It didn't matter what Mike Havers knew or didn't know. Didn't *really* matter. Kingman was there—*had* to have been. He'd been there when Private Havers sucked down his last breath. When Patrick Beale sucked down his. I *knew* it; every fiber of my being believed it to be true. And my fingernails ripped into the Bronco's plastic-wrapped steering wheel when I thought about why Kingman knew my daughter and what he would do to her. What he had already done. What I was going to do when I caught him.

Out in the county, as I sped past the fields and the houses and the apple trees, I watched for Jimmy King. I watched for the unusual, the odd, the suspicious. Whatever it was that would solve the puzzle, that would right the wrong. I didn't know where I would find it—whether I *would* find it—but I knew it was out there, somewhere, among the kids playing in sprinklers, the neighbors eating ice cream on the front lawn of the church. Somewhere, I would find that last bit of evidence that would take him down.

The truck rolled to a stop at an intersection. Without thinking, I drove straight ahead. I almost didn't see the road sign, but when I did, my stomach dropped, my heart leapt into my throat. Still, I drove on, studying each of the little houses I passed every quarter of a mile, straining to see them in the last crimson rays of the sun just peeking over the hills. And then I was there: little brown house, big oak tree, sheriff's cruiser in the drive. I pulled in behind it and turned off the engine, sat there for ages, watching the blue light of the television flashing through the flowered curtains as the evening deepened. Sat there until a cool breeze swept through the leaves and the open windows of the Bronco, until the crickets started to hum and sing.

The first time I had been there was a few years back, two, maybe three. There had been a barbecue, and there were people, lots of people: Meredith's friends from the tribe, Darren's from the Sheriff's Office. A few people we had all been in school with. And me. But I'm not good at parties anymore. Haven't been since the war.

I got there late, long after a line of vehicles had strung out along the road, late enough for me to study everything, to get comfortable enough to approach the house. The front door was open, but narrow and crowded. So I went around the side, a six-pack of weepy beer bottles in my left hand, my right hand free like my drill instructor always said it should be: free to salute, free to defend. But even the backyard was a mistake, with the coolers full of alcohol and the drunk cops and the sober Indians and the loud classic rock and the strings of Christmas lights shining dully in a tree dripping with overripe plums. I put the beer down and left, and when I slipped into my truck, I saw Darren watching me from the porch, one hand holding the screen door open, the other waving at someone leaving, but his eyes on me. And I knew I shouldn't have come.

That night in August, there was no one. I was alone.

Darren wanted to know where I was. He wanted to know if I was safe. He wanted . . .

I took the keys out of the ignition and slid to the ground, closed the Bronco's door as quietly as its ancient hinges allowed. Then I walked up to the front porch, still not sure if I should have come. But I knocked anyway, and the television went mute, then soft footsteps, bare footsteps, approached the door.

"Who is it?" Darren's voice said loudly, clearly. His sheriff voice.

"It's me," I said, my voice catching in my throat. "Camille."

The door opened, a little at first, then fully when he saw my face. He was still pulling on a rumpled white undershirt; his feet were bare below a pair of worn-out jeans. Quickly, he shifted the gun in his right hand behind his back.

"You got any sandwiches?" I said awkwardly, then smiled.

He held the door open. I walked in, my arm brushing against his. He closed the door, locked it. I stood in the tiny entrance hall, my back pressed up against the wall, watching him. He stepped into the living room, set his weapon down on the coffee table, the muscles on his back tight and lean through his thin shirt.

When he turned back, he started to say something but stopped. In the dim light of the hallway, I saw on his face that look, the one from the lot, from after the explosion, after I lost it, after I swore at him.

I looked away.

"You, uh . . ." he said quietly. "You want—"

"I should go," I said abruptly, but I didn't reach for the door.

"What?" Darren said, surprised.

I fumbled for words, so instead of saying it—saying anything—I just shook my head. I turned back toward the door, but before I could touch the doorknob, his hand wrapped around my wrist.

"Stay," he whispered.

I breathed quickly, my chest barely moving. His fingers loosened, but I could feel the heat of his chest behind me, radiating against my shoulder. I turned toward him, and his fingers fell away. Mine reached out, touched the skin of his forearm, slid across the lean muscle there up to his bicep, relaxed and long. Below my fingers, his arm flexed; his hand slipped over my hip, and he pulled me closer.

I tilted my chin up and saw that look again, the one that was just for me. And I knew I shouldn't have come.

18

I woke gasping for air.

My fists were clenched, arms rigid, lungs straining for oxygen. Blood burned in my cheeks. The stink of a campfire drifted past my nostrils, the snap of a belt faded from my ears. And twisted in the threads of my nightmare, hovering in my mind's eye was Oren, grinning greedily, viciously. My own personal demon.

Then faintly, the sound of something small and light—*leaves?*— smacking against glass. Painfully, I turned my head, my hair grinding beneath my scalp, fabric brushing against my earlobe. Window panes. Glass window panes flexing in a stiff wind, and beyond them, a line of hills—the eastern hills that roll into the Res—stained a sick yellow-gray in the predawn. Far off to the north, thunderclouds vomited thick streams of rain, a dark stain on the lightening sky.

I pushed myself up on my elbow, and a flowered sheet fell away from my bare chest. In the yard, unripe plums became projectiles.

Slowly, soundlessly, I rolled out of bed, stood tall, and looked down at my flat belly. I traced my fingers over the faded, shiny stretch marks that still shot across my hips, still snaked along the side of my breasts. I closed my eyes, ran my hands through my hair, pulled the tangles free. And when I opened them again, when I turned around, there was Darren, sleeping on his back, one arm tucked under his head, the sheet rising and falling with each deep breath. But in the half-light, in the silence, he could have been anyone. He could have been—

Ice ran down my spine.

I had to leave. A few moments later, I was in the living room, whipping on my clothes as I went. I was moving so fast I almost missed it. But when

I sat on the leather couch and leaned forward to tie my boots, I discovered Darren's secret. Files, four of them, stacked untidily, his white undershirt hastily thrown on top. I glanced over my shoulder at the bedroom door. I held my breath and listened for Darren's slow inhale, his even exhale. Then I lifted off the shirt.

The first file was all notes: disorganized, cryptic, written in tiny, tidy handwriting. Darren's.

The second file contained incident reports, dozens of them, going back years. For the most part, they were nothing exciting: a coke deal here, a small meth lab there. Besides the drugs, the only common thread was that the incidents *had* no common threads; they involved different people, different parts of the county, even the Res. The last report was about a fire and a death a few months back. The official conclusion was asphyxiation from smoke inhalation, but on the yellow sticky notes peppering the file, Darren called it suspicious, maybe homicide.

The third file contained other official documents: property deeds and legal documents at first. Then pay dirt. A Washington driver's license report for James Kingman, his photo staring out at me from the page, like a mug shot. A California license for a Victor Calzón who looked eerily like the tattooed jackass Nick. Similar reports for other names I'd never heard: Leon Palmer, Garrison Taylor, half a dozen others. And a Form DD-214 discharging Captain James Kingman from active duty in the U.S. Army, effective January 26, 2010.

The fourth file was even better: transcripts. Most for conversations between Sergeant Darren Moses and an unnamed CI, a criminal informant. A couple of the more recent ones featured an unnamed federal agent, who was dangling witness protection in front of the increasingly fearful CI. Someplace far away, Texas maybe. Houston was a possibility. But all the transcripts had something to do with a large operation, an operation that the CI saw only through a keyhole, but a keyhole just big enough to reach through and pluck at the strings of a very sticky web.

The last transcript was for August 6. In it, the CI mentioned that something had the manager—whoever that was—spooked, so spooked that he'd ordered the immediate destruction of one of the most profitable labs. The CI said the manager hadn't attended himself, but he'd sent his right hand, someone described only as the sergeant, and the CI to take care of it.

He—the CI—described how they'd done it, how they'd piled up the lab equipment and all the ingredients that hadn't been moved already into the living room, like a bonfire before a football game in the fall, how they'd taken a couple of machetes and cut down the tinder-dry plants near the outside walls, taken them into the little house and piled them around the stuff from the lab. How they'd torched the place with a few cheap matches and some high-tech propellant the sergeant had laid out ever so carefully and then, ever so carefully, lit, watching constantly, manically, fire extinguisher in hand. He and the CI prowled around the little house like cougars in the tall grass to control the burn in that very dry season in that very dry country so close to the town of Little Falls.

I raised my eyes to the open door of Darren Moses's bedroom.

He hadn't told me.

He had told me to stop, to lay low, to stay out of it. He had told me none of it had anything to do with Patrick Beale. That none of it had anything to do with me. Or my kid. But here, in his living room, was the proof.

No shit he wanted to know if I was safe.

When my blood stopped pounding, when my fists unclenched, I put the files back, threw the undershirt on top. Outside, the sky was as light as it was going to get behind those clouds. In the next room, Darren's breathing was as steady as his lies.

I stood up and reached back, yanked my hair into a ponytail, pulled the rubber band off my wrist, and twisted once, twice. It snapped on my fingertips, caught in the loops, but I pulled them out and tugged my hair tight.

I was right and he had done wrong.

Time to go.

*   *   *

Visiting hours that Tuesday began at one o'clock, security clearance at twelve thirty. I got there at noon and ate a sandwich in the truck, parked under a tree. At the other end of the parking lot, behind a series of chain-link fences, the stained concrete prison loomed large and colorless; eight stories of rapists, murderers, drug traffickers, and worse—all of them bad enough for the feds. While I ate, a steady trickle of their family and friends—black, Latino, Asian, white—swung out of crappy cars and Audis, shuffled to the doors with the same angry glances around the parking lot, the same tinge of shame. I was the last one in.

Inside, the guards checked my ID and wrote my name in a logbook filled with curled pages. Then came the metal detector and the mandatory check-in for my stuff. Afterward, all of us—the visitors—filed into a long, narrow room flanked by guards on one side, pea-green desks and bullet-proof glass on the other.

And then we waited.

A young woman bit her nails, glanced at one of the guards like she knew him, feared him. An older man dozed, his neatly shaved chin resting on a brown sweater vest that was fuzzed and unraveling at the hem. A toddler fussed and squirmed, tried to break free; his mother scolded quietly, like she was too exhausted to do even that.

On the other side of the glass, a thick steel door opened, and in walked two male guards, tall, hawk-eyed, their electronic keycards swinging from thick black belts. They were followed by a line of prisoners wearing orange jumpsuits and shiny handcuffs and wary, watchful looks. When they were all in, they stopped suddenly, then turned as one man and stood behind stools bolted into the ground. One of them made a face at the toddler, who giggled gleefully. Then a guard said something, a command barely audible through the glass, and the room was suddenly buzzing.

I picked up the phone receiver hanging beside the thick glass barrier.

"Camille Waresch," said a voice I barely recognized.

"Billy Boykin."

He smiled—smirked—his canines long and narrow and yellowed. But on the counter his pale hand, thin like a woman's, rested calmly on the scarred Formica.

"How are you?" I asked.

"Can't complain," he said.

"How's the food?"

He shrugged. "I've lost twenty pounds."

"I thought you looked different."

"Yeah, I look like hell."

He did. We were the same age, but his black hair was shot through with gray, and the wrinkles on his face weren't laugh lines. When he was young, when I'd known him, when he'd been Oren's second in command, he'd been in the sun all year, his Irish skin baked brown, like he was just another boy from the Colville Res. Prison had made him pale, like a dirty sheet.

"I want to talk to you about something."

"No shit," he said and looked down, flexed his fingers.

"Something's going on back home."

"I been away a long time, Camille."

He had, I knew he had. I'd heard he'd left the Okanogan, gone out to Seattle for a job—given where he was, I could imagine what kind—two, maybe three years before. Maybe longer. I just hoped it wasn't too long.

"There was this kid—" I said. Started to say anyway.

"Yeah, I heard about it." Billy tucked the phone receiver into the crook of his neck, began to pick at his fingernails. "The Beale kid, right?"

"Who told you?" I demanded.

He smiled slyly. "Oh, just one of my connections."

"Who?"

Billy laughed. "Jesus Christ. Relax. My brother was down here a few days ago."

"Right," I said and tried to laugh. "Do you know what it was about?"

"*About?*" he said, curiously. "It was suicide, wasn't it?"

"That what your brother told you?"

Billy shrugged. "Cops found the kid strung up in a barn. Looked pretty bad, but looked like suicide. Open and shut."

"It wasn't."

"Yeah?"

"Yeah."

Billy's thin fingers gripped the phone receiver as he straightened his neck and leaned in, his mouth almost on the glass. "How do you know?"

I leaned back, my free hand curled into a fist on my thigh, and stared him down. His tongue traced the front of his teeth, lifted his lip, flashed pink.

"Why you comin' to me?" he said, settling back a little.

"You always knew what was going on. Back when, I mean."

"I been gone more than a year. Hell," he snorted, "*two* years. I been gone two years and you think I know what's goin' on up in the O-ka-no-gan," he said, drawing out the county name like he was making fun of somebody.

"Sorry to hear that, Billy," I said quietly. "Two years isn't much time to make a profit."

He stopped, grimacing mid-jeer. Then he laughed, grinned like the Big Bad Wolf. "Okay, Camille. For old times' sake. *For Oren*," he said quietly, his lips half open, salivating, those narrow canines pressing against his bottom lip. "How is the old bastard anyway?"

"I'm not here to talk about Oren."

"No," he said, all matter-of-fact. "Ain't seen him for fifteen years, have you? That how old the kid is, right?"

I must have flinched then, because his grin grew wider, redder in his pale face.

"He found my money yet?" Billy said.

"I don't know what you're talking about," I lied.

"You do," he said, nodding, still grinning. "I bet you know where he put it too. Hell, maybe you took it after he blew out of town."

I clenched my jaw and on my lap, my fist shook, it was curled so tight. "I'm not here to talk about Oren," I growled.

He laughed again, a laugh like a bark, like a coyote snuffling around the door on a hungry night.

Then he said, "What d'ya wanna know?"

"Who's in the business back there?" I said it quietly so my voice didn't tremble, didn't rage.

He leaned back, rested his free hand on his sunken belly, his smile widening. "I don't know what you mean."

"Patrick was into something—something big. I got an idea, but you know better than me."

"I don't know what you mean," he repeated.

"Who—" I started, but it was clear Billy was just going to protest again. He was toying with me. He was going to play the laughing con, deny everything until I had something solid, then he would deny that too. What had I expected? He hadn't changed, wasn't ever going to.

"I mean, if you had to guess, what do you think he might have been into?" I tried.

"Who says he was into anything?"

I put the phone down, pulled my backpack onto my lap, and pulled a piece of paper out of the front pocket, unfolded it, pressed it against the glass with one hand. With the other, I grabbed the receiver. "What about them?" I said and watched Billy focus on the photo, watched his eyes widen, his eyebrows arch, then knit, his lips press thinly together.

It took just a glance, less than a moment, and then he was looking away like nothing had happened, like he hadn't seen King standing at the pump in front of the mart or Nick in the front seat of the truck or Sophie, her head turned, in the back.

"Where's that?" he said, his chin jerking ever so slightly toward the photo I was still holding against the glass.

"You don't recognize my mart?" I simpered. "I'm hurt."

"Looks like LA," he mumbled into the phone. "Like fucking Compton."

He shrugged, looked over my head to the room behind me. I watched the wheels turn behind his flat blue eyes and I waited.

"What's this really about?" he finally said. The receiver was back in the crook of his neck, and he was picking at his fingernails again. A little smile had crept back onto his lips, but his voice was low and cautious.

I folded the photo, put it on the ledge between my chest and the window. "You tell me."

"Do you know who those guys are?" Billy said quietly.

"I've got names."

"What you got?"

"You know them?"

"Tell me," Billy demanded.

But that didn't seem like a good idea.

Billy broke first. He glanced around, shifted the receiver to his other ear, slouched, and watched me, studied me. "You don't have any fucking clue what you're into, do you?"

"I'm looking for Patrick Beale's murderer. That's what I'm into."

"And you think King and Victor put him down?"

I must have betrayed myself, looked confused or surprised or shocked or something. But I stopped myself from asking, "Who?"

"Yeah," I said instead.

Billy smirked, unconvinced. "How come?"

"It's personal."

"Personal?" he said doubtfully.

"If you'd seen what they did . . ." I shook my head. "It lacked elegance, Billy. It was messy."

"You saw it?"

I nodded once.

"That why it's personal?"

I shook my head, rolled my eyes. "I can tell it was personal, why they killed him. You don't do that kind of damage unless it's personal, unless you're trying to make a point. Otherwise, it's one shot—*bam*—you're done."

"And you'd know," he said, but he didn't flinch, didn't move a muscle; he didn't even blink. Just sat there, smirking.

"Yeah," I said, letting the insult go. Then I bluffed; it's what I had thought until that morning anyway. "I think he was into the business with them, and then he did something wrong. Pissed them off somehow. Lost a shipment, lost a client. Something."

Billy smiled, those yellow canines almost piercing his bottom lip. "Or maybe they were just having fun with all them electrical cords."

I leaned forward, my fist in my lap quivering—angry, too angry—and growled, "Or maybe Patrick was gonna turn them in."

I shouldn't have said it. I know I shouldn't have. I've wondered so many times about what would have happened if I hadn't opened my mouth, if I'd only kept my suspicions about why Darren's files ended so abruptly to myself. If I had stopped long enough to wonder why Billy Boykin knew anything about electrical cords in the context of Patrick Beale, why he would *ever* tell me he knew these bastards and knew how they operated, how they handled infractions. Why he'd tell me where he had seen them before. But I didn't and I hadn't: the words were spoken, and there was no taking them back.

Billy blinked once, ponderously. Then a slow smile spread like melting tar across his face, and he chuckled. He actually chuckled. "What do the cops think?"

I shrugged.

Behind the glass, Billy grinned viciously. He looked down, scraped imaginary dirt from under his pristine pink nails. "Why do you want to know about the kid? You ain't a cop."

"I just do."

"What's it about, Camille?"

I sat back, tried to read the expression on his face, but it was a blank wall. "I've seen it before. What they did to him. I've seen it before."

Billy's grin widened. "So, it's personal to *you*. It ain't personal to the kid."

"They fucked him up, Billy," I spat, blood pounding in my ears, pulsing at the edge of my vision. "They fucked him up bad."

Billy leaned into the glass, so close he might have kissed me through it. "What does it matter to you, little sister? What does it matter to *you*?"

"He was a kid, Billy. Christ, he was Sophie's friend."

He leered. "How *is* my sweet little godchild?"

"She isn't your godchild."

"Yeah, but Oren always said she would be."

"He was a fucking heathen, Billy. He never went to church a day in his life."

"Maybe so," he said, leaning back as much as he could on the crappy stool. "Maybe so," he said again. "But he fathered a pretty little thing."

I slammed my hand against the glass and stood up fast—too fast. A guard's voice—firm, clear—from behind said, "Ma'am. You need to sit down, ma'am."

But I barely heard him. I couldn't hear anything except Billy laughing, taunting me; Billy telling me, in a singsongy little voice, "You gonna play the game, Camille," as he stumbled from the glass, dragged backward by two guards with their hands clamped around his arms, "you gotta learn the rules. You better learn 'em *fast*, little sister."

* * *

Omak at seven thirty was brown and orange, the sky that deep blue you get after a storm, when the air has been scrubbed clean.

I went to Patrick's apartment again. I sat there behind the wheel in the parking lot and stared at the building, waited for the stained yellow brick to reveal the secret, for Patrick's ghost to come down the stairs and tell me what the hell was going on. It didn't.

I thought about Christine Beale and her horror and pain. I tried to feel it too, tried to figure out how I'd feel if I were in her shoes. I imagined the ache I should have in my chest. I imagined the rawness I should have in my throat, the sting I should have in my eyes. The hollowness in my soul. But as much as I missed Sophie, as much as I thought I loved her, wanted to protect her . . . I couldn't. Not that day. It was like a whole part of my soul, my heart, was numb. Forgotten. Fragmented.

For a while, I waited. I told myself I would talk to a neighbor. I would see if someone—the devil, maybe—would show up and tell me I was right, that this was Havers again, this was all a repeat of history, *my* history, and that if I kept pushing, if I didn't back down, if I put a bullet in the right brain this time, it would all end. That the nightmares would stop and Sophie could come home. That I would feel something more, something better than numbness and fear and anger. That I would be whole.

Instead, I drove, the Bronco rattling at low speed through Omak's tidy residential streets, rattling even more up the hill toward the highway. And then I parked in a blacktop lot too big for half the town, got a burger, and sat down in the front window of the restaurant, a jet of air-conditioning blowing down my shirt. Around me were more fast-food places, all fluorescent lights and play structures and plastic cheese. And teenagers hanging out in clusters, texting and laughing like idiots, like Sophie. But she wasn't with them. I looked away and past the parking lot, past the traffic light, watched semis tearing up the highway to the Canadian border and the eastern horizon darkening as the sun fell below the mountains.

After a while, I went out to the truck and watched the restaurant in reverse, from the outside looking in. The dark-haired girl behind the counter exhausted, her face lined with every one of her twenty-odd years. The kid flipping burgers in the back, his eyes rimmed red from pot, his hands slow, a sloppy smile on his face. They were just like the people at the prison that morning. Strung out, strung up, nowhere to go but inside.

I wondered whether it was all really so ugly or if it was just like that through my eyes.

I wondered what the point was.

Sleep. I needed sleep.

I got into the Bronco, shifted it into gear and adjusted the rearview. Halfway out of the parking space, I hit the brakes hard, stared into the rearview harder. In an alley between a service station and an old strip mall, in the dim wash of the surrounding lights, a Chevy Suburban—black and red and beat up—idled. Someone tall and lean slipped into its back seat, and then it rolled out of the alley, out under the lights, and into the street, slow and steady, its turn signal blinking like a sleepy old man. As it passed, I saw a familiar silhouette through the partly rolled-down window: buzz cut, chiseled jaw, thick shoulders. A soldier's silhouette.

I followed the Suburban from a distance, gave it a good quarter-mile lead, pulling back and forward randomly, like a normal person on their way home, a normal person paying more attention to the radio than the road. But I watched the truck carefully, waited for it to turn off onto one of the county roads, go east to the Res or west over the river, and up into the mountains huddled by its shores. When it finally did, it was dark, but I saw its headlights cut left and strafe a dirty white shack beside the road.

Maintaining my distance, I followed, the Bronc's rumble echoing off the river below the metal grid of the low bridge, then deepening to a dull roar as I pulled it right and powered up the hill. I crept closer and closer, trying to keep the Suburban in sight as we climbed into the hills. Eventually, it turned onto a long gravel path, a driveway soon enough hidden in the woods. I kept going through the next bend and then the next, then stopped, my mind racing. Following would be reckless, probably stupid too, but if I let it go, if I was right and I didn't do anything, it would haunt me for the rest of my life. So, when I had a story and the M9 ready in the door panel, I went back.

A quarter mile up the gravel road and past the first few trees, crouched a low hut sprouting a long CB whip that swayed like a drunk in the breeze. And beside the hut, waiting, a sentry in a brown T-shirt with the sleeves ripped off and an old pair of camo pants stuffed into scuffed black boots, a rifle—an AR-15—held loosely in his left hand. I stopped the truck.

"This is private property, ma'am," he said, a wad of chew in his lip.

"I'm so sorry," I gushed, and pushed my hair behind my ear. "I just— Look, I'm sorry, but I can't get a signal out here, and I'm really late getting home. The kids are with a sitter, and I was supposed to be there half an hour ago."

His sun-browned face softened just a little, but he still said gruffly, "Where you headed?"

I blurted out the first place I thought of: "Loomis."

"You shouldn't have turned onto the road. Shoulda kept going up the highway."

"I know. I got stuck behind a line of semis, thought this might be faster."

He spat a long brown stream of tobacco juice into the dirt. "It ain't."

"I know, I know. It was stupid. But listen"—I pushed my hair back again—"I just need to use a phone, call my sitter and let her know I'm on my way."

"Can't do that."

"Come on, this is the first place I've passed in five miles. Please? Listen, I can pay you for the trouble."

"Sorry. There ain't no phone here," he said and spat again.

"What?" I said more angrily than I meant to, too angrily to keep up the act. "Really, I've got to get in touch with her."

"Sorry, lady." He shifted the rifle to his right hand. "You're gonna have to try somewhere else."

I revved the engine a little, played with fire, just to see what he would do. He sighted his weapon and backed away in the same movement, like clockwork, like a clockwork soldier. And suddenly the smell of dirt and pine and sweat filled my nostrils, the dust pricked at my eyes, the heat crushed my chest. And I needed to feel the weight of an M16 in my hands, feel the trigger nestled under the skin of my index finger, needed it like I need to breathe.

But it was too late. Too late to draw my weapon before he pulled the trigger.

"Hey, hey," I said shakily, my voice unrecognizable, distant in my ears. I lifted my hands up high. "I'm gonna back away, okay?"

He nodded slightly and I threw the Bronco into reverse, then let it roll slowly, slowly, down the drive, one eye on the sentry, the other on the rear-view mirror. When the wheels touched tarmac, I swung the truck around and flew back the way I'd come.

*   *   *

Late that night, I sat on one of the hard wooden chairs in my apartment, my jaw set, my head pounding. I stared at the wall, at the big black-and-white assessor's map of the county held up with packing tape, at the locations marked with different colors. Blue for Patrick Beale's known movements. Green for Jimmy King's properties and his and Nick's—Victor's, Billy had said—known movements. Red for damage: the burnt meth house, the bleached torture chamber, my mart. And circled so many times it looked like a tornado had hit, the boundary line between Jeremy Leamon's ranch and Don McEnroe's old place, over the place where Patrick Beale breathed his last.

On the table in front of me, my notes were stacked high, piles of paper covered in my neat block handwriting. Notes about where and when and how. What I'd seen. Where I'd been. What I'd been told. Who told me. The sheets of paper were creased and wrinkled, read and reread, mangled in trying to find the bombshell that would blow King away.

I pushed a stack of papers to one side, pulled another toward me, and scanned the top sheet.

Paul Havers: 19
Narcotics: theft, distribution
Associates: unknown, infantry, Kingman?

Patrick Beale: 19
Meth: distribution, cooking
Associates: Nick (Victor Calzón?), Jimmy King (Kingman?), Sophie

Sophie.

I hadn't spoken to her since Sunday, since she'd called from the airport. I had heard someone laughing in the terminal near her, and I remember thinking that was fucked up, like the lady on the other end of the phone had no right to laugh, had *no fucking right* to be happy.

Later that day, there had been a text: *here.* I asked if she was with Martha, my mother's sister, the one who had stayed in Michigan to mind the family orchards when my mother fell in love and moved to Washington and had a kid she left to fend for herself while she did sit-ins with students and protests with office workers and strikes with factory workers, and devoted herself to everyone else. Martha, the one I told when I got pregnant my first term at the University of Michigan. The one who told me to not pack my bags, that she'd help me, that blood is thicker than everything else. The one I didn't listen to.

Sophie texted me back, said she was with Martha, that they were on the way home.

Home.

I hadn't responded.

I was a shitty mother. I know it now. I knew it then. Protection makes sense; it's just another mission. But everything else—the nurturing, the teaching, the joy . . . I just couldn't.

But I still felt—still *feel*—the guilt. It's like a lead ball you swallowed, a concrete block poured around your legs, and you're drowning, sinking deeper and deeper into the deepest ocean because you know you can't do anything about it now and you have to live with it, you have to just keep going, knowing that you—*you*, not your kid, *only you*—fucked up. And she paid for it.

My work phone was on the table. For those long minutes I sat there staring, I wanted nothing more than for it to ring, for Sophie's phone number—my personal cell phone number—to appear on the screen. But it didn't.

I could have dialed. I *should* have dialed.

But I didn't.

19

In real life, it happened in a town in the north; not even a town—more like a cluster of mud-brick houses with dirty children running through alleys caked in yellow dust. In real life, it went down like this: me, the medic who asked too many questions, who didn't get her head straight, banished to the front line with my M16 and my emergency kit, waiting with the driver while the real soldiers went through the houses, confiscating weapons those people needed to protect themselves from the raiders, from the insurgents, the real enemy. And because I was not green, because it was not my first time at that rodeo, I watched the people watching us. I watched the houses, the cars, the dead dog crawling with flies on the side of the road. And then I saw them, the pinpricks along the upper wall down the street: a jagged row of Kalashnikov barrels and behind them, tossed in the wind like a kite, a fringe of camo netting hiding our assassins.

But in my dreams, in my dream that night, *all I can see is the black barrel of a rifle winking at me, and all I can feel is the stock of my M16, firm and heavy against my shoulder, my finger firm and steady on the trigger. And I fire round after round, tearing the camo netting, blasting through the mud bricks, hoping like hell to see a spray of blood.*

Instead, out of nowhere, there's a bullet. And I'm thrown back against the doorframe of the Humvee and I can't breathe, but for a moment, I can see the chaos, see the patrol pour into the street and storm the buildings where the snipers are holed up, see the grimy children scatter, crying, see the explosion when the last of the soldiers goes in. And I hear someone, somewhere close, screaming. Maybe me.

And then: nothing.

Nothing.

20

When I stopped running that Wednesday morning—exhausted, sweat pouring out of my skin—Darren was there. I saw the cruiser first, then him, his mirrored *Top Gun* sunglasses dull and dark in the shade of the mart. He was sitting behind the wheel, watching, waiting for me.

My first thought was that he was there to arrest me, that the feds were pressing charges for my little outburst at the prison or that the sentry from the night before had reported me for trespassing. But when he stepped out of the car, his hands were empty, and he strode toward me with long, loose steps. When he took off his sunglasses, he looked relieved.

"Hi," I panted, hands on my hips.

"Hi."

Darren stepped closer and I swear every muscle under his dark brown uniform moved like they had two nights before, like they had when he was—

My cheeks burned hotter, my jaw tightened. I turned away, walked over to the wall of the mart and steadied myself, stretched my quads. He stayed where he was.

"What's going on?" I asked. "Why are you here?"

He frowned. "I've been calling you."

I frowned in return, then remembered. "Oh, right. Sophie has my phone."

"What?"

"She busted her phone before she left. I gave her mine."

"Oh."

"Sorry."

"You just—" He stepped toward me again, lowered his voice. "You left so early yesterday and . . ."

"Yeah. I had something to do."

He drew his head back, his nostrils flared: shocked, annoyed, I don't know. I didn't care.

"The coffee should be ready," I said, then unlocked the door, climbed the stairs. In my kitchen, I poured a cup for him, set it on the counter, then pulled off my shirt.

"I need a shower."

When I returned, one towel wrapped around my hair, a second around my body, he was leaning against the counter, his arms crossed, watching something out back behind the mart. Then his head turned and he was watching me, his eyes curious, hungry, but wary, as though I were a caged beast, one that might leap through the bars if he got too close.

I went to the sink, filled a glass of water, drained it, filled another.

Darren still hadn't spoken, just turned around, one hand lightly touching the handle of his coffee cup, the other loose, relaxed, resting on the counter. But his eyes . . .

"So, what's going on?" I asked again.

"Nothing."

"That's why you're here at five thirty in the morning. Because of nothing."

Darren held his ground, remained grave. "I wanted to make sure you were okay."

I narrowed my eyes. "Why wouldn't I be okay?"

"You were upset," he said levelly, his hands still loose, relaxed on the counter. "Your truck, your computer. I thought you might . . . I don't know."

"I might what?" I said, clenching my glass of water so tightly it should have shattered.

"Look," he said and glanced at the door. "I know you've been asking around about the kid, about Patrick Beale."

I didn't answer.

"You talked to that lawyer, Jack Wyatt," Darren said.

"Not about Patrick."

Darren nodded. "And you've been talking to Lyle."

I balked. "I've been talking to Lyle for almost twenty years, Darren. Whether I wanted to or not."

Darren sighed, looked away. "Where did you go yesterday?"

"Why does that matter?"

"Where did you go?" he said again.

I shrugged. "Seattle."

"Seattle."

"Yeah. Went to see a friend."

"I didn't know you counted Billy Boykin as a friend."

I tried to calculate what he knew, how he knew it. Goddamnit. *The files. The feds. Boykin must have been on some watch list.*

Briefly, Darren closed his eyes. When he opened them, they had this urgent look, this fear. "You need to be more careful, Camille."

I tightened the towel around my breasts, tightened my jaw.

"This is bigger than you realize," he said.

I cocked my head, raised my eyebrows. "Big enough for the feds?"

I picked up my water glass, watched Darren out of the corner of my eye while I drained it again. His eyes were dark and deep, but the muscles of his face were smooth, untroubled. If he suspected I had read his files, he wasn't letting on.

I wiped my mouth with the back of my hand, then cleared my throat, tried a different approach. "You think Victor is going to have me picked up. Or King. One of the two."

And he did react, just a little. He was surprised I knew those names, or at least surprised I'd said them. "Who are they?" he asked carefully.

"You know," I said just as carefully.

"Billy tell you about them?"

"No," I lied.

"Jeremy Leamon?"

"You mean before or after they blew his head off?"

"It might have been suicide," Darren said softly, then frowned when I laughed.

"Suicide?" I said and laughed again. "Like hell."

"Doc Fleischman hasn't finished the autopsy."

"Why? Not enough of his head left?"

"That's not funny."

"No. But there's no way you're going to convince me that level of response was for a suicide."

Darren's eyes narrowed. "Response?"

"I saw it, Darren." I nodded, glad for a trump card, any trump card. "Sat there for five minutes chatting with Deputy Walker while the EMTs brought his body out."

He clenched his jaw, looked away, his eyes now stormy and black. "Camille," he said, his voice low and threatening.

"It wasn't suicide."

"You shouldn't have been there."

"It wasn't suicide."

"We don't know that."

I didn't think Leamon was scared enough to pull the trigger himself. I figured he knew the writing was on the wall, but I also knew—knew in my gut—that the old man wouldn't go down without a fight. But then I remembered sitting in his kitchen that day with the whiskey and the dirty curtains and the shotgun leaning against the wall by the back door. There had been a wedding picture in the front room, the silver frame polished, the only thing in the house that was clean. But no wife. She'd been in the ground for years now. I remembered how good the barrel of a gun looked during my own bad times. And I doubted myself.

"Have you spoken with them?" Darren said.

"What?" I said, startled.

"Victor and King."

"Don't you already know?" I said, my lip curling. "I would have thought you'd heard."

Darren looked away and when he looked back, his face was hard, forbidding. "You don't know what you're getting yourself into, Camille. I don't want you to get hurt."

I snorted. "I've already been hurt, Darren. They broke into my place, they blew up my truck while my kid was sleeping thirty feet away."

"And if you would leave it alone, they'd stop."

"Leave what, Darren? I can't leave it alone if I don't know what it is."

"Stop asking questions," he said quietly. "Stop talking to people."

"Then tell me this," I said and leaned into the counter. "Tell me where he fits into soldier boy's little network. What was he doing for them? Why did he have ephedrine caked into his jeans? Because he was cooking for them, right? But if that's all, why kill him? Why string him up, why fry him with a fucking car battery?"

Darren stared at my fury and rage, and absorbed it all and didn't open his mouth once, just held his jaw tightly, blood pumping, roaring through the vessels in his neck.

"And while you're at it, tell me this: Why was he in here looking anxious a few days before he died?" I continued. "Why were King and Victor here a couple of days after that? Were they out at the place behind Jeremy Leamon's? Were they burning down a lab?"

I waited for his reaction, but his face was blank, chiseled stone.

"And why," I said, well aware that I was shouting now. I lowered my voice to ask, "Why was my *daughter* with them?"

"I can't . . ." Darren said, his mouth barely moving.

"What? You can't what?"

"I can't tell you."

"But you know."

Darren looked down at the counter, looked at his fist balled up and resting on it.

"Or *do* you know?" I shouted. "Am I the only one asking questions anymore? Is that the problem? Are you trying to cover something up? Are the *feds* trying to cover something up?"

"It's a live investigation, Camille," Darren said evenly.

"And I found his body, Darren," I breathed. "I found Havers."

Darren's chin jerked up, his brow creased. "Who?"

I stopped, stepped back, stunned. Confused. "Patrick," I said quietly. "I found Patrick."

"Who is Havers?"

But I was already gone, back in Iraq, back with *the heat and the dust and the flies buzzing in that dark, mud-brick room, the stench that hit me in the face as soon as the corporal kicked open the door. I was standing to the side while the other guys went in, rifles at the ready. And when the first soldier put his arm over his mouth and stepped to the side, when the second dropped his weapon and started to heave, I saw him—Havers— hanging from a heavy metal hook screwed into the ceiling; hanging, bloated, blackened, unrecognizable, his chest bare, his feet bare, the strings of his BDU pants loose around his ankles in the spotlight of one soldier's headlamp, a soldier who stood there transfixed. Horrified. And when that soldier looked away, there was nothing but—*

"Camille?" Darren said softly. His hand was on my shoulder, the skin of his palm cool and dry on my still-damp skin. I jumped, looked up quickly, wildly.

"Tell me what happens if I *stop* asking questions?" I said fiercely. "How long before the next one? How long before *Sophie* ends up hanging in a barn?"

Darren wrapped me in his arms, but I stood there stiffly, my spine like iron, my chin dry against the abrasive cloth of his uniform.

"I'm not afraid," I said, my voice solid, icy. "I've been there. I've seen things."

Darren's lungs filled and then emptied, his breath hot against my neck. "This isn't Afghanistan, Camille," he said. "These guys make the Taliban look like Boy Scouts."

I shook my head. He held me closer.

"They'll kill you, Camille," Darren said, his lips on my hair. "They'll kill Sophie."

I clenched my jaw and pushed him away.

* * *

Rhonda fed me that morning, made me stand there like a little kid in front of the counter in the mart while she watched me eat a cinnamon roll and drink a cup of coffee.

"You look like hell, boss," she said. "When was the last time you slept?"

"Where did you see Patrick Beale?" I asked.

She frowned, wiped my crumbs off the counter for the fifth time. "You mean up in Oroville?"

"Yeah, with that guy."

"That restaurant on the way into town."

"The pizza place?"

"No, the north end of town. It's a diner or something."

"On the way in from Canada," I muttered.

"Yeah. Maybe."

I ate some more of the cinnamon roll, waited for her to keep talking. When she didn't, I asked her what Patrick and the other guy—Nick, Victor, whatever his name was—were doing.

"Eating."

"And?"

"I don't know. I just saw them through the window."

"Were they talking?"

"Maybe," Rhonda said, got snotty with me. "It's not like I stood there and watched them."

I sighed, looked over at the door, looked through it at the road baking in the early sun.

"They were just eating," Rhonda said more patiently. "Patrick looked kind of scared and the other guy looked sort of . . . I don't know, *preoccupied*."

I raised my eyebrows.

"You know, sort of pissed off and thinking hard about something."

Rhonda picked up a pair of plastic tongs and rearranged the cinnamon rolls on their red plastic platter, filled the hole from the one I had taken, and scraped up the frosting that had dripped off.

She shrugged, then said, "Maybe he was just tired. It was—God—a month ago, I think."

"There wasn't anyone else with them?" I asked.

"No," she said, then tilted her head. "Well . . ."

"What?"

"There was a lot of food on the table."

"So?" I said. "They're guys."

"No, like *a lot*. Like there was another person with them."

"But you didn't see him?" I said, then remembered the video and my daughter in the back seat of that truck. "Or her?"

Rhonda shook her head, then stopped like she thought better of it. "There was someone walking toward the table. A blond guy. Looked like an asshole."

"Tall, buzz cut?"

"Yeah. Pretty ripped too."

Captain Jimmy Kingman. I would have bet anything it was King.

"And the other one?" I said. "You said he had dark hair."

Rhonda nodded, then pointed to her neck, right where it sloped down into her tanned shoulder. "And a tat, right here."

And that was Victor. Or Nick, depending on who you asked.

I nodded, shoved the last of the cinnamon roll in my mouth. When I had swallowed it, I borrowed Rhonda's car on the excuse that the Bronco was acting up, but really because no one had seen me in it before. Then I slipped out while the mart was still empty.

Ten minutes later my phone rang. I glanced at the number and slammed on the brakes, jerked the wheel to the right, and just as the car shuddered to a stop—

"I need a favor."

"Well, thank *you*, Camille. I'm doin' just fine. How you doin', friend?"

"Harry," I said sternly. "I'm not fucking around."

Laughter, Harry German's trademark rumble, deep and bassy, like he was at the bottom of a barrel. "You never do, woman."

"I need a service record."

Silence.

"Camille—" Harry said quietly, his voice cautious.

"I need it, Harry. He was Army. Discharged as a captain in 2010. I'll send you a photo of the DD-214."

"You know I can't—"

"Yes, you can. I know you still have the contacts."

"I *can't*, Camille. I wish I could, but—"

"This is important. Life or death."

Silence.

"Harry?"

A longer silence.

Then: a sigh, big and deep.

"What's so important about it?" he asked.

"You know those properties? The ones you found? He's behind it. Meth. And it's big time. It's vicious."

"So what? Let the cops deal with it. This ain't your—"

"*No*," I snapped. "Don't tell me to—"

"That's what they do, they—"

"*No!*" I shouted.

"Whoa," Harry said quickly. "*Whoa.*"

I was clenching the phone in my fist; it was smashed against my cheek. But my eyes were closed, my throat was closed. And the tears burned when they traced down my cheeks.

On the other end of the line, a chair creaked, a door closed. Then Harry said, "What's this really about?"

"Sophie," I said, my voice choking. "She's in it . . . somehow. I don't know how. But she's involved; she knew that dead kid, and he's . . . this guy has got her involved."

Harry was quiet then, but it was a busy sort of quiet. He breathed rapidly in short, sharp bursts. And in the background, a pencil tapped on a wooden surface.

"Give me the name," he said, his voice barely more than a whisper.

"I'll send you the photo."

"*No,*" he said quickly. "No photos. No emails. No records. Just give me his name."

"Kingman. James Kingman, Captain."

"I'll see what I can do."

"Thanks," I said, but Harry had already hung up.

Alone in the car on the side of the road, I rolled down the window, listened to the wind, felt it scour my face. Sweat trickled between my breasts. A single question preyed on my mind: Why was I alive?

Darren had said they would kill me. He was right. I had gotten close enough for threats, for intimidation: the laptop, my truck, maybe even the asshole who tried to run me off the road the Friday before. But I hadn't gotten close enough to try to kill. Not yet. That meant I hadn't gotten close enough to the truth about Patrick Beale.

That had to change.

On my work laptop, I scanned through the maps I had saved, duplicates of the ones I had hung on the wall of my apartment, then burned in a fit of paranoia. I flipped through them, layered the data, unlayered it, racking my brain to find a pattern, a central location where they congregated. Someplace convenient, but hidden, maybe in plain sight. Someplace for me to start again, to reevaluate. But almost everything was a one-off. I had seen the Suburban once in Omak by the fast-food places, once on the road out to Little Falls, once at the football field where Patrick Beale had been laid in a box. I had seen Nick or King twice in my mart, three times in Chelan. Rhonda had seen them once in Oroville. I had seen their dirty work twice in the hills above Little Falls and twice north of the Res.

I traced my finger over the roads and smack in the middle, on the way to everywhere else, I saw the link: the Chelan airfield.

The helicopter.

It was essential equipment. It was how they got product out, probably how they got supplies in too. If I could find out when they were using it—*who* was using it—I would be that much closer to the truth.

* * *

The airfield looked the same as it had a week before: gray sheds lining the gravel road, tufts of yellow-brown grass waving in the breeze. A dog, something big and golden and panting in the heat, watched me drive slowly toward the office. It smiled, but didn't get up when I climbed out of Rhonda's little red sedan.

"Hello?" I called when the tinkling bells died down. That was new. The bells, I mean. Or, maybe I just hadn't noticed them before.

There was no response. I waited a minute, then wandered through the small office and down a short hallway past the bathroom to the back room and back again. I shivered, my arms going all pimply in the AC, so I went out the other door, toward the airfield, and scanned the wide expanse of grass and cracked tarmac.

I didn't see the male I had spoken with before, but at the other end of the airstrip was a female wearing a green ball cap. She was talking to a guy with shiny silver hair and a gold watch that flashed like a beacon in the sun. He signed something on a clipboard and handed it back to her, then grimaced when she kept talking. Words like "safety" and "on my watch" drifted back on the breeze.

I waited. Eventually, the old guy waved her off and climbed into his little four-seater and started the engine.

The female with the green cap stood on the grass beside the apron, her arms crossed over her chest, the clipboard clutched in one hand. She watched the old guy steer his plane down to the runway and wait as the propellers turned faster and faster until the plane, wobbling on its stork-like legs, sped down the airstrip and caught the breeze. Her head swung up, watching the plane wing toward the mountains, climbing up and up and up before banking toward the north, then toward the east, and finally toward the southeast. That was when she saw me.

"Mornin'," she shouted, then began the long walk back toward me and the office.

"Good morning."

"Nice one, isn't it?" she said when she was within spitting distance. "Hasn't been this clear since June."

"Yeah." I inclined my head toward the runway. "That guy giving you some kind of problem?"

"Naw. Just needs to be a little more careful on my airfield. You know how it can be with folks who aren't from here."

How the hell she knew I was local, I had no idea, but I nodded and followed her into the office. She placed the clipboard on the desk, took off her ball cap, and tightened her graying ponytail.

"What can I do for you?" she said, still standing.

"You've got a helicopter here I'd like to see."

The woman frowned. "Don't think any of our airframes are for sale at the moment."

I shook my head, tried the same lie that had worked so well with her colleague. "No, I'm from the Assessor's Office. I need to follow up on something."

"Oh, sure." She sat at the desk, pulled a battered notebook toward herself and flipped to the front. "What did you want to look at?"

"Helicopter. It's a Sikorsky S-76, registered to CLA LLC."

She frowned. "Don't think we got one of those."

"Could you please check?"

The woman shrugged, then scanned the page, ran her finger down the margins. When she looked up, she shook her head. "Nope. Don't have any Sikorsky."

I went to the desk, looked at the register myself. "Well," I said and shrugged. "It was here last week. Hangar seven."

"Last week?" she echoed, her brow furrowed.

"Yeah. Tuesday. Your colleague opened the hangar for me."

"Who's that then?"

"Big guy, orange shirt. Didn't get his name."

The woman glanced at the phone, glanced back at me. "Ma'am, I'm the only employee here. Maybe he was the owner?"

"Well, I don't know what to tell you," I said, shaking my head. "But he went into the back room and got a couple of keys and took me out to hangar seven. And that Sikorsky was in there."

"No, ma'am. I don't have any records for a Sikorsky. The only helicopters we've ever had have been two-seaters anyway."

"Look, maybe I'm remembering wrong. Can I just show you what I'm talking about? I know what it looks like."

She studied me for a few seconds. She had laugh lines around her eyes: pale in the shallows, deep brown at the peaks. She brushed a few wisps of her hair behind her ear, then shrugged again, pulled on her cap, and stood up. "Alright. I'll follow you."

"Don't you need the key?" I said.

"Got 'em right here," she said and patted a lump in her jeans.

We went outside—I led—and strode down the apron past hangars one through six. Hangar seven was exactly as it had been before: trim and well-painted in the same dark gray I'd seen at bases from Georgia to Baghdad.

The woman from the office turned the key in the lock, opened the door wide, and stepped aside. Inside the hangar, the air was stifling. No air-conditioning that day. The banks of fluorescent lights buzzed and sputtered to life, but under them: nothing. No helicopter, no lift, not even a drop of oil. Just a wide expanse of scrubbed concrete.

"This what you wanted to see?" the woman said, her voice gentle and wondering. But when I turned toward her, she stepped back.

"It must be out," I said shortly. "It must be out on a run."

"No, ma'am. The only airframe supposed to be in this hangar is a little orange Ag-Cat, one of them old crop dusters. That's what I been trying to tell you."

"Where is it?"

"No idea. This isn't a library, ma'am. Owners can come and go as they please."

"I want to see your flight records."

"Well, now." She squared her shoulders, squared off her hips. "I'm not supposed to share those with the public."

"*Now.*"

She looked at me thoughtfully, her head tilted a little to the right, her tiny blue eyes sparkling like diamond chips. "You said you're from the county?"

I nodded. She did as well.

When we stepped outside to go back to the office, the sun was almost directly overhead, almost hot enough to burn through my hair. Way up in the stratosphere, it dazzled on the wings of an airliner.

In the office, the woman unlocked a cabinet under the desk and pulled out a big black binder. She pointed at it with her chin and said, "Here you go. They're organized by hangar number."

I thanked her and flipped through the first few pages. The handwriting at the top of the pages was all in one person's tiny, neat style, but the handwriting for the list of flights below that varied.

"Who signs out the aircraft?"

"The pilot's supposed to."

"They don't always?"

"Like I said, this ain't a library."

When I reached the page for hangar seven, I sputtered. "Why is this blank?"

The woman in the John Deere hat shook her head. "I've never seen it go out."

I rifled through the pages, trying to find any entries for a helicopter or, hell, a crop duster. There was nothing.

"You got what you need, hon'?"

"When are the planes allowed to fly?" I demanded. "What time of day?"

"Most everybody flies during the day. This airfield isn't equipped for night landings."

"But could someone go out at night?"

The woman shrugged again. "I suppose."

"Would anyone see them? Is anyone here at night?"

"No, ma'am." She glanced at her watch, a tiny, delicate golden model. "There's no one here after five."

* * *

I'd say I returned to that party house that afternoon, but that would mean I intended to go back there, that I'd had a plan and executed it. I didn't.

After I left the airfield, I was on autopilot, watching the scenery pass by, rather than going anywhere in particular. First, I drove up the hill to Chelan from the airfield, then into town. Before I knew it, I had blown through Chelan entirely, gone past the campgrounds and the boat launches and the ritzy houses sprawled along the lake's shore. And then I was there, like my gut knew better than my head where I needed to be. It was the same house, the same off-white paint and dark gray trim and bushes lining the front walk. But now there was also a realtor's sign, swaying gently in the breeze blowing off the water.

I parked the car and got out, climbed up the concrete front steps, approached the long, frosted window stretched alongside the door—and halted.

The door was ajar.

For a long moment, I listened, the breeze washing over one ear, the other straining to hear anything from inside the house. Finally, faintly, indistinctly, I heard a female voice lilting at the end of each statement, straining to sound enthusiastic. Then creaking from above: footsteps. And a man's voice, questioning, and the same female voice, responding.

I reached out and pushed the door open, stepped soundlessly inside the front entrance. Three pairs of shoes stood on hardwood floors that extended through a living room wider and deeper than my entire apartment, with a ceiling that soared to the roof. A massive stone fireplace rose up one wall, and a grand staircase, the railing studded with antlers, wound down another.

I straightened my ponytail, smoothed the front of my tank top, and ran my tongue over my teeth. Then I reached back and knocked on the front door.

"Hello?" I called out toward the staircase. "Is there an open house today?"

There wasn't, but the real estate agent—a short woman with a blonde blowout that added more inches to her height than the stiletto heels parked beside the door—reluctantly let me tag along with her expensive-looking clients.

I followed them through the luxe kitchen with windows that looked out on the water, the marble-tiled bathroom, the sleek modern den with a projection screen. I walked out the folding glass doors with them to take in the view I hadn't had time to notice when I had been there searching for Sophie the week before. There was nothing in the house that hinted at the shotgun or the booze or the drugs I was sure were there that night. It was just a house, a fancy, bland house that would sell for more money than I'd ever earn, more money than I could ever get for the hundreds of acres of orchards I had inherited from my father. But even fancy houses have places to hide skeletons. So after the expensive clients drove away in their big, black BMW, I asked to see the basement.

"There isn't one," the blonde agent said.

"Oh, but I saw some windows outside?" I said as innocently as I could.

She waved her hand, fluttered her blood-red nails. "That's just a crawl space."

"I'd like to see it."

The agent sighed. "There isn't anything to see. And"—she glanced at the slim gold watch on her wrist—"I need to meet someone in ten minutes."

"I'll be quick." I smiled and crossed my arms across my chest.

She sighed again, but turned back toward the kitchen. "It's through here."

I followed her past the sparkling appliances and down a short hall to the door of what I had assumed was a closet. She turned the knob and pulled open the door, stepping in front to try to hide the two inches of solid wood door, the heavy steel knob, the thick deadbolt, all of them pointless for a crawl space that went nowhere, but perfect for stashing your drugs or your guns. Or a kid who's gone narc.

"I just need to make a call," the agent said and glanced away. She bit her glossy pink lower lip.

"I'd rather you went down there with me." I laughed haltingly, my nerves on fire, my paranoia acute. "It's silly, but I'm a little afraid of the dark."

The blonde rolled her eyes but didn't put her phone back into her monogrammed purse. I stepped aside, then followed her down. And while she stood and sulked at the bottom of the stairs, holding her phone out this way and that to get enough bars to make her call, I did a circuit of an unfinished room that reeked of bleach and Pine-Sol. A wide drain, covered with a cross-hatched grate, punctured the cold, gray concrete floor. Heavy steel brackets, spaced perfectly for shotguns, studded the longest wall. In the harsh light of the single bare bulb, it was clear the lowest row of brackets had been removed and the drywall repaired almost perfectly—except at the farthest point from the door, the perfect place to shackle a man seated with his back against the wall. I looked up, trailed my hand across the sill of the high window—no dust or cobwebs. Pristine. But outside, caught between the low branches of a spiky shrub and the concrete foundation, a red plastic cup.

I glanced over my shoulder at the agent. She was standing at the foot of the stairs, her spiky fingernails flashing over her phone, her pedicured toes curled on the cold concrete floor. Who was she texting so frantically? She'd said she had another appointment. Maybe she was just saying she would be late. Maybe my paranoia was winning.

She hit "Send" and looked up at me, my fingertips still on the windowsill, watching her. She shifted, stepped back, and put her heel on the bottom step, her hand on the flimsy wooden rail. Something dark—fearful, desperate, and dark—flickered across her eyes.

In a breath, I'd closed the space between us. She threw up her arm, phone in hand, to bar my path. *No. Not paranoid.* I pushed past her and pounded up the steps, two at a time.

"Wait," the agent shouted up the stairs, her bare feet slapping on the concrete. "Don't you want to see the second floor?"

"Don't want to make you late for your appointment," I tossed over my shoulder.

She scrambled up the rest of the stairs, shouting, "Wait!" and something about the view. I detoured, darted left out the kitchen door, jumped over the deck railing, then sprinted up the hill to the car, pausing only to snatch the red plastic cup.

I couldn't be sure I wasn't imagining everything, that my fractured mind wasn't making it all up: the party, the helicopter, the real estate agent's clumsy attempt to lock me in the basement. I couldn't be sure I wasn't just desperate for a solution, for something to make the nightmares and the paranoia and the terror stop.

Still, I knew what I had seen. A hole where a nineteen-year-old kid could have been locked up. The cheap red plastic cup, evidence of the party where some asshole had gotten a shotgun out because my teenage daughter gave his boss the finger. And the text message on the agent's phone when she'd raised her hand to block me: *Keep her there. On my way.*

No, motherfucker. I'm on my way.

I sped through the shiny suburbs, then past the lakefront, past the kitschy little stores selling kitschy little shit, when, almost at the eastern edge of Chelan, I caught a glimpse of a sheriff's cruiser headed the other way. Stuck at a light, I strained to see who was driving, hoping—*needing*—to see Darren's black buzz cut, his chiseled brown face still and impassive, always the calm in the storm.

The distance between me and the cruiser closed to three blocks, two blocks, one. The cruiser turned down a side street and I saw the driver clearly: red hair, face tanned and freckled and smiling, always smiling, even with the worst news. Even for the dirtiest jobs. Lucky Phillips. And two cars behind him, a black and red Suburban.

* * *

I got a call from an unlisted number that afternoon. I glanced at the screen of my phone while I drove through the dry hills, then put it down, ignored it. But then it rang again. And again.

"You got a pen?" a man's voice said.

"Who is this?" I shouted over the wind sweeping in through the windows.

"Just get a pen, Waresch," the man said, like he was trying to be quiet and quick.

The windows squeaked shut. "Who is this?" I said again, my suspicion sharpening.

"Pull over."

He sounded pissed off, anxious, stressed. Like someone who had just broken a rule he knew he shouldn't have.

"Harry?"

"Pull the fucking car over and get a pen."

I swerved and let the engine idle on the narrow shoulder. Then I rummaged.

"Go ahead," I said seconds later, a pink pen from under Rhonda's passenger seat held at the ready over a fast-food napkin spread over the center of the wheel.

"Indian valley meats at unipoint dot cn one niner six three kennedy."

I stared at what I had written. I blinked. *"What?"*

"Indian valley meats at unipoint dot cn one niner six three kennedy," Harry repeated.

"The hell are you talking about?"

"Log in at twenty-three twenty-two tonight. The record will be in the draft mail folder."

My brow unfurrowed, my jaw dropped. "You got Kingman's record?"

"Five minutes, Waresch. It will be there for *five minutes only.*"

"Okay." I reread my scrawl. "Okay."

"What are you going to do?" Harry said urgently.

"Log in at unipoint dot cn. Address is Indian Valley Meats. Password is one niner six three kennedy."

"And?"

"At twenty-three twenty-two precisely."

The line went silent.

"Harry?" Frantically, I shifted the phone. The call had ended, the screen just a black background with the county seal. I scrolled through my calls, wanting to call him back, but you can't call an unlisted number. That's the point. I had a feeling no one would answer now anyway.

I spent that night in the basement of the county building, pawing through property records—tax filings, deed transfers, tax inspection records, parcel maps—everything. What I found on the computer, I checked in the files. What I found in the files, I checked on the computer. And the longer I spent, the deeper I dove, the more confused, the more on edge I became. Because everything had changed.

Sure, Jeremy Leamon's ranch was still deeded in his name, but where the parcel map had been blank before, there was now a barn. On the neighboring property, the one with the burn circle, the one where Don McEnroe had lived until he sold up to Leamon's bogeyman, there was no barn. And the other properties, all the places on Harry German's list, were registered in the names of ordinary people, a bunch of Bobs and Sues and Mikes, not Gorgon Four or CLA or any other LLC. But those names, that barn—they were all in my memory, clear and bright as day. Hell, they were written in my notebook, the one that had quickly filled with scrawled notes on Patrick Beale's murder, the one I had gone back out to the truck to retrieve hours before it went up in flames. In the property tax records, nothing. No records for CLA LLC; no trace of the helicopter or the forklift or the black Dodge truck that Patrick Beale had driven.

But that was impossible. Even Harry had records. Even Harry found those names—

Harry.

I grabbed my phone, checked the time: 11:07. I turned to my laptop, entered the site, and waited for it to load. After it had, I typed the address and the password into the only boxes that made sense on a page full of Chinese. The screen changed. An email account opened, everything labeled again in Chinese. I clicked on the folders, clicked on everything with a link. The minutes on the clock slowly turned over. 11:18, 11:19. There was nothing there. Nothing behind the links. Just more Chinese. I glanced at the clock in the corner of the screen. 11:21. I went to a web translator, typed in "draft," and matched the characters to what I saw on the screen. Found the right folder, clicked on it. But there was nothing.

Reload. Reload. Reload—and then, there it was. One draft email. No text. Three attachments, all jpegs. Three photos of sheets of paper arranged on a deeply scratched wooden table. Government issue. And when I zoomed in, I saw the name: Kingman, James Lionel.

I plugged my USB into the laptop and saved the photos. Two minutes later, they were gone.

For hours, I stared at the screen, squinting at the grainy photographs of Captain James Kingman's personnel record, then plotting points on a map, then diving back into the county databases again. Each time, I came up empty-handed.

The personnel record was a model: physical fitness outstanding, educational achievements unsurpassed. Record-breaking advancement in ranks. More medals than I wanted to count. All in eight years of service: 2002 to 2010. But this Kingman, this version of him, had never been to Iraq. I searched online for *that* record, the obituary that stated he had survived in Iraq while his brother died at home in Oklahoma in 2005. The last year I was in Iraq, the last year Havers had been alive. The obit I would swear on a Bible I had seen before—but there was nothing. Not even a historical record.

I searched for Nick, for a Latino called Nick in California or Washington, then searched Victor Calzón, the name I had found in Darren's records, the name that Billy Boykin had used at the prison. Still nothing.

The maps were just scattered dots. No pattern. No rhyme. No reason.

The county databases were blank. There were no companies registered under the names Harry had found less than a week before. There were no records of anything I had seen or heard or written down and saved to the same USB that flashed green every time I dumped more files onto it.

I buried my face in my hands. I scraped my nails through my hair. I pounded my fist on the table. And then I got up and paced back and forth across the cold concrete floor.

The files were wrong. They had to be wrong.

The data was there, the information was there. *It was.* Why else would I have written it in my notebook? Why else would I have gone out to that trailer where Patrick Beale had been tortured? Why would I have gone to the lake house and the airfield? Why would I have gone all the way to see Billy Boykin in that concrete prison? Why would I have gotten Harry to dig up Jimmy King's records at all?

I wouldn't have. *No way.*

I wasn't just crazy.

I couldn't be just crazy.

I couldn't be broken.

Not like that.

In the numbing silence, deep in the back of my head, the whirr of rockets, the staccato burst of M16s, the buzzing of the desert wind began. But at the fringe, at the edge of hearing, a tiny voice spoke: *Think, Camille.* Don't just react. *Think.*

Who could change the records? A lawyer, someone like Jack Wyatt. But that would take too long, that would leave a trace. To hide your tracks, you'd need someone on the inside.

Who had access?

I jerked my head up from my keyboard, scanned the room, scrutinized the dark corners, my nerves on fire. There was the guy in charge of records. His coffee cup—always half empty—was on the wide oak desk by the door, the one with an old desktop computer on it. *Maybe.* Who else? IT. The mousy woman with hair the same dirty gray as her cardigan and glasses thicker than the bottom of a high ball. *Yeah, right.* Who else? The land use guy, who sat in the office next to mine, who had back issues of some hippy magazine stacked on his desk. *No way.* The assessor, my boss, my father's boyhood buddy—an old man who didn't know how to turn on a computer. *No.* Gene. *Ha.* Me.

Me.

I looked down at the screen of my computer. The cursor flashed on and off—green, then nothing—in our old database program. It was at the end of someone's name. Not just someone, a property owner. A name that could have been Gorgon Six LLC the week before. *Off and on.* All I needed was the delete key. *On and off.* And a new map shoved in the file drawer late at night. *Off and on.* And then, *boom.*

No fucking way. No fucking way I was that crazy.

But the records on my laptop—

That was it, that *had* to be it. The laptop. It had logins and passwords, but how hard would they be to break? How hard would it be to hack into the records of a backwoods county with systems that had been around longer than me? Not hard at all. And if someone went looking, if they dug through the ones and zeroes, would they find my fingerprints? Would they see my login? Would they believe me when I said that I didn't do it?

I slammed the laptop shut.

21

The eastern horizon was just starting to lighten when I stopped the car outside Omak: the moon was still out, the stars were fading fast, and the sky was that velvety blue-black you get before the hottest days. The clean scent of the Okanogan at dawn mingled with the funk of gasoline as I filled the tank.

My brain buzzed, trying to make sense of the cover-up —because that's what it was, what it had to be. But *why*? It wasn't like the Sheriff's Office was any closer to the truth. It wasn't like *I* was any closer. Or maybe that was it; maybe I was closer to finding out what had really happened with Patrick. But what did it matter now? I had seen the originals, I knew the records on the system and in the drawers were fake.

But I couldn't *prove* they were fake. I couldn't prove anything. Every time I went looking, at every place I visited, with every person I spoke to . . . it was only me. *Alone.* There was no one to back me up, no one to corroborate what I had seen. Not Darren. Not Harry. Not Sophie. Not even Lyle. If I went to Darren with what I knew, with just my memory and notes about what the record showed, I'd look like just another damaged vet. Seeing things. Hearing things. Believing things that weren't real.

The pump handle clicked; the gasoline stopped flowing.

It was Iraq again. It was Havers again.

I held my head in my hands and sunk to my heels, my ass sliding down the side of Rhonda's little red car.

Could I even trust myself?

The night I sent Sophie away flashed through my head. Had I done something like that before? Had I dreamed something and made it real? *Had I* blacked out and done something terrible? Stolen my own laptop, blown up my own truck, changed the county records? Purged the evidence of Patrick Beale's torture? Trashed the recording he made? Was it me?

I rocked on my heels, slamming my head against the steel quarter panel of the car, my arms crossed over my knees, my fingers digging into my shoulders, my thumb digging into the scar under my left clavicle, willing it to hurt, willing it to scream like it did in the desert, something else to focus on, something else to worry—

The hospital. There were machines everywhere: whirring, beeping, clicking. And it smelled. Bleach and BO and that soap we used—chemical bubblegum. I moved my head to the left, opened my eyes a crack, as far as I could. Bandages. My shoulder was covered in white gauze bandages, wrapped tightly and stained with blood. My blood.

Then.

The hospital again, but this time I was sitting up, this time I was in the first sergeant's office. He was saying something about access to records—no, he was denying me access to records. And I was reporting that something was wrong, that documents were missing, that I just wanted to see if what I remembered was real. I just wanted to know if the other soldiers, the three who were with me when I found Havers, remembered what I did.

He shook his head, glanced at the door. I stood and shut it. He closed his eyes. He sighed, then said, "You know nothing about this, understand? This never happened." And I nodded and hoped. But then, a few minutes later, his brow creased, his eyes darkened. He looked up from the computer and said, "They're dead."

I shook my head, wouldn't believe it.

But the first sergeant said, "Their convoy was attacked. A few weeks ago. All three of them, they're dead."

Then.

The mortuary, the front entrance, a heavy steel door painted gray. Inside, a tiny office with a photo of the president next to the door. Bush the Second. No one there remembered me; I didn't remember them. All new. They were all new, rotated onto base the same day the surgical team extracted a bullet half an inch away from my heart.

Then.

The first sergeant's office again. "I'm not obsessed," I said.

But the first sergeant frowned; he wasn't convinced. "Take it easy, find something else to focus on," he said. "You're almost healed. You'll be off light duty soon."

Then.

A few days later, Major Brittan's beige steel door again. The major himself, sitting behind his scratched desk again, his intense, crackling blue eyes again, ordering me to stop asking questions, to stop interfering. With what, I wanted to know. Was he saying there was an official investigation into Private Havers's death?

"I'm doing you a favor, Sergeant," he said. "You won't like the answers anyway."

I countered, "I want the truth."

The major smiled, a patronizing smile, a Sunday school teacher's smile. "You'll feel better after you get back to work, Sergeant. Work makes you free."

The next morning, a sheet of paper delivered to my desk: new orders, temporary orders, signed by Major Brittan. Germany. No argument. No resistance. So I went to Germany, and for five weeks of rainy mornings, I cut grass and raked leaves and polished brass, my fingers itching for my M16. And for an hour every afternoon, I sat on a scratchy yellow sofa and stared at the wall of an Army psychologist's office, never opening my mouth. Then I went back to the sandbox.

Then.

In Iraq, I was shunned, ignored. I was that big, bad monster, the one we all feared we would become: a broken soldier, battle-crazed and shipped off to the shrinks. No one would talk to me, no one would even look me in the eye. And every record, every document I could get my hands on had been purged. The bare facts about Havers were there, yeah, but nothing else. No flight record for when we went out to retrieve him, no journal entries in the hospital for when we brought him in. It was like his corpse appeared out of nowhere, a bloated gift left on the doorstep of the morgue.

I stopped asking questions, but I didn't stop looking for answers.

Then.

I got the message to go home. The message that my mother had been smeared across the highway.

I don't remember driving from the gas station to the cemetery, but I remember being there at daybreak, staring at Patrick Beale's tombstone. It's small and gray. Granite, I guess. And carved into it are his name and his dates and a baseball diamond. It's out in the open, near the edge of the cemetery, not far from the edge of the bluff. If he had been alive just then, alive at the end of August, he could have stood on his grave and looked out over the valley, looked out at the blue river and the lines of green and gold and red climbing up the flanks of the hills.

The valley had been white when we buried my mother. White and pink and pale, pale green, the color of apple orchards blooming, the color of pear trees unfurling their first leaves.

When we buried Dad, it was electric green, the green of trees pumping sap into branches and leaves and new fruit.

They were there too, rotting under headstones like Patrick Beale's: small and gray, flush with the grass. The white lilies on Patrick's had browned in the sun. And someone had left a six-pack of cheap beer, all the bottles empty except one. I didn't know what was on my parents' graves, whether there were flowers, whether they were real or fake. I didn't remember what was written on their stones—can't remember what I've never seen. But I knew they were there, fifty yards away on the other side of the cemetery, lying in the dirt under the camellia I could see from the parking lot, the camellia my father and my daughter had planted one Saturday long, long before, while I sat alone with a bottle and the memories screaming through my head and my mother's voice echoing, telling me that someday, someday, I would under-stand. Someday I would stop looking for revenge. Someday I would regret—

"What are you doing here?"

I jumped, turned fast, my hand on the holster just inside my jacket, the M9 almost out before I stopped myself, before I realized who was there.

"Todd," I said. *Patrick's brother.* I slid the pistol back into its holster, slid my hand out of my jacket, casually, like I hadn't been about to blow him away.

"I asked you what you're doing here," Todd said. His voice had more menace in it than he could ever deliver.

"Just paying my respects," I said between ragged breaths, fevered blood still racing through my veins. I breathed again, forced myself to focus, to *calm down.*

"Yeah?" he said sarcastically. His face was screwed up, creased with anger. He turned his head to the side, spat on a grave.

"It was a nice funeral," I said. "Lot of people there."

"Why do you even care? You didn't know him."

I frowned, studied the kid in the pale light of the rising sun. He was panting. Sweat shone on his face, dampened his dark blond hair, soaked his gray shirt. Out for a run. I could relate.

I shrugged. "My daughter did."

His jaw tightened, his eyes narrowed. "You didn't even know that until I told you."

"Yes, I did."

"No, *you didn't.* I told you."

I stiffened, clenched my fists.

"Look, kid—"

"You didn't know he was fucking her," Todd snarled. "That's illegal, you know. It's called statutory rape. You didn't care about that."

I ground my teeth, flexed my hands. I tasted the rage—metallic, raw, like fresh blood—rising quickly in my throat. And I wanted to let it go, wanted it so badly. I wanted to rage at him, the little punk, questioning me, condemning me. Rage at Sophie for putting me in that position, for being the little bitch she had been for months—hell, for *years*. Rage at Sophie for being so goddamn stupid, so selfish. So much like me.

Todd stepped forward. He was breathing in short bursts, a vein in his neck throbbing. He felt the rage too. But why?

"Do you even care about Sophie?" he shouted.

He took several more steps forward, got up in my face. My lungs burned; stars burst in my vision. I sucked down air, closed my eyes, and saw Sophie at the funeral, her glossy black hair flashing in the sun as she moved through the crowd. And I saw Todd sitting on the bench. He should have been staring at the casket or his parents or the brown-haired girl next to him, the one who held his hand like she wanted to own it. But he wasn't. He was staring out at the field, at the people. *Wait. No.* He was staring beyond them. He was staring at Sophie.

I opened my eyes and he was glaring at me, his eyes hard and red, vicious, his mouth twisted.

Oh.

"You—" Todd said.

"You hated him, didn't you?" I interrupted.

"*What?*"

"You hated your brother," I said, nodding. "He got Sophie and you hated him for it."

Todd's face reddened. "He was my brother."

"Yeah. Made you hate him even more."

"He was my *brother*," Todd said, anger and resentment surging through every word.

"How did you even know they were dating?" I said. "Sophie can't drive. She couldn't have gone to your parents' place."

"I saw them. In Omak. At his—" He grimaced, realized his mistake too late. "I saw them at school."

"You saw them at his apartment."

Todd's chin jutted forward, his fists shook like an infant's. "I said at school. And at graduation," he added hurriedly, his face lighting up like that information was his ace. "She was at his graduation."

"You said you hadn't been to his apartment."

Todd's eyes narrowed. "No, I didn't."

"You did: at the mart that Monday after I—" I stopped myself abruptly. That wasn't something I was ready to tell. "After Patrick was found."

That's when he threw his punch. Sweat sprayed from his hair, caught the golden early light like a halo. But I caught his fist and pivoted, twisted his arm up and around his back, secured it between his shoulder blades. He struggled, thrashed; I held him tighter.

"He's dead, Todd," I said, my chin lodged into the back of his sweat-slicked neck. "It's over."

Todd laughed then, that kind of thick, throaty laugh like he was really sobbing. So when I let him break free, when he turned on me, I expected to see grief in his eyes. Instead, there was anger there, shining like a hot coal. And gloating. And *pride*.

Todd lunged forward. I stepped back and to the side. He fell to his knees, then shot up like a wrestler and came for more. I caught his fist again, swung him in a wide arc and, my other hand twisting his shoulder, pushed him to the dirt, ground my knee into the small of his back, his face into the thick grass, still damp from the sprinklers.

"What else did you see, Todd?" I barked.

He groaned. *"Fuck you."*

His arm was locked in the crook of my neck; I leaned into it, forced his shoulder until he screamed.

"What else did you see?"

He yelped. "Nothing!"

"Did you see Vic—" I remembered what Sophie called him. "Did you see Nick?"

He shook his head, then thought better of it, said too quickly, "I—I don't know what you're talking about."

"Who else? Who else did you see?" I lessened the pressure on his shoulder. "Sophie? Other girls? King?"

His hips bucked as he tried to throw me off. When he was done screaming that time, when he had learned to submit, he glared at me from the ground, dirt smeared over his face, a gash over his eye seeping blood, hate blazing in his eyes. He still hadn't confirmed anything. Hadn't denied it either.

So I took a stab in the dark. "Lyle?"

Todd glowered, spat.

I took another stab. "Sergeant Moses?"

The corners of Todd's mouth flicked up, a wicked light entered his eyes. Fear? No. Triumph.

My stomach dropped. *He didn't.* But the notes in the files, the ones sitting on Darren's coffee table, swam in my memory. Information about a lab, about trafficking routes. Records for King and Victor and a dozen other men. And an encounter with the terrified criminal informant on August 6, then nothing. Blank. Until August 13, when I found him, wrecked. Patrick was the informant. He had to be. Todd had ratted him out; he'd tattled on his big brother. And he was still smiling about it. *You sick fuck.*

Then: voices. Shouts.

I leapt up, stepped away, pulled my gun out of its holster and didn't bother to hide it.

Todd Beale laughed. He sat back on his haunches, massaged his shoulder, wiped the blood from his eye. And laughed.

"How much do you know?" I said urgently.

Like a golden-haired lizard, Todd swiveled his head toward me. "Where is she?" he parried, razors in his voice. Then he stood, unfolded his wiry arms and skinny legs. "No one at school knows where she is."

Behind him, on the road from town, other kids, all of them in gray shirts like Todd Beale's, were running up the hill. I slid the gun behind my back.

"Who did you tell?" I said, my voice rising, panicking.

"Where is she?" he said more loudly. I glanced at the runners again. A few had crested the hill; the leader was approaching the cemetery gates. Todd followed my eyes, stepped toward me, his rage electrifying the space between us. "Tell me where she is or I'll—"

"Did you know they would kill him?" I said. "Is that what you hoped?"

The lead runner—a female—was in the cemetery now. She was small and slight, her brown hair pulled back in a stubby ponytail. The girl from the funeral, the one holding Todd's hand. And now she was calling his name.

He glanced over his shoulder, shouted cheerfully, buoyantly, "Go on to the Milgards' orchard. I'll catch up in a minute."

The brown-haired girl nodded, waved, a pretty smile blooming on her plain face. She bounded over to the rest of the group, half of them leaning on their knees, then passed them. A couple of the girls broke off, then more followed, and soon there were just a few kids standing around, watching, staring. One of them shouted to Todd, said it was getting late. But Todd waved and yelled that he'd still beat them back to the school.

When they were gone, Todd spun around like a tornado and lunged. But this time, I just tripped him up, watched him sprawl on the ground. When he rolled over, he was at the wrong end of my gun.

"We're done," I said, suddenly exhausted. "*You're* done."

From the ground, his head a few inches from his brother's gravestone, Todd shook his head and grinned. "You have no idea."

* * *

Todd.

I watched him down the barrel of my gun. I watched him run. When he'd gone beyond the orchard down the road, when he'd disappeared, I lowered my weapon.

Todd.

Was it that simple? Patrick was the informant. Todd was the jealous younger brother. Sophie was the chip in their little game.

It couldn't be that simple. If it was that simple, I'd be dead. And even if it *were* that simple, there still wasn't anything to tie it all to Jimmy King. And I knew—knew like I knew my name—that he was holding the strings.

But Todd had given me something important, something vital: my sanity. I couldn't prove he tipped off Jimmy King. I couldn't prove *any-thing*. But his anger and viciousness toward me meant I wasn't wrong, despite what the records didn't say. Now I just needed proof. There had to be something I had missed somewhere out there. Even if they could change the records, they couldn't clean *everything* up that quickly.

I started retracing my steps way back in the county, to the place where Patrick Beale had been tortured. But where a gutted vehicle had been melt-ing into the undergrowth the week before and a double-wide had squatted low, there was nothing. Now there was only an empty clearing dappled with the first rays of the weak morning sun, dotted with patches of brown grass, padded with long pine needles. And there was me: prowling the perimeter, scrutinizing the dirt, and finally crouching in the middle, head in my hands.

I drove again, farther out into the other corner of the county, out to that place with the smart-ass supervisor and what I figured would be a pot farm someday. But it was deserted, the coils of electrical wire and the piles of steel piping for the fence gone. Even the postholes the crew had been drilling when I was there had disappeared into the dust and the tall, dried-out grass. And the house next door, the one the man on the highway had said was his, was deserted, curtains drawn against the blazing sun, the driveway empty, no sign of the battered truck he had been sitting in.

By the time I got to Jeremy Leamon's place, it was getting bad. Adren-aline was ripping through my bloodstream, my brain was buzzing like a wasp's nest. I watched everything, every blade of grass, every branch that jumped in the dry wind sweeping in from the east. In my right hand, I clenched the Beretta M9 I'd bought two weeks after I was discharged, that I had slept with under my pillow until my father took it from me and hid it in his safe. Those were the bad days, the days when he wasn't sure who I'd use it on, when he was afraid it would be on me. The days when

I didn't know when the demons I had tried to leave in Iraq would be back.

And now . . . now, they were coming for me.

I was sure Todd Beale had squealed again, sure he'd made another visit to Victor to tell him I knew too much. I wasn't afraid; that's not why I was waiting. I'm still not sure *what* I was. Ready, I guess. Ready for the attack, ready to fight. Or ready for Victor's or King's or somebody's bullet to crash through the windshield and penetrate my skull. Ready for the darkness. For the end. No matter who pulled the trigger.

I looked down. My hand—tanned and dirty skin, ragged fingernails—clutching the Beretta was steady, but my trigger finger twitched. I stared at the black barrel, the rich, brown wood on the grip, the gold lettering . . . It was beautiful, in a way. A beautiful way to die.

Oh my God.

Slowly, fearfully, I put the gun down and withdrew my hand.

I was cracking up.

I took a deep breath, all the way to the bottom of my lungs, and glanced up at the house beyond my windshield.

Cracking up like Jeremy Leamon.

I swung the car door open, stepped out, and filled my lungs again and again with that dry, hot air that smelled like pines and dust and fertilizer. Like the Okanogan. Like home. I closed my eyes and leaned into the wind.

I wouldn't end it, but they still could. They could kill me. Then. There.

No.

They could try.

My eyes flew open. The hills in the distance were golden, studded with narrow trees, black and green like onyx and emeralds. The sky was blisteringly blue. And I was alive. For now. For the fight.

*   *   *

That night, Mike Havers finally came through for me.

I had asked him to send copies of his brother's records: personnel, medical, whatever he had. I had told him I wanted to see if anything rang a bell, if something would jog my memory. I wanted to fill in the gaps. I wanted to see if I remembered what was real.

The personnel record Mike sent was unremarkable: boot camp at Benning, training at Fort Sam. Deployed less than three months later. Service record terminated not long after.

The medical record was brief and ended abruptly with a death certificate: cerebral hemorrhage. I squeezed my eyes shut, opened them, and looked again.

Decedent: Paul Kerry Havers
Rank: Private
DOB: 04/29/86
DOD: 08/13/05
Cause of death: cerebral hemorrhage

Not asphyxiation.

I paged through the document again, but there was nothing else except his boot camp physical and a round of vaccines before he deployed. The trauma I recalled, the viciously inflicted damage I had seen so clearly in my dreams, was nowhere.

But records can lie.

No one would tell me if I was right about Patrick Beale, but someone could tell me if I was right about Private Havers: Major Jack Brittan, the man who had gotten me reassigned for my own good, who had said that work would *set me free.*

Online, Brittan's obituary said he was killed when a mortar hit the base. The article by his hometown newspaper said he was missing in action, presumed dead. His name was on the official list of the fallen.

The first sergeant then. But an obit said he had died of natural causes the year before, in the hospital in his hometown in Florida.

The pretty undertaker? But I never knew his name, or that of the doc who did the autopsy. And neither one was listed in the file.

Goddamnit.

The chair crashed to the floor when I rocked to my feet. Papers were spread over the surface of the table: I swept them onto the floor. Maps were displayed on my laptop screen: they flickered and faded to black when I threw the machine against the wall. Photos I had pulled off Sophie's phone, stills from the video camera, shots I had taken since the whole thing started were sorted and stacked tidily—I shoved them into one pile, picked them up, held them above my head, and—

The photos.

We all had photos in Iraq. We all *took* photos too, back in the day when you'd use a disposable point-and-click and send the whole thing home. To your family.

I lowered my arms, stared at the photos in my hands. Mike Havers had said he hadn't heard the name Jimmy or Kingman or King. Said his brother didn't know any officers, just a bunch of infantry guys who took him out to the field to shoot up shit. But maybe he had *seen* King and just didn't know who he was looking at.

I dropped the stack back onto the table and pawed through the images until I found the still from the mart's video that I had left on the table for Sophie to find the week before. Then I retrieved the laptop, prayed silently while the screen righted itself, then pulled up that moment on the video record and emailed a screen shot to Mike Havers: *Do you recognize these men?*

Ten long minutes later, Mike Havers responded with another photo, a cell phone photo of an old glossy of three guys in cheap sunglasses and brown tees standing in front of a blown-out truck.

Got this the day they told us he was dead, the next message said. *The one on the right. He your man?*

Even with the sunglasses, even with his BDU blouse off, even without his name tape stretched across his chest, there was no way the tall blond bastard with his hand on Private Havers's shoulder wasn't Captain James Kingman.

That's him, I typed. *That's who murdered your brother.*

22

Dawn.

I stood in front of the window, one hand on the kitchen counter, one hand around a cooling cup of coffee, watching the sun rise trembling and furious and raw over the Res.

It was time.

I had been avoiding it—I knew I had. I kept telling myself I needed a plan, needed a strategy. Kept telling myself it wasn't likely anyway: one sighting of that black and red Suburban meant nothing. It didn't have the same weight as a property record I could tie back to Jack Wyatt, which didn't exist. And, hell, I hadn't met a trigger-happy sentry at any of the other properties, so that was another good reason to save the place out in the foothills for last.

I finally found the driveway just after noon. I had gone looking official, in case the sentry was posted during the day, in case they had tightened security even more. And if that strategy failed, I had decided to storm the gates, so to speak, just gun the engine of Rhonda's sedan—which they hadn't seen me in before—up the hill and take my chances, bad as they were.

After I turned off the road, I pulled my ball cap down low over my eyes, checked that the strap of my holster was loose, the safety was off my Beretta, my county ID was still tucked under my thigh. Then I took it slow down the gravel drive, slow and respectful. Let them get a shot of me on the video cameras I was sure were hung out there somewhere. Let them get a shot of the binder I'd casually left on the dash. Let them see the county seal and the inch-high letters that spelled out "Okanogan County Assessor's Office" in gold across the front.

It had been dark the first time I was there, so I hadn't noticed that the first part of the drive was surrounded by brown fields studded with wheat way past its harvest date, the stalks bent over from the weight of the golden brown kernels that had spilled out of the seed heads to litter the ground. To the right of the drive, an irrigator stood idle in the center of the field, like its operator had abandoned it mid-season, mid-thought.

Past the field, a thick stand of trees began: ponderosas, their long green needles tipped with brown, caked with dust. But the drive had been graveled recently: the thin trail that rose behind Rhonda's little red sedan disappeared within moments. Any time now, any second, I'd stop at the sentry post, give the asshole my line about county business, wait for him to radio to the guys in charge, learn if they recognized me, discover whether I was likely to be shot down that day.

I turned at a slight bend in the drive and slammed on the brakes.

The car ground to a stop inches away from a tree lying across the drive like a dead drunk. Off to my right, a few feet back into the woods, was its stump, split and splintered, jagged and damp. It was a new wound, a new carcass.

Damn. I tapped my fingers on the steering wheel. I tried to think of a plan, a wise alternative, but my sleep-starved brain was blank, empty as a chalkboard in summertime. I needed something that would avoid their sight lines, just in case someone was watching. Or . . . I could give them a show.

I killed the engine and stepped out of the car, binder in hand, Beretta in its holster under a light jacket. I inspected the tree, walked up and down it and back to the car. I opened the binder on the hood, made a couple of notes, shut it. Then I opened the door, tossed the binder onto the passenger seat, and grabbed a roll of toilet paper from the back. I looked left, right, and then plunged into the woods, toilet roll held prominently in my hand. But I didn't stop at the first bush or the second; I kept going deeper and deeper and then farther up the hill, skirting the gravel drive as closely as I dared.

There was no note in my binder about the flattened hut, the shards of lumber just visible through the lower branches of the fallen pine, or the bite of a chainsaw on its trunk. There was nothing about the CB whip that someone had too hastily tried to cover with fallen leaves a few feet back into the woods. And there sure as hell wasn't a note about the tiny black video camera wired to one of the branches that pointed straight at the sky. Why give them anything interesting to read in my absence?

Fifteen minutes. I figured I had fifteen minutes to see as much as I could of whatever the sentry had been guarding. I could explain that much time with a strategically placed pile of crumpled toilet paper, and I could explain my presence away from it as confusion, disorientation: *Sorry, sir. I guess I went too far into the woods. Didn't want to give anyone a show.* It would probably work for a little while, long enough to get out of there. And maybe it would be worth it.

I had been slogging through the undergrowth for five minutes when I saw a clearing up ahead. I hunkered down, crept closer. Trees and scrub gave way to a shady opening about a hundred feet across, but a lot longer than that. Within it sat a long, low, metal-sided building with a camera above a solid metal door. A wooden barn several yards away had cracked windows and weather-beaten wood, but no camera as far as I could see. The clearing was still, no sign of any people, sentries or otherwise.

Cautiously, I picked my way around the perimeter to the rear of the metal shed. Twenty feet away I got my first whiff: chemicals, thick and toxic, blown out by a line of fans that studded the building up near the roofline. My eyes watered, the inside of my nose burned. Meth—had to be. So this was the new cookhouse. I snapped a few photos, but that was all I could do. There were no gaps in the walls, no windows. And there was no way I was going to walk into that camera's view.

I retreated to the rear of the barn, then sidled along the side wall to the first of the windows. I crouched down, positioned the viewfinder of my phone's camera in the corner where it wasn't likely to be seen by anyone inside. The screen showed the view: roof beams strung with spider webs sagging under a thick layer of dirt, and below them, a black Dodge pickup and a black and red Chevy Suburban. In the corner of the screen, just barely visible, was a floor-to-ceiling cabinet. I tilted the phone to see more of the rear wall: more cabinets—a whole wall of them, in fact. But only one was locked tight with a shiny new padlock.

I tested the window, but it was wedged tight. So were all the others on that wall. I skirted the backside of the barn, peered around the corner and—*shit*. The windows on that side of the barn were within view of the camera on the other building. Which meant that the front of the barn was also within view. I retreated, tested the windows again, and when that failed, snapped several photos through them. *Better than nothing.*

That's when I heard the familiar crackle of static on a CB radio, the familiar thump of a steel-toed boot on packed dirt.

I halted, crouched. Waited.

A male voice drawled on the radio, but the volume was too low to make out what was said. There was no response, just more footsteps. Then, a moment later, the jangling of keys.

I darted to the other side of the barn, the one within camera range, threw myself to the ground, and squinted through a clump of tall, brown grass out into the clearing.

A tall kid in jeans that billowed around his bony legs and a dirty yellow T-shirt that hung loose off his shoulders stood at the door to the metal building. He selected a key, slid it into the lock. He looked right, looked left. I lay in the dirt perfectly still, perfectly motionless; his eyes slid right over the barn and I risked adjusting my phone to try to get a photo. He turned the key, opened the door outward, and paused. There was another transmission over the radio, this one clearer, though I still heard only two words: "county" and "visitor." I held my breath.

The guy in yellow lifted the radio to his mouth and said, "This is Donovan. I'll take care of it—gimme a minute."

Like hell I would.

I ran.

*　*　*

Closer. I was getting closer.

On my phone, I had photos of the truck and the Suburban, even a few of the guy called Donovan. But time was short. I had been careful to take Rhonda's car and I had worn a ball cap pulled down low, but someone would recognize me. Maybe not immediately, but they would. I said I was paranoid. I was—still am—paranoid. But I felt this in my bones, knew in the pit of my stomach that this *was* personal and that someone *was* determined to shut me down. I didn't know why they hadn't already killed me, but I knew I had a target on my back now.

Omak.

The brakes squealed when I tapped them on the hill on the way in and again at every stop sign on the shady residential streets on the west side of downtown. Kids in new clothes for the new school year strolled down the streets in threes and twos and on their own. They were mostly young, twelve or thirteen. A dirty, dented brown hatchback passed, a couple of older kids in the front seat. The girl in the passenger seat looked like Sophie—long black hair, creamy brown skin—but her face was clean, glowing, her hair pulled back in a tight ponytail. And instead of a skimpy top, she wore a soccer jersey.

A crossing guard in an orange reflective vest held up a limp yellow flag, carelessly entered the crosswalk. I slammed on the brakes and felt them give way before they grabbed. The guard—a pimply, skinny kid who probably waved a flag around just to feel important—shot me a dirty look. But I was busy watching the kids loitering outside the high school across the street. They were just kids, flirting and talking and carrying on. Glad to be back after the summer break, gladder to be done for the day. I had been there once—there, standing right where they were standing now, under that tree, next to that bike rack. And my daughter—

The crossing guard was shouting. The horn of the car behind me blared. I lifted my foot from the brake; the car behind me jumped, swerved around me. A kid with scruffy blond hair and a football jersey leaned out the window, shouting. A couple of girls on the other side of the intersection jumped back onto the curb, yelled after him.

I coasted through the intersection, took it slow past the high school, then punched the gas and beat it out of town.

Forty minutes later, I pulled into the back lot of my mart in Little Falls. Rhonda was waiting for me on a plastic green and white folding chair set in the middle of the gravel lot, her face glowing like coal. She started yelling at me before I stopped the car, closed the distance to the driver's door before I had it open, and held her hand out for the keys. I dropped them into her palm.

She threw the keys of the Bronco against the wall of the building while chewing me out for stealing her car. "Borrow for a couple of hours doesn't mean a couple of days, Camille!"

I closed the driver's door of her little red sedan and walked to the building, stooped to retrieve the keys to the truck. She kept screaming about how I was supposed to call and tell her when she'd get her car back. How I was supposed to at least tell someone that I was still alive.

I nodded as I got to my feet and said, "Alright, I will. Next time."

She sputtered, declared that there would be no next time, that I had a kid to think of, demanded to know where Sophie was, anyway.

At the door to the apartment, my shoulders tensed as I inserted the key into the deadbolt. Quietly, I said, "In Michigan. With my aunt."

That shut Rhonda up, at least for a moment. But as I slipped inside the door, she called after me.

"Your boss has called three times this week. He wants to know if you're ever gonna do any more inspections. He wants to know if you quit or he should fire you."

I stopped just long enough to say, "Tell him I'll call him back." Then I shut the door.

Upstairs in the apartment, I dropped my keys on the table, opened the windows, and collapsed onto the sofa. I don't know how long I sat there, head in my hands, staring at the cheap, fuzzed carpet, but when I looked up, it was almost dark.

Snatches of television—some sitcom with a manic laugh track—drifted through the open windows with the smoky, thick scent of burgers grilling over charcoal. My stomach growled. But the apartment was empty. Silent. Stale. On the table, my notes were shoved into folders. In the kitchen, the counters were bare. There was just me, breathing in the dark. Just like it had always been. Before Sophie, anyway.

The blank white door to her room was shut; I hadn't gone in since she'd left. But now I crept inside, softly, tentatively, like it was a holy shrine. I picked up a T-shirt she'd tossed aside and held it to my chest. I sat down on her unmade bed and stared out the window and watched the shadows of the houses across the street lengthen. And then I pulled my phone out of my pocket and dialed.

She answered on the last ring, out of breath, distracted. She wasn't happy to hear my voice, not that she should have been. I'd abandoned her again, left her with an aunt she barely knew. Hell, I hadn't even spoken to her since I'd sent her away. And before that . . . before that, she'd been at the wrong end of my rifle.

"How are you?" I asked, hesitantly.

"Fine," she said.

"Everything going okay with Aunt Martha?"

"Yeah."

Silence. I listened to her breathe.

"What do you want?" she said eventually. But she wasn't angry, not even annoyed. She sounded bored, like she had much better things to do.

"Nothing," I said. Then, before she could say anything else, before she could hang up, "What do you, uh . . . what do you think of Ann Arbor?"

"Oh, it's," Sophie said distantly, distractedly. "It's nice, I guess."

"Have you met any other kids yet?"

"Kids?" she said, like she was insulted by the very term. "Yeah, I've met lots of *people*."

"Oh. I didn't realize classes had started."

Silence, but I could almost hear the wheels turning in her brain. "Well . . . maybe? The ones I've met are, like, eighteen. Maybe they start earlier?"

"Tell me about them," I prompted. "These kids you've met. Tell me about them."

"They're just, you know, people."

"And they're college students?"

"Some of them," she said defensively. "Yeah, one of them's a history major."

"That's a life skill."

She laughed a little. Back then, she had this laugh that was buoyant, but deep and strong. A laugh that didn't hold back. It was a lot like her grandmother's. My mother's. But then there was other laughter, other voices in the background, indistinct, muffled, like a party someone was trying to keep quiet.

"What's going on? It sounds like there are people over."

"What? No, no one's here. It's just the TV," she said, then shouted away from the phone, "Hey, can you turn it down?" There was another voice then, a male voice, gruff and angry. Sophie, her voice soft, submissive, answering, "Yeah, sure. I'll just—I'll just go outside."

A screen door opened, the metal latch clattering, then the door squeaked and shut with a bang. Her heels—bare, I would have guessed—thudded softly on wooden boards that whined even under her slight weight. A hush fell.

"Who was that?" I said.

"No one," she snapped. But at least she didn't tell me it was the TV.

"Martha have a boyfriend?" I asked, laughing a little despite—or maybe because of—the growing tension.

"What?" Sophie said, distracted. "Uh, yeah. Sure."

For a few seconds, I listened to the whoosh of her breath on the phone's receiver. She was breathing fast, like I'd caught her in the middle of something. In the background, the wind sighed and a hawk screamed and—

"Hey, what happened to all the numbers on your phone?" Sophie asked suddenly.

"What do you mean?" I said, startled.

"The numbers. You know, like my phone number and Grandpa's."

"I don't save them," I said carefully. "Why?"

"Oh," Sophie said. "So you, um, you know everyone's numbers by heart?"

"Yeah, it helps me to remember," I said. "Why?"

"Oh, nothing," she said dismissively. "It's just that someone's been calling today. It's a local number, but I didn't answer it."

"A local number?" I said, confused.

"Yeah, I mean, local back home. You know, five-oh-nine—whatever."

"Oh," I said. "But you answered when I called."

"Well, yeah. I recognize your work cell."

I frowned, glanced around her room. There were photos of her friends tacked to the walls. A few paperback books—pages splayed, spines bent beyond repair—were on the floor with her dirty clothes. Her ridiculous pink backpack sat open on the floor, a couple of glossy new spiral-bound notebooks spilling out of it. My frown deepened, my mind spun.

"Who do you need to get ahold of?" I asked.

"No one," she said quickly. "I was just—I was just wondering who it was. They just kept calling and calling."

"Huh," I said. "What was the number?"

"Just a sec," she said, then recited the number, her voice distant like she was reading it off the phone. *Darren.* It was his cell number. But he knew Sophie had my personal phone. He *knew* I only had my county cell. Why was he calling Sophie?

I stood up, paced the room.

"Do you recognize it?" Sophie asked.

"No," I lied. Then I halted, staring at the shelf above Sophie's desk. The photo she had had on her phone—the phone that had been run over—was tacked to the edge of the shelf. Except it was bigger than it had been on her phone. In the copy on the shelf, Patrick and Sophie stared out, their eyes glazed—just drunk, I hoped—but in the background, other kids were laughing and drinking from red plastic cups. And far behind Patrick and Sophie, standing in the yellow pool of somebody's back porch light, was a kid who looked very, very familiar.

"I saw Todd Beale yesterday," I said, interrupting Sophie's attempt to hang up.

Silence.

"Who?" Sophie said, cautiously.

"Todd Beale."

"Oh. Where?"

"At the cemetery."

"Oh," she said, like she was happy he was there.

"You go to school with him, don't you?"

"Yeah. He, uh, he tutored me in Spanish last year."

"You ever hang out with him?" I took the photo off the shelf, studied it under the light. "Socially, I mean. Maybe when you were seeing Patrick."

Silence. Then Sophie said quietly, quiet as a mouse, "No."

Really.

"What's he like?" I said.

"Okay, I guess."

"He and Patrick hang out a lot? Go to the same parties, maybe?"

"I—I don't know."

Sure.

"You know, I never asked you," I said casually, "how did you meet Patrick anyway? Did Todd introduce you to him?"

"No." Then she added, irritably, "Anyway, why does it matter? Patrick's dead."

"I thought—"

"You thought *what*?"

I had thought a lot of things. About how I was shocked that my daughter had been fucking a nineteen-year-old who had his own place, how she had been out partying all the time, with God knew what substances flowing through her bloodstream. How she had gotten so cold, so angry, and so wild. But at that moment, the only thing I was thinking was how messed up it was that she didn't care that Patrick Beale was dead. That she had put his death into a box, tied it with a neat bow, and put it on the shelf with all her other memories and dreams. That she had taken so much after me.

"Nothing," I lied.

The screen door on Sophie's end of the line opened again, then she muffled the phone, exchanged a few words with a male. I strained to hear, to figure out if it was the same voice I had heard a few minutes before, but he was too quiet or too far from the phone. And again, Sophie's voice was soft, submissive, like when she was little and she wanted something. But this time, I noticed the fear.

"Who is that?" I demanded.

Sophie didn't respond, but then I heard all I needed to hear: from somewhere inside the building she had walked out of—a laugh, a unique laugh that was shrill and braying like a donkey that had been sucking down helium. A stoner's laugh. A loser's laugh. I knew that laugh. And it didn't belong in Michigan.

"So, tell me about Ann Arbor," I said, careful in case I was wrong. "What do you like about the campus?"

"Um . . ." She stalled, panic saturating her voice. "It's, uh, really green."

Like every college campus in every photo everywhere.

"What do you think about Weatherford Hall?" I said, baiting her. "Aunt Martha shows everyone Weatherford Hall. It's her favorite building on campus."

"Yeah, it's great," Sophie said. "Really, um, classic and stuff. Great columns."

She was lying. There is no Weatherford Hall at the University of Michigan. At least there hadn't been when I'd spent a semester there.

"Where are you, Sophie?" I said, my voice low, threatening.

"At Aunt Martha's place," she said quickly. "In Ann Arbor."

"Her house is in Milan."

"Yeah, I mean—I meant *near* Ann Arbor."

"Is she still up?" I said nicely, almost syrupy. "I'd like to say hello."

"*No!*" Sophie said. "No, she's already in bed."

"So who was watching TV?"

"She was. She was watching TV, but she went up to bed right after I went outside. That was her at the door a minute ago. That was her saying good night."

That, at least, was almost believable. Under other circumstances, anyway. "Alright."

"And I should go to bed too." Sophie yawned dramatically. "It's late."

"Alright," I said again, squeezing the word through clenched teeth, thin lips.

"So, good night." Then as though she was asking permission—something she never did—she added, "Okay?"

"Yeah. Good night."

I called my aunt, called her even though it was almost eleven in Michigan. She was surprised to hear my voice and still up, still watching the news. But Sophie wasn't. And no one was laughing.

* * *

I got to the Beale house a little before ten. I had already called all of Sophie's friends, the ones I knew about anyway. No one knew anything, or at least nothing they would tell me. Maybe Sophie had pulled the wool over their eyes as well, spun them a story just like she had for my aunt.

I got it all from Martha that night. How Sophie had called a few hours after my panicked call the night my truck had gone up in flames. She'd told Martha I'd calmed down and changed my mind. We were both okay, but I was busy with the mart and finding a new truck, and Martha shouldn't worry. How Sophie had even called her again the next day, sounding sweet and upbeat, and they had talked for fifteen minutes about nothing in particular, just like old friends. How Sophie reminded Martha so much of me, and I should be careful of her and keep her close. I should remember the choices my own mother had made and learn from them. I thanked her and hung up, her words ringing in my ears like a funeral bell.

I called the airline, tried to pry out of them whether Sophie had ever even boarded the plane to Detroit. They wouldn't tell me anything—privacy laws or some shit like that required a birth certificate and someone to review it, to check that I was really her mother. But there was no time for that, even if I had had a way to send it to them electronically. I called the cellular company, but the phone I had given Sophie was too old to track.

Then I called Lyle. I called him more times that night than I ever had before. He never answered. And I called Sophie, but the phone went straight to voicemail, my voicemail—*Camille Waresch. Leave a message*— over and over again.

I didn't call Darren or any of his buddies at the Sheriff's Office. Not about this. Not about exactly what he had warned me about, exactly what he had told me to not bring on myself. Besides, I wasn't even sure I could trust him. He had withheld information from me, lots of it, and all the evidence I had given him—Patrick's USB drive, the stuff at that trailer out in the middle of nowhere—had gone missing. Where did he stand anyway? Whose side was he fucking on?

When I had run out of ideas, when there was nothing left except blinding rage and fear, I got in the Bronco and tore down the highway.

Ed Beale answered the door in a threadbare yellowed undershirt and a pair of old shorts. Behind him, the blue glow of a television danced, a sitcom droned, a fan buzzed. He was surprised to see anyone on his doorstep at that time of night, even more surprised it was me. But he was shocked when I asked to speak with Todd.

"I don't think that's a good idea, Camille," he said and shook his head. "We all been through a lot and—"

"It isn't about Patrick, Ed," I said. "It's about Sophie. My daughter."

Ed frowned. "Todd don't know Sophie."

"He does. He tutored her in Spanish last year."

"Who is it, Ed?" Christine—her voice tired, drained—said from further inside the house.

"You know Camille Waresch's girl, Sophie?" Ed shouted over his shoulder, but he kept his eyes on me.

"Sure. Patrick—" she said, then faltered. Somewhere beyond the living room, something splashed, a faucet was turned on, then off. "Patrick knew her," Christine said faintly.

"See?" Ed said. "She was Patrick's friend."

"Look, I know he's here," I said impatiently. I pointed out past the bushes at the little blue sedan parked beside the driveway. "His car is right there."

Ed stared at me for a few long seconds, sizing me up, I guess. I'd never given him any cause for alarm, but having a child taken changes you, makes you more wary, more scared. More protective of what you've got left.

But he turned his head again and shouted over his shoulder: "Todd! Come out here a minute."

The sitcom went to commercial. The faucet turned on again, turned off.

"Todd!" Ed shouted again, louder.

When Todd replied, it was somewhere deep within the house. "What is it? I've got an exam tomorrow."

"Come out here a minute, I said. You got a visitor."

"Alright, alright. I'm coming."

A minute, maybe more, passed before I heard footsteps. Ed heard them too; he left the door open, stepped away, went back to the living room and turned down the volume on the TV. Todd appeared in the doorway.

"Ms. Waresch, hi," he said, his voice all light and cheerful, like the perfect kid on a sitcom. Or a psychopath in a horror film. Even his eyes were smiling. "How are you?"

I narrowed my eyes. "Fine."

"What can I do for you, Ms. Waresch?"

I stepped away from the stoop, hoping he would follow me outside. He didn't.

I mirrored his smile, clenched my fist. "Have you seen Sophie lately, Todd?" I said.

He thought for a moment, his nose screwed up like a baby that smelled its own fart. "Don't think so, Ms. Waresch. I don't think I've seen her at school at all this term." He laughed lightly, then smiled. "Not that we've been back more than a couple of days!"

"And an exam so soon?" I said icily.

His smile widened. "AP U.S. History."

"Your brother ever take that class?" I said viciously.

Anger—no, disgust—flashed across his face, was replaced by a plastic imitation of grief. "I don't want to talk about Patrick."

That was the end of the line.

"Listen, boy," I said, my voice low, a maternal growl. "Where have they got her? Where is my daughter?"

"I'm sorry," he said. "I haven't seen Sophie all summer."

"Where are your little friends hiding out?"

"I don't know what you mean. My friends all live at home," he said, then paused. "With their parents."

"Don't fuck with me, kid." I shifted my weight. "Tell me where King and Nick are."

"Who?" he simpered.

I stepped closer, got right up in his face. "If they've done anything to her, I swear I'll—"

"You've made a mistake," he said slowly, clearly, and not for my benefit.

Then my gun was in his face, millimeters from his mouth. I could feel the trigger pressed into the pad of my index finger, feel the blood pounding in my temples. In his face, deep in his eyes, the devil was back.

"Tell me," I breathed.

He smirked. My index finger twitched. A grin spread across his face, daring me to do it, to shoot him on the front doorstep of his parents' home.

Footsteps.

"Todd, get back to your studying." Christine's voice from beyond the door, in the hall. "I'll talk to Camille."

Todd flashed one last smile. "Nice to see you, Ms. Waresch."

By the time Christine appeared in the doorway, the Beretta was tucked into my holster, but I was still shaking with anger.

"Camille?" Christine said, wiping her hands on a dish towel. "What's going on with Sophie? She all right?"

"Ask your son," I shouted, leaning against the doorframe with one hand, one foot on the stoop, the other on the dirt, caught between going after him, beating the information out of him, and . . . and nothing.

I stepped back from the door, focused on Christine—Christine in white shorts and a water-splashed blue tank top with ruffles at the hem.

"And while you're at it," I said, more quietly, but no less angrily, "ask him what he told Patrick's other friends."

Christine shook her head. Strands of her graying bangs stuck to her sweaty, creased brow. "I don't understand. What friends?"

I looked her in the eye. "Ask him who killed your boy, Christine."

Her face blanched, the dish towel hung limply in her hand. Then I heard her say, her voice small and tight, "Why?"

But I didn't answer. I was already gone.

23

"**O**pen the door, Lyle!" I shouted, beating the door with my fists.

When he answered—his eyes bloodshot, his hair tangled—I pushed him aside, back against a wall. I wanted to take him by the throat, to shake him like a rag doll, but I kept my fists low and bared my teeth instead.

"Where is she?"

He fumbled for the door handle, eyes screwed tightly against the morning light. "Jesus, would you close the door?"

Instead, I slammed it into his shoulder, into the wall. Plaster showered onto the frayed brown carpeting.

"What the hell are you doing?" he yelled, clutching his shoulder. "I've got a deposit on this place."

I grabbed the torn collar of his T-shirt, clutched it in my fist, and leaned into him. "Where is my daughter, Lyle?"

"How the hell should I know? I took her to the airport. You said she was in Michigan."

"Bullshit," I said. "I heard you last night. I heard your ridiculous fucking laugh on her phone."

"What?"

"*You heard me.*"

"It wasn't me. I was down at the casino last night, *all* night. Go ask. George Entenman was at the bar."

"*It was you!*" I shouted.

"Hey!" he shouted back at me. He was wide awake now. "Maybe she made some friends out there. Maybe she was out with some friends."

I could have told him everything. I could have told him I knew damn well she had never shown up in Michigan. I could have told him I knew about his buddies, about Captain Jimmy King and Nick, who was really Victor Calzón from California. And Todd. That I knew Sophie was in deep.

"I don't care how you're involved in this, Lyle," I growled. "I don't give a fuck what your angle is. Just tell me where she is."

He shook his head, his eyes disbelieving and passive, like this was all some big joke. "You're insane, Sis," he said. "You've gone fucking insane."

Maybe I had, maybe I hadn't. But he knew—I *knew* he knew—and I wasn't going to stop until he told me.

"Whoa," he said, his eyes suddenly wide and fearful. He raised his arms up the wall like a stinking crucifixion. "Okay, I get it. I get you. Just take that piece out of my ribs and I'll tell you. Okay?"

I moved the M9 an inch, but I kept my grip on Lyle's shoulder, pinned to the wall.

"You know that guy, Nick?" he said quietly.

I nodded, didn't add that I knew more about him than that.

"There's this place up in the mountains."

"She's there?"

"Maybe. I don't know." He shrugged and I thought about how easy it would be to break his clavicle. "But they're close, you know?"

"As close as he was to Patrick?"

"No," he said awkwardly, then blushed even more awkwardly. "I mean, they're *really* close."

"He's fucking my daughter?"

Lyle shrugged.

"And what about Jimmy King?" I said.

Uncertainty distorted Lyle's face, like an abused puppy that's been offered a bone.

"Is he up in the mountains too?" I said.

Lyle shrugged again but couldn't talk fast enough when I pressed the muzzle of my gun under his rib cage. "Yeah, it's King's place. There are parties sometimes."

"Like the one last night?" I purred.

And for a moment, it seemed he would trip up. But, then: "I was at the casino."

"You said."

"I don't know nothing about a party last night."

"Or whether my daughter was there?"

He shook his head. I relaxed my grip, let him breathe. His eyes were flat and pale, empty, but knowing, like a feral dog's. He breathed raggedly at first, but after a while he was calm again, pliant.

"How well did King know Patrick, Lyle?"

He blinked quickly, narrowed his eyes, then tried to hide the wariness there. He turned his head, rubbed the stubble on his jaw with his knuckles. "Pretty good, I guess."

"Did he work for him?"

"Sometimes," Lyle said, like everyone knew. Like it was no big deal.

"What did he do?"

Lyle shrugged.

"I know Patrick pissed him off," I said.

A chunk of Lyle's hair, greasy, dirty blond, fell from where it was tucked behind his ear. He reached up, brushed it back again, but then he turned his head, stared blindly into the brown living room.

"And I know someone else told King something that pissed him off even more," I added, careful not to say too much. Lyle raised his eyebrows, but he didn't look back at me.

"Did he do it, Lyle?"

He looked at me then, but his face was a mask: carefully blank, and beneath it, something more. Always something more.

"I don't know what you're talking about," he said.

"Did he kill him, Lyle? Did King kill Patrick?"

"Why would he do that?" Lyle's voice was leaden, a little leaden smile on his lips.

"What is he going to do to Sophie?" I said, my voice thick in my throat.

"She's fine," he said. "She's a big girl."

"*She's fifteen,*" I snarled.

Lyle shrugged.

My elbow hit him first, under the chin, snapped his mouth closed. The butt of the M9 followed, caught him beside his left eye on the way down the wall, sent him sprawling.

I wanted to scream at him that I knew what King was doing, that I knew what he, Lyle, was doing. I wanted to tell him that I knew he knew.

And I wanted to ask, to know, how he could stand by with Sophie, his precious little niece, in the crosshairs.

Instead, I pinned him, ground his fresh wound into the dirty carpet and bruised his tender neck with the muzzle of my gun.

"Where are they?"

*　*　*

Lyle gave me directions, landmarks, claimed he didn't know the address. It didn't matter; I already knew where he was sending me. And by the time I got there, I had sunk down into that blackness you get in the field—if you're lucky, that is. It blocks out everything else. Morality. Justice. Mercy. In the blackness, there is only the mission. Out there, in Iraq, Afghanistan, Somalia, wherever, sinking down into that blackness is how you survive. That day, that night, it was the only reason *anyone* survived.

*　*　*

09:03 PDT.

I pitched the Bronco in a stand of trees half a mile away from the property line. My brown jeans faded into the shadows. My long-sleeve green camo faded into the branches. The CamelBak I had strapped on had enough water for twenty-four hours; same for the pouch of energy bars. Would it take that long? I had no idea. I had no idea what was waiting for me, whether I had finally gotten close enough to kill, whether there would be a patrol or a guard or just rabid Captain Jimmy, waiting for me with a shotgun. Maybe it was a trap; maybe it was my day of reckoning. I didn't care. There was only the mission. There was only Sophie.

I hiked in along the boundary lines, staying as close to due south and as far from any buildings as I could. The big Okanogan complex fire was still a couple of years off, and the trees in the foothills were still green, lush, the ground still thick with long, thin pine needles dried to a rusty orange. And it was quiet, so quiet. Just the whispering of the breeze in the branches overhead, the screams of hawks riding the thermals, the manic chittering of chipmunks in the undergrowth. The steady swish-swish-swish of fabric as I climbed higher and higher.

10:12 PDT.

I had been hiking for an hour when I finally heard footsteps up the hill. I retraced my steps, took cover. The patrol was young, green: wearing a brown T-shirt and BDUs that had never been stained with anyone's blood or sweat or piss, an AR-15 resting on his shoulder like he was in the god-damn color guard. Swaggering, with a cigarette hanging out of the corner of his mouth. Playing soldier.

And while I watched, hunkered down in prone, my M9 at the ready, I wondered why Jimmy King would bother to set a patrol who didn't even swing his head in my direction as he passed. But that's the reflex, the Army reflex. You set a watch, you set a patrol. You protect what you got, even if your protection is just a dirtbag kid. *So why do you need a patrol, Captain Jimmy? What do you have back in those woods that you need a brat with a gun in the middle of nowhere? How much you got in that shed, Captain Jimmy?*

I picked up the pace.

11:19 PDT.

I carried on through the trees, headed southwest. The GPS I had taken from the county office indicated there was about a mile left until I reached the vicinity of the barn and the shed I had seen the previous day. The barn was on the county map, two houses about a half mile away were, too, but the shed wasn't. With a patrol out that far, who knew what else I would find on the way.

I picked my way slowly up the hill, stopping frequently to listen. The second and third patrols I saw weren't much better than the first. Seemed King kept the good ones, the ones with a clue, for the gates. Or maybe I'd find my trigger-happy friend from the other night lurking closer to the lab. Either way, I had decided to go in under cover of darkness—this was the time to assess the field, to listen, to find out what I was up against. And so far, I was smiling.

12:27 PDT.

I located the barn and the shed. The black Dodge was still there, but where the Suburban had been the day before, there was only an oil stain on the packed dirt floor. The metal shed was still closed tight, not even a break in the siding as far as I could tell, and nothing except two empty wooden pallets to see outside. But chemicals hung thickly in the still air, and over the whirring of the powerful fans up by the shed's roofline was the faint, very faint, bass thump of a stereo inside. Jimmy King was making a new batch, a potent one by the smell of it.

13:21 PDT.

I located the two houses that showed up on the property records. One was older, wooden, and spare. It sat in a brown, weedy garden beside the gravel drive that came up from the road and then snaked back into the woods to the barn and the metal shed. Across a wide clearing, dug into the side of the hill, was a newer building, its long wall of windows facing the valley to the east. Each house had a wooden porch that could have whined under Sophie's bare feet the night before. Each had a screen door. Both looked deserted.

Uphill from the clearing, I squatted in the underbrush, slowly sweeping my binoculars across every square foot of visible space and growing more and more anxious, doubting more and more that I was in the right place, that the compound was where my daughter was being held or holing up or whatever the hell she was doing. Where were the vehicles for the guys out on patrol? Where were the empty booze bottles, the sticky plastic cups, the other trash from the party Sophie had been at the night before? I pulled out the map I had printed from the county records and checked the layout again. There were no other roads, no other buildings recorded, no other areas that would support a building either. Immediately to the east was a cliff just waiting to sheer off in the next landslide. To the west, another steep slope rose into the mountains. To the south and down the hill was a thick stand of woods and the county road I had turned off of the Tuesday before. And to the north was territory I had already covered.

I circled the clearing, scoping for any sign of life, any flicker of movement at a window or on the gravel drive, anything that indicated these buildings were inhabited, any sign of Sophie. At the bottom of the clearing, too near the gravel drive for comfort, I saw it: the door of a small red shed pushed ajar by a black plastic garbage bag that had fallen off a much larger pile. Garbage. Evidence of the party? It wasn't like I had a better option. The entrance was exposed, but if I was fast . . .

13:57 PDT.

Inside, the wooden shed stank of stale beer and food rotting in the dark, close heat. At first, it was rank and sour, like a garbage dump, but then a wave of sweet ammonia, like meat, like bodies, swept up my nostrils. Sweat prickled on my skin. My chest tightened, squeezed until I couldn't breathe. My ears filled with the buzzing of flies feasting, flicking against the plastic bags, dive-bombing my face, my eyes. And when I closed my eyes, there was Patrick, there was Havers, there were the flies crawling—

I opened my eyes wide, dropped to a crouch, then fell further, scooted backward on my ass, my hands flailing, swatting at flies that wouldn't—

Stop.

Male voices, heavy footsteps, the jingle-jangle of keys being tossed in the air.

"I heard that blonde chick is coming tonight," one said. His voice was still faint, muffled by the trees, but he sounded like a local.

"Yeah? The one you did last time?" A second voice, deeper, brasher, and definitely not from the Okanogan.

"Yeah," the first said, his voice louder, closer. "Wouldn't mind some of that again. You should try her, man. Nothin' she won't do."

Gravel crunched under their boots. They were moving at a relaxed pace, but thirty feet away became twenty, became fifteen—

"Nah," the second said.

"Why? You got watch tonight?" the first said. One of them spat a long stream of liquid—probably chew—into the dirt. "Fucking crazy setting a watch out here. Ain't no one gonna come all the way out here."

"Dude. The party?" The second one said it sharply, bluntly, like it was the most obvious thing in the world. But I still couldn't place his accent.

"Whatever. Everyone's gonna be trashed. No one's gonna do anything. Besides, they all know King don't fuck around."

"Yeah."

"Anyway. Sucks that you got watch tonight. This blonde, man . . ."

"I'm not on watch," the second said. "I got other plans."

"Yeah? Jerking off in the bunkhouse?" the first said, then laughed like a dog.

"Fuck off, Dougie."

The footsteps stopped. My breathing was shallow, quiet. Theirs was loud, rapid, like they had been running moments before. They had to be just outside the shed, standing on the gravel drive. Then the door swung open and sunlight spilled onto the garbage bags.

"I got dibs on that little Indian girl," the second said, like it was supposed to be confidential information. When he bent down and grabbed the necks of two garbage bags, his head and shoulders came through the door. His black hair glowed in the sunshine. "You know, that hot Pocahontas chick that's been hanging around the last few days."

My daughter. He was talking about my daughter and calling her a *Pocahontas*? It didn't quite narrow down where he was from, but at least now I knew he was a racist fuck.

Silently, I maneuvered to the corner closest to the other door. It was the darkest corner, but I wasn't out of sight, not if one of them turned, not if they really looked. Slowly, I flicked open the strap on the holster under my left arm, wrapped my fingers around the butt of the M9.

"Dude," the first one—Dougie—said, his voice suddenly quiet like he didn't want to be overheard. "You wanna think about that."

"Why?" the other asked. He stepped into the shed, his back to me, and grabbed another garbage bag. He was tall and thin—wiry, really—and tan, just like Billy Boykin. They could have been brothers. Sewn onto the back of his BDU pants was a name tape: "Ibensen." God knew if it was his name, but maybe it was.

Dougie—stubby and thick with mud-blond hair clipped short—stepped inside, facing me and Ibensen, then took the garbage bag from his buddy and stepped out. I heard the trash settle on the gravel and then he was back.

"Nick's claimed her," Dougie said, his eyes on the ground as he took another bag.

My grip on my weapon tightened.

"That fuckin' beaner's got plenty of women," Ibensen said. "He ain't gonna miss one girl for one night."

Dougie shook his head.

"Ain't you heard about California?" Dougie said, taking another bag.

"Yeah. Nice place."

Standing in the doorway, Dougie looked both ways down the gravel drive, then stepped closer to Ibensen, lowered his voice: "Not if you fuck with Nick. He's killed guys. Like, lots. For screwing him, you know. Screwing his women too."

Ibensen paused, then shrugged. "Yeah, right. He ain't gonna care about one fucked-up little red."

In one movement, I pulled the Beretta free of its holster; slid my thumb over its safety, releasing it; aimed my weapon. *Fucked up?* I'd show him fucked up. Fucked up was his brains sprayed all over the inside of a crap shed.

Just inside the doorway, Dougie shook his head. "Your funeral."

They shifted a couple more garbage bags. My hand was shaking, I wanted to pull the trigger so badly, but the one brain cell that was still coherent screamed at me, wouldn't let me do it. Firing shots at that stage would alert everyone within a mile. It would sabotage the mission, keep me from finding my daughter.

"Dude, she's always with him," Dougie said as though he'd had a bright idea. "How you gonna get her to go with you?"

Ibensen picked up the last garbage bag and grunted. "I can be pretty persuasive," he said. "Shouldn't be too hard anyway. She's always lit."

"Yeah, but, dude," Dougie said.

Ibensen stepped past him, the muscles on his arms rippling with the weight of the garbage bag. Briefly, I saw his profile in the light of the doorway: long nose, thin lips, high cheekbones. Dougie followed him out of the shed.

"What if she won't fuckin' go with you?" Dougie said. "She makes a scene and you're a dead man."

The door of the shed swung closed. A shaft of sunlight pushed through the crack, fell on the packed earth floor. In the corner, in the dark, I stood up, pivoted toward the door.

"She'll do it," Ibensen said. He cracked his knuckles. "And if she don't want to, it'll be even more fun."

My entire body shook with the effort of resisting the urge to go out the door and empty my magazine into that motherfucker's head.

Minutes crawled past. Through the crack in the door, I watched Ibensen walk away while Dougie stayed, smoking a cigarette just outside. A few minutes later, a truck rumbled up, gravel crunching under its tires until it came to a halt beside the shed. The two grunts tossed garbage bags into the bed, the crackle of plastic and aluminum buckling against steel punctuated by the pounding of blood in my ears. They finished and jumped in the truck. The truck's engine started, diesel gurgled, tires lurched forward and gathered speed.

Silence.

I closed my eyes, breathed—*in, out, in, out*—until the battle cry in my throat settled in my stomach. I flicked on the Beretta's safety and slid the gun back into its holster. I sank back into a crouch, shuddered, stayed there until the stream of hate and terror ripping through my brain faded. Until the horror film stopped playing in my head. When I opened my eyes, I saw what I needed to see: a cell phone, its screen glittering in the sliver of sunlight that slanted in under the door.

I stood up, crossed the floor of the shed, and picked it up. The screen was crushed, half the glass turned to dust. It looked like Sophie's, the one she had left on the counter after Patrick Beale's funeral, the one that had been destroyed. But when I turned it over to inspect the back of the case, I saw that it was *my* phone, the one I had pushed into Sophie's hand that night when she was slumped—stunned and terrified—in the passenger seat of Lyle's car. My personal phone. The one I had closed her fingers around while she stared at me, her eyes wide and black with fear, her face as pale as mine.

15:01 PDT.

I retreated, picking my way methodically through the underbrush, pausing periodically to survey the clearing. There was still no sign of Sophie, but at least I knew she had been there. I reached a high point, a small rise just outside the southwestern quadrant of the clearing. It wasn't the best reconnaissance point, but it was the best within striking distance.

Sophie was still there—had to still be there—but there were few options for extracting her. The clearing was one big open space. Both houses had several vantage points, good sniper holes if Captain Jimmy was as paranoid as me. Nowhere to hide except in a crowd, but I doubted I would fit in with the party people. There were the woods—thick, dark, choked with underbrush—but it was difficult to maneuver in them quickly and even more difficult to get close to anything in the clearing. My best option would be to wait for her to show up, track her movements, and try something after dark, after they were all shitfaced.

So I waited.

16:22 PDT.

Several vehicles had arrived. A van carrying supplies for the party: a couple of kegs, some handles of cheap booze. Ice. Tiki torches. The rest of the vehicles had been filled with foot soldiers coming in from God knew where. Maybe the bunkhouses Dougie had mentioned. Why Jimmy King needed twenty dumbass kids to run his operation, how their vehicles had gotten past the fallen tree on the drive, why King would even throw a party out there, I didn't know. I didn't care. I only cared about Sophie.

16:31 PDT.

A long black lowrider rumbled up the hill and turned onto the dirt track that snaked past the older house and up the hill, terminated at the front porch of the newer house. It was familiar, that car. King had gotten into it at the lawyer's office; it had been at Patrick Beale's funeral. And the male who stepped out of it was familiar as well. I clenched my jaw, ground my teeth, when he slammed the vehicle door behind him and walked toward the house. The late afternoon sun shone on the black hair he had pulled into a man bun, flashed off his mirrored sunglasses, glowed on his brown skin. And on his neck, a serpent twisted.

Victor, alias Nick.

Jimmy King's number two. *My* number two.

17:11 PDT.

The shadows of the trees had lengthened into black spears piercing the clearing, their forward assault moving closer and closer to the houses, to the vehicles parked beside them. There was still no sign of Sophie, little sign of anyone except a few of the younger males pushing tiki torches into the ground, layering bottles of booze and ice in massive tubs. No additional vehicles had arrived, none had left. But it was early yet.

17:47 PDT.

I had forced down an energy bar and was reaching for the mouthpiece of my CamelBak when I heard helicopter rotors, their steady thump-thump-thump bouncing off the hills. I scanned the air. One moment there was nothing but blue sky; the next, the bird swept in from the north, the evening sun flashing off its windshield, its windows, its mud-brown paint.

It was a Sikorsky and it was coming in fast. Suddenly, it slowed, crawled over the treetops, swept through the air immediately above me, the down-wash pounding against my scalp. Even after I couldn't see it through the trees, I could still hear it: the tempo of the rotors quickening, then the scream of the engine powering down and the roar of the rotors steadily slowing, fading.

Half a mile, maybe three-quarters. It couldn't be far. The helicopter existed. Even if it wasn't at the airfield, even it had been scrubbed from all the records, it existed.

I shoved my binoculars into my vest and scrambled down the rise. When I reached the bottom, I heard a shout, a girl, crying, "Hey!" like a valley girl on TV. Dropping to a crouch, I strained to hear, every nerve on fire. A few males shouted something, their words unclear over the last of the helicopter's noise, but testosterone dripping from their voices. Then more girlish babble, squealing. Two girls, maybe three. But none sounded like Sophie, none had the gravel in her voice she had had since she was tiny. No bird voice for my girl.

I still had the photo I had taken to boot camp; I took it with me that night. It had gone on every tour, every mission, taped to a piece of card-stock and laminated with plastic wrap. During the war, I'd kept it in my helmet so it wouldn't be damaged if I caught a round or if someone bled out on me. In the photo, she was perfect: chubby cheeks and wispy black hair, bright black eyes, toothless grin. In it, she was the perfect baby I hadn't wanted. The perfect baby I loved fiercely. The perfect baby I left behind. It was the only photo I had.

The helicopter was still. The trees were still. The party had gone inside. For now.

18:09 PDT.

The helicopter sat idle in a long clearing, its rotors drooping, a wide circle of brittle, golden grass flattened by the downwash. It was the same one I had seen at the Chelan airfield: a Sikorsky S-76, gritty with dust, the brown paint shiny where the dirt had been wiped away.

I stayed back in the trees, panting, catching my breath after running through the heavy undergrowth to where I suspected the helo had landed. I could hardly believe what I saw: no guard, no cameras. It was a temporary site, had to be. Something hasty, so quickly used that even Jimmy King thought he could get by without security. But there were other tracks in the grass, long and narrow and just wide enough for a helicopter. This wasn't the Sikorsky's first trip out there.

Slowly, I circled the clearing, photographing the bird from all angles with my phone. But I had to stay too far back in the trees to maintain cover, and I couldn't get a shot of the open cargo door without crossing a track wide enough for a Jeep. So I got as close to the path as I could without breaking cover, then low-crawled until I was even closer, pulled some dead branches over my back, and waited in prone, the Beretta in one hand, my phone in the other. Someone would come to get whatever was in the bird, or maybe they'd come and load it up. Either way, I would get the evidence I needed to put these bastards away.

But, God, I was exhausted. I hadn't slept—really slept—for weeks, not since I had found Patrick Beale's body. And I couldn't remember the last thing I'd eaten that hadn't come wrapped in plastic. I rested my chin on the ground for just a moment. Twigs dug into my ribs, my stomach. A beetle crawled over my hand. Dry, sharp pine needles burrowed into the skin of my face. And then—

I was running, the metal pole of the gurney digging into my shoulder, the weight of the soldier on it weighing me further down with every step. There was blood everywhere, bone fragments too. We had done what we could, but the only thing for him now was the operating room. And he was the lucky one; his buddies were still out on the sand, their bodies waiting to be collected.

The orderlies met us just outside the hospital, with a table. We set our lucky soldier down and stood back, watched the white coats wheel him in, poking him, prodding him, prepping what was left of his leg for surgery.

I rubbed my shoulder, rotated it to get the blood flowing again. That had been the fifth trip of the day, the fifth ambush or IED or whatever else that made Americans bleed in the desert. Me, the pilot, the doctor—we were all exhausted, the kind of weary that feels like the hand of God pushing you into the ground.

It was time for a break. On the other side of the airstrip was an air-conditioned shed with sodas and a huge box of cheap crackers someone had brought back from Baghdad, and behind the desk, a fat civilian in an orange shirt who always scoped my boobs. I loosened my chin strap as I walked through the door, took it off after bolting the latrine door. In the mirror, I was a stranger; dirty, spiky blonde hair and a deep tan on the band of skin between my sunglasses and my chin strap, deep purple blotches like bruises under my eyes.

I splashed water on my face, wiped it off with a rough paper towel, the kind that's already so brown it doesn't show the dirt. Leaning against the steel sink, I closed my eyes and the day replayed, the day before replayed, and the day before that and before that and before that and before that . . . My eyelids flew open, and there I was again, a stranger in the mirror. Slowly, I ran my hand through my hair, broke up the dirt-crusted chunks. Then I picked up my helmet and saw my baby, her photo taped inside so I would see her every time I put on my gear. So I would remember. I kissed the pad of my index finger, touched it to the photo, and tucked my helmet under my arm.

Back in the lounge, my pilot was watching a telenovela; my doctor was sprawled on the fake leather couch, one arm over his face. The door opened and a cloud of dust and heat puffed in ahead of our commanding officer.

I sounded off: "Major Brittan." The doc was already on his feet. The pilot was standing at attention in front of a black screen.

"Waresch," the major said, "you're standing down."

"Sir?"

But he wasn't talking to me anymore, he was talking to the doc: "Thompson will go with you on the next mission. Waresch is coming with me."

The major turned on his heel, marched through the door.

"I don't understand, sir," I said, stunned. Had I screwed up? Did the guy die? But there hadn't been much I could do about his wounds, not much the doctor could either. There were just too many pieces to put together again.

"Sergeant!" the doc said, pointing out the door. "Major Brittan said you're with him."

I took off, slipped my helmet onto my head, and tightened the chin strap as I jogged out the door and across the tarmac.

"Sir," I said. "Permission to speak, sir?"

"Go ahead."

"Is there anything more about Private Havers, sir?" I shouted over the grinding of the trucks nearby, and the staccato slap of helicopter rotors rotating, preparing to take off.

Major Brittan kept striding across the airfield.

"Sir! Is there anything about Havers, sir?" I repeated, more loudly this time.

"Not now!" But then he turned, flashed a bright, pearly-white smile. "Patience, Sergeant."

"But, sir—"

"Not now, Sergeant."

"But, sir, I know who killed Havers. Sir!"

That's when he began to whistle, a lilting back-and-forth, up-and-down tune that steadily quickened his steps, that had me running after him. Whistling like—

Whistling like a bird. My eyes flew open, my head jerked up. How long had I been out? But it was still light, still hot, even down in the dirt. Still quiet. But then, again: whistling. To my left, toward the west. The same lilt, the same back and forth, and up and down, and steady quickening. And then footsteps, like heavy boots swung casually, carelessly. I dug in, readied my camera.

A moment later, the skinny kid from the day before walked onto the screen of my phone. Donovan, he'd said into the walkie-talkie. He was wearing the same jeans, the same shit-kicker boots. Dirty white hoodie instead of the yellow T-shirt. Strapped to his back was a canister and strapped to that, a spray wand. Just like my dad had used to spray pesticides. He was whistling.

He walked right past me; dirt puffed up from his boots and blew away on a gentle breeze, into my face. I wiped off the camera lens, tracked him to the helicopter's open door. He reached up, pulled a heavy-duty gas mask—the kind that scares children—over his head, adjusted it, then pulled on a pair of bright yellow dishwashing gloves.

And then . . . fragments.

It was like I was there, but I wasn't there. It was like I was seeing the helicopter, that Sikorsky S-76, for the first time, like it hadn't been at the airfield the first time I went. Like the woman who was there the second time really was the only employee and the fat civilian in orange . . . maybe he was only in Iraq. Had I gone to the airfield? Had I seen the brown bird in that hangar, cold and gray as a tomb? Or had I imagined it? But I remembered the dog, that shaggy golden mongrel that was too fat, too pretty to have been in Iraq. The dog that smiled at me . . .

I looked up from the screen of my phone and stared hard at the mud-brown Sikorsky in the clearing, willing it to be real. From my position, buried deep in the brush, I couldn't see Donovan. I couldn't see the tail number or what was inside the passenger compartment. But I saw the four long, spindly blades of the rotor hanging limply, like a dead eagle's wings. I saw a narrow red racing stripe like a bloody gash down the side of the airframe. I hadn't noticed that before. I heard spurts of liquid spraying onto a hard surface: psssh, pssssshhhh, pssssshhh. And when the breeze gusted, I smelled that slick tang of bleach.

That was real; as real as Patrick Beale's tortured corpse.

19:17 PDT.

I backtracked past the first clearing I had come to earlier, took a look since I was there. The old barn was glowing gold, the low roof of the metal shed flashing silver in the last rays of the setting sun. I approached the barn, stepped out of the trees, and stood silently at the rear corner of the building. The Beretta was in my hands, the safety off. I nosed around the corner: no one in sight. I got to my knees to pass under the windows, then stopped mid-crawl.

Voices, inside the barn.

"See? It's all there," a male said. "Just like he wanted."

The barn had thin wooden outer walls, but his voice carried clearly, like the doors of the barn were open. I was too pessimistic to hope for the evidence from the trailer where Patrick Beale had been tortured, but by then I would have taken anything incriminating, anything that proved I wasn't delusional.

I pulled out my phone, hit the video button, and held the viewfinder just above the windowsill. The screen was mostly brown fuzz, the dust on the windowpanes catching the last of the sun. A few feet away, the black and red Suburban—recently returned home—blocked the rest of the interior of the barn. There was no visual of the people speaking, but at least I'd get the audio.

"Where's the wire?" a second male said, his voice dead calm.

"There," the first said. "There's about thirty feet left."

"The battery?" the second said.

"On the floor."

"What about the tarp?"

"We burned it."

"The fuck you do that for?" the second said, his voice flat, almost whining. But it had this edge, this . . . twang that sounded familiar, like I knew it a long, long time ago. "You had orders."

"It was—"

"Forget it. You got his shirt, don't you?"

His shirt?

"In that box," the first said. "With the pliers and the battery leads."

Bile rose in my throat. *They kept his shirt. They kept Patrick Beale's shirt. With the pliers they used to pull out his fingernails. With the leads they used to electrocute him. My God.*

"The hell does he want with this stuff anyway? The kid's *dead.* I took care of it," the first said, his voice a little too hardy, a little too macho. Captain Jimmy Kingman. Had to be.

"For him to know," the second said, his voice still emotionless.

"Fucking weird, man."

"Like I said, for him to know." A pause. Then, "The product ready?"

"Yeah."

"You gonna show me?"

"We gotta do this tonight?" King said, clearly annoyed. "You said he wanted it Monday."

"Timeline's changed."

"Since when?"

"Since your little fuck-up."

"Jesus Christ. I told you," King said, "this site is secure. That little prick didn't know about it. No way he could have told the feds."

They knew. Todd Beale *had* ratted on his brother. I had never been more sick about being right.

"Yeah, like I'm gonna take your word for it," the second man—the mystery man—said sarcastically. "You *fucked up,* Jimmy. You're makin' it hard for the boss. And he's makin' it hard for me. He's makin' me clean up a lotta shit because of you."

"What the fuck, man? You *know* me. You know I'm gonna do it right."

"All I know is you let in one helluva shitbird, and I got orders to unfuck the operation."

"What are you trying to say?" Kingman said, his voice louder, aggressive and harsh. "What you gotta unfuck?"

"You got the product or not?" the second snapped.

Silence. I watched the screen of my phone for movement. Still nothing. But a moment later King, his voice like a rubber band ready to snap, said, "Look. I got so many guys out on patrol . . . I'm short-handed. Donovan can't—"

"You saying you failed?"

"*No.*" King's voice took on a dangerous edge. "I can give you ten kilos."

"It's supposed to be thirteen," the second said, his voice low and razor sharp.

"I got *ten*. You want it or not?"

Silence.

Kingman, backtracking: "Give me a couple of days and I'll—"

"Show me," the second growled.

Wooden doors slammed closed, metal scraped against metal, then the heavy click of a padlock snapping shut. Two sets of footsteps on packed earth, on the screen of my phone, two men walked quickly past the windows of the Suburban. Bent over to clear the lower sill of the windows, I darted to the corner of the barn, then dove to the dirt. The men were walking toward the metal shed. One wore faded jeans and a faded black T-shirt, his long hair an unkempt fringe below the rim of a dusty ball cap. The other was taller and wore pressed BDUs cinched tight at the waist and a brown T-shirt that rippled over the muscles in his back. His hair was cut so short his scalp shone in the fading sun, and when they reached the shed, when he reached forward to unlock the door, for a moment before they disappeared inside, I saw his profile: James Kingman, Captain, U.S. Army. Jimmy King. I was right.

And the other guy? I didn't care.

I waited. The fans on the metal shed spun, their white noise drowning out the sounds of the night.

Eventually, I checked my watch: almost eight o'clock. When I looked up again, a shaft of light spilled out of the closing door of the metal shed and cast a shadow in front of one man walking down the gravel drive. His back was turned toward me, and as he walked away, the door of the metal shed swung shut. I listened to his footsteps until I couldn't hear the crunch of the gravel anymore.

Was it King? I couldn't be sure, but I didn't think so. The frame was wrong and he was too short, didn't carry himself like an officer, even a bent one. So it must have been the other one, the one who wanted his thirteen kilos of meth. But he hadn't been carrying anything, and he hadn't been headed back to the helicopter. A third man? Perhaps.

I held my position. As the last of the light drained out of the clearing, the shed faded into the background until it was only a darker blot against the trees.

A few minutes after eight, a truck rumbled into the clearing, and two guys in camo jumped out. They carried AR-15s and moved with the reluctance of teenagers who have been ordered to get out of bed. One of them wandered around the clearing in a vague circle, then grabbed his radio and stated he'd completed a perimeter check. The other rattled the door handle on the shed. Locked. Had I missed King? Had I fallen asleep again? Or maybe the door just locked automatically and he was still in there, busy making the other three kilos.

Night deepened, the stars clustered above; there was still no sign of King. But I had to move. The bass was rumbling, shrieks of laughter carried on the still air from the party down the road. King was not the mission; Sophie was.

21:03 PDT.

I shadowed the gravel track, retraced the route I had taken through the trees earlier that day. The music grew louder until it was deafening, echoing off the walls of the cliff that rose to the west; and shooting through it, the shouting, the screams, the squeals of the party people. Then I was at the edge of the clearing. The older house was to my right, the newer one to my left. Tiki torches flickered on the lawn between them. Kids—a hundred, maybe two hundred, maybe more—clustered around them, drinking and dancing and gyrating. A thick fog of marijuana and tobacco smoke hung in the pocket of air.

I shrugged off my pack, retrieved the binoculars. Through the lenses I saw a party that made my wildest look like a Girl Scout sleepover: drugs, lots of them, and not just the bongs being handed around; keg stands; sex, lots of it, mostly in the shadows.

I spotted Dougie first. He was on the porch of the older house, his face and God knew what else mashed into a bleached blonde leaning against the rail.

I scanned the crowd, changed positions. Minutes passed without recognizing anyone. Then I saw Ibensen, loitering beside the patio near the newer house. He was with a group of people shouting and carrying on, watching something at the center of the crowd.

After shifting a hundred feet to the east, I focused again on Ibensen. My trigger finger itched, my mind spun out all the targets. *His heart? Too clean. His head? Too quick. His stomach? Too slow, too much chance of making it to the hospital. His lungs? Now that's a possibility.*

I shook my head, pulled my hand away from my holster. Ibensen was only a lead, a lead to Sophie.

He was still on the patio, his long nose silhouetted against the light of a Tiki torch, but where the house had blocked part of the circle before, my view was now clear. At the northern end of the patio, close to the house, Nick sat with one arm around a girl with light hair and a bikini. In his other hand, a bottle of booze glinted amber in the torchlight. The girl was giggling and teasing him, her fingers tangled in his long black hair. He didn't seem to notice. Why? Because in front of him, in the center of the circle, was another girl, the waterfall of her thick dark hair shimmering in the porch light of the older house as a hula hoop swept around her bare midriff and bounced off the waist of her ripped denim shorts. Her hips gyrated to the left, and she slowly turned around, her hair whipping around her bare shoulders and her small bare breasts until she had completed the circle and I could just see her face.

Sophie.

The crowd closed, but I knew what I had seen. My daughter: fifteen, trashed, nearly nude.

I shoved the binos in my pack and crashed through the woods. Two hundred yards, one hundred, twenty. Twenty yards was the closest I could get without breaking cover. The Beretta was in my hand, but I had no idea how it got there. I saw nothing except that circle, watched no one except Ibensen. Ibensen was the key. He would follow Sophie; I would follow him.

The hula hoop flew up into the night sky, circled the stars, then fell to earth. Again it flew, and again it fell. Until finally someone held it up briefly, shook it like a prize. And then the circle broke; people trickled away until I saw Sophie again. She was on the ground at Nick's feet—asleep, passed out maybe. A smaller group of people lounged around them. Ibensen and a few others stood at the fringe, passing a bottle around.

22:11 PDT.
Minutes crawled by; an hour disappeared. Every muscle in my body was tense, my teeth ground together until my jaw burned. She was right there and I couldn't do anything, couldn't grab her without bringing the entire compound down on both of us.

Finally, she stirred, rose up on one elbow. I couldn't see her face, just her hair streaming down to the ground. Then Nick spoke, leaned down. Sophie rose unsteadily, sat on his knee. She leaned into him, pressed her bare chest into him.

Acid bubbled into my throat. I gulped in cool mountain air, quieted my heaving stomach. But when I turned my attention back to the patio, Sophie was gone.

My adrenaline surged, my nerves screaming like I was under live fire in a minefield. Nick was still there, his face buried in the light-haired girl's neck. But his lap was empty, the ground at his feet was empty. And Ibensen . . . Ibensen was gone.

I was moving before I knew where I was going, gun in my hand, racing through the trees with no thought to maintaining my cover. I passed the house, darted around to the other side, to the rear entrance, the only entry point where I might slip in undetected. But before I got there, there was a scream in the woods, ten yards from where I was about to break cover. I stopped and listened. When I heard another, I dove back into the trees.

There was a fight, the sound of skin smacking against skin, a male shouting harshly, a female pleading. I changed course, plunged farther to the north. Outlined in the darkness, a male: tall, rangy, broad-shouldered. He was standing, elbows cocked, unbuckling his belt. And at his feet—

In the darkness, in the heavy shadows, I didn't see the branch that caught my running foot. I didn't see the rock that hit my head when I crashed to the ground. But I heard her scream. It tore through the night, through the fog in my head, through the bass thumping and the shouts and the crackling of the fires. Drowned it out. Until—*silence.*

I opened my eyes. Blood in my mouth. Dirt in my eyes. I was on the ground, panting, my heart bursting in my chest. And my hands were empty. *Mother fuck.* I needed a weapon, any weapon. *Now.*

My fingers, scrabbling in the dirt—gritty, dry—brushed against something cold and hard. A rock maybe. A rock was better than nothing.

I reached, I grabbed. Then hands closed over my ankles.

Another scream. A wail. Terrified. Pleading.

Thrashing and kicking, I turned toward that scream. Toward him. When he looked back at me, even in the gloom of the forest I saw the viciousness in his eyes, the ice in his soul.

He rocked back onto his knees, then his heels, his feet.

I flipped, flailed frantically for the rock I had touched moments before. I'd throw it if I had to, charge him if I could. Beat it into his skull, if I was lucky.

But there was no rock.

My fingers closed around the barrel of a gun.

I rolled. I aimed. I fired.

The void collapsed; sound rushed in.

And I was standing. My chest heaved. There was blood—slick and warm—on my face. On my hands. On my gun.

At my feet, a shape, a—just a shape in the dark. Crumpled, still. And crouching beside it, a girl, her long hair tangled and dull in the dappled moonlight. She was whimpering, sobbing, but when I bent down, when I wiped the blood off on my jeans, when I reached out to push her hair out of her eyes, she fell back, her arms splayed behind her, her bare chest raised to the night sky. She twisted, scurried away.

"Sophie," I said, desperate even to my own ears.

A branch snapped.

"What the fuck?" she yelled, hysterical, her voice breaking with fear.

"It's okay," I said. "It's okay," I said again to myself.

"Who are you?" she said, farther away this time, her voice muted by the party and the trees. I followed it anyway.

"It's me," I said more loudly, then paused, waited for the next sound, the next indicator of her location. When there was nothing, I said more loudly still, "Camille." Then, even though it sounded strange in my head, felt strange in my mouth: "Your mother."

"You're lying!" she shrieked. "You're fucking lying!"

She was gaining distance, heading away from the clearing, north into the forest. Into the wild. I ran after her.

"No!" I shouted into the darkness. Branches whipped my face, underbrush tore at my jeans as I pounded through the trees. "You're not—you can't—"

"I don't have a mother!" she shouted, closer now, her voice dark and hoarse.

"*I am!*" I yelled, the words bursting from my chest. "I am your mother!"

"*No!*" she screamed, her voice breaking again. In pain, in fear, in anguish? I didn't know. I flew over a felled tree, crashed through a thicket of brush, and—

And there she was.

She was bent double, her hands on her knees, her shoulders heaving, retching. When she was done, she fell to the ground, her thin legs bent at the knee, spread in front of her while she leaned over them, her head in her hands. I broke cover.

"I am," I said quietly.

Her head jerked up. In the moonlight, she was feral.

"What the fuck are you doing?" she said, mania rising again. "Why are you here?"

"To save you." I advanced quietly, cautiously toward her. She pushed herself to her hands and knees, scrambled to a tree. "To take you home."

"I don't need to be saved! I don't *want* you to save me!" she screamed. But she was sobbing, her voice was catching in her throat.

"You do."

"You're fucking psychotic," she yelled. "Did you shoot him? Is he dead?"

But even then, it was all . . . static. Static like on the old black-and-white television set we had when I was a kid. Black lines, white lines, rolling over the screen. Glimpses of color, snatches of sound. The deafening roar of the void.

"*Did you?*" she screamed.

She was kneeling, trying to conceal her body behind the tree. And she was rocking back and forth, her long hair swaying, jerking, her hands covering her face, then sliding over her head like she expected incoming fire.

I crouched in front of her, touched her shoulder gently. "I'm—"

She threw her head up, bucked, struggled. "No!" she screamed again. Her eyes were wild, her face contorted.

I pulled her toward me, held her against my chest until she stopped struggling, until she stopped thrashing, stopped pounding her fists into my shoulders, my face, my neck. And then I held her until she stopped crying, held her tight like when she was a baby. I put my jacket on her and zipped it up. Still holding her with one arm, I rummaged in my pack with the other. On my county-issued sat phone, I dialed a number I knew by heart.

"Darren," I barked when he answered.

"Camille," he said urgently. "What the hell is going on? I've been calling you all day."

"I'm out on the Sinlahekin Road, number one-five-one-three-four. The drive may be blocked; you'll need to come by helicopter."

"*What?*" he said, panicked. "What the fuck are you doing there? Get out *now*! You don't—"

"*No,*" I said fiercely. "Everything is here: the helicopter, the Suburban, that truck, the new lab. And everything from that house, everything they used to torture Patrick. And they're here: Kingman and Victor and—"

"Stop! You can't just go in there!" Darren shouted.

"You don't understand. I saw it, Darren. I saw *them*." In the dark, I touched the pocket where my county cell phone was secured. "I have video of them talking about a job. Spraying the helicopter down with bleach. *Hard evidence.* It's everything you need to put them down."

"*No!*" Darren commanded, his voice cold and hard as steel. "You don't understand how much is at stake!"

I paused. The wind had picked up, was cutting through the trees. Sophie was sniffling, her head still on my shoulder, her forehead nestled into the curve of my neck. But in the background, faintly now, was the thumping music and the laughing and the shouting and the squealing of dozens of people who had stood by, who had partied on while my daughter was—

My chest tightened. I understood *exactly* how much was at stake.

"Camille!" Darren shouted, his voice distorted, scratchy over the tenuous connection. *"Camille!"*

A fragment fell into place.

The file on Darren's coffee table. The FBI and the informant and the carefully assembled case notes. The years of criminal records. The patterns. *The dead.* And I realized what I had done, the ball I had pushed off the cliff. What would happen when they realized Sophie was gone. What would happen when they found Ibensen. And how small, how insignificant Patrick Beale was to Darren's mission. How much of his mission I had compromised.

But Sophie was *my* mission. I clenched my jaw and held her tighter.

"It's too late," I growled. "It's too late for that."

"Jesus fucking Christ, Camille. Do you have any idea what you've done?"

"Just get out here," I said, my voice sounding distant and dead calm in my ears. Sounding like someone else's, someone who was in control. "And bring the feds."

23:41 PDT.

We were nearly back to the Bronco when I heard the helicopters, four of them, I'd guess. Then the megaphones, booming and indistinct, echoing off the hills. Then the screams—whispering faintly in the wind—as the party people scattered. Gunshots. Single fire. Small arms. Repeated. *King. Victor. Dougie.* Followed by multiple rounds, the staccato crack of an AR-15. *The patrols.*

I stopped, turned back. Saw the spotlights strafing the trees, then swoop wide as the helicopters maneuvered out of range. Saw the flash of the rifles responding from the air. The screams grew louder.

Sophie, shivering in my jacket and my socks, her legs torn by the underbrush, started to say something. I shook my head and for once, she let it go.

24

When I opened the door to Sophie's room the next morning, the first rays of sun were creeping across the floor. I pulled the white curtains shut, turned and watched her sleep, waiting for her to stir, to wake. But she was in deep, her blue T-shirt gently rising and falling, her hair knotted, still damp on the pillow.

I'd made her shower when we got back. I knew I shouldn't have. I knew I should have taken her to the hospital, had an exam done, made sure she was all right. But the doctors would ask questions I didn't want to answer, questions I didn't want Sophie to answer. Not now. Not ever. And then the cops would come, and I couldn't allow that. They couldn't know she had been there, couldn't know what she had been doing. *No one could know.* And Ibensen . . . no one could know anything about him either.

When Sophie left the bathroom that night, so late it was almost morning, waves of steam trailed after her. She slammed her bedroom door and didn't say a word to me, not to scream, not to rail, not to blame or hate. She was in shock. Maybe. Shock because she had nearly been raped or because her mother had come out of nowhere, swooped in, did damage. Claimed her. Or maybe she was just rigid with anger.

I stood in the kitchen, my fingertips grazing the counter, my thighs tensed to run. I didn't say anything. But I stayed awake, on watch. Cleaned the Beretta, bleached every inch of it, then reloaded. Burned our clothes and my supplies slowly, carefully, in my old Weber and scattered the hot ashes in the gravel behind the mart. Sprayed down the Bronco's fake leather seats and rusting doors. Prowled the dark windows, listened for tires on the cracked tarmac. But there was no truck, no sheriff's cruiser, no boots on gravel, no helicopter. No crack of gunshots. No whistling of incoming rockets. No roar of incendiaries. Just the wind rattling the window screens and, in the distance, the flash and bang of dry lightning arcing from the clouds, striking the hills of the Okanogan.

25

Rhonda Faye walked into the mart just before seven. She told me I looked like hell. She told me to go back to bed. I nodded, said, "Maybe tomorrow."

She did her thing: quarterly Sunday inventory and a deep clean. I told her it was pointless. She insisted, every time. I retreated to the office, booted up my new laptop, and stared mindlessly at the home screen. The background was water, churning white and crashing into the ocean, a thousand little falls. And above the water, rocks, craggy and orange, untouched by the spray.

Stiffly, I rested my elbows on the desk and sank my head into my hands. In the field, after a mission, you return to your home base. If you're lucky, you go to a green zone, someplace safe where other soldiers are on watch. Someplace you can relax and let your guard down. Recover. Without that, you get more and more exhausted, closer to the water, closer to its icy embrace and pounding waves. Until, eventually, you jump from the rocks into the churn.

I wanted to climb back to the top, to stand in the sun and look out at the ocean, to see into forever. But I needed a toehold, some way to scale the rocks, to make myself whole.

Slowly, I opened my eyes, fumbled for the mouse, and opened Facebook. In the few days since I had logged in, Mike Havers had sent five messages, asking more questions, asking for an update. Telling me that his momma had hope, that *I* had given her hope on her sickbed. I smiled a little, even while I cringed. I was no one's savior, no one's giver of hope. But maybe I could return to them some kind of peace. So I told Mike Havers what I thought was true: that James Kingman had been arrested, that he would face justice for someone's death, if not Paul Havers's. When I was done, I deleted the account. I had nothing else to say to him.

What next? I needed to talk to the Beales, to tell Christine it was over, that she could stop crying, at least for Patrick. But my bones were heavy, my brain fogged. I needed sleep, needed to check on Sophie, to make sure she was still there. Unsteadily, I stood, but before I reached the door, there was a sharp knock.

Rhonda's voice, muffled by the solid wood door: "Boss." Just outside, she stood tensely, her eyes narrowed, her lips tight. "Someone here to see you."

In front of the ice cream cooler was a woman, a stranger with a blue suit and black skin and a tight knot of braids on the crown of her head.

"Camille Waresch," she drawled, her accent straight out of New York. "Darlene Oyinwe, FBI. You got a few minutes for me this morning?"

Standing in the doorway to the office, I swallowed, nodded. Without breaking eye contact, I said to Rhonda, "Sophie's not feeling well; she's asleep upstairs. Take care of her."

* * *

At the Sheriff's Office in Okanogan, the deputy driving the cruiser let us off in the back of the building, then pulled away before Agent Oyinwe had even entered the code on the keypad next to the heavy steel door. She held the door, then took the lead down the hallway and on through a set of double doors with another keypad. Down that hallway were four rooms with four numbers mounted at the top. Between them, two doors marked "Observation." At the end, a blank wall.

Agent Oyinwe held the door of room two open, then offered me a cup of coffee. I refused.

"Take a seat," she said, then sat down in one of the metal chairs herself.

I stood there for a moment, taking it all in: the one-way mirror on one wall, the cameras mounted in two corners of the ceiling, the fluorescent tube lighting. The paint, brown and beige, like a white man in Darren's uniform.

I retrieved my phone from my pocket, sat down, and slid it across the steel table.

"What's this?" Oyinwe said and glanced at the phone like it was an amusing toy.

"It's all on there," I said. "The evidence you want."

"Is it?" she said. "And what's that, then?"

"The photos. The *video*."

Oyinwe was still smiling faintly.

"I told Darren about them last night," I said. "Isn't that what you brought me down here for?"

"Well, thank you, Ms. Waresch," she said, her voice lazy and calm. "I'll just see if one of my colleagues can take a look at this while we're talking."

She stood, scooped up the phone, then passed it to someone just outside the door.

"How long will it take?" I asked.

"Not long," she said.

The second hand swept over the face of the clock mounted over the mirror. I was exhausted, running on vapor. Paranoid without my weapon, taken "for everyone's safety" before I'd even walked into the building. Anxious about my kid who was alone, still vulnerable.

"Is that all?" I snapped.

Oyinwe frowned. "Oh, I'm sorry about the delay. My colleague will be here very soon."

And then, on cue, the door handle turned, the door opened into the room, and from behind it stepped a man with sun-browned skin and flaming orange hair, wearing a swanky gray suit.

"Lucky Phillips?"

"Camille," he said and bent toward me, his hand outstretched, his white teeth dazzling behind a wide smile. "Special Agent Phil Paulsen. My friends call me Lucky." He tilted his head. "Are you my friend?"

* * *

Hours later, I had lost my cool.

"This is a waste of time!" I shouted from the corner of the interview room. My shoulders were braced against the wall, my heels dug into the brown linoleum floor.

At the table, Lucky and Oyinwe had removed their jackets, pushed their open laptops to the edges of the table.

"These people weren't there," I said, pointing at the stacks of photographs—grainy surveillance, crystal-clear mugshots, distorted photocopies—in front of the agents. "I don't have any clue who they are. They're not the ones you want!"

Oyinwe leaned forward, her hands folded on the table. "Who *do* we want, Ms. Waresch?"

"Kingman!" I groaned. "Victor. *They* killed that kid. *They* killed Patrick Beale. And his brother—that little shit Todd. He told them Patrick was an informant. He tattled."

"No, Camille." Lucky sighed.

"He did! He told . . ."

Me, I started to say. But he hadn't. That morning in the cemetery replayed in my head. Todd in his gray shirt, on the green grass, blood seeping out of his face where I had hit him on the way down. There was a look in his eye, an evil, knowing look. But he didn't confirm what I had accused him of. No, Todd was too smart for that.

Lucky shook his head. "Todd doesn't matter. And even if he told them, that's not a crime. He's not law enforcement. He's just a kid."

"*Fine.* Todd doesn't matter, but the rest of it is true. It's all on the video I gave you!" I scraped my fingernails through my hair. "It's all in the photographs!"

Lucky shook his head. "They're not enough."

"Then what *is* enough? What do you people want?"

"We want them all," Oyinwe said.

Then Lucky, his eyes hard as flint: "And we would have had them."

Fury burned through my shredded nerves. Words I could never say rose in my throat: "My d—" I clamped my mouth shut.

"Your what?" Oyinwe snapped.

"Fuck this," I spat. "Why don't you fucking ask them? Ask Kingman. *Interrogate* him. Fucking torture him if you have to. *Turn* him. Isn't that what the feds do?"

Oyinwe and Lucky exchanged glances. He raised his eyebrows. She opened her mouth.

"James Kingman is dead."

I blinked. "You shot him."

Oyinwe shook her head. "No."

"I heard you open fire."

"Our colleagues *returned* fire, Ms. Waresch."

"Whatever." I shrugged. "You shot him."

Lucky leaned forward. "He was dead when they got to the compound, Camille. Executed."

"*What?*"

"Taken out. Taken down." Lucky gripped an imaginary pistol and pulled the trigger. "*Boom.* Single shot to the head."

"What, like in the movies? Kneeling and begging for his life?"

"No. He was standing, probably walking away."

"But close range?"

"Yeah."

"A handgun," I murmured.

Lucky nodded. "Probably. Initial ballistics are iffy, but it was probably a Glock."

I shook my head. "When? Where?"

"Afternoon, probably. Maybe early evening," Oyinwe said. "In the building you identified as a lab."

"That's impossible. I was there. I would have heard the shot."

"Maybe, maybe not," she said. "The shooter may have used a suppressor—"

"*Yes*, I would," I said, but then I paused. Remembered. "There were fans, several of them venting the lab. They were really loud."

"Yeah, and they were running last night, weren't they?" Lucky said, like he was speaking to a child. "They were manufacturing around the clock."

"Yeah," I said sarcastically. Then a memory slotted into place. "Kingman didn't leave the building," I said slowly. "No, I didn't *see* him leave the building."

I pressed the palms of my hands into my eyes. What else had I missed? My memory flashed, another fragment fell into place.

"But the other man went in with him." I opened my eyes. "And *he* came out."

"Tell us more," Lucky said quickly.

"The other guy, he was a buyer . . . or something. You can hear him on my video. He was going to buy thirteen kilos of meth, but Kingman only had ten. He, the second man . . . he wanted the tarp and Patrick Beale's shirt." I shivered. "He wanted the pliers they used to torture him."

Hastily, Oyinwe began laying out the photographs again.

"I didn't see him in those," I said, waving my hand.

"Look at them again," Oyinwe insisted, her fingers flashing as she flipped through the photos.

Glaring at the top of her bent head, I slowly stood, walked back to the table, and looked. I shook my head while sitting down.

"Can you describe him?" Lucky asked.

"Shorter than Kingman . . . two, three inches shorter maybe. He was wearing a ball cap and his hair was a little long."

"Black, white, Latino, Asian?" Lucky prompted.

"White," I said quickly. "His hair was dark, though. And he was thin, I guess. Or just not fat." In my mind's eye, the man faded, blurred. I pressed my fingers into my eyes, stretched the lids to the corners. Stars burst, blood pounded in my temples. "I don't know. *I don't know.* But his voice . . ."

"You recognized his voice," Lucky said eagerly.

"Maybe." Slowly, I shook my head, opened my eyes. "I don't know."

"If we played a recording, could you identify him?" Lucky asked.

"I . . . I don't know."

Oyinwe raised an eyebrow at Lucky.

He swallowed. "Yeah," he said.

Next to him, Oyinwe pulled her laptop closer. For a moment, her fingers flew over the keyboard, then audio began. Fabric rustled. Wind blew. White noise—a fan, maybe—droned. And distantly, a man spoke.

". . . about thirty feet left."

"That's Kingman," I said swiftly.

A pause on the recording was filled with the steady in, out, in, out of breathing. *My* breathing.

". . . floor."

Another pause. Longer.

"The fuck you do that for? . . . orders."

"That's him," I said. "The second man."

Oyinwe nodded. Lucky was leaning back in his chair, his arms folded, his eyes closed.

Another pause, then the second man's voice, but his words were unclear, only "... shirt ..." drifting to the microphone.

Kingman responded, "... pliers and the battery leads."

A few moments later: "The hell does he want with this stuff anyway? The kid's *dead*."

Then, the second man, his voice angry, taunting: "You *fucked up*, Jimmy ..."

A gust of wind swept across the microphone.

"—the fuck, man?" Kingman again. "You *know* me. You know I'm gonna do it right."

A pause, then the second man: " ... orders to unfuck the operation."

"What are you trying to say?" Kingman again, his voice loud and combative. "What you gotta unfuck?"

White noise and, distantly, murmuring.

The audio ended.

"That was them," I said. "Kingman and the buyer. In the barn. Can't you get better audio? Enhance it or something?"

"No," Oyinwe said shortly.

"What are you talking about?" I said quickly. "You're the FBI, for Chrissake."

"I said, *no*," Oyinwe snapped.

I threw up my hands. "You're missing everything. Everything important." I searched my memory, but it was fuzzy at best. "They ... they fought. The second guy, he was really pissed about Patrick leaking information. He said—"

But I couldn't remember what he said, couldn't remember much more than what had just played on Oyinwe's laptop. So, hurriedly, I repeated that: "He just said he had orders to unfuck the operation. You heard that, right? Don't you see? He was gonna *shoot* Kingman, tie up loose ends. Make sure you couldn't get to him and his boss through Kingman."

Oyinwe stared at me, unblinking. "Try this one."

Another audio file played, a man and a woman speaking urgently about a grocery list with bizarre quantities, some kind of amateur code. I didn't recognize either voice. Oyinwe played another and another and another. Fifteen, twenty recordings, the sounds washing over me. The rumbling of engines and whirring of fans. The distortions and skipping of microphones placed too closely to electronic equipment. On one, the steady ping of an open car door with the keys left in the ignition. And voices, lots of voices. But I didn't recognize any of those.

When Oyinwe was out of audio, she shut the laptop and sat back in her chair.

Lucky, his eyes still closed, said, "Did you see his face?"

I hesitated, searched the corners of my memory. I shook my head.

Lucky's eyes opened a crack. "Was that a 'no'?"

"No," I said. "I didn't see his face."

Lucky's jaw tightened. Oyinwe's head dropped. With one short magenta nail, she scratched her scalp between two braids.

"You said you saw the second man leave. Did you?" Oyinwe said. When I nodded, she asked, "Are you *sure* it was him?"

"No," I said, my jaw rigid.

"Did *you* kill Kingman?" Oyinwe said it quietly, but her brow was creased, her lips tight and pointed. Sparks ignited in her eyes.

"*No.*"

"The problem I have, Ms. Waresch," Oyinwe said, leaning on her forearms and carefully twinning the tips of her long fingers, "is that my key target, the man I was trying to turn into an informant, is dead, and I have only guesses about who killed him. My problem is that I no longer have an entry point into one of the largest domestic cartels my colleagues and I have ever seen. *I no longer—*"

She closed her eyes, interlaced her fingers, and clenched her hands so tightly that light-colored blotches rose on her skin. "I no longer have a case at all." Oyinwe's eyes burst open. "But I *do* have a *stupid* person, a *civilian*, who thinks she knows better than I do. Who thinks she *alone* can solve a murder, eliminate one tiny, insignificant manufacturing operation, and bring some kind of vigilante justice to the *O-ka-no-gan*. And that *stupid* person, Ms. Waresch, is *you*."

My fists shook and my legs screamed with tension, with the sheer effort of holding myself back. My vision shrank to pinpricks. At the center was Oyinwe, vibrating, shining with righteous anger. *Breathe.* I forced my eyes closed. *Breathe. Let it go.*

"Camille." Lucky's voice. The kind of voice you want in commercials for condoms or caramels. But hardened. Like there would be consequences if you *didn't* buy the candy. "We have one more photograph."

Slowly, I lifted my eyelids. "Hit me."

The last one. The last photograph. It was grainy, a shot from a surveillance camera like the one I had at the mart. Black and white. Pixelated. Distant. The person in the photo was male, wearing sunglasses, the cheap wraparound kind. Bony. Shaggy-haired. Looking away from the camera, only his profile visible, the rest of his body in shadow.

"Who's he?"

"That's a good question," Oyinwe said.

"No," I said. "I mean, *what* is he? Another dealer?"

"A courier," Lucky responded.

I studied the photo again. When I had seen enough, I shook my head, looked up at the agents, and lied. "No idea."

*   *   *

Another agent—young, barely out of training wheels—brought back my phone and my gun. Lucky and Oyinwe shook my hand, but neither meant it. I understood. I didn't either.

*   *   *

Midafternoon heat hit me like a sandstorm when the kid agent opened the door to the back lot of the Sheriff's Office. I squinted into the orange light, shielded my eyes as a black Suburban pulled into a parking spot fifty feet to my left. A man with salt-and-pepper hair and a blood-red tie stepped out of the driver's door, then held the back door open for a passenger. A woman in her Sunday best emerged. Christine Beale. And behind her, Ed, his too-long hair combed and curling, his white buttondown open at the neck.

"Christine!" I shouted before I could stop myself.

She turned, her face surprised and scared. When it crumpled, her hand was halfway up and cupped like she was about to wave. Ed wrapped his arm around her shoulders, tucked her under his wing. She folded into him and he glanced at me. His eyes were hollow, his face haggard and pale and warning.

"I'm sorry," I whispered. And I was. I am. Sorry for Patrick. For Kingman. For having no one to rail against, to condemn or hate. Or forgive. For their emptiness. For having my child still.

Then, from the other side of the vehicle came Todd, playacting. Pretending to be the dutiful child, the grieving brother. The good boy with red-rimmed eyes, placing his strong hands on his parents' arms as they shuffled to the gray door of the Sheriff's Office. When he looked over his shoulder at me, he didn't smile or nod or anything, but when his eyes met mine . . . there was that sick gleam, that triumph. That *evil*.

"Ms. Waresch?" the kid agent said.

"*What?*" I demanded, swiveling toward him.

"Could you please get in the vehicle?" he said impatiently, gesturing to a black sedan parked nearby. "I have to be back in an hour."

I frowned more deeply, took a step toward him. "Look, junior detective. *Those people—*"

"Camille!"

Startled, I looked right. Across the street was a spotless green Four Runner, and leaning against the hood was Darren Moses.

"Need a ride?" he shouted.

I squinted, shielded my eyes again. I didn't trust him, wasn't sure I'd ever be able to trust him again, but he was still better than a disrespectful kid. And worse come to worst, I had my Beretta back. I nodded and jogged across the street without a backward glance.

"You're not out with the troops," I said when I had buckled my seat belt. The AC was on high, but sweat prickled on my brow.

"Just got back," he said.

"That was fast."

"Naw. That compound is crawling."

"Really."

"Yeah, we just got the fire out a couple of hours ago."

I snapped my head toward him. "*Fire?*"

"Yeah, whole clearing burned. We thought we were going to lose the whole mountainside. Looks like someone threw a tiki torch into one of the houses. Dry as tinder."

"What about the lab?"

"Untouched. Wind was going the opposite direction."

"Lucky."

"Yeah. He was relieved."

Darren drove; I rode and silently rejoiced. Forest fires burned hot. Hot enough to cover up anything Sophie had left behind. Hot enough to bury whatever I had left behind too. I didn't know then—still don't—exactly what happened to Ibensen. Exactly what I did to him. Not that it mattered, because either way, I was glad.

But that gladness comes with a sickness. You can tell yourself hundreds of times—*millions* of times—that you did the right thing. You can tell yourself that inflicting death is human nature, that you won by staying alive. But words don't get the taste of blood out of your mouth, the feel of it off your fingers. Not even time can do that.

The town sign came into view. "Little Falls, Population 72." Darren slowed down. I tensed up.

"Listen," Darren said. "About the other night."

My jaw tightened.

"I meant it."

My neck was rigid, my eyes fixed on the parade of rundown houses, the scrubby yards of my two-street town.

"This has been tough," he said. "Keeping things from you, I mean." The truck slowed, the turn signal chirped. "I'm sorry. I didn't have a choice."

The front of the mart, then the side, then the rear came into view as he steered into the back lot. The truck rolled to a stop, idled. My hand was on the door handle. My fingernails needed to be filed.

"I'm sorry about last night. About yelling at you. You understand, right?"

My gaze fixed on the door of his truck, I nodded. Once.

"I want to try again," Darren said.

I raised my head, narrowed my eyes and met his.

"Why?"

I opened the door. I walked away.

＊　＊　＊

In the mart, Rhonda Faye was sweeping the floor. Her head snapped up when my heels hit the concrete outside the door, but she didn't stop.

"Everything okay, boss?"

I nodded. "How's Sophie?"

"Okay. She came down for a while."

"Did she say anything?"

Rhonda paused, shook her head. "Just sat on the stool. Watched TV."

"She's not feeling well."

Leaning on the broom, Rhonda watched me, scrutinized me. "You said."

"Where is she now?"

Rhonda jerked her chin up. "Upstairs. Conked out."

"Good." I fingered the keys in my pocket, their jagged edges. "Can you stay a couple more hours? I gotta run an errand. It can't wait."

* * *

Five o'clock in Riverside. Quitting time.

Kids were playing in the parking lot at Lyle's apartment building. Some game with a bouncy ball and uneven squares chalked on the uneven pavement. They scattered when I swerved into the lot. Stared warily when the Bronco jerked to a stop and I vaulted out, took the stairs two at a time, and pounded on the door.

No answer.

I stepped aside to the window, M9 in hand, ready to crash through the glass, but stopped short. The curtains were open. Lyle never left his curtains open; he was a creature of shadows, just like in the last photograph the feds had shown me.

I cupped my hands around my eyes, pressed against the glass. The place had been ransacked. Cupboards, drawers open. Clothes and debris scattered over the floor. Sofa cut like a cadaver, its stuffing spilling out like intestines. I holstered my weapon, turned, and gripped the peeling railing. In the lot was his crappy dirt bike, but there was no sign of his junker car. Just like a courier to take only what he would need.

He was gone. *Cut and run.*

Just like his father. Just like his brother. It was the Scott way.

* * *

Back in Little Falls, I sent Rhonda home, then crept upstairs.

In front of the apartment door, my key in the lock, I listened for Sophie. Listened for her footsteps, her voice. But there was only silence.

In front of her door, I listened again, my hand raised, my fingers on the smooth white paint. Silence. I pushed the door open. Dressed in pink pajamas, on her white bedspread, she slept.

At the foot of the bed, I listened for her breath, held my own, watched her chest rise and fall. She slept like a baby. Like she did when she was a baby. Deep and quiet, her breathing so light, so faint, my ears strained for each gentle puff. In the golden evening, her face was smooth, calm. Her cheeks were still rounded, still dusted with freckles. My Sophie. My baby.

I slipped away. I closed the door.

In the living room, I stood at the table and cried.

I felt stupid. I felt frayed. Betrayed. Adrift. Broken.

Glad.

Time to reset.

For the third time in twenty-four hours, I sat down and cleaned my weapon. Methodically. Cleared it. Removed the slide. Removed the recoil. Wiped it down. Lubed it up. Then I put it away in the closet.

On the shelf was the case for the gun that had burned up with my truck a week before. It had been a Glock 19, a good weapon. A useful weapon. Maybe I would get another, teach Sophie how to shoot it, just like my dad had taught me. In my mind's eye, I saw his weathered hands on the black grip, his strong finger pointing out the parts of the weapon while we huddled in the October wind in the back field, where there was a hill that ate the bullets even when they flew wide.

I would teach her how to kill.

Acknowledgments

Little Falls is the result of years of study, sweat, and tears. I am incredibly lucky to have been accompanied on my mission to bring Camille to you by a number of terrific people who have provided moral support, constructive criticism, and helpful comments.

Seattle is home to one of the best chapters of Mystery Writers of America. Of the many members who have offered a ready ear and quick response, I'm most indebted to my fellow sailor, Brian Thornton, and Colonel Larry Keegan (USA, Ret.). I am also very grateful to Larry for introducing me to Brigadier General Bill Bester (USA, Ret.), who in turn introduced me to the incredible Pam Wall. Pam generously shared with me some of her experiences as an officer in the Army Nurse Corps and her deep knowledge of the psychiatric consequences of combat.

Special Agent Luke Thomas unwittingly inspired the location of Little Falls and wittingly provided valuable feedback on my interpretation of FBI procedure. He's also been a great friend for more than a decade.

Many of the stories about life after deployment that Melissa and Ryan Will have shared have stuck with me almost as long as they have over the years. Anj Jurich fed me lots of details about life in the green zone. Dr. Ron Grewenow spent a lifetime as a Veterans Affairs physician learning about post-traumatic stress disorder and influenced a lot of details in Little Falls by recounting his day over dinner during the thirty years he has been my stepfather. Many other experiences of combat veterans came to life for me in the books I read for research. These authors are too numerous to count, but Kayla Williams' and Ryan Leigh Dostie's memoirs stand out as exceptional.

My sisters, Madeline Grewenow and Sarah Grewenow Blumthal, have supported me every step of the way with handgun tutorials, wry suggestions, chocolate, and insightful social media guidance. (That is, all the essentials.) My best friend, Elisabeth Yandell McNeil, has been a valuable sounding board for everything important to this book and Camille's development, as well as providing cover at work so many times. My mother, Melissa Coe Grewenow, is terrific, and I guess I can't stop her from reading this book now. Same for my father, Richard Crouse, who has always supported my writing and made sure I had a steady diet of British mysteries growing up.

In publishing, I'm grateful to have found my agent, Sandy Lu, and my initial editor, Chelsey Emmelhainz, both of whom just got Camille from the start. Stacy Robinson of The Next Chapter helped me see in early drafts where I didn't. And I'm very appreciative of the staff at Crooked Lane Books who helped to bring Camille to you.

Finally, my husband, who always looked hottest in his Air Force blues, is an inexhaustible well of support, patience, and tolerance. And he makes a damn fine cup of coffee, too.